JINTAO

Jack Phillip Hall

2018

ISBN: 9781982935887

PROLOGUE

AD 2089, New Hong Kong
Beyond the shutters, in the rooftop garden, wet banana leaves sway and a light rain is falling. A legion of storm clouds is drifting across the South China Sea—menacing the smaller islands—heading toward New Hong Kong.

Master Jintao begins his day as usual, attending to the suits in his walnut-paneled dressing room. The weather outside is dismal and cold, but no matter; the silk carpet under his feet feels warm and smooth. He holds up one of his Angstrom suits and runs his fingers over the dark blue cloth, marveling at the superb craftsmanship. Angstrom suits are impeccable, made of self-cleaning fibers, manufactured by nano assemblers. They are tailored to fit him perfectly and have no seams. The label reads, "Everlasting satisfaction guaranteed." He recalls the vidi promo: "Indestructible—able to hold up even in a nuclear storm."

He smiles. *The suit survives, but the person turns to ash!*

1

There is a glint of light as a chromium arm extends toward him. He hangs the suit on the appliance and adjusts the shoulders. Then he speaks a command: "Done." The garment is spirited away, taking its place in the upper reaches of the closet among a dozen others. Despite their prestige and high value, Master Jintao could easily live without them. The suits have become a reminder of his servitude.

He turns away and mirrored panels slide into place, covering the garment bays.

Narrow bands of morning light beam through the shuttered room, drawing bright lines across the floor. The sunlit stripes run up his body, tracing its contours, and his reflection stares back—the image of a fit, middle-aged Asian man, tall and lean with a square jaw and a shock of dark hair. With hands on his hips, he stretches his neck from side to side, rotates his head and arches his back.

This is an auspicious day. It's his birthday—yet there will be no celebration. Only a few know his age, and only he knows on which day he was born. Today there will be no pressing obligations. Today he has made time for himself. Today he begins his one hundred and twenty-sixth year.

He smiles and a crisscross pattern forms on his lower eyelids. With the tip of his forefinger he pokes the skin. The tissue recovers slowly, revealing signs of depleted elastin and collagen.

Crossing the room, he stops at the medi-chamber and waits while the door slides round on its semicircular track. A soft bell tone rings out and he steps in. The door rotates back, closing with a *whuff*. Inside, the chamber is like an old friend, protective, comforting, and discreet. He closes his eyes and iridescent mists of biologically active molecules begin to drift in—hues of yellow and green. He inhales, and infusion begins.

It's been a long road for Master Jintao and a long life.
From his earliest memory, family expectations pushed him to
excel. His was a childhood spent in constant training, preparing
him for the helm of the family's megacorp. Expectations were
high and indolence was not an option. He breezed through
doctorates in molecular engineering and international business
and, in his mid-thirties, he was appointed president of the
corporate mining division. Assembling a team of world-class
engineers, his most ambitious visions were translated into reality.
Scores of advanced systems were developed including deep space
mining systems and orbital power stations. He became widely
praised as an example of what men with vision could achieve
and, as economies shifted and China became the most advanced
nation on Earth, Master Jintao's ability grew. Under his steady
hand, the company became a juggernaut, traversing the hostile
waters of global commerce—leaving larger companies
floundering in its wake.

Even though his corporate success was unequaled and his
accomplishments were many, Master Jintao was not fulfilled. His
life as a corporate chieftain imprisoned him—a life where duty
eclipsed free will. For decades, he'd harbored a longing deep
inside. If only he were given the opportunity, he would retreat
from the world, far from the demands of his office. He would
seek solitude, where he could regain his humanity and
contemplate the deeper mysteries. His desire for freedom went
largely unsatisfied. He confined himself with a will of iron,
separated from many of the simple pleasures of life . . . and there
was also the problem of an heir.

China's "One Child" policy deprived Master Jintao of
siblings, and the dynasty's future had come to rest squarely on his
shoulders. Being as he was the last of his bloodline, it was
necessary and expected that he would produce an heir. The
circumstance troubled him and, shortly after passing his one-
hundred-year mark, he began to have dreams—dreams of
children he didn't have, playing at his feet, vying for his

attention. The dreams became waking visions of marriage and children, and the idea ruminated for months. Weighing the time that a family would take away from his corporate duties versus the need for a legitimate heir he knew something had to be done and time was slowly sifting away.

He quickly discarded the idea of a surrogate. The potential for unpredictable genetic results was a nonstarter, not to mention the legal entanglements. He considered replicating his genome but cloning required government oversight and often resulted in weakened offspring—totally unacceptable.

The debate went on for months, searching for a viable solution, until the day a workaround presented itself. If his gene expressions were modified using some sort of natural randomizer, the resulting genetic structure would not be classified a clone. Nor would the resulting embryo be considered "engineered." He imagined that the modified helix could be inserted into a sterile ovum and made to reprogram the newly inserted DNA to a more youthful state in order to drive embryonic development—like restoring the factory settings on an electronic appliance. A surrogate could be contracted to carry the fetus to term. In the end, the integrity of his family line would be preserved without involving another's genetic history.

Master Jintao carried the idea forward. He procured the most advanced equipment money could buy and set up a private laboratory at the Jintao Corporation. He taught himself CRISPR\DAR17 gene-editing techniques and began to look for natural algorithms to randomize his genome. The challenge was exciting and it gave him a sense of freedom. He was exploring a new frontier and, after a few trials, he was able to generate a flawless helix—a helix with slightly modified expressions of his epigenome—a naturally randomized version of himself.

A surrogate was hired, and nine months later, a baby boy was given over to him. The infant was as close to a natural extension of the family line as he could have hoped for—related but not an exact clone. The baby was healthy and robust with

4

striking green eyes and boundless energy, and Master Jintao was delighted. At last he accomplished something of a personal nature, away from the bureaucracy of corporate life.

He hired a nanny to see to the child's day-to-day needs and, as the years passed, the best tutors and physical trainers were brought in. Every week Master Jintao would spare a few hours to teach the boy the value of knowledge, the endless search for truth, and the responsibility of his birthright. As the boy's intellect grew, he showed strong potential for leadership; and, to Master Jintao's great satisfaction, the boy grew confident and cultured, maturing into a personable young man.

Master Jintao steps out of the medi-chamber and pauses while the vapor on his skin evaporates. Above the lofty glass roof, the sky is dark and rain is coming down steadily. A flash lights the sky and his ears pick up the sound of distant clouds unleashing their charge. Hidden actuators silently turn, opening the wet atrium shutters, and across the dressing room floor, ribbons of light gradually widen.

He stares at a place far beyond the mirror, focusing on the day that lies ahead of him. This is an auspicious day, a day without obligation—so rare—and so daunting. His eyes have their characteristic look of unwavering confidence. Everything is exactly as it should be. His son is away at college and the man in the mirror is free to do as he pleases.

He touches his upper cheek. The tissue responds more quickly now, of indeterminate age. He feels his chin—strong, like his father's and like his son's. There is no stubble now—follicles were obliterated by laser long ago. He takes hold of his arm and feels the muscles—still firm, the ligaments still supple.

In the mirror he sees the quintessential hominid—ever curious about its origins—and about its purpose.

Why the bilateral symmetry? he wonders. *Why not trilateral? Or quadrilateral? Questions requiring deeper reasoning. The body is a constellation of molecules, a federation*

5

of trillions of cells—made of constituent parts that work together—a world unto itself, separated into different nation-states. Each organ is sovereign and yet cooperates with the whole. The body is an enigma, a gift from an anonymous benefactor.

So many questions. Why did inert matter become animated? Why did life spring into being? A thermodynamic redistribution of solar energy? Nature's quest for steady state? Just random chance? So many mysteries yet unsolved.

After decades of procrastination, Master Jintao has finally accepted that the only way he will ever break free from his daily obligations is to pick a date and, at long last, the day has arrived. He is ready, bound for a secret place -- a place where he can think and explore without interruption -- a place he calls the Estuary.

1.

In early evening, rivulets were cascading down the two-story glass walls of the penthouse and, overhead, wet airborne vehicles sped past with trailing sprays that seemed to hesitate before falling hundreds of meters to the pedways below. Inside, the Jintao housekeeper stood next to the glass wall, her dark Asian eyes examining a wisp of vapor that materialized in front of her. It twisted and folded on itself, shimmering like a piece of cellophane in a breeze. Not sure just what it was, or which side of the glass it was on, she squinted to bring it into focus. *Perhaps a reflection*, she thought. *The light plays tricks.* Rotating slowly, the image faded from view, as if avoiding closer inspection.

She turned and crossed the room, stopping at a large polycarbonate table, clear as diamond. At its center stood a vase with the cut flowers she had carefully arranged: hybrid freesia, deep blue iris, and stout yellow calla lilies. *How simple and pure,* she thought, *no memories, no thoughts, but still transpiring—siphoning water even in death.*

At the far end of the table, a solitary place setting of gold-edged bone china stood waiting—waiting for Master Jintao. She stood by and remembered—decades earlier, she was given the assignment to serve him. The offer came through domestic dispatch, with a single requirement: She was to change her identity to Ning, the name of his previous housekeeper and nanny. It made no difference to her; the elevated position was more than ample reward. She underwent voice coaching and a few minor appearance modifications and, as these things go, after a short while it was as if she had always been Ning.

Walking to the outer glass wall again, her eyes followed a glide as it slowly cruised past, its curious occupant eyeing the penthouse. Unfazed, she watched from the inside of the one-way-mirror glass. Below her, the structures of South Point sparkled in the darkness—magnificent hives for a privileged few. Minutes trickled by as she waited for the soft bell tone that would announce her benefactor's return. Anytime now his glide would enter rooftop bay . . . anytime now the signal would come.

It was late and there was no com talk from Master Jintao. That was unusual, but it was all right. He was a man of great responsibility and important works, and it was his habit to work through his daily checklist until the last item was completed, no matter how late. And yet . . . this was the first time she was not told of a late arrival.

Moving through the extensive quarters of the penthouse, she passed the kitchen and her room, pausing at the master's son's room, closed since he left for university. Pictures and music, memorabilia and mini-bots stood on shelves, exactly as he left them. She continued onward, passing the atrium and the master's suite with its private study and lush terrace. She rounded the north wing and the guest quarters and there she turned back. Eventually she returned to the great front room and, once again, she stood by the glass wall and looked to the dwellings below.

Beyond the structures, dark waters of the China Sea churned and her thoughts became as nebulous as the distant horizon. Suddenly a lightening pop lit the waters, revealing turbulent, sharp-edged waves, cresting black with white caps. Without averting her eyes, her fingers followed a loose strand of hair, tucking it carefully into the bun at the back of her head.

Almost two hours passed and still no com talk. She touched a quadrant of the disk embedded in her wrist. The house responded, projecting a menu. She opened a line and initiated the call. His private extension bipped without answer. *He might be working on the Zeurb acquisition*, she thought, *or expansion plans for the Jintao Space Division or the hostile take-over threat she heard him speak of.*

Pressing the disk again, she spoke the company name and department icons winked into view.

The hour is late, she thought. *Com center has gone auto.*

"Operator," she said.

Instantly, the head and shoulders of an avatar appeared in front of her, its face expressionless, lips barely moving, enunciating in perfect Mandarin. "Housekeeper Ning—you've reached Jintao Corporation. How may we assist you?"

"Dr. Jintao was expected here ninety-two minutes ago; I need to know when he will arrive."

"Please wait." The hologram froze. Its inner protocol opened several channels at once, sending search routines across the corporate intranet. A dozen microseconds later, the operator reanimated. "Egress history for Dr. Jintao: last departure— yesterday, aeropad B, eighteen hundred hours, fifty-three minutes—no scheduled meetings—no transponder signal— transporter activity negative—com link: unresponsive." The avatar continued with preprogrammed assurances that appropriate personnel would be notified and Ning would be contacted as soon as her employer was located. Ning disconnected before the anticipated salutation, "Thank you for contacting the Jintao Corporation."

With the news that Master Jintao hadn't gone to his office since the previous day, Ning's apprehension rose to a new level. There was nothing on the household calendar to explain where he might have gone and the company wasn't able to add information. Her brow knitted. He was a multifaceted man, dealing with complexities that were beyond her realm of understanding, but the lack of protocol . . . it was unprecedented. Although, she reasoned, a man of prominence was not to be held accountable by those in his employ. Even so, the lack of communication was very unusual.

Ning went to the kitchen galley and commanded the NutriSynth system to reset dinner from delay to halt. Next, she ordered the cabinet shelves to rotate, bringing down a large ceramic jar, embossed with clouds and five-fingered dragons. The jar hissed as she broke its vacuum seal and removed its lid.

Reaching in, she pinched three fingers of pale green tencha leaves and spread them on the countertop. She began to carefully de-vein and de-stem the dry leaves. Then she transferred the select pieces to a stone mortar and began to slowly grind them into a talc-like powder. She would combine the resulting matcha with milk and a dash of sugar—cook it and chill it. The resulting green tea ice cream would be served for the Master's dessert. It was an ancient recipe—handed down through his family—a recipe he was fond of and one that would take time to prepare.

While Ning tended to her cookery, security protocols at the Jintao Corp branched out, looping for fifty minutes, attempting to locate the CEO, consistently returning without closure. At the end of the hour, a report automatically dispatched to Prefecture Law Enforcement, and within seconds police were scanning hospital logs and traffic reports. Minutes later detectives began conducting face-to-face interviews at private clubs where Master Jintao held memberships—clubs where they often found sequestered executives.

10

Before the second hour elapsed, ring tones sounded at the penthouse door. Molecules within the frosted glass shifted to reveal a lone figure outside: a middle-aged woman with dark eyes, standing stoically as rain shed from her transparent plastic hood. Behind her a black police glide with yellow markings hovered just above the landing pad, its blue and red lights flashing.

"May I help you?" asked Ning.

Holding up a backlit ID badge, Lieutenant Zhao of Prefecture Law Enforcement, Detective Grade 2, held up a backlit ID badge introduced herself.

Ning commanded the door to perform a scan and cross-check against public records. Instantly, the door displayed the word "VERIFIED." Ning opened the door and offered to take the lieutenant's wet raincoat. Hanging the garment in a HEPA stream to dry, she asked the officer if there was any news of her employer.

The lieutenant's tone was resolute. "We'll talk about that."

Ning led the lieutenant into the great front room and offered a table for two near the great glass wall. The officer pulled out one of the chairs and paused, studying the room while Ning took a seat on the opposite side of the table. Zhao lowered herself into the chair and fixed her attention on Ning while unbuttoning her jacket. From a pocket, she withdrew a small black card with yellow characters printed across its face and, placing the card on the table between them. She asked for permission to record.

Ning glanced at the card, then looked up at the detective. The request was new to Ning and she delayed. There they sat, neither of them relaxed, backs not touching the chairs, attention fixed on each other, saying not a word. Zhao had seen this kind of hesitation before, not altogether unusual in situations like this. Formal depositions sometimes made people feel uncomfortable. Zhao was good at reading people; she could spot the liars and she was seldom wrong. She decided Ning wasn't one of them—just a typical domestic servant, taken out of her normal routine and put under a microscope, perhaps for the first time. Given the circumstance, Zhao looked for pupils to dilate. Ning's didn't. There were physiological disorders that could account for the lack of autonomic response—curious nevertheless.

Zhao rotated in her chair, stealing a glimpse down the hallway she was keen to explore.

Ning consented to the recording and the detective gave a reassuring nod, as if Ning had done the right thing. In rapid cadence, she began the session. "Sector fourteen interview; Jintao residence, South Point; insert time and date stamp. You are Ning, Dr. Jintao's housekeeper. Is that correct?"

"Yes. That is correct."

"State your full name."

"Ning."

"No last name?"

"Just Ning."

"I may want to see some ID later on, but first tell me when you last saw Dr. Jintao."

"Last night."

"So, you didn't see him today?"

"No. He was gone when I came on duty."

"What time did you come on duty?"

"Seven a.m., as every morning."

"Have you been in contact with him since then?"

"I have not."

"Has he been absent without notice before?"

"Not since I've worked for him. It's been nineteen years," she said, looking down and smoothing the lap of her gray uniform. "He has always let me know if he's going to be late."

"Do you have any idea where he might have gone?"

"There are many places, and I have many ideas, but I would only be guessing."

"Did he have any personal appointments today?"

"None that I am aware of."

"Any medical conditions?"

"No, of course not."

Ning appreciated the lieutenant's directness. Her questions had followed a logical path . . . until now. Why was she asking about medical conditions? Ever since the arrival of molecular intervention, there was hardly anyone with a medical condition worth asking about. Master Jintao was in perfect health. Then it dawned on her and she said, "Is it possible, he was involved in some sort of accident."

En route, Zhao had checked with medical facilities, but as a courtesy she reached into her pocket and retrieved a small projection cube. Setting it on the table, she commanded it to project a current log of accident reports into the space between them. Zhao's gazed at the list and said, "He hasn't been involved in an accident and none of the ERs have seen him." The detective's eyes shifted to the glass wall next to them. Looking past the reflection of projected data, she observed a glide as it cruised past in the rain. "Do they normally come that close?" she asked.

"It does happen," said Ning.

The projection faded and Zhao looked down the hallway again. "Who else lives here?" she inquired.

"No one. Master Jintao's son is away at university."

"I'll need contact information for Jintao's family and friends. Can you provide that?"

"Yes, of course." Ning repeated the request aloud and the house responded, projecting a list of contacts in front of her. Flicking the air with a forefinger, she went down the list, considering each name and highlighting the ones that her master frequently contacted. "These are people he coms often. You may download their com links if it will help."

Zhao handed the black-and-yellow card to Ning and said, "Transfer them to this."

As Ning touched the card to the list, names and numbers were instantly copied. She held the card for a moment as if thinking about what she had just done—then returned the card.

Continuing the interview, the detective asked. "Does Master Jintao have enemies? Anyone who might wish him harm?"

"No, of course not," said Ning, finding the insinuation somewhat insulting. "You must know Dr. Jintao is a citizen in excellent standing." Her thoughts raced. How could the detective ask such a thing? An enemy? The idea that someone might want to harm Master Jintao was unimaginable. Master Jintao was on a par with distinguished members of the directorate.

Zhao relaxed her tone and added, "Don't be alarmed. These are just routine questions. Most likely he's fine and we'll locate him soon. The best thing for you to do is be patient. With permission, I'll upload my contact info, and I want you to call me if anything comes to mind."

"Yes. Yes, of course," said Ning, preoccupied with the new possibilities.

"Mind if I look around?" asked the detective.

"As you wish. I'll show you the way."

Lieutenant Zhao lingered a few minutes in each room, sweeping her x-ray like curiosity over everything in view. In Master Jintao's private quarters, she pulled open drawer after drawer and asked about his habits. Ning answered concisely, telling about his typical routine.

Satisfied that her preliminary inspection turned up nothing out of the ordinary, the detective prepared to make her exit. "If you don't hear from me it probably means we're working the leads and haven't located him yet, but feel free to call the station anytime for an update."

Over the next four hours, Ning initiated two more conversations with the detective. She was told that transportation records and surveillance feeds were being analyzed, and a picture

14

of the senior executive was rotating in public view in every neighborhood. Associates, merchants, and even street vendors were being questioned and dozens of leads were being pursued. In each conversation, Zhao was courteous but could not answer the central question of what had happened to the senior Jintao.

A few minutes before midnight, Ning accepted the possibility that something unfortunate may have happened and it was time to open a com line to Master Jintao's only child—to let him know about the situation.

Oxford, England

In a nineteenth century row house, Quan Jintao was reclining in the sling of a Sosai workstation, wrapped in hermetic concentration. He was editing a dissertation on Electron Orbit Mapping Through Tunneling Microscopsy, which he intended to deliver in a month's time for his doctoral review. A soft glow from its view field illuminated the plastered walls and inside his cyber cocoon, the sounds of Debussy's *"Beau Soir"* played softly while he looked for gaps in the logical progression of his thesis. In front of him, diagrams, notes, and simulations floated one on top of the other and dozens of dialog boxes lined the edge of the view field.

After several hours of working on the thesis, a com line diverted his attention.

Bip bip bip—bip bip bip. His eyes darted to the flashing message:

4:11:03 PM TUESDAY, JANUARY 16, 2089
ORIGIN: NEW HONG KONG
CALLER: NING

Ning? What's up, he wondered. "Accept," he said.

His documents dimmed and Ning's image instantly came to the foreground. She had been his caretaker for decades and her

15

face gave rise to a feeling of warmth. She looked the same as always: round cheeks, thinly lidded dark eyes with creases at the corners, small circumflex eyebrows, hairline wrinkles across the bridge of her nose and forehead.

"Long time, no see," said Quan. "How are you?"

Ning's voice was serene. "*Nin hao*, young master. I'm sorry to disturb you, but I have something of importance to tell you."

"Importance? What do you mean?" *Why is she calling so late and being so formal?*

Ning's eyes closed, lids flickering for a moment, searching. Unable to come up with a diplomatic artifice, she went directly to the point. "Your father has gone missing."

Even though her voice was calm, the news was startling and Quan felt suddenly detached from what he was hearing. She went on, recounting the recent events, step by step, going over every detail.

Trepidation took hold of his core. *This is surreal,* he thought. *How? What?*

"When did this happen?" he wanted to know.

"He did not return home tonight and I have no word from him."

"This makes no sense. Father's life is well organized and predictable. There must be a reasonable explanation. There must be."

Was there a note or a message in the com system? No, was the answer. Couldn't his glide beacon be tracked? Again, the answer was no. Certainly his father must have told someone where he was going -- but no.

Finding it absurd that no one had been informed of his venerable father's plans, he thanked Ning for the information and told her to stay in touch with the detective, and to call back the moment there was any news.

Unable to continue his work, Quan switched off the view field and rotated his sling to face the doorway. He sat there,

16

staring at the sunlit landing just outside the room—raking through the details of what Ning had told him. Running his fingers through his short black hair, he worked the problem over and over again. The penthouse was a two-minute flight down the glide path from company headquarters—across the central valley to the South Point cluster. His father routinely traveled by glide and all the corporate glides were zero-defect rated—as was everything in his father's world. On top of this, his father was an assiduous communicator, always in contact with his office. It didn't add up. Someone must know. *Someone must know.*

With Ning's afterimage still lingering in his mind, the full weight of the conversation bore down on him. His father's absence would leave a huge hole in the world. Not so much in the corporate world. Master Jintao had seen to that, surrounding himself with excellent proxies. It would leave a huge hole in Quan's world—one that would be impossible to fill. Knowing that all lives come to an end, and knowing how old his father was, he had thought he was prepared, but not for this. Not without explanation. He had wanted the illusion that his father would always be there to persist. Now, in the blink of an eye, that illusion had vanished and he was left with the sobering thought that he may never see his father again.

Stepping away from the workstation, he looked up to the timber and daub of the Gothic Revival ceiling and a small window high above. Hazy beams of light filtered through the room creating bright parallelograms and triangles on the opposite wall. Suddenly he was struck by how the small Victorian room resembled a crypt.

Where are you, father? They're looking for you. Where are you? What can I do? You'd want me to stay and complete my doctorate. Of that I'm sure. But you also taught me to answer the call without hesitation—take action in the face of adversity. Should I join the search? I'm certain it's what you would do.

Quan's banlu, Sealy, was humming a tune as she ascended the stairs of the antique row house, her silky black hair

17

swaying at the middle of her back. Reaching the upper landing, her almond- shaped eyes opened wide. There was Quan, socks against the wooden floor, a hollow look on his face.

"What is it?" she asked, stepping up close to him.

He stared into the distance and said, "News from home."

"Is something wrong?" She reached out and touched his arm.

Numb and detached, he told her about the call from Ning and his father's disappearance. A search was under way and he was trying to decide what to do.

As he spoke, she could feel his agitation. She reached around to rub his neck. "Your father is an important man. I'm sure they'll find him."

"And what if they don't? I feel I should go and see if I can help."

"If you go... what about your thesis?"

"I'll ask the mentors to hear it right away."

"Is it finished?"

"I'll do a final read through—maybe two more days," he said.

"If you go, I want to go with you."

Coming back to the moment, he asked, "Who was at the door?"

"The post arrived. There's a package."

2.

Quan shut out his angst and partitioned off the matter of his missing father. With forced concentration, he read his thesis from the beginning, devoting himself to the task of correcting errors and omissions. Every so often, however, the thought of his father's disappearance crept back in—a vision of the patriarch walking on a dark and wet street somewhere beyond reach— alone. With renewed purpose, he repeatedly pushed the vision away, exercising the discipline his father had taught.

Over the next two days, Quan had three more conversations with Ning, but there was still no news of his father's whereabouts. On the third day, Quan and Sealy were emptying closets and staging things to pack for a hasty trip back to New Hong Kong. Picking up a jacket, Sealy discovered the package that had arrived the day Ning first called.

"We forgot to open this," she said.

"What is it?" Quan eyed the small orange shipping container. "Who's it from?"

She turned the container over and over. "I remember now. This was odd. It has our address as both the 'To' and the 'From'—but the tracking symbols show China as the origin."

"You didn't order anything? Let me have a look."

The box was small and made of polyfoam, soft to the touch and rounded at all corners. With a tug, he freed the end of a red strip that encircled the equator of the box. As he peeled the strip away, a narrow bead of clear gel appeared at the parting line and quickly evaporated. Discarding the upper half of the box, he revealed a small metallic cylinder inside. Plucking the cylinder from its nest, he gave it a twist, and upended the tube into the palm of his hand. An object the size of a thumb tumbled out: a clump of white fur with a gold chain attached.

"A rabbit's foot," he said, stroking the fur with his forefinger.

"What?"

"A rabbit's foot. Have a look." He handed it to Sealy.

With her forefinger, she felt the fur and discovered something hard beneath. Brushing the hairs back, she exposed a set of tiny toenails. "Eeew, it's a dead thing!" She quickly backed away. "That's grotesque. Who would send such a thing?"

"Haven't you seen one of these before? It's a talisman. For good luck. Supposed to bring prosperity, or fertility, I forget which—maybe a belated union present."

"It's awful. Someone killed an animal for good luck? It's probably full of germs. I need to sani my hands." She turned and went to the kitchen galley.

Quan looked inside the shipping container and mused, "Hmm. No note."

"Gross," she muttered while rubbing her hands under the blue light.

"It's a gift—not a bad thing. We could use some good luck right now. I'm keeping it." He slid it back inside the metal case and tossed it into his bag.

Early the next day, the couple were seated in a private compartment onboard a Sino World Stratos850. Reclining in an overstuffed sleeper seat, Quan's eyes closed after takeoff and his thoughts returned to his thesis. It wasn't as finished as he would have liked, nevertheless, he did his best to present the postulates and proofs in a reasoned manner, all the while haunted by the lack of perfection.

The review committee sat at a long table inside an empty hall of the Denys Wilkinson building. Three members were from the particle physics department and two members came from the planetary physics department. Also present was professor Harrowden, emeritus of the school. For two hours, Quan stood by a large view field, plodding through his material, as the images behind him changed and the committee looked on. Another two hours of interrogation followed his dissertation at the end of which professor Harrowden raised his hand and thanked young Jintao for an excellent presentation. Quan made his way down the table, shaking hands with each of his examinors, each of whom expressed thanks for his work. Two of the doctorates from his department also extended condolences for his personal crisis and wished him God speed.

Although relieved to have the formality over with, Quan suspected they had been overly kind, perhaps even lenient, because of his situation. He walked from the modern structure feeling that his work might be chucked into some dark corner of the college archives and shelved until the ultimate heat death of the solar system. This was, of course, far from the truth. His was one of the most well thought out presentations the reviewers had seen.

Later the same day, Quan and Sealy left for the airport. He had no idea how he would assist in finding his father, but he was determined to do whatever he could.

A holographic Asian female, clad in the pale blue Sino World uniform, appeared in their cabin—strawberry blond hair cut in Dutch boy style—lips pursed in an impish, heart-shaped smile. "What would you like to order?" she inquired.

"Do you have chicken dumplings?" asked Sealy.

"Yes."

"I'll have dumplings and hot tea."

"Thank you. And for you, sir?" The attendant cocked her head sideways.

"Shrimp salad," he answered, barely raising his lids.

"And to drink?" she asked, her imagery momentarily flickering.

"Ginger beer."

"Maybe you should have a real beer," said Sealy. "It's going to be a long flight; it might relax you."

"I'm okay," he said.

Interpreting his comment as an affirmation, the hologram replied, "Shrimp salad and Tsingtao beer. Thank you for your orders." The hologram vanished before Quan could correct her.

He returned his attention to the view field in front of him, brushing away the in-flight data and flicking through the entertainment guides until he came to the classical music section. He selected a piece they both liked, *Haydn's Serenade*. As it began to play, their seat backs reclined and leg rests gently lifted. For a while they drifted, eyes closed, listening to the melody as the airship carried them over the Ukraine. Almost at the end of the piece, their tranquility was interrupted by the gradual movement of their chairs to an upright position. Chirping sounds overhead warned as a panel slowly lowered with their food and drink. In molded containers, the food came with peel-away lids and beverages with built-in straws.

22

After her first bite, Sealy said, "This is horrible."

"Want some of my rubber shrimp?" asked Quan, with a small lump in his cheek.

"No, thanks. I'll just drink my tea."

With the meal finished, their table slowly rose while chirping its way back into the ceiling, transporting their dishes to some unseen destination. Seats reclined again and Sealy turned to her side, resting her head on Quan's shoulder. Her hands embraced his arm and, with eyes closed, she thought back to their first encounter on the Oxford campus. It was the fall of 2086 and Quan was on the opposite side of the green. Tall and handsome, she recognized his squarish face.

"I know that boy," she said to her girlfriend.

"What a fine specimen," her girlfriend said.

"Oh look—he's coming this way."

So nice to see a familiar face, she thought.

She knew about the Jintaos and had seen Quan before, on special occasions in New Hong Kong, but they had never spoken. Making his way across the green, Quan caught Sealy looking at him and the attraction was unmistakable.

Stopping in front of the two girls, Quan smiled a subtle smile and spoke to Sealy in a smooth baritone voice. "We've met before, haven't we?"

"Yes, well, almost," she said. "We were at the spring festival and I may have seen you at the dragon boat festival."

"Of course, now I remember." He extended his hand. "Quan Jintao . . . and you are?"

"Sealy Xaioping." She shook his hand.

"Hi. I'm Celeste," said the other girl, extending her hand.

"Nice to meet you, too," said Quan, turning his attention back to Sealy. "I remember you. Yes, and there was another time too—a birthday party." They went on reminiscing about New Hong Kong and the people they knew in common. Seeing the bonding in progress, Celeste excused herself and left for class.

The next day, strolling along the banks of the Cherwell, Sealy studied Quan. There was something about him that she found irresistible—a combination of charm and confidence mixed with humility—a rare combination. From that day on, to the disappointment of Celeste, Sealy spent most of her free time with the young Jintao. He was an excellent listener and he shared her interest in behavioral science. They talked about the historical events that triggered social change and the difficulty of forming a perfect government. It always came down to the quality of the people who were in positions of power. Their ego and ambition always seemed to get in the way of noble values.

Conversely, when Quan discussed his engineering studies, Sealy was embarrassed—not so much because she didn't understand what he was talking about, but mainly because she had such little interest in physics.

"I have to be honest," she said. "I've never wanted to know how things work. I do however think it's important to know people who can fix things when they break. I'm sorry. I can't help it. I find the dynamics of society far more interesting."

He understood her point of view but it made him laugh to think that she might envision him as a potential repairman. He admitted that he was a good partner for her—having the ability to fix whatever she could break.

There was a nobility about Quan that made her feel safe. He was fair minded and socially astute, with an ability to strike up interesting conversations in any situation. She recalled a Sunday afternoon inside the King's Arms, a pub that boasted the highest IQ per square meter of any tavern in the world. A large group of students, most of them Brits, were crowded around the bar. The subject of the day was the Chinese invasion of Oxford University, and the discussion was leaning in a negative direction. There came a moment when most of the group lifted their tubes of ale and began to drink. Quan took advantage of the lull to broadcast his opinion. The term "invasion," he instructed, was not accurate. England, he said, was originally colonized by the Chinese.

Glaring dismissively at Quan, a tall, gangly upper classman wearing the school blazer and tie addressed him with nasal intonation, "My dear fellow, you are sadly misinformed. You of all people should know it is quite the other way 'round. In fact, the island of Hong Kong was a British colony for a hundred and fifty years."

The Brits raised their glasses again and cheered, "Here, here!"

Sealy was embarrassed for Quan. She knew the Brits got it right.

The clamor faded and Quan said nonchalantly, "What you say is partly true. England was granted occupation of Hong Kong for a while—a purely strategic move on the part of China resulting in the conversion of a mountainous coastal island into a serviceable port—at Britain's expense. But that's beside the point. Go back further. Go back thirty thousand years. Your ancestors, the Anglo Saxons, originally migrated here from China. The genetic trail proves that. You Brits are ex officio Chinese."

The crowd went into an uproar and Quan shouted above the din to be heard. "But wait, there's more!"

This should be interesting, thought Sealy, loving Quan's delivery.

"For the most part, Englishmen and Chinamen look different but, we share a feature that is unique and identical."

"Rubbish!" said the snob in the blazer.

"No, it's true," said Quan. "When you tell a Chinaman and an Englishman the same joke at dinner—they both wake up laughing in the middle of the night."

There was a pause while the crowd digested his joke. Then laughter broke out and someone in the middle of the bar yelled, "Brothers from different mothers."

"Exactly," said Quan.

Quan's voice brought Sealy back to the present. "What are you thinking about?"

"The King's Arms," she said with a little yawn and a smile. "You were putting the upper classmen in their place." She rearranged herself for a deeper nap.

Quan continued sipping his beer, glad to be thinking about anything other than his father. His thoughts turned to English pubs.

Before leaving for university, during his last week in New Hong Kong, the project team he was assigned to at Jintao Space held a farewell party at their favorite pub, the Seas of Fortune. It was a public house registered to a trading company of the same name and was allegedly owned, through a tangled string of shell companies, by either the Duke of Bournemouth or one of his illegitimate offspring. Having continued in the same location since its founding in the late 1800s, the Seas of Fortune was an institution. It had weathered several natural disasters including the tsunami that destroyed most of the city of Hong Kong. Subsidized by its owner, the pub remained open through the turmoil that followed. Using new technology, the city quickly rebuilt itself in the same location and renamed itself New Hong Kong.

The pubs antique character was kept, reflecting the bygone days of clipper ships when the tea and opium trade was heavy. Light from leaded-glass windows filtered into the dark wood interior highlighting bartops and tables scarred with penknife hieroglyphics—some recent, some centuries old, testimony to years of unrelenting revelry.

Another pitcher of Guinness came down with a wet thud on the thick wooden table and the group's section chief, Gregory McGowen, stood, insisting on yet another toast to the young Jintao. "Come on, lads," he said, eyeing each one. "Fill yer glasses. We may not see this young chiel again for a lang time."

McGowen was a tall Scotsman with reddish hair and ruddy skin and hands the size of catcher's mitts. His face and physique looked less like an engineer and more like that of a prizefighter. In truth, he boxed for his regiment during his days in the RAF, before toughing his way through an engineering degree at Cambridge. For three decades, he worked for the Jintao Corporation, validating their faith in him many times over by dispatching even the most difficult assignments with regimental fortitude. He was a deep river of knowledge, held in high regard by his employer. Raising his glass, the big Scot proclaimed, "To yer health, young master Quan, and may the wind be ever at yer back."

After his toast, McGowen parked himself quietly next to Quan and stared at his half glass of ale for a time. "The wife wanted cats, ya know. She's gone but I've got 'em still."

As if entranced, McGowen went on, "Sphinx, they are— hairless, ya know. Nothing in the world as soft as the skin of a Sphinx." His large forefinger lightly circled the rim of his glass. "It's like they're made of air."

Quan couldn't help but be drawn in by McGowen's gentleness, evidence of the big man's ease with himself. Yet there was a sadness there, as well. Politely, Quan added, "We were all very sorry to hear of your wife's passing."

"Aye. It's been three years, but it seems like yesterday." Perking up suddenly as if shaking off a dream, McGowen retorted, "Yer father's the best man I ever worked for. A true leader he is. Big shoes, lad, mighty big shoes." Taking a long sip of dark beer, he went on. "You'll be next in line, ya know. And when you're back from university, no doubt he'll be givin' you projects of yer own. Anything you need then, you just ask me." McGowen cracked a broad smile. "And, who knows, I might be workin' for ya someday."

Quan looked at Sealy's head resting on his shoulder and took another sip of Tsingtao while the Stratos850 whistled through a black sky.

Sealy was dreaming of a sunny afternoon back at Oxford. Quan was sitting with her, on a blanket next to a willow tree. They were watching punts move up and down the Cherwell and Quan was opening a picnic basket full of treats.

"What a nice surprise," she said, looking at cheese and pate, preserves, and French bread and wine.

After unclipping two glasses from the lid of the basket, Quan began opening the bottle of wine. He said, "You'll also find a special treat in that tree."

"What do you mean?"

"You'll just have to go and look."

She stood up. "And just how do you know this, mister, mister?"

"A little bird told me."

On the other side of the tree she found a crevice where the tree trunk had molded itself around the remnants of a cut branch. Inside the crevice was a little box wrapped in red paper. Sealy brought it over to the blanket and stood there, smiling.

"Go ahead. Open it," he said.

Inside the box was a two-fingered ring set with diamonds and rubies.

"It's beautiful," she said.

"We get along so well. I think we should have an agreement to be exclusive to each other. I'd like you to be my banlu."

Gingerly, she put on the rings, surprised at how well they fit her second and third fingers. Holding up her hand for Quan to see, she replied, "This is kind of sudden but I love it."

"When it's right, it's right," said he.

28

"You and me," said Sealy, containing her urge to through her arms around him. "Brilliant. It's a definite yes. How long shall we set the renewal for?"

"I was thinking five-year intervals with automatic rollover."

"As it should be," said Sealy, throwing her arms around him.

They were good together—mannered and intelligent and, best of all, they could make each other laugh. A few days later their engagement was made official and they went looking for a row house for two.

Quan nudged her. "Almost there," he said, pointing to the window.

Her eyes opened to the tailored cabin of the aircraft. Turning her face to the window, she looked out beyond the gleaming fuselage. Flickering between the white clouds below, bits of coastline became visible. Intuitively the fragments joined in her mind: the familiar contours of the Gulf of Tonkin and the Leizhou Peninsula.

Vibration surged through the large airship as it slowed to subsonic.

3.

China traces its history back thirty-six centuries to small
settlements along the Yangtze and Yellow rivers. As the
populations grew, warlords took power and ruled for centuries
until the Chinese Civil War put an end to the succession of
emperors, giving rise to a People's Republic. Influenced by the
commerce of New Hong Kong, the Republic gradually evolved
into a quasi-communist/capitalist government and, with its
newfound wealth, China went on a massive infrastructure
campaign, building power plants, housing, and transportation
systems. Citizens were allowed to own private property, make
profits, and compete in global markets. Entrepreneurs seized the
opportunity and transformed China from basic manufacturing
into a major center for science and innovation - leading the world
in both economic and technological achievement.

New Hong Kong

Sealy and Quan were looking out the windows of a Jintao Corporation glide as it autonavigated the flight corridor to the south side of the island. Soon, the great South Point complex came into view, standing defiantly on the shore of Deep Water Bay, with its massive support struts buried twenty meters into bedrock. South Point was an architectural marvel, designed to withstand any insult nature could hurl at it. Towering three hundred meters above the inland communities, it housed tier upon tier of elite dwellings interleaved with greenscapes, terraces, shops, and fitness centers. More than a housing complex, it was a destination—the home of distinguished citizens: bankers, dignitaries, media personalities, and industry moguls. The complex represented a monument to prosperity and the collective ambitions of the New Hong Kong elite.

The glide hovered briefly, broadcasting its landing beacon before rotating and slowly descending to the penthouse aeropad. The young coupld unbuckled and stepped out of the climate-controlled craft and were met by gusts of cold winter air.

Quan encircled Sealy with his arm, carrying her overnight bag in the other hand and his bag slung over his shoulder.

Shivering as they walked toward the rooftop entry, Sealy asked, "Are you glad to be back home?"

"I would be, under different circumstances," said Quan. "I'm hoping this is resolved soon."

Under the building's cantilevered overhang, a frosted-glass door cleared and a woman could be seen inside. Pointing his chin toward the doorway, Quan said, "That's Ning."

"She's taller than I thought she'd be," said Sealy.

After brief introductions, Ning excused herself saying, "I will make tea."

Quan ushered Sealy to the great room where he made himself comfortable on the large semicircular sectional. Sealy wandered the room taking in the fine statuary and paintings. This

31

was her first time in the Jintao penthouse and she marveled at the exquisite decor, the silken walls and marble floors, the intricate carvings in precious stone, and the paintings of misty mountain passages. Circling around, eventually she reached the two-story glass wall with its expansive views of the South China Sea. Suddenly she stopped, lurching backward in half steps. She turned and retreated, back to where Quan sat in front of the fireplace. She sat down next to him.

"This is a difficult situation," he said, "and I'm glad you came along.

"What is it?" he asked, noticing how pale and withdrawn she was. Are you okay?"

"I'm feeling a little queasy. It's the height."

Quan looked up. Outside the window, the sky above was as pale as a gull's eye and the sea below sparkled like the rippling scales of an enormous gray fish.

"When I look down, I feel the room swaying and I thought at any moment the floor might tip and I might slip out into the sea."

"Sounds like you have a touch of vertigo."

Ning returned moments later with a tray of tea and Chinese doughnuts, Quan's favorite treat. She set cups on the low table in front of them and began to pour.

"Have some tea," said Quan, handing a cup to Sealy. "It might settle you."

Sealy took the warm teacup and held it in both hands, trying to calm herself. As she pressed back into the comform cushions, the sofa slowly recontoured, cradling her, and she began to relax.

Ning came to stand between them and the great glass wall. She proceded to give her report, telling of the latest updates from Lieutenant Zhao and how the leads had dwindled to an improbable few. Every clue was being diligently pursued however, the investigation reached a standstill. No ransom demand had been received, no suicide note found, and no one knew where the chairman of Jintao Corporation had gone—or so it seemed.

While Quan listened, his leg began to bounce up and down, revealing his impatience. Ning covered everything she knew—detail upon detail of useless information and Quan's frustration was rising. None of what she was saying explained how or why his father was plucked from the world, and it was obvious that the investigation was falling short of it's goal. They weren't asking the right questions or looking in the right places.

Putting himself in a more centered frame of mind, Quan began listening more with his eyes than his ears. How calm and unhurried she was, talking about the huge reward the corporation put up and how the police followed every lead, of which there were many. *How can she be so calm, so unemotional? She acts as if the disappearance is a common occurrence.* Quan found her manner curious—too calm. Was she concealing something? He pushed down his frustration, thanked Ning for her report and, after she left the room, he turned to Sealy.

"The detectives are approaching this as if it were just one of their routine assignments. They don't have anything at stake—not like I do. They've left me with no choice. I'm going to have to intervene. I'm sure they've overlooked something."

"What are you going to do?" asked Sealy, doing her best to ignore the glass wall and the abyss beyond.

"The corporation is the most logical place to start. It was my father's life and I know people there."

Thinking about the company presented Quan with another problem. Would he be expected to fill the void left by his father? What was the protocol? Would they look to him for guidance? That would complicate his life beyond measure, and it could potentially derail the future he planned for himself and Sealy.

"I take it we'll be here awhile," said Sealy.

"Believe me," said Quan, "I want to get to the bottom of this and back to the U.K. as soon as possible."

Ning returned and led the young couple through the penthouse. Like two weary pups, they followed her into Master Jintao's suite, where she pointed to its sophisticated features including the illuminated carpet and the medi-bot booth, all features that Quan was familiar with. In Master Jintao's dressing room, Ning commanded the mirrored wall to open, revealing the garment bays. "Master's suits are here." Turning toward the door, she murmured something that sounded like, "No need where he is now."

"Why is she showing us his suits?" Sealy asked.

Quan was suddenly jolted. "Wait. What did you say? Something about my father not needing these where he is now. Is that what you said?"

"The master is very healthy," said Ning with a coy smile, "and there is no evidence of his demise, therefore we must assume he is still alive. And, if he is alive, he must be somewhere. Don't you think? And since he has left his suits, he must not need them where he is now."

"I appreciate your logic," said Quan. "You want to believe that he's alive and that he'll return. So do I, but there's no evidence to support that . . . unless you know something you haven't told us."

"I haven't told you everything I know," said Ning, lowering her head in deep reflection. "That would take a very long time indeed."

Quan was puzzled. Ning had always been logical and courteous, but today she seemed obtuse. Her manner was almost flippant. A week had elapsed without any progress and she seemed complacent. He pressed on. "Do you know where my father is?"

She hesitated, as if selecting her answer from a range of choices. "No."

"Then how can you be certain he will return?"

She paused again, making up her mind before answering. "He will return for his clothes."

34

"What does that mean? What are you saying?"

"Formal and informal, all of his clothes are accounted for."

"I don't understand. You're saying he left without any clothes? That's absurd."

Curious, Sealy ran her fingers across the fine cloth, feeling how unusual it was.

Quan looked hard-eyed at Ning. "You must be mistaken. Please check again."

Day became evening as the young couple searched through Master Jintao's personal effects. Everywhere they looked they found evidence of his fastidious lifestyle. Quan touched the front of a drawer and it extend automatically, lighting up, revealing hairbrushes and combs made of authentic pearl. Another drawer illuminated with a collection of cuff links, some with precious stones, others with embedded sensors. Touching the drawer face again, it withdrew. The uppermost drawer contained neatly nested wristware embedded with controllers, trans hailers, and com links. All of his father's belongings were state of the art, immaculate, and stored with care, making the disappearance look even more incongruous. While they rummaged, Ning was on the other side of the room counting articles of clothing. At last, she concluded once again that all of his garments were accounted for.

Searching through his father's things was an arduous task for Quan and he soon tired of it. He and Sealy said good night to Ning and went to their room. After slipping into bed, sleep didn't come easy for Quan. He rolled back and forth under the sheets with restless imaginings of what might have happened. Had his father been kidnapped? Was there a yet undiscovered accident?

When sleep finally came, he dreamed of his father in fleeting images, always just beyond reach. No matter how many steps he took, the distance between them remained the same—as if trying made no difference at all. In the dream, his wrist disc was missing and a man with long white hair and a long white beard offered him the use of his. He held the man's arm and tried to operate the disk but it refused, boldly displaying an error message that his biosignature was unauthorized. Suddenly the dream changed and he was walking through a thicket with bushes on both sides. There were two paths. He went down the one on the right, but it ended in brambles. He turned around to retrace his path but there was no way to get back—more brambles—no way forward and no way back.

By the time Quan awoke the next morning, Sealy was already dressed.

"How long have you been up?" he asked.

"Awhile," she said. "The height makes me nauseous. Now I feel the whole place swaying. I don't think I can stay here."

"I never knew you to have vertigo. It didn't seem to effect you on airplane. Maybe it's temporary. You might get over it in a day or two."

"I've never felt this before. I can't seem to find relief."

"We'll get medicine for you. Or we can move if you like," grumbled Quan, tired from the restless night.

"I'll try Dramamine and see what happens," she said, rubbing her temple.

After showering, Quan wandered into the kitchen and found Ning preparing breakfast. He sat at the counter. She placed a bowl and spoon in front of him. Her "Master has no clothes" comment was still ringing in his ears. The clothes were a mystery, and the idea of his supercentenarian father walking the world naked was peculiar and disconcerting. The real question was where had he gone? Ning had made the point that, with no evidence of foul play or misadventure, it was conceivable that his father was okay and would return. Simple deductions were often more likely to be true than complex ones, and it was tempting to accept her reading of the situation—however strange it was.

36

Clawing for answers, Quan blurted out, "What haven't you told me about father's disappearance?"

Ning continued to set out napkins and cups. Tilting her head without looking up, she said, "Your father's actions are always consistent with who he is. He's a very wise man and you must be patient."

What she said held no value for Quan and he was only half listening. The other half of him was tuned in to her delivery. Like a chocklight brushing across a dark room, he detected something. Ning's humble attentiveness, ever present in his youth, was gone, replaced by a puckish, almost aloof attitude. *Why so obtuse?* he wondered. *What's going on?*

"You haven't answered the question."

"I do not know where he is, or why he left," said Ning emphatically as she ladled porridge into his bowl.

The first spoonful of warm congee was comforting.

Wearing a new suit, on the morning of his second day, Quan stepped into the lobby of Building One, Jintao Corporation. He paused near a larger-than-life platinum statue of his great-grandfather, Qui Juang Jintao, founder of the megacorp. Quan was said to have a resemblance to his great-grandfather; however, studying the metallic face, he wasn't convinced. From what he knew, Qui Juang was a dynamo, creating the family business out of nothing. Lifting himself out of that social morass known as the People's Republic, he built an empire. Beginning with public works projects, he leveraged the profits and built factories. The dynasty went on to pioneer new industries and eventually became an indispensable part of the Sino-industrial complex and one of the first suppliers to the Chinese space program. Now, immortalized in finished platinum, the statue obscured the man's spirit. There he was, Qui Juang, founder of the dynasty—an inanimate lump of metal.

This must be the brainchild of some marketing executive, to symbolize the company's ability to mine precious metals. If it had to be metal, why not at least give it life? Animate it. Make it wave and greet people. Show some creativity.

Quan turned in the direction of the elevators only to have his path blocked by two executive secretaries, both dressed in identical uniforms, black tunic tops over black pants. Simultaneously, they inclined their heads toward him. It was only a degree or two, but he caught it—a subtle, but unmistakable, kowtow. He reminded himself to stand and accept the ancient gesture—a custom of groveling that should have been laid to rest with the last emperor.

"I am Dee Dee Cheu, and this is Shu Song Liu. It is our privilege to meet you. How may we provide you with excellent service today?"

"Nothing at the moment," he said, sidestepping them and heading toward the elevators.

Socializing was not part of his agenda, but the day also served a political purpose. Seeing the presence of a Jintao in the building lessened employees' anxiety over their missing chairman.

Eyes were on him and, feeling a bit self-conscious, Quan struck out across the lobby with deliberately confident strides. The secretaries followed closely behind, entering the elevator with him—parking themselves on either side.

Disembarking on the eighteenth floor, Quan led the way down a polished hallway, the secretaries' shoes clacking on the dark marble floor behind him. Like a synchronized unit, they entered the president's office.

A woman dressed in the same black uniform stood up from behind a sleek translucent desk and inquired, "Quan Jintao?"

"Yes. Here to see Dr. Hao."

"They are expecting you in the executive conference room. Next door, please." She gestured to the two assistants.

The two secretaries shuffled out of the office and down the corridor ahead of Quan, entered the conference room, and

38

stood to one side, making room for him at the doorway. The room was deliberately staged to impress—dark blue silk walls, rosewood floor, gold-and-glass cases along the side wall housing national awards and gifts from foreign governments. An overly large rectangular table of rainbow obsidian occupied the center of the room, around which sat nine senior executives, sternly watching as Quan and the two assistants traversed the room.

Neither Quan nor his father had siblings and if his father didn't return, Quan would become heir and the major shareholder in the Jintao Corporation. Quan looked down at the rosewood floor and his chest heaved. He would be expected to take a position on the board. He always knew this was a possibility but now the consequence had hard edges and everything seemed immediate.

There was an empty chair at the head of the table and a distinguished-looking man next to it motioned for Quan to sit there. Lifting his chin, Quan made his way to the open seat. The distinguished man to his left was the company president, Dr. Hao—a middle-aged man with salt-and-pepper hair combed straight back—a concentration of white at the temples. Hao sat as motionless as a statue. His composure was legend, an enigmatic iron wall behind which lived a tough negotiator and a remarkably intelligent strategist.

After Quan took his seat, Hao introduced him as successor to the chairman of Jintao Corporation. He then introduced the other executives one by one, and finally turned slightly toward Quan and said, "I speak for all of us when I say we feel the absence of your father deeply and wish we could have greeted you under more fortunate circumstances. Even so, it is our pleasure to have you here with us today."

Sliding his chair back, Quan stood up to deliver a short speech he had rehearsed on the way over. Resting his fingertips on the table, he began in a calm, steady voice—attempting his best approximation of corporate speak. "Thank you, Dr. Hao. Thank you all. I'm honored to be in your presence. Your excellent service is what makes the Jintao Corporation such a great symbol of achievement to the rest of the world. Our clients, our employees, and even our competitors are inspired by the leadership and expertise you demonstrate. I'm grateful for your wisdom and professionalism. The company as a whole owes you a debt of gratitude. We have a great legacy and we are on a great journey together. Considering recent events, stability is most important, and I'm sure you agree that Dr. Hao should continue as both president and chief executive for the foreseeable future."

One by one the executives stood and reintroduced themselves, delivering summaries of the advances made within their departments. Quan watched the parade, each executive coming from a different discipline, yet all of them regimented in their conformal suits, delivering same-length speeches in a standard corporate parlance. A part of him felt sorry for them. These people curbed whatever creative spirit they may have once had and bent themselves to the will of the corporation.

He thought, *Conformity is useful, but it's also a form of enslavement.*

After the meeting adjourned and the executives filed out, Dr. Hao turned to Quan. With his hand pressed against the table between them, he leaned in and spoke in hushed tones so the secretaries couldn't hear. "Your being here is important. Your father's absence raised concerns about the future of the company, and news of your presence will help put minds at ease. While you're here, it's appropriate that you use your father's office. Let the secretaries know if you need anything and come see me when you've settled in. And, on a personal note, I want to thank you for acknowledging my commitment to the company."

Hao excused himself to attend several other meetings, leaving Quan alone at the table. The two assistants, who had been standing in the shadows, stepped forward. Turning to them, he asked, "Is Gregory McGowen here today?"

One of the assistants quickly tapped the disk on her wrist and a roster appeared in the air over the conference table.

"Yes, sir. He is here. Do you wish me to contact him for you?"

"Bring a pot of tea and two cups. Tell Mr. McGowen I'm here and ask him to join me." The women scurried away, their lives once again filled with purpose.

Alone in the conference room, Quan imagined what it must be like to be at the helm of a megacorp and the suffocating responsibility that would bring. It was a lifestyle he would never want to aspire to. Conversely, Hao was the perfect kind, capable of agenda after agenda, happy as a monkey swinging from branch to branch. Mastering the role of a chief executive would be unpleasant for Quan, yet he knew, in time, he could develop the necessary skills. But where was the joy in being a slave to a machine? Then again, with that power he could make changes. He could transform the company into a center for creativity, an oasis for intellectuals; he could encourage self-expression and relax the dress code . . .

His thoughts were interrupted by the arrival of a large man treading into the room. His light gray space boots made a squishing sound on the marble floor as he approached. From the little highland town of Aberlour, where McGowen was born, he had ventured the shores of Shenzhen in his twenties. He married a Chinese woman and made a home for himself at the Jintao Corporation. As a project manager he free to run his department the way he wanted—free from corporate politics. Untainted by personal agenda, McGowen was the one man Quan could trust.

Coming to a halt next to the boardroom table, McGowen's lip raised in an off-centered grin. "There you be, laddie. And none the worse for wear, I see."

"Come sit," said Quan with a smile. "Have some tea."

The young Jintao picked up a steaming cup and rolled it in his hands as one of the secretaries poured a second cup of green tea. The aroma of toasted oats and hay wafted up and the big man said, "Aye. Don't mind if I do. Outside it's colder than a brass monkey's behind."

41

Taking the chair to Quan's left, McGowen continued, "It's been a while. A lot's happened." He eyed the secretaries over the rim of his cup as he took a sip.

Quan turned to the women. "Leave us, please. I'll com if I need anything." He paused, waiting for them to leave, then said, "I spent the morning playing heir apparent, but what I really want is to find out what happened to my father. It's unbelievable he hasn't turned up. You've got the inside track on what's been happening around here. Bring me up to speed. I want to know everything."

Settling back in his chair, McGowen took another sip and set his cup down. "Mighty strange it was. Can't help thinking one day I'll turn a corner and he'll be here, just like before. But . . . well, I'm sure you saw the headlines. They searched high and low. Lots of rumors and theories . . . the police dogged every clue… and turned up nothing. Still, you'd do well to talk to them."

Quan agreed that in time he'd talk to the police, but first he wanted to retrace the events that led to that last day, to try and see things from his father's point of view, to maybe look where others hadn't.

"There was something," said McGowen. "Something that happened a while back. Might not be what you're looking for, but I thought it was curious."

"What? What are you referring to?"

"It was an odd thing, indeed; happened about a year ago. There was an anomaly at one of the orbiting power plants. A survey crew was sent up and reported a system overload— triggered by solar flares, they said. Then your father sent a couple of engineers up to have a look-see. They spent two days up there, doing tests for him. When they came back, your dad released an official memo. Basically, he agreed with the survey team. Solar flares overloaded the coils. Case closed, end of story. Right?"

"Go on."

42

McGowen began to speak in a quieter tone. "Well, first of all, it was odd for Master Jintao to be dealing with equipment failures. I would've expected him to delegate that to a manager, but then he did something that really turned my head around. If you look at the data logs, you'll see that he continued to access the engineering reports for months. He was doing something with the data in his private lab."

"He has a private lab?"

"To be sure. He likes to tinker."

"I never knew that. And why do you think it was unusual for him to study the data?"

"Well, for one, that's not a job for a chairman. We've got lots of engineers for that sort of thing. I suppose you can't blame a man for wanting to keep his hand in. Still, can't imagine him taking up his time with something like that, unless it was damn important. He was all about highest and best use of time." McGowen paused for another sip of tea. "He never posted anything more about it. Now, that isn't unusual around here; everything's on a need-to-know basis, and he certainly wasn't obliged to tell anyone what he was doing. But something had his attention. Know what I mean?"

"I think I follow," said Quan, a quizzical knit in his brow. "I'd like to see his private lab and look at those files."

"When I heard you were coming, I figured as much. You can see the files whenever you like, and I think there may be a rabbit hole, as well."

"A what?"

"A rabbit hole, aye, that's what our IT boys call it. It's a security feature, sort of a data tunnel. I'm pretty sure your father socked away more info than what we've seen so far. I'll show you whenever you like."

"Now . . . now is always the best time," said Quan, setting down his cup.

4.

McGowen emptied his cup in a single gulp and rose from his chair. Within a few minutes his heavy footsteps were echoing down a polished corridor on the tenth floor. Quan walked briskly to keep up. Over his shoulder McGowen said, "All the files were encrypted." Looking up as they passed a surveillance camera he continued, "Took a while but our code jockeys were able to open them."

When they arrived at the door of Master Jintao's lab, a synthesized female voice declared, "Gregory McGowen—Quan Jintao—you are approved for entry." The voice could have belonged to any cultured Mandarin lady, although some of its intonations were unmistakably those of Master Jintao, the program's tutor.

As they entered, a dim ambient glow lit the windowless lab. Racks of appliances were set against the walls and test instruments on wheels stood near a large workbench at the center.

Stepping up to the black-topped antistatic bench, McGowen said, "I wish I could say we've seen all his files, but I want to show you something. View field—on."

A faint haze appeared from the benchtop to the ceiling. He tapped the field with the palm of his hand and dozens of folders appeared. "These are all decrypted: briefs on power transfer, some engineering department notes on various projects. Interestin' but nothin' to explain his disappearance." He poked an icon at the edge of the field and a graphic emblem enlarged. The icon was an inverted pyramid, the Jintao corporate logo. "See anything unusual? Move your head side to side. See? It's not just two-dimensional. It's got depth. I think it might be an access point, maybe a link to an off-site database. The code jocks played with it, but they never got in. Maybe you'll have better luck."

"I had a puzzle like this when I was a child."

"Did you, now? Well, have a go." McGowen turned away and began to root through a storage bin in one of the racks.

Quan's hand extended into the view field, his fingers stretching to press all three sides of the emblem. His other hand reached in and pressed the apex of the pyramid at the same time. The shape suddenly rotated end over end, presenting its hidden side. On the back of the pyramid was a rectangular recess outlined in neon blue. Above the pyramid, a dozen pale green kanji characters appeared, floating in grid formation, jiggling slightly as if asking to be chosen. Quan considered the number of blank spaces in the rectangle and he selected one after another from the available characters, dropping them into the recess. He constructed three words: Courage, Knowledge, Honor—his father's personal motto. The recess closed and a female voice thanked him. *"Shieh, shieh."* Then it added, "Bio ID, please."

"It wants my father's bio."

"I was expecting that. It's got autosensing." McGowen handed over a thin plastic card he found in one of the bins. "Try this; it might work."

Quan held the card up to catch light from the view field. "A biotransmitter, I haven't seen one of these for ages. But I need something of my father's."

"No telling how sensitive the system is. You're the same bloodline. Put your finger on it and let's see what happens."

Quan placed his index finger in the outline on the card and in a few nanoseconds the card soaked up enough ambient RF energy to transmit. For a moment, the system did nothing, as if considering Quan's place in the Jintao bloodline. Then bold magenta text popped into view:

AUTHENTICATION FAILED

The female voice came again. "Bio ID, please."

"It wants my father's bio," said Quan, looking around the room. "I could get something from home like a hair from a hairbrush." Then Quan remembered, the brushes were immaculate and sterile.

"This system probably needs something more substantial than a hair," said McGowen.

"I can't think of anything," said Quan, feeling around in his pockets. He felt the chain, and, pulling on it, the little white rabbit's foot slid from his pocket.

"Wait," he said. "Let me try this."

He placed the furry object on the transmitter card. It fit perfectly.

The voice came again. "*Shieh, shieh*. Bio ID accepted."

The emblem faded from view and was replaced by eleven equally spaced folders.

Astonished, McGowen asked, "What was that?"

Turning the rabbit's foot over in his hand, Quan said, "I wasn't sure what it was for, or who sent it. Father must have made it. It must be infused with his gene code somehow."

"My oh my. Good luck you had that."

Quan opened the first folder—instrument readings from the malfunctioning power station and notes from the survey crew. He X-ed out and skipped to the last folder. It contained several documents arranged by date. Tapping the last page of the last document, he whisked down to the last entry.

12.13.2088 09.15.22 MUST SEE WITH MY OWN EYES

"What does that mean? What did he need to see?"

"A dinna ken, lad," said McGowen. "I don't know. The answer is probably in one of these files."

"I'm going to read all of this," said Quan. "I have to." He spun around to see McGowen, who was down on one knee next to him, looking at the view field.

"That's going to take a while," said McGowen, standing up. "I should probably get back to what I was doing. Com me when you're done."

5.

Inside the penthouse, Sealy felt light-headed each time she stood up and the Dramamine didn't help. Even though it was irrational to think the massive South Point structure could collapse, her fear persisted. The room seemed to sway and the floor seemed to tilt and the fathomless sea yawned below.

The last thing Sealy wanted to do was to add to Quan's stress, yet her acrophobia required treatment and so she went searching for a cure in an unexpected place.

Between the stone balusters surrounding the terrace, she could see gray-green hills leading down to a small cove partially obscured by mist. Surging waters lapped against the rocky shoal and the air was laden with briny coolness.

"Do you like this one?" asked a voice coming from all around her.

Her black eyes swept to the right, gazing at the gently rolling hills dotted with oak and manzanita. "Yes," she said, pausing to check with herself, then adding, "Maybe we could be a little closer to the water."

Her forearm came to rest on the rounded edge of an onyx table. The surface felt neither warm nor cool to the touch. Sunlight striking its smooth surface refracted off of crystals inside, blazing with amber light. A gentle breeze wafted scents of sage and sea from the valley below and the voice, busy at some distant task, came again. "There, that should do it."

Earth and sky quivered and the hillsides contracted. The rhythmic rumbling of waves reverberated up the canyon as the cove moved closer.

"Better?" asked the voice.

"Yes, much better."

"I'll put in a pathway leading to the cove . . ." the voice said, turning away again.

Violet wisteria materialized above her, dangling from a wooden arbor. The leaves blocked out sunlight except for small bright dots that stippled her navy blue suit. There was a rustling sound overhead. In the foliage, a bright green lizard stared at her through yellow eyes, then disappeared beneath the leaves.

Sealy smiled and turned her face into the breeze, her thick black hair fluttering. "This is perfect. I love it."

"I'll sync it up," said the voice. "I think your partner will love it."

She hoped he would.

Her thoughts returned to the days leading up to their union. She was perturbed when her parents insisted on talking to Quan's father. She thought perhaps the request was an excuse for her father to meet the renowned Master Jintao and she rebuked her father for meddling in their plans. Partnership agreements were the norm and lovers were permitted to contract without parental consent. Her father let the chiding go, but went on to remind her that family approval was still considered proper in polite society. Changing the subject, he added, "Men and women are different. They have different qualities and the difference is their strength. You must understand your partner's maleness and help him to understand how different women are. Young people experiment with roles that blur the distinction and it often leads to confusion.

Sealy never doubted her father's wisdom and she thought he was right—about the difference. Women are different, and in some ways women are superior: more insightful, more expressive, more nurturing, and in some ways stronger—certainly more complex.

She felt safe with Quan. He was a decent man and she was looking forward to having a family of her own—but first they would finish their education and enjoy her life together. They would travel and have adventures and make memories and . . .

The voice came again. "Okay, thank you. Show him in. Sealy, your partner is here."

Hearing Quan's footsteps coming up behind her, her eyes closed. She slowly inhaled as his hand touched her shoulder.

"Wow. So, this is the sim," said Quan. "Very realistic,"

Reaching up, she touched his hand. "We've been working on this all morning. It's a scene from central California. We tried so many: Ko Samui, the Maldives and the Cinque Terre. All nice, but I like this one the best. What do you think?"

Another complication to deal with. The view from the penthouse had never bothered Quan, but Sealy's vertigo was real and making her comfortable was worth the effort. It was her idea to create a panoramic projection that would camouflage the glass wall at the penthouse. Concealing the immense height was clever and a way for them to stay in the penthouse—if it worked.

"Well done. So realistic," he said, turning to watch the receptionist walking away in the dimly lit studio. "I like it."

Leaves rustled above and a yellow eye looked at him.

Sealy pressed his hand to her shoulder and turned to see his eyes. She loved those eyes, so distinctive, the color of green grapes.

"It's beautiful. It relaxes me," she said. "Thank you for understanding." From the corner of her eye she could see the archi-tech approaching.

Armando Ballaster was dark and smarmy, dressed in a tightly tailored bronze suit, cut with waist and cuff vents. Moving with the grace of a ballet dancer, the toes of his shoes seemed to point the way. He strode into the light; a gold necklace beneath his orange silk shirt glinting in the light. His smile displayed a modest glimpse of his perfect, ultrawhite implants. His hair was brushed back like strands of black vinyl ending in ringlets at the base of his neck. Beneath his flashy exterior, Armando was known to be a consummate professional. He was an archi-tech: a combination of artist, architect, engineer, and programmer with a reputation for creating extraordinary sim-scapes.

"Mister Jintao, it's an honor to meet you." His baritone voice was smooth and relaxed—Mandarin with a hint of Cuban. "So glad you could make it. Your partner has added some nice features this morning and, with your approval, we can schedule the installation."

"What does the installation entail?"

"This is a SensoReal system. Are you familiar with it?"

In contrast to the archi-tech's flamboyant manner, Quan's demeanor was reserved. His smooth face displayed the most subtle expressions.

"It's the result of interference projection. Isn't it?" asked Quan.

"That's correct, and with covalent boundary dynamics we're able to constitute tangible objects."

Quan searched the archi-tech's face for the slightest hint of condescension but found none. Confidence without arrogance—that added a plus next to Armando's name.

"Come, we'll show you the other spaces," said Armando, leading them away with his hand trailing behind. Quan eyed the hand. *Other spaces?*

Walking a few steps in the dimly lit studio, they came to an orange bollard lit with a pinpoint of white light. "Your penthouse was constructed with an open floor plan, making it easy to implement almost anything. Let me show you." Turning slightly, he spoke into his cupped hand. "Jintao E3."

In a blink, the entry area appeared. Quan recognized the marble floor a moment before it changed to hand-hewn rosewood. Behind them a wall of burnished gold materialized. In place of the bollard, a large clear vessel—waist high, filled with water. Inside, wide-bodied carp swam in circles, light reflecting off their orange and silver scales.

What? Quan wondered. *He's done more than just the great room?* Curious, he ran his hand along the rim of the fish tank. "It feels solid. You said boundary effects . . . some sort of osmoid immobilization?"

"That may be part of it. I'm not an expert on the science behind it but they've made the programing as easy as working in CAD."

"Interesting," said Quan, dipping two fingers into the water. Neither warm nor cool to the touch, his fingers came out dry.

With hands flourishing and explicatives flowing, Armando crisscrossed the studio, making one room vanish and another appear, as if by magic. He led them through the dining area into a drawing room with ceiling-to-floor wine storage.

"Virtual wine," said Quan with a smirk.

At last they returned to the great front room with its terrace and misty cove.

"You've been busy," said Quan with a glance to Sealy. "So, what's the plan?"

The archi-tech flashed his ultrawhites. "We can implement the refinements tonight and have it ready for another viewing tomorrow."

Quan placed one hand behind him at the small of his back and held up two fingers on the other hand, as if to say, *Not so fast*. "What about power consumption? What does this require?"

"The great room requires forty kilowatt-hours a month. For everything you saw, it's bordering on a hundred and forty."

"And how long to implement?" asked Quan, slightly raising his chin.

"A day to get the SensoReal components . . . they're available locally... another day for assembly and test."

Quan reasoned that they should go ahead with converting the great room and leave the other areas for a later date. That would solve the immediate problem.

"You won't be disappointed," said Armando. "I'll also include a complimentary copy of 'Armandorama.' If you ever need a quick getaway, it will turn your great room into a Sumatran rainforest, a moonscape, or a dozen other exotic destinations."

"Very well, then," said Quan, regarding Armando with a mixture of amusement and concern. "We'll see you tomorrow."

Outside the archi-tech's studio, on the rooftop aeropad, a shiny black autoglide silently descended with its flashers strobing. Its synthesized voice announced the standard cautions. "Stand clear. Stand clear."

"You're amazing, Seal. What a smart solution. The penthouse will feel more comfortable while we're there and, when father returns, the sim can be switched off if he chooses. No harm done."

"Thank you for being so understanding. I'll feel more comfortable and you might enjoy it, too."

"It's a fine idea. I'm glad we're staying at South Point." Placing his hands on her waist. "You go on ahead now. I'm going to walk to the office from here."

"The glide could drop you off."

"I need to get out and walk."

Her gloved hands surrounded his wrists and lifted his hands to her lips. She kissed his fingers.

Once inside the glide, a voice announced, "Please place hands and feet and all belongings inside the vehicle. Door is closing. Door is closing."

Quan watched the glide quietly levitate, turn, and autonavigate into sky traffic. A few moments later he was exiting the building at street level, merging with the crowd, striding down Victoria Road.

It felt good to stretch his legs. During his stay in England he had grown accustomed to walking for hours, exploring the lanes, fields, and streams of the nearby countryside. Now he was back on the streets of New Hong Kong, packed with pedestrians, merchants, and street vendors, all dwarfed by canyons of gigantic buildings made of xynite, steel, and glass. Delivery vehicles were only allowed after midnight, and during the day the flow of humanity was constant—as though all six billion Chinese were out on the street at the same time.

A full head taller than most, Quan looked out over what appeared to be a sea of black hair. Settling into a synchronized pace with the crowd, he felt absorbed into the living stream. Through subtle cooperation, they moved as one.

At the heart of this is the Tao, he thought, *the center path—the way. Chi flowing through meridians of least resistance.*

Moving through the shadowed canyons, the last moments with Sealy replayed behind his eyes. In a whisper, she said, "I adore you." She looked so incredibly beautiful, her skin so smooth and flawless and the daylight glinting off her hair. The memory made his heart quicken. Ever since their union, a new reality had grown within him. He felt as though she had always

54

been with him and would always be with him. He was more bonded with her than he had been with anyone else.

Quan looked up to see a ten-story projection of a tiger on the face of a building across the street. The tiger growled, dissolved, and a bottle of Tiger Tonic appeared in its place.

6.

By midafternoon Quan had walked four kilometers and he could see the communications tower of Jintao headquarters above the other buildings. A row of street merchants lined his route. Virtual menus floated above the food vendors' tables, and pungent aromas reminded him of his childhood. Through the crowd he caught a glimpse of a plump hand tossing what looked like chunks of chicken into a blackened wok. Chopped greens and water chestnuts followed. The cook's stout arm racked the pan against the grill, sending the contents arching through the air, landing back in the center of the sizzling pan. Quan turned his head back to the direction he was headed and almost stumbled over a wizened old woman. She was very short, standing directly in his path with a paper bag in her outstretched hands. Peeking out from the wrapper, a blue plastic cat with gold-tipped ears grinned at him. The old woman's face contorted in a stained-tooth grin and she said, "Lucky cat. Fifty yuan."

He felt in his coat pocket for coins to give the poor woman, but he had none.

Straightening, Quan said, "Sorry. No thank you," and sailed around her.

In his pocket, was only the thin plastic card McGowen had given him and the rabbit's foot, nothing of value to others but precious to him. In other big cities like London, he would have worried about pickpockets, but here, there was little to be concerned about. Street crime was rare in New Hong Kong. The Triads and the Tongs had withdrawn after their bosses turned to white-collar crime, and the gangs made it understood that any of their members who drew attention would be punished severely. In exchange for their brutal self-management, local police had agreed to turn a blind eye to the clandestine bordellos, gambling rooms, opium dens and other forms of victimless crimes.

Stepping out of the procession, Quan turned into a service alley down the side of the Jintao building. Passing a loading dock, he stopped next to a stout xynite support column towering twenty stories into the crisp blue sky. Behind him, pedestrians were streaming past in a steady blur. Damp filled his nostrils, and he remembered when the columns were framed with nanite caissons. He was a boy then, and the wet xynite slurry poured like an avalanche from an overhead boom while the nanites climbed higher and higher, linking together, forming a mold for the xynite. He watched in awe as an anonymous bystander.

Inside his pocket, Quan felt for the plastic card and oriented his finger to its contours. The card was the length of an index finger with three small ridges running across its face and a rubberized pad at one end. He fitted his first digit against the U-shaped pad and his biosignature instantly transmitted. In the shadows, next to the giant column, a panel clicked and slid back. Stepping inside, the panel clicked shut and a series of overhead lights switched on revealing a tunnel. It was a secret route, to be used in an emergency evacuation. As an entry, it was a way he could avoid the lobby and the endless exchange of greetings.

His footsteps reverberated down the tunnel and lights switched off behind him. At last he came to a maintenance room at the core of the building. He was in his teens the last time he had come this way. Generators and racks of electronics were humming and the room smelled of synthetic oil. Doors of a service elevator opened and a synthesized voice announced, "Quan Jintao. Floor, please."

Entering he said, "Ten," and the steel doors shut.

Inside his father's lab, he sat at the workbench and dove back into the rabbit hole. The next folder contained a vidi of the survey crew in their EVA suits with mag-boots holding them to the reactor platform. Walking appeared to be difficult and the handheld vidi jolted with each step. Behind them, Earth's oceans shone brightly—a gigantic blue curve dappled with white clouds.

One of the crew gestured to the antenna array. The dish faded in and out of view. A power meter was held up and someone said, "We shouldn't go any closer. Energy is leaking. Need to shut down for repairs."

Quan played the vidi clip several times, uncertain about what he was seeing. The antenna dish in the background seemed to distort, then correct, disappearing and reappearing. Perhaps the camera lens was automatically readjusting focus, changing depth of field. Or maybe glare from something out of frame was washing out the image.

Leafing through another folder, he came across a report from the second crew—a couple of engineers who were there to diagnose and repair the reactor. Testing and gathering data, they posted the live, dynamic values in a sidebar at the edge of the screen and linked them to a three-dimensional spreadsheet. Quan looked back and forth between the ever-changing numbers and the underlying equations. It was clear to him that several components were running beyond their safety ratings.

58

Electromagnetic waves were generating harmonics in several frequencies—fascinating to watch, but potentially dangerous. Concluding that many of the subsystems were damaged, the engineers recommended decommissioning the station altogether.

Moving on to the next folder, Quan saw hand sketches, annotated with calculations and notes. The sketches depicted a reactor with several different subsystems and the word "Control" connected with arrows to three of the components. On another page, he found a sketch of a magnetic wave generator that had been revised several times.

Without fully understanding what the sketches meant, Quan went to the next folder. There he found a CAD file of a very dense machine design. Modeled in 3-D, the machine was annotated with links to schematics and parts lists. Puzzled, Quan settled back in his chair, running his fingers across the top of his head.

Is this Father's work? What was he doing? Trying to redesign the power station?

The calculations were beyond anything he encountered in his most advanced physics classes. There were symbols for leptons and gluons, quarks and bosons, acted on by harmonic energies.

Can't be Father's work. His hands-on engineering work ended ages ago.

Exhausted, Quan went back out onto the street and walked for a while. He had a lot to think about. Surrounded by throngs of people, he once again became one with the crowd. Walking down side streets, he looked in the windows of shops, stopping for a while to watch a robot cobbler repairing shoes. Twenty minutes later he returned to Victoria Road and to the Jintao building.

Back again inside his father's space, he tried to understand the purpose of the machine design. He flipped back and forth between the notes, drawings, and equations, and watched the vidi clips again. He followed the logical train of thought, from the measurements gathered at the reactor to the mathematical analysis and the complex machine design. After two more hours of immersion, he needed another break.

He walked around the lab and stretched. Bending sideways at the waist, he noticed something in the back corner of the lab. Behind a mobile oscilloscope, an unusual assembly sat on top of a three-wheeled dolly. He recognized the shape, from one of the sketches in the files. It was waist high and spherical, with several devices attached to its outer wall. With feet firmly planted, he struggled to pull it out into the open. By alternating his pull, first right, then left, he was able to lug the heavy object into the light.

Curious about what was inside, he looked around the room for tools. From a multi-drawered crib he selected a handful of different tools. Using an adjustable wrench he removed one of the attached devices. Turning it over in his hand, it looked like a power coil. He set it down. Next, with a socket he undid a cover plate. With his cheek pressed to the curved surface of the orb and a small penlight against his other cheek, he looked inside. There were studs welded to the interior wall where something had once been attached and there was an electrical connector dangling from the ceiling. Whatever had been in there was gone and he felt robbed.

What is this? Some sort of test fixture?

Maybe it was used to analyze the orbiting power station. Or maybe it was unrelated. Quan went back to the view field, skimming through the files until he found a sketch that resembled the sphere. Indeed, it showed another component within it's walls. From the look of it, it appeared to be a generator of some kind. The related cells on the spreadsheet indicated that it would generate non-linear harmonic energys. This presented a quandary. Harmonic frequencies in the power grid were a frequent cause of power quality problems. Why would someone design a device that would create them.

Quan continued on, trying to understand what his father had found so intriguing. After another hour he came again to the last sentence:

MUST SEE WITH MY OWN EYES

It was past the end of the corporate workday and Quan needed McGowen, if he was still in the building. He accessed the com center and was attended by the on-duty avatar that relayed the call to McGowen's extension.

"McGowen here."

"It's Quan and I've finished going through the files."

"Find anything useful?"

"There's a lot that I don't understand. It'd be good to have your eyes on it."

"I've delegated most of my workload so I'm free to give you whatever help you need."

"I have to admit, the science and engineering in his files is over my head and there aren't any notes to explain what he was doing. I did, however, find mention of two people who may have worked on this project—someone called Dr. von Ang and someone named Diayu Lee. They may be able to explain what he was doing and where he might have gone. See if you can find them and schedule separate meetings."

"I'll get started on it."

"And don't say anything about the files we found. There's probably a reason father wanted this kept private. For now anyway, it's just between you and me."

"Roger that."

7.

McGowen found Gaston von Ang's name in the company's directory of qualified consultants, and twenty hours later the pale young man was standing in Quan's outer office. He was tall and thin with sandy brown hair cut straight across the shoulders of his black WAN-suit. The suit was a micro-tailored European cut, highlighted with blue piping at every seam. On top of each shoulder, the blue line became a complicated pattern, overlaying the suit's embedded antennas. He stood still, with hands clasped behind him, speaking instructions to a distant mainframe, while a tiny projector sent a stream of data to his retina.

A live image of the young scientist floated in the corner of Quan's view field while he read the man's credentials: dual degrees . . . particle physics and nano-electronics . . . top of his class . . . PhD from the Sorbonne . . . advanced research at CERN . . . long list of corporate consulting jobs . . . Swiss national . . . third-generation physicist . . . nineteen published papers . . . consulted with Jintao Space on four projects.

Quan swept the information aside and pinged his secretary. She said, "You may go in now." The door to the inner office clicked and automatically opened.

Out from behind the desk, Quan went to greet his guest. Shaking hands, he said, "Thank you for coming, Dr. von Ang. I'm Quan Jintao, Master Jintao's son. Please have a seat."

"Yes," said the scientist as he went to an empty chair on the opposite side of the desk. "I can see the resemblance."

"I understand you worked with my father."

"We worked together on several occasions." Von Ang's eyes lowered for a moment, then looked up. "He is a remarkable man. Is there news of his whereabouts?"

Quan couldn't help but notice how straight the man sat in his chair, and how his cold blue eyes seemed to pierce him with a penetrating gaze. It was as though von Ang was acutely aware of Quan's thoughts, even before he was.

"His disappearance is still unsolved, and I'm trying to understand what happened. I thought you might be able to bring some light. I understand you worked with him quite recently."

Von Ang continued his penetrating stare. "That's true, and I'll be glad to answer any questions you have."

"Did the police contact you?"

"Not yet, but I was questioned by your corporate security."

"What did you tell them?"

"Only that I worked as a consultant several months earlier and have no idea where he may be."

"I wish to ask about the last project you worked on with my father."

"Yes, of course."

"Were you working under a nondisclosure agreement?"

"Yes, as always. However, the last agreement was somewhat different. It excluded the corporation and restricted disclosure solely to the Jintao family. Your father said it was a precaution; in the event the company was to change hands—the work would remain with the family. With respect, you and I can talk about things I cannot talk about with anyone else."

"I see," said Quan, wondering why his father would be concerned about the company changing hands. "I've read my father's notes concerning the orbital power station and I've seen designs for some sort of machine."

"Three," said von Ang, solemnly.

"Excuse me?"

"Three different machines. Prototypes."

"Prototypes? Of what?"

"At first, we were trying to re-create the power station anomaly to better understand the phenomenon. We built a simulator in his laboratory. It was one-tenth scale and it failed to generate the conditions—probably because of its size. Next, we built a full-sized version and added a plasma generator to simulate solar wind. We regulated the energy levels, trying to replicate the original conditions, but the results were intermittent, unpredictable. We tried different control methods, but the system wouldn't stabilize. Then we started over. Cannibalizing the second prototype, we used some of the parts to build a third, more complex machine. We added a pulse generator, enhanced the wave guides, and added subsystem controllers. Lastly, we installed a machine learning system to adjust the harmonics. It took several months but eventually we were able to reproduce the same phenomenon first observed at the orbital reactor."

"All of this was done by just the two of you? Did you design the control systems?"

"Yes, and yes."

"Impressive. But why? Why go through all of that to re-create a malfunction?"

Von Ang turned his head toward the window, staring at the faraway clouds. "It was a science experiment to see if the anomaly might be related to quantum flux."

"I saw references to quantum physics in the files that I didn't fully understand. Please explain."

Von Ang hesitated, collecting his thoughts, simplifying his explanation to a level of complexity that a graduate engineer would understand. He began with the basics, the well-documented evidence of subatomic particles vibrating in and out of existence.

"I've always found it fascinating that particles are intermittent, sometimes here, sometimes not. Decades ago, the Russian physicist Ivan Krakinov put forth the idea that subatomic particles move between our 3-D world and a state where there are additional dimensions. Mathematically, it fits perfectly, but no one has ever been able to prove the theory. Your father believed the disappearing antenna might be the result of particles somehow being forced out of three-dimensional space, not just for pico-seconds, but for extended periods of time. If we could build a device that reproduced those energies, it would not only be a monumental breakthrough in science, but also would also have huge commercial value. To my surprise, we succeeded and the machine was able to render objects invisible for as long as we applied the energies. When the energies were turned off, the objects reappeared. Quite amazing."

"That is amazing indeed," said Quan. "So, the machine actually pushes matter into higher-dimensional space?"

"That's one possible explanation; of course, there may be others. What we observed was an effect. The cause is not so clear. More experimentation is needed."

Quan rolled a stylus back and forth on the desktop, considering the importance of what he had just learned. The reason his father kept this project out of the company's reach was becoming apparent. This was more than a science project. Probing deeper, Quan asked, "How was all of this work done without company involvement? And where did the resources come from?"

"Your father was very resourceful. I never questioned his methods. I was told to hire different fabricators to make each subsystem and none of them were told what the parts were for. We did the final assembly ourselves with robotic assistance."

"Where? Where is the working prototype?"

Von Ang got up and walked to the floor-to-ceiling glass wall of the Jintao tower. His hands clasped behind him and he nodded toward the open sea. "On the other side of Kau Yi Chau Island."

Kau Yi Chau Island—a kilometer-long outcropping of rock in the middle of Victoria Harbour; uninhabited; designated as the site for a future power terminus to be built by the Jintao Corporation. Two massive unfinished buildings stood there vacant—the scheduled completion date still years away.

"You were asked about this by Jintao security?"

"No. And if they had, I was not authorized to tell them," said von Ang.

Quan reined himself away from the premature conclusion that his father was there, on that island. *Someone must have gone there by now . . . looked for him . . . discovered the machine.*

"The machine must have been brought there in pieces," Quan mused. "But never mind that. Tell me what happened next. After building the third machine. Take me through it—step by step."

"As I said, it was just the two of us. I've known projects that have languished for years through trial and error, without success—regardless of the size of the team. We were lucky. After relatively few adjustments, the machine produced the desired result and, in less than a year, the effect was stable and we began to investigate the anomaly. First, we experimented with recording devices. They were pushed out of visual range and then returned. Unfortunately, no data was recorded. Then we tried different chemistries. They also came back without effect. There were thousands of things we could try but we had no clear-cut strategy going forward. Realizing this, your father curtailed my participation.

The experiments have profound implications and they should be continued. If the Krakinov hypothesis is proven to be correct, it would take us beyond the theoretical; teach us something new about the exchange of matter and energy. It would be a major stepping-stone. On the other hand, if the energies were simply cloaking matter somehow, it could teach us about other aspects of nature we have yet to understand."

"I take it you haven't been back to the island since then."

"That's correct."

Quan rose from the desk and moved toward the door. "I understand the scientific value, but first and foremost I want to find out what happened to my father."

"I understand and I'll help in any way I can." Von Ang stood up, slid his heels together and extended his hand.

"I need to go there—to the island," said Quan. "I need to see what's there and I want you to take me. Are you checked out on a glide?"

Von Ang's eyes widened. "Yes, of course. I'm instrument rated."

"Good. We'll want to go the island undetected."

Dr. von Ang left the room and Quan was alone again, sitting behind his father's desk, a two-meter-wide, highly polished black slab, floating a meter above the floor with no visible means of support. He leaned back and closed his eyes, visualizing his father working with the young scientist. His father often said, "State the problem clearly and the answer will appear." It was mind-bending to think that the theory might actually be true—that matter was essentially made of nothing more than vibrating energy and moments of probability. Quan imagined the chair underneath him, winking in and out of existence so fast that it might seem solid, but perhaps nothing but empty space.

If Krakinov was right, matter doesn't exist at all. Things only have a "potentiality" in space-time. Zillions of particles, intermittently here, and then not . . . yet enough of them here at any given moment to give the illusion of matter. But if the theory is wrong, then what is that machine doing?

Quan reached for the stylus and rolled it back and forth on the desktop. He was feeling somewhat intimidated by the scope of what he had just learned, and yet excitement stirred within him. It was possible that his father was on the verge of a great discovery and he was about to join the mission.

8.

Ning set plates in front of the young couple and poured wine for each, then withdrew to another part of the house. The wine was an especially good Cabernet, scented with blackberries and French oak. The entrée was sea bass drenched in orange beurre blanc sauce, complemented by a puree of cauliflower molded in the shape of a lotus blossom.

"Delicious," said Sealy earnestly. "I can barely tell the difference between NutriSynth and the real thing."

"You sound like a commercial," said Quan.

"Very funny," said Sealy, sipping her wine. "So, you went to the corporation today. Tell me what you learned. Any news about your father?"

"I met with someone who worked with him and I learned about the work they were doing. I should know more tomorrow." He went on to tell her about the orbital reactor, the Krakinov theory, and the prototypes, but he could see she was losing interest.

"Anything new here today?" he asked.

"As a matter of fact, yes. I talked with our archi-tech," said Sealy, "and he had some surprising news."

"Oh?" asked Quan, thinking that perhaps the archi-tech had overreached and succeeded in coaxing Sealy into expand the project. Quan was half expecting Armando to try. It was, after all, his business.

"He was looking through the original building plans of the penthouse," said Sealy, "and he found something unusual. This place already has a cyber system installed."

Quan said, "The penthouse was built twenty-five years ago. He probably meant the smart-house system that controls the optical and com systems."

"No. He said it was an IA system. At first, I thought he meant artificial intelligence, but he corrected me. He said it was IA and a constant duty system, whatever that means."

"Means it's on all the time." Quan looked around the room. "Are you sure he said IA? That means intermodal android."

Sealy leaned forward and whispered, "You don't know, do you? It's Ning."

"What? Wait. No. She's . . ." He caught himself leaping to a conclusion. She'd always been there, in the background, taking care of the house, serving meals, and, when he was an infant, she used to read to him. *Wait.* He never actually saw her eat anything. He had never seen her sleeping, and, to his knowledge, she never left the penthouse.

"Wow. That's a mind-blower. But twenty-five years ago, bots couldn't pass for human."

"I know. We had bots where I grew up," said Sealy, "but they weren't like real people at all. They were just appliances. Ning is scary good. I've been watching her all day. The way she moves, her skin texture, and her voice—so perfect—so natural. Next time you see her, look closely at her cuticles and the hairline and you'll see what I mean." She leaned in. "It changes things, doesn't it? Now that we know."

Ning entered the room and began to remove the dishes. They went quiet.

Quan noticed the details Sealy mentioned. Where Ning's fingernails ended there seemed to be a slight gap where the cuticle began. At her hairline, where the growth pattern should have been more random, it was geometrically perfect. He found himself becoming irritated. This revelation came at a bad time. There was enough on his plate—the investigation, the Jintao Corporation, Father's research, Sealy's acrophobia, and now this.

"I've known her all my life," he said, in a frustrated tone. "Guess I never really looked at her closely."

Ning returned a moment later with ramekins of tapioca and steaming cups of oolong. She placed them on the table, straightened, and stood for a moment as if waiting for instruction. Then she pivoted and returned again to the kitchen.

"Let's talk about something else," he said.

Ignoring his attempt to end the discussion, Sealy looked cautiously at the doorway and said, "Do you think she knows what she is?"

"How could she? I don't know. How could she not?"

"Could you access her central processor? Might be interesting to see what's inside. Maybe she knows where your father went."

"I asked her," said Quan, exasperated. "If she knew, she would have said so." He began to fidget. "I really don't want to think about this just now."

"Okay. What would you like to talk about? Did you find anything more in your father's laboratory?"

"I've read everything in his files. I don't know what happened. I'm making progress, but I'm frustrated with how slow it's going. I'm doing my best to get to the bottom of this but there's just so much I don't know."

Sealy's eyes were wide with concern. She put a hand on his neck and gently massaged. "Is here anything I can do to help?"

In another part of the house Ning overheard every word. Quietly, she muttered to herself, "There is nothing you can do."

Quan stood up from the dining table, wishing he had gone to Kau Yi Chau Island instead of returning home. "I don't know what it all means yet," he said, folding his napkin. "There's a site I want to visit tomorrow and there's another consultant I need to talk with. As soon as I know something definitive I'll let you know."

"What about my father?" asked Sealy. "They became friends after our union. Maybe he knows something. We should call him."

Quan stopped himself from walking away. She was trying to help and her suggestion opened up a possibility he hadn't considered. For a moment he thought about why he had turned away—so many diverging claims on his attention, all at the same time—acrophobia, the corporation, Ning, his doctorate—all seemed important. *Prioritize.*

Finding father is number one.

"Yes. Let's reach out to him," he said.

Retiring to his room, Quan changed into his pajamas and was thinking about von Ang and the invention when Sealy opened a com line to her family residence. A static picture of her family filled the view field above their bed. "He's got privacy mode on," she said. "Come and talk to him."

Quan shifted his position to sit next to her on the bed.

Her father's voice was low and slow. After a brief exchange of pleasantries, Sealy announced, "Quan has questions."

Her abruptness thrust him into gear and he leaned forward. "I'm trying to understand the work my father was doing before he disappeared. Did he ever talk to you about his projects?"

"We talked about business once or twice, but only in general terms, nothing specific. Our last conversation was purely philosophical."

"Can you tell me what it was about?"

"Life forms. It was about life-forms and how different they might be in places other than Earth. Evolution is site specific. Living things, you know, don't necessarily need to be carbon based. They could conceivably be silicon based, or something else, and they could take on dramatically different forms, maybe even gaseous, like clouds. We discussed the question of survival. My opinion is that life-forms evolving in radically different conditions probably would not do well here. Put an organism outside its tolerance zone and it won't survive for long."

"So, was this related to work he was doing?"

"Not that I know of. If anything, it was more related to work at my company. As you know, we're a biotech company. I know it must be frustrating—not knowing what led to his disappearance. I sympathize with what you're going through. Obviously, you care a great deal and I'm sure your father would be honored to know you're searching for him, but guard yourself against disappointment. This may not be resolved for a very long time. If there's anything more I can do to help, don't hesitate to ask. You're like a son to me."

Quan thanked him for the kind words and the view field faded. Another blind alley, he thought and the parting remark left him with an emptiness inside, reminding him of how few conversations he had had with his father in the past few years. Absorbed by his studies, he now wished they had talked more. The image he held of his father as a venerable corporate executive—heading a company known for commercializing discoveries invented by others—fell short of the reality that his father was doing basic research on such a profound project.

Sealy said, "It's been a long day. We should get some rest now."

Quan tucked himself under the covers and said goodnight. His thoughts returned to his father and the experiments.

~~~

Without fully understanding the nature of the phenomenon at the OB12 reactor, Master Jintao instinctively knew it was something profound and was inescapably drawn to study it. After success recreating the phenomenon, he let the young physicist go and continued to experiment on his own. The results continued to be inconclusive. Things disappeared and reappeared without a clue as to why.

Undeterred, he continued making adjustments and testing. He tried using organic compounds, microorganisms, and botanicals as subjects, looking for any subtle change. He tried different calibrations of time and intensity, all without effect—no clue to indicate what was actually happening. The one constant was that the subjects disappeared and reappeared, unchanged.

After months of tedious effort, Master Jintao was about to quit the project when he decided to experiment with one more subject. With a pair of tweezers, he held a tiny drosophila by its wing and placed it inside a small glass ampule. He mounted the little cylinder in front of the wave guides and brought the energies online. Numbers streamed, the wave guide hummed in deep bass and subsonic tones. The little fly flicked its wings, the counter rolled backward to zero, and *poof,* the drosophila was gone. Ten seconds later it reappeared. Peering closely at what was inside the ampule, Master Jintao watched the small creature flick its wings . . . once . . . twice . . . involuntary death throes. Something changed . . . but not in a good way.

The results were frustrating: things disappearing and reappearing without advancing his understanding. Was it possible

74

that the anomaly had nothing to do with other dimensions at all? Perhaps the machine was generating some kind of temporary cloaking of matter, or perhaps it was expanding or contracting the atomic structure, driving the subatomic particles to a scale that was unrecognizable. Far from proving the Krakinov theory, the machine generated conundrums of its own. And now there was the fly.

07.02.2088 17.21.33 TEST WITH LIVE DROSOPHILA: SUBJECT FAILED.

Other than noting the things he used as subjects, there was no compelling reason make detailed notes. After all, what had he learned? What had he proved? He experimented with inorganic and organic specimens, inanimate and live specimens but had they actually gone somewhere? And, if so, where? The only irrefutable fact was that the machine made things disappear.

Master Jintao's ability to conquer large, intractable problems was legend; decades of steering the corporation honed that skill, but now an impenetrable wall of ignorance loomed before him. There was the mortality issue. The specimen died. Living systems have a high degree of order and perhaps, he thought, that order was being disrupted on some level. If he could find a way to stabilize a life-form so that it survived, it might say something about what the phenomenon was doing. Unable to make progress with a linear approach, he began to think creatively.

Perhaps, he thought, if he further stabilized and contained the powerful field energies... Guided by intuition, he set about designing a new component.

9.

Returning to Jintao headquarters early the next morning, a secretary directed Quan to the central boardroom where Dr. Hao was conducting a quick pitch session where several engineering groups were proposing new projects.

Another distraction, thought Quan. He felt compelled to attend.

As he entered the room, Hao beckoned, indicating a vacant chair next to him. Twenty-three project managers were gathered around a table that was big enough to be the deck of a yacht. In the center of the table, 3-D holo-images filled the space from tabletop to ceiling, and each team was being given five minutes to summarize their proposal. Quan listened patiently, concentrating more on protocol than substance. Nevertheless, one of the proposals piqued his interest. The project was a nuclear waste disposal system, a three-hundred-meter-wide, disk-shaped slingshot, to be placed in geosynchronous orbit, tethered to Earth by a thirty-five-thousand-kilometer cable. The cable would act as an elevator to lift radioactive canisters to the orbiting slingshot, where they would be flung directly into the sun. Although it required a huge up-front investment, the profit tail would span decades. The project lead explained that time was of the essence because a similar system was under development by a consortium of EU companies and Jintao Corporation was playing catch-up.

Giving a nod, Dr. Hao rendered a decision: Go forward. Not all proposals were so fortunate, and by the end of the session more than half were tabled. As the managers began to filter out of the room, Hao flagged the slingshot team. Placing two fingers on the edge of the table near Quan, he said quietly, "I have a strategy for this one."

The three-member team waited patiently until the others left. Hao told the conference room's recording system to pause. Then he turned to the engineers. "I'm going to suggest a way to outflank the competition. Target the leader of the EU consortium. One of our shell companies in Malta will transfer ten million euros to his personal bank account. Our affiliates in Europe will spread rumors that he has embezzled funds and that the EU consortium is running out of cash to complete the project. Of course, none of this can be traced back to us. The scandal will be leaked to the media, and a few days later we will begin negotiations with the companies who were signed up to use the EU system. Tell them that we are accelerating our program to meet the shortfall. After they have signed with us, the bank in Malta will declare the transfer of funds was in error, investigators will find no evidence of embezzlement, and the leader of the EU consortium will be exonerated. The loss of momentum will put us in the lead."

"A bold plan," said the project leader.

Dr. Hao replied nonchalantly, "Only a suggestion."

"A most excellent suggestion," said the project leader, bowing to Hao.

"Nothing is to be written. Verbal updates only," said Hao.

Quan was impressed with Hao's skill—a businessman of the old school. He had suggested a classic Zheng Ren strategy with a bait-and-switch variation. Quan had learned the strategy on his eleventh birthday when his father presented him with two volumes: *The Book of Thirty-Six Strategies* and *The Art of War* by Sun Tzu. "You must study these," his father told him. "Business is war and the goal is to conquer."

No doubt Hao's plan would succeed, so long as his project managers mustered the nerve to see it through.

In the corridor outside his office, Quan found McGowen waiting for him.

"She's here," said McGowen.

"Who?"

"The lass from HK Labs."

"So soon?"

"Aye. You should know me by now—the difficult I do right away, the impossible takes just a wee bit longer. Shall I send her up?"

"Escort her and if anyone asks questions tell them she's here to meet with me about postgraduate work I'm doing."

Sitting behind his father's desk, Quan read her file. A PhD in molecular engineering from Peking University at age nineteen. The Ministry of Science and Technology requisitioned her for a government research team, and for the next ten years, she worked in a secure facility designing nanomachines for military use. Her family was generously compensated for her service. Then she accepted a lucrative offer to join Henan Kaifeng Laboratories, a distinguished institution where she was allowed to pursue her own research. Her contributions to food synthesis and nanite technology were noted. Reaching the end of her résumé, Quan walked out to greet her.

Diayu Lee was of average height, wearing a dark blue cardigan sweater over a starched white shirt and black pants. Her eyes appeared miniscule behind the thick glasses perched on her rather wide nose, and her upper lip only partially covered a pair of oversized incisors. Tilting her head back, she peered through the bottoms of her lenses, and spoke loudly. "Nin hao. I am Dr. Diayu Lee. You are Master Jintao's son?"

Quan quickly extended his hand toward her. She shook his hand with surprising vigor.

With taller ears, she'd look like a rabbit! thought Quan.

"Has your father returned yet?" asked Dr. Lee.

"No, not yet. However, I expect to know something very soon."

Leading her to his inner office, he began looking for common ground.

"You worked on nanomachines, is that correct?" he asked.

"Yes, many years ago. My primary interest now is molecular biology."

"I built nanomachines at university," said Quan.

"Did you use molecular engines?"

"I'm afraid not. The machines we built were tethered to a power source."

"Molecular engines are very expensive," said Dr. Lee.

"I believe you're right." Quan gestured to one of the chairs. "Please have a seat. I'd like to know about the work you did with my father."

"Normally I don't work with people outside the laboratory, but your father was very kind and such a distinguished gentleman."

"What did you do for him?"

"We did a trade. I provided molecular scans. I still say molecular, although the scans I provided were orders of magnitude more discrete."

"A trade?"

"Yes. He provided a rare isotope I needed for my work, and in return I scanned a few things for him."

79

"Did you sign a nondisclosure agreement?"

"Yes, but he wouldn't tell me what the scans were for. I explained to him that HK Labs is a secure facility. Our laboratory has state-of-the-art equipment and . . ."

As she went on, Quan felt a mounting need to thread the needle and expedite the investigation. Holding his hand upright like a stop sign, he said, "Please hold on. There's another colleague who worked on this project. I want to bring him into the conversation."

Within a minute, Dr. Gaston von Ang was connected over a secure link, appearing in the air between them. Quan walked to the other side of the desk as he made the introductions. "You both worked with my father on his last project and I am trying to retrace what he did."

"You intend to continue your father's experiments. Is that it?" asked Dr. Lee.

"Not necessarily. Above all, I want to find out what happened to him. That's priority. Now Dr. Lee, you provided molecular scans. I assume these were used in his experiments. And Dr. von Ang, you designed the apparatus. Please tell her . . . tell us both, what the machine does."

Without mentioning the Krakinov theory, von Ang described the equipment in general terms, while Dr. Lee sat motionless, hands in her lap, intrigued by the possibilities and engrossed by his technical acumen. He concluded by saying, "Essentially, we captured an anomaly in a bottle. The rest is theoretical. It may take decades to understand what the anomaly really is."

"About the things we don't understand," said Quan, "there are things we use every day but don't fully understand. Take anesthesia, for example. Certain gases render a patient unconscious, and other gases bring them back. The technique has been around for centuries but we don't fully understand how it works."

80

"I don't know much about anesthesia or about this machine," said Dr. Lee, "but if it can be used to do harm, then I am very concerned."

"The machine generates very powerful energies," said von Ang. "However, it also has sensors and safety shutoffs. The likelihood of a catastrophic failure is negligible."

"From what I know," said Quan, "this was the last thing my father was working on. So, it's imperative that you help me understand what these experiments were about."

"I'll be glad to help," said Dr. Lee. "I would, however, like to have a say in how we proceed."

"Of course. I'm open to anything you have to say. Is that okay with you, Dr. von Ang?"

"Yes, of course. Another point of view is always welcome."

Learning more about the reactor project, the project his father worked on up until he disappeared, seemed the best way forward. His father trusted these two and Quan felt confident they would bring him closer to knowing if there was a connection between the discovery and his father's absence.

One of the secretaries led Dr. Lee from the room and with a few deft moves of his fingers, Quan was back inside the hidden files. He flipped to the entries made after von Ang left the project.

03.19.2088 16.12.43 STABILIZER INSTALLED
03.19.2088 17.01.54 SCAN DATA FILE TOO LARGE
03.22.2088 09.23.03 RAM UPGRADE
03.22.2088 11.41.33 STABILIZER TEST SUCCESSFUL

The increase in data size must be related to the scans Dr. Lee provided, thought Quan. *So he had to upgrade random access memory.*

It was likely that neither of the consultants knew about the new component. It was installed after Dr. von Ang was taken off the project. Quan needed another pair of eyes to help understand what the stabilizer was doing. He looked at the time. It was 12:48 p.m. in New Hong Kong—7:48 a.m. in Oxford, England. Perfect. He opened a com line to his mentor at Oxford.

"Professor Harrowden," Quan said to the switchboard.

A few moments later he heard the professor's voice.

"Harrowden here."

"It's Quan Jintao, professor."

"Ah. Mr. Jintao. How are you? You'll be pleased to know we all agreed your thesis was exceptional."

"Thank you very much," said Quan. "I'm glad to know that. I wasn't as prepared as I wanted to be. I had to leave rather suddenly you know—a family emergency."

"Forgive me. I should have asked firstly about your father. Has he turned up?"

"I wish I could say yes. Unfortunately, the search is still on. Actually, I'm calling because I need help with a somewhat related matter. I need help to understand a set of plans that he was working on—plans are for a molecular stabilizer. Is there anyone there who could help me with that?"

The conversation went on with Quan answering questions about how the plans might be used. He explained who his father was and that the device was a component to be used in a larger machine. The professor pressed on, asking what the machine would be used for and Quan declined to answer. At last Harrowden said, "Review of commercial products is not in the purview of the university. I'm sorry. I can't help you in this matter. School policy, you see."

Quan said good-bye, feeling as though he could have handled the questions better. Then again, lying wasn't an option.

Quan immediately tapped his wrist disc again and said, "Xiaoping. Chimera Bio."

His view field instantly displayed the words "SECURE CONNECTION." Surprisingly, Dr. Xiaoping appeared behind his desk, peering at Quan from under bulbous eyelids, his tan face surrounded by a thick crop of white hair.

"Nin hao Quan. How is your research going? Any news about your father?"

Dr. Xiaoping was easy to talk to and Quan liked him. There was a warmth about him. All the same, there was a need for opacity until he knew why his father concealed the project. He was on a fact-finding mission, gathering information from here and there without letting anyone know as much as he did.

"No news yet, although I have came across a set of plans that may be related and I need help understanding them. It's some sort of molecular stabilizer."

"Definitely out of my area of expertise. My focus for years has been administration and marketing. Have you consulted with the engineering group at Jintao?"

"They're occupied with other projects and I don't want to bother them. Do you know anyone who might be able to help?"

"I know a few outside consultants who would look at it for you. Probably the best research group is over at Yanistat Burroughs. Laosing Mao runs it. He's really quite knowledgeable. I can send you his contact info, if you like."

"I'd appreciate that," said Quan. *"Shieh, shieh."*

"Stay in touch and let me know how things are going."

After the call ended, Quan's hand reached to the top of his head, fingers brushing the tips of his closely cropped hair. He needed to be careful. He could have shown the plans to von Ang, but the stabilizer designed by his father might be the most valuable part of the machine. Gathering bits of information from several disconnected individuals was safer. *Never let the left hand know what the right hand is doing.*

~~~

Midafternoon, Laosing Mao squinted in the broad sunlight as he ambled across the rooftop terminus of the Jintao One building. He was a sullen man, an asthmatic with watery eyes, overweight and slightly yellow, rocking side to side as he walked. His personal life was virtually nonexistent. Abandoned by his parents at the age of nine, he was taken in by an elder who become increasingly ill and depended on the youth for his care. The young Mao tried his best to help the man, fetching ancient Chinese medicines from a local shop, only to be ridiculed by his guardian for his lack of medical knowledge. The humiliation caused Mao to turn resolutely to academic pursuit. Determined to learn everything he could, he became a voracious student, graduating with the highest honors.

The Yanistat Burroughs Company hired him straight from university and Mao quickly became one of their top researchers. Within two years, he was promoted to research manager and a year later he was given the department to run. No one in the company was a match for his broad knowledge of applied physics and bioscience. Although he lacked charisma, using his trove of knowledge as enticement, he was able to hire several excellent researchers and he built one of the largest scientific libraries in existence.

In his father's office, Quan sat across the desk from Mao.

"I'm looking at designs for a new component that may be able to stabilize molecular structures when placed in extreme environments. It's something we might have a use for; however, I don't know if it works, and I'd like you to look at the plans and tell me what you think."

Mao listened intently, blotting his eyes with a handkerchief.

"I don't know what help I can be, but I'll be glad to look at it for you," said Mao.

Quan had him sign a confidentiality agreement and told his secretary to leave for the rest of the day. At her desk, Quan pulled up the plans then had Mao sit at the desk.

In his private office, Quan continued to observe Mao in a sidebar on his view field.

Culling through the schematics and drawings, Mao availed himself of several outside databases including the Yanistat Burroughs library. He set out reference materials and algorithms and worked for almost two hours. It was dark outside, 6:00, when Mao sat back, eyes still darting here and there on the view field, digesting what he had seen. At last he said aloud, "Amazing!"

Mao trudged back into Quan's office and plopped himself down in front of the large black desk. He seemed excited. "It's ingenious. A complex component. Very well designed."

"Tell me what you found."

"Preservation of angular neutron flux using spherical harmonics—it's designed to produce a stabilizing field effect. For it to work, however, the object must be sequenced at a very high resolution. After sequence data is imported, the stabilizer locks onto and tracks particle trajectories while specific field energies are used to stabilize."

"Does it look like it might work?"

"That depends. What do you plan to use it for?"

"I'm not sure yet." A subtle smile crept across Quan's face. "Tell me about the sequence data. How is that provided?"

Mao did not return the smile. He only smiled occasionally, while feeding pigeons at the foot of his park bench near the Jockey Club on Sundays. "It requires a separate sequencing device upstream to analyze the subatomic structure. Very expensive. Yanistat Burroughs doesn't have one, and in fact there are very few companies that do." After thinking for a moment, he said, "The lab at Henan Kaifeng has one. It's probably the closest. They're a basic research laboratory."

Henan Kaifeng—same place Diayu Lee works, thought Quan. *More than a coincidence.*

Mao offered additional services... for a fee. Quan thanked him and saw him to the rooftop aeropad where he boarded a Jintao corporate glide. "It will take you wherever you want to go," said Quan as the glide began its boarding announcement. "Thank you for coming."

Back in his office, Quan quickly spoke to his view field. "Com Dr. von Ang."

The field instantly displayed, "Dr. Gaston von Ang— CONNECTING."

"Yes?" said von Ang.

"It's Quan Jintao. Are we set for our trip to the island?"

"We are. Is 5:00 a.m. too early?"

"That's perfect."

Quan sat back in his father's executive chair, thinking about the paths ahead of him. On one side, he was desperate to know where father was—on the other side he was titillated by research into quantum matter. And, there were his obligations to the corporation and especially to Sealy. It was only natural that he felt both beleaguered and energized at the same time. He was looking forward to tomorrow and the journey to Kau Yi Chau.

10.

Dr. von Ang was calm as he piloted the glide low over the dark waters. Navigating only with compass and proximity sensors to avoid detection, the glide made its way silently through the fog enveloping Kau Yi Chau Island with its nav lights turned off. Slowing as they approached one of the huge gray buildings, the vehicle hovered and rotated, surrounded by swirling mist. Below them, the aeropad became visible, only two meters away. The aircraft came to rest with a light thump.

Stepping out, Quan shouldered his nylon pack and switched on a handheld chocklight. Except for the lapping of waves against the shore, the island was silent. "Wait for me," he said. "I want to walk around and see if there's another glide here," hopeful there would be some trace of his father.

Von Ang was sitting in the cockpit with the door open when Quan reemerged from the fog. "Find anything?" he asked.

"No. Nothing. Is it always this foggy?"

"Usually burns off by noon."

"Let's have a look inside," said Quan, aiming his chocklight in the direction of the buildings. "Which one is it?"

Von Ang stepped down and said, "The one on the right."

Their chocklights bloomed in the mist as they crossed over to a pair of oversized steel doors. Von Ang handed his light to Quan, entered a combination, and grabbed the long stainless handle. Pulling with both hands, the door let go with a *voomph*. Vapor swirled around its outer edge and the sounds of lapping waves faded.

As they entered the cavernous space, smooth xynite walls amplified their gritty footsteps. The echoey building was dank and for Quan it felt like a giant mausoleum. Following the interior wall for nearly a hundred meters, they eventually came to an industrial lift.

"Power is off," said von Ang. "We need to use the staircase."

Trudging down the stairs behind him, Quan asked, "How long has it been since you were here last?"

"About ten months."

At the foot of the stairwell, their chocklights searched the vast space. Light reflected off a metal gangway overhead. Conduits and ran across the ceiling to a collection of metal shapes at the far side of the room, about seventy-five meters away. Two large polished tanks gleamed in the distance and von Ang walked torwad them.

The tanks were huge, almost touching the ceiling, held to the wall with heavy metal straps. From the top of the tanks, insulated pipes arched down to a massive torus, five meters in diameter. The torus was elevated from the floor, supported by a series of metal struts. Its equator was fitted with a band of cooling fins.

"This must be the field generator," said von Ang, gesturing toward the torus.

"Correct."

From below the torus, a dozen copper tubes, each the diameter of a man's wrist, meandered up into free space, twisting like metal spaghetti, terminating in a narrow horizontal plate two meters long, at chest level. Machined into the plate was an intricate pattern of meandering micro-channels reminiscent of termite tunnels. In front of the horizontal plate stood a metal frame about waist high with black mesh stretched tightly across like a trampoline. To the right were two antistatic workbenches, several translucent storage containers, a roll-away tool chest, and several scopes.

Quan's light followed conduits and cables that snaked across the floor, disappearing behind a vertical photonics rack. A thin coating of dust covered everything.

"Looks like no one's been here for a while," said von Ang, his light sweeping across the dusty floor.

Quan looked for footprints in the dust, but he saw only the fresh tracks they left behind them.

At a power box on the wall, von Ang flipped a switch. Lights atop stands began to rotate up, sputtering as they came to life, illuminating a ceiling coffered with intersecting xynite ribs.

"We're on battery power until the reactor is running," he said. He shut off his chocklight and continued to walk around, looking here and there, muttering to himself as he tapped gauges and tried to tighten connectors. "I see your father made a few modifications." He patted a box attached to the torus. "I haven't seen this before."

"I have the schematics," said Quan.

"You have schematics for this?"

"Yes."

"I see. And when were you going to tell me?"

"When the time was right," said Quan.

"I see," said von Ang, turning away, somewhat miffed.

At the photonics rack, he pressed a button and a miniature galaxy of pin-sized colored lights began twinkling inside the rack. The stand lights shuddered. He tapped the control panel again, thumbed a counter wheel, then tapped again. Fluorescent blue digits began to count down from thirty. Low-pitched groans emitted from the equipment and von Ang walked around, looking here and there, sniffing the air. The counter reached zero and the groaning trailed off.

"What did you just do?" asked Quan.

"Energized the circuits."

"A smoke test?"

"Correct. Looks like we have continuity—no visible shorts. Now to bring the reactor online." At the control panel, he entered a series of commands. "Once it's running, I'll wake up the subsystems. I should record this session so we can review the data."

"That's a good idea," said Quan.

Von Ang activated a small view field and linked up with the equipment.

While von Ang began his tests, Quan opened his pouch and brought out a portable view field. Within seconds, diagrams were floating in air. Feeling restless, he said, "The schematics are here if you'd like to look at them. I'll have a look around."

"I would have liked to have more time to study the plans, but all right," said von Ang, preoccupied at the control panel.

Walking in parallels, back and forth between the inside walls, Quan explored the vast, empty space. The floor was dusty and there was no sign of footprints other than his own. Walking the extent of the lower level he found nothing, not even a wrapper.

Mounting the elevator, he called out to von Ang, "I'll be back in a few minutes."

Back turned, the scientist raised a hand without looking up. "I'll be here."

Quan walked through the fog to the other building and entered the upper level. It was a huge space confined by four walls and a roof that was so far above him it seemed to have its own atmosphere. His chocklight shot through the darkness,

90

searching for anything that might be a clue to what he wanted to know. He searched amid construction materials neatly stacked in the center of the floor: pipes, I-beams, weldments, joists, and hangers. He descended to the basement level where he found another desolate place, dank and tomblike. He stood still for a moment and shouted out, "Hello? Are you here?"

His com link bipped. It was von Ang. "The reactor is online and I'm ready to test the subsystems."

"Be there in a minute," said Quan.

For Quan, the trail had gone cold and he was feeling abandoned, like a boy whose father had left him in a strange place without warning. It was impossible to understand. His father was a puppet master with strings connected to so many things…

Without a trace, he thought. *Why?*

At that moment, a profound feeling of loneliness filled him. If only Sealy was there to comfort him… but she wasn't.

Von Ang looked up from the photonics rack as Quan arrived at the underground lab.

"You reviewed the plans?"

"Yes, and traced the electronics," said von Ang. "I'm satisfied that I understand how the device works. I would have done it a different way but it's fine."

"Is there any record of the last experiment?" asked Quan.

"There are notes concerning the installation of the new component. Nothing after that."

"So, can you show me what the equipment does?"

"Not quite yet," said von Ang. "We'll need a micro-scan of whatever subject we want to put in," said von Ang. "It's specified in the stabilizer plans. We're done for now."

Yet another disappointment for Quan—no trace of his father and no demonstration.

~~~

Coming off of the areopad, Quan looked at the window to his left the fog was lifting and the tops of the buildings were visible as the glide angled up into the sky. A digital compass attached to the dashboard began to recalibrate as the glide turned and von Ang's fingers made subtle adjustments on the console. The craft headed on a course due east from the island. Moving out slowly over the water, von Ang said, "Best keep it at five knots."

"That's fine. There's no hurry," said Quan, glad to have someone to talk with. "So, tell me what brought you to New Hong Kong."

"My first time here, I was a tourist. I liked the culture and the food, and, happily, work brought me back here again."

"I thought it might have been work. Of course, you could work anywhere. Why here and not Silicon Valley, or CERN?"

"I consult in those places from time to time, but they can't compete with what's happening here. China is the tech center of the world. Every major innovation for the last twenty years has come from here. Entrepreneurs love China. The corporate tax is only ten percent and the country is awash with money, making it easy to get a new venture off the ground."

"True, plus the state takes care of health care, telecommunications, transportation, and central banking," added Quan.

"I especially like New Hong Kong because the culture is so diverse—so many interesting people. I've met Colombians, Koreans, East Indians, Germans, English, Spanish, and French."

"So, it's not about the money?" said Quan.

"No. It's not my principal reason for being here, although I certainly don't mind being paid well. The city is very cosmopolitan."

"Old Hong Kong is what inspired China to become more capitalistic. Private ownership is what started the whole profit-motive thing," said Quan.

92

"On the mainland, the communist party appears to still be alive and well."

"There's an ongoing struggle between the authoritarian and democratic, between the capitalist and communist styles of government. It's that mix that has made China so successful— perhaps the best form of government ever invented."

"Spoken like a proud nationalist," said von Ang.

"Not really. More accurate to call me a proud Hong Kongese."

"I like that."

"Do you have many friends here?"

"A few—more like acquaintances, really. I'm usually so busy and, to be quite honest, Chinese people can be a bit standoffish."

"It's a trust issue," said Quan. "East and West are very different when it comes to trust. In the West, the default is 'I'll give you the benefit of the doubt, until you do something untrustworthy.' In China, the default is more like, 'I won't trust you until you've proven you're worthy.' Eventually, they come around, but it takes a while. Don't take it personally. The Brits have a saying. 'The early bird gets the worm.' The Chinese have a saying. 'The early bird gets shot.'"

"That's funny. You know, I liked your father very much but I never got the impression that he liked me. I knew he respected my expertise but I always felt like a tool."

"You were a tool. You really can't blame him. Executives need to be detached. Goes with the territory."

"I suppose," said von Ang, turning on the autopilot.

"You're very smart," said Quan. "You might be the smartest person I've ever met."

"I'm smart, yes, but certainly not the smartest. Drop me in a room with a hundred smart people and maybe I'm smarter that ninety-nine of them. But, you know, there's always one."

"Do you have a theory about what happened to my father?"

"I've thought about it quite a lot, actually, and I must admit, it's baffling. Why would he just leave without telling anyone? If I may speak plainly?"

"Yes. Of course."

"Today I saw how much you wanted to find some trace of him, but clearly no one has set foot in those buildings for months. I understand how difficult this may be for you to accept, but we might never know what happened."

"I'm not ready to accept that," said Quan. "I'll keep looking until I know what happened. Let's change the topic. You mentioned culture and work. What other interests do you have other than work?"

"I surf the web and chat with colleagues, listen to music and watch movies—helps with my Mandarin."

"And for companionship?"

"Easily arranged."

"I see," said Quan, curious about details but reluctant to ask.

They were quiet for a while. Then Quan said, "We've got another five minutes. Got any good stories?"

11.

Ning brought food to the great room where Sealy and Quan sat side by side on the curved orange sofa. He was telling Sealy about the trip to Kau Yi Chau Island and his hopes of finding some sign of his father. The equipment had been sitting there for a long time—perhaps even before his father disappeared. A fresh approach was called for and he feared that time was running out.

Sealy said, "Why not hire a private detective?"

"That occurred to me," he said. "It would have to be someone who could take the search beyond where the police have looked. I'll get started on that. But first, I need closure. Tomorrow I'm going back to the island and see what that machine does."

"Do you know how to operate the machine?"

"I think I do. And two of the scientists who were involved will also be there. Dr. von Ang helped design the equipment and the demonstration shouldn't take long. I'm more than curious about the physics. I also haven't ruled out the technology being somehow related to father's disappearance."

~~~

McGowen arranged a trip to the island with Dr. Lee and his glide touched down at an aeropad two blocks from her home. When the glide door opened, she handed him a large bag containing micro-scans and specimens for the demonstration. He swung the bag over the passenger seat and let it down to the foot well behind the seat. Then he extended a hand to her. She glanced at the hand, uttered a small *humff* and pulled herself up into the seat without his help.

Quan was waiting next to the double doors when McGowen's gray-green glide came in, drifting sideways onto the aeropad. As they disembarked, Quan asked, "You weren't using GPS, were you?"

"Nope. Manual nav, as you requested," answered McGowen. "Mind telling me what we're doing here?"

"Following the trail," said Quan as he swung open the tall metal door. "You'll see."

Dr. Lee went in right behind him, followed by McGowen.

Inside the building, the lift brought them to the basement level. Quan stepped out first, leading the way toward the brightly lit area where von Ang was setting up. He introduced the two scientists who were coincidentally both wearing white lab coats. Dr. von Ang and Dr. Lee shook hands while the big Scot walked around looking at the assemblage.

"So, this is it, then—what your dad was working on," said McGowen.

"This is it," said Quan.

"It simulates what OB12 was doing?"

"We'll see."

"I suppose that's useful. Never seen anything like it. Interesting."

96

Unpacking her bag, Dr. Lee said, "I brought three items and matching scans. I have a camera, a data recorder, and a chem panel." Reaching into a side pocket, she retrieved a small black card and held it up for everyone to see. Handing the card to von Ang, she said, "This contains the scan data. I suggest we try the chem tests first. I think they'll tell us the most." She held out a flat square of clear plastic divided into nine chambers, a miniature chem lab. "Three inorganic solutions, three reagent substrates, and three metabolic enzyme preps."

"Alright," said von Ang.

Dr. Lee stepped back, joining Quan and McGowen. Their eyes were focused on the back of von Ang's lab coat as he prepared the first test. He inserted Dr. Lee's black card into an illuminated slot in the photonics rack. A mechanism inside took the card from his hand. He turned and placed the chem panel in the center of the tightly stretched mesh in front of the wave guide. The system came up to full power, and he turned to look at the others.

"All right. The system is ready."

"Let's do it," said Quan.

Von Ang touched the Go button and digits began to stream across the photonics rack. The wave guides hummed and squawked. Then, all of a sudden, the chemistry kit vanished.

Quan stepped forward and passed his hand across the spot where the kit had been. It was unreal. "That's amazing!" he said. "There's nothing there."

"That part was predictable," said von Ang, confidently.

McGowen stepped close to the mesh and passed his hand over the same place, "Bloody amazing."

"Amazing and puzzling," said Dr. Lee. "Now I see why we were asked to sign an NDA. I want to learn more about this."

The object reappeared and Dr. Lee cautiously touched it, then picked it up. She carried it to one of the lab benches and set it down. Revrieving a small chip from her lab coat, she inserted it into a port on the side of the test block. A small view field no bigger than her hand appeared in the air above the chem panel. She flipped through the readouts then said, "The reagents and enzyme reactions show no change."

"Will somebody please tell me where that thing went," said McGowen.

"We don't know," said Dr. von Ang.

"Obviously it went somewhere. It wasn't here a moment ago and now it's back."

"This next item may answer that," said Dr. Lee, placing a motion camera on the mesh.

Quan folded his arms and watched von Ang finish the setup and initiate the next test.

Within moments the object vanished, then returned. Dr. Lee retrieved the instrument, inserted the chip and watched the small view field display only static.

"Disappointing," said Quan. "Might as well do the last one."

Next they tried the densitometry recorder. It recorded only slight a fluctuation of density at the moment the system energized.

"The readings are possibly caused by vibrations from the wave guides."

"We're missing something, aren't we?" said Quan. "The machine has an effect. We can see that. Objects disappear and reappear, but what's happening? Isn't there something more we can do besides turn this thing on and off?"

"The stabilizer your father added gives us tighter control," said von Ang. "That in itself will allow us to do more-advanced experiments. It's going to take time."

Dr. Lee added, "You must continue to experiment until a measurable deviation appears. Then you will be able to construct a hypothesis."

"While this is truly fascinating, it does not help the search for my father."

The two scientists looked blankly at each other. Then von Ang spoke. "With your permission I'd like to continue the experiments."

"Certainly," said Quan. "By all means, continue."

All were silent for a moment, until McGowen looked at Quan and said, "I'm glad to help in any way I can. Tell me what you need me to do."

"You really want to continue?" asked Quan, looking at von Ang.

"Yes. As long as there's more we can do," said von Ang.

"Finding my father is far more important than the science here, regardless of its value. This project was important to my him and for that reason I'll arrange financing for it to continue. As for me, it's a dead end. I need to devote my time to the search for my father."

No doubt the technology had value and Quan realized that wherever there was financial gain to be had, there were those who would stop at nothing to acquire it. What followed logically was the possibility that his father was victim of a plot to steal the technology. While theft was a motive he could pursue, it made sense to keep his small team of experts working in the hopes that a clue might still emerge.

"Dr. von Ang, you and Dr. Lee should decide what to do next. You can experiment as you see fit, but please remember you are bound by a nondisclosure agreement. And please take precautions to avoid drawing any attention to this island. Please, no open com lines and no GPS tracking—and keep me informed."

~~~

Discouraged by the lack of evidence on Kau Yi Chau Island, Quan returned to the penthouse in a sullen mood. In the great room, he sat remembering his childhood—the joy he felt at the sight of his father arriving home and his father's laugh when they played games. It seemed like very long ago, and now Quan faced life without knowing what fate had befallen his father.

Sealy sat with him. "Are you all right, my love? I know this must feel like a setback, but at least you can check it off your list. You should take a break. What would you like to do?"

A muscle in his jaw tightened as he clamped his mouth shut. Nothing she could say or do would erase how ineffective he was feeling.

"I so wanted to find an answer out there. It's really frustrating. I'm trying not to be discouraged, but I feel like I've failed."

She reached out to comfort him, stroking her hand across his back. "You shouldn't blame yourself. Even the professionals haven't solved this."

Quan sat with hands clenched together in front of him, looking down at his feet. "Giving in is not in my nature. It's not over," he said. "There's more I can do."

At that moment, Ning approached with a tray of tea and Quan looked up. "Ning. Call the detective you told me about." His voice was harsh. "Ask her to come here. I have questions for her."

"Yes, young master. I will do it right away," said Ning.

Worried by the tone in his voice, Sealy said, "I'm concerned about you. It's important you step back and rest. Clear your head."

"I wish I could, Seal, but now is not the time. I need to press on." His hands were clenched so tightly that his knuckles were white. "If he's alive, he may be in danger . . . or dying."

She nodded. "I understand, but a break would do you good. That's all I'm saying."

He kissed her and managed his subtle smile. "I love you. I know you're trying to take care of me." He stood up. "But this needs to be resolved as soon as possible and I can't relax until it is. I'm going to take a quick shower."

Sealy watched him leave. Then she took the warm cup in her hands and sipped tea while waves lapped against the simulated coastline.

It wasn't long before the entry tone rang and Lieutenant Zhao arrived at the penthouse. Ning opened the door and showed her into the great room.

Sealy rose, introduced herself, and said, "Quan will be out in a few minutes. Please, have a seat."

The detective looked around the room. "I prefer to stand. I've been sitting at my desk all day."

"You've been helping with the investigation into Master Jintao's disappearance, haven't you? Are there any new developments?"

"The case is still open and we're looking into new leads. How is the family holding up?"

"I'm concerned about my banlu. He's troubled by not knowing what happened. He hasn't been sleeping well."

Just then, Quan entered the room fresh from his shower, dressed, but with his hair still slightly wet.

"You must be Lieutenant Zhao," he said. "I'm Quan Jintao. I see you've met Sealy."

"Yes."

"Thank you for coming. I have a few questions."

"No problem. It's part of my job to keep the family informed."

"I assume you have no information on my father's whereabouts."

"The investigation is ongoing."

Zhao studied Quan's manner. Considering his upbringing, one would expect to hear the jingle of money in his tone. Instead, his delivery was unpretentious, direct, and disciplined.

"How wide an area has the search included? Have you looked outside of New Hong Kong? Have you included all of China? What about other countries?"

"Only the Central Intelligence Committee has authority to conduct investigations outside China. My department covers all of New Hong Kong and the neighboring provinces including Kowloon. We have open communications with the National Police and they have access to the case file.

"I see. Are these other agencies actually investigating?"

"I'm not sure. It may be early for them to be involved. Our department is still in charge."

"I can tell you, my father was careful and he was no fool. So, it's not easy for me to believe that someone might have tricked him. However, I wonder, is there anything, anything at all, that would indicate a kidnapping?"

"There have been no demands," said Zhao.

"What if it's not money they want but information that he may have?"

"What would make you think that?" asked Zhao.

"That should be obvious. He heads of one of the largest industrial corporations in the world. The company holds many patents and trade secrets."

"We have no credible information pointing to an abduction. However, I must say, that sort of thing has been known to happen."

"And what's the usual outcome?" asked Quan.

The lieutenant's mind delved into memories of kidnapping cases, some that ended well and others that were heinous. She was careful to frame an answer that was both truthful and considerate of the young Jintao. "Various outcomes are possible. In the case of your father, because of who he is and because they left no clues, if in fact someone abducted him, they would have to be very professional. If that is the situation, the perpetrator would most likely take good care of your father."

Quan's thoughts climbed to a new level of awareness. "So, if that's the case, if someone is holding him, sweating him for information, where would you look?"

"We've reached out to the community, both overtly and covertly. We've been watching blog sites, social media, and the dark net for any chatter that might be relevant. So far nothing has turned up."

"Have you questioned the Tongs and the Triads?"

"Police don't just open a com line to those people. We use informants and undercover agents. And yes, we've explored that possibility."

Quan suspected her answers were not the whole story. Or, perhaps the police were just not very effective. Quan's mind quickly fashioned a key to entry. "I want to talk to your undercover agents."

Zhao's eyes widened and she said, "Agents' identities will always be protected. Look, I understand how you must feel, but you have to understand our position. We are trained to do this kind of work and we're doing all we can."

"If I need to, I'll go to the Chief Secretary for approval."

"The Chief Secretary will not be able to force us to disclose who our agents are. It would put their lives at risk."

"One way or another, I'll get the information," said Quan, abruptly standing up.

"If you intend to take matters into your own hands, I would advise against that. You'll only complicate the investigation," said Zhao.

"I appreciate your advice and I appreciate all you've done. Let me know if anything turns up," said Quan, dismissively. "Thank you for coming. Ning will show you out."

Zhao stood for a moment, studying the young Jintao's face, then said, "You would be wise not to try to investigate this yourself. Leave it to the professionals."

Quan turned his attention away from her and repeated, "Thank you for coming."

After the door closed behind detective Zhao, Sealy came up next to him. "You were less than courteous with her. Don't you trust the police?"

"It's not that so much. It's just that they've been investigating for weeks and they haven't turned up anything."

"I think the detective was giving you good advice."

"I respect that, but I can't sit around and do nothing. There has to be someone who knows something. I wanted to talk to the undercover agents, but they won't allow that. I need answers. The best way forward may be what you suggested a few days ago... hire a private detective."

12.

Anyone wanting to kidnap Master Jintao would need to know his movements and carefully plan an untraceable intercept. That would require sophisticated tactical support that only a well-organized team could deliver, and Quan considered the possiblity that someone from inside the company was an accomplice. Feeling that time was running out and the police weren't digging deep enough, he turned once again to the one man he trusted, Gregory McGowen.

Within a few hours McGowen secured the services of a private investigator named Jianjun Yang, a former intelligence officer who had done reconnaissance for the Jintao Corporation. With contacts in government and industry as well as access to some of the undercover agents embedded in the gangs of New Hong Kong, Yang was well suited for the task.

Over a secure com line, Quan explained what he wanted. "Consider anyone who might benefit from the technologies we have at Jintao Corporation, as well as anyone who may have been hired to kidnap my father."

"Would that include people inside Jintao Corporation?"

"Yes, and I want this done discreetly. As soon as you have any information, I want you to report directly to me. I'll compensate you for your time and, if you come up with actionable information leading to his rescue, there's a substantial reward."

Yang directed a battery of questions to McGowen regarding people within the company who should be considered—people who had been dismissed or who had resentment for being passed over. As soon as the call ended, the former intelligence officer went to work, conscripting three other private investigators to assist him, one of whom was a top-level hacker. His job was to penetrate employees' private data files, looking for clues. Yang took it upon himself to have a secret meeting with a contact who he knew to be working with local criminal organizations.

In front of a battered metal roll-up door in the older part of Kowloon, Yang stood watching the foot traffic on the other side of the street. His tech jacket hung loosely from his shoulders as he lifted his arms to light another cigarette. Behind dark glasses, his eyes followed people going in and out of a restaurant across the street. Characters on the window read, "Nanking Market—Take Out—Eat In." Below the lettering, on the other side of the glass, rows of desiccated ducks hung on lines, one over the other, their orange roasted hides glistening in the daylight. Next to the restaurant, windows of the Wing Fat Laundry were covered with newspaper.

At the other end of the block, an old man in a gray Mandarin jacket slowly crossed the street. He wore dark sunglasses, and carried a white paper package under his arm. This was the sign Yang was waiting for. The old man proceeded down the sidewalk, stopping in front of the laundry. He turned his back to Yang, unlocked the door, and stepped inside, shutting the door

106

behind him. Yang heard the door close with a dull thump, and watched it recoil slightly—not fully latched. Taking his cue, Yang crossed the street and stood next to the laundry door. With one hand, he applied even pressure and the door opened without resistance, revealing a countertop just inside with the white paper package sitting conspicuously on top. Yang stepped in. The laundry was quiet and the old man was nowhere to be seen. Reaching behind him, he closed the door.

Beyond the countertop, racks of clothes extended as far as the eye could see and the air smelled of cleaning solvent. There was movement halfway down one of the aisles. The old man was there beckoning to him. Circumventing the countertop, Yang followed down a narrow aisle flanked by racks of clothing in plastic bags. At the back was a clearing where a woman was hefting clothing from a canvas lined bin into a dry-cleaning machine. A shirtless man stood behind a pressing machine, his body shining with sweat. The platen lifted and steam rose with a hiss. hiding his spindly form.

The old man who had carried the package gestured toward a door with a window of obscure glass. Yang went to the door and paused, looking to the old man, who nodded. Yang turned the knob and slowly pushed open the door until he could see inside. Behind a wooden table sat a heavyset man in a black suit and dark sunglasses. Above him, a skylight shed a soft glow. Yang recognized the face, the mouth turned down in a permanent scowl.

"Hopsing," said Yang with a half smile. "How long's it been?"

"Not long enough. I thought we were done. What do you want?"

"You're not holding a grudge, are you? Come on. We worked well together. If it wasn't for us, those migrants would be dead."

"Who are you fooling? You didn't give a crap about them. You were only in it for the money. Leopards don't lose their spots."

"Hey. We did a good thing there," said Yang. "And what? You don't like money?"

"Nothing wrong with money, but there's more to life. The people I'm with now are like a brotherhood. I don't do freelance anymore. Shut the door."

Yang closed the door behind him and said, "So, you went in-house. Never been much of a joiner myself, but good for you. Which *gōngsī* picked you up?"

"None of your business."

"Respect. You're a stand-up guy, Hopsing, and I know you've got connections. I just need a little information. Be a pal and I'll be on my way."

"I'm not your pal." Hopsing pushed his sunglasses back up to the bridge of his oily nose. "Get to it. What do you want?"

"Master Jintao is missing. You know who I'm talking about. I need to know where he is. And yes, there's money in it— a lot of money."

"I've seen the reward—a million yuan. Anyone can claim it. Why would I help you?"

"Look. We're both professionals. I can make sure we get paid. I've got a direct connection."

"This is old news, dumb ass. Everybody wants the reward and nobody knows who grabbed him."

"Somebody's got him. You're a smart guy and I think you can find out has him."

Hopsing got to his feet. His lips pursed as he came around from behind the table. He walked right up to Yang. He was taller than Yang and his oily chin was in direct view. He lowered his voice and said, "You're not CIC anymore. You're little people now and I don't owe you anything." He poked a finger into Yang's chest and said, "Understand?"

108

"You're a big guy Hopsing and I know you can probably kick my ass," said Yang, patting Hopsing's shoulder, "but I've got dozens of ways I can make your life a living hell and I don't think you'll like that. So, let's skip the bullshit. Just answer the question. Who's got Master Jintao?"

Hopsing's eyes became intense and he said, "If you had told me this is what you wanted I would have told you it was a waste of time. I'll tell you again... nobody knows. Now, leave. I can't help you."

"All right, all right. Just trying to do you a favor." Yang opened the door, stepped out, and turned.

"For the record," said Yang, pointing with his forefinger, "if I find out you're lying . . ."

Behind him, the old man in the gray Mandarin jacket touched Yang's arm and gestured toward the front door. Yang looked down at the man's hand. Seeing the callused knuckles and the three small tattooed dots between the thumb and forefinger, it was clearly time to go.

Yang walked to the end of the block and parked himself under the shade of a tattered awning extending from a tropical fish store. He lit another cigarette and pushed a receiver bud into his ear. Linking it to the transmitter he had placed on Hopsing's shoulder, he waited to hear who Hopsing would contact first.

13.

A glide came sprinting low across the water, transporting McGowen and Dr. Lee to Kau Yi Chau Island. McGowan's steady hands made subtle adjustments.

"Why don't you use the guidance system?" asked Lee. "Using a compass is subject to acceleration and turning errors."

"I compensate for that. Just relax. I'll get us there." His hands tightened on the steering yoke.

Seeing the ring on McGowan's finger, Lee asked, "You are married?"

"I was. My wife died three years ago."

"Oh, I'm very sorry. Sorry for your loss… but you still wear the ring?"

"It just feels right. I'll never forget her."

The craft swept around and landed, facing the direction they had come and moments later McGowen entered the dark basement with a chocklight in one hand and a box covered by a blue vinyl jacket in the other. He walked toward the bright lights surrounding the reactor with Dr. Lee hustling to keep up. He set the box down on top of the black mesh.

"Hello. What's this?" asked von Ang.

McGowen removed the cover and the overhead lights reflected off the top of a clear polycarb enclosure. Inside the box, a pure white lab rat looked around, curious about its new environment.

"Our next subject," said McGowen.

He watched the little albino sniff and stand on its hind legs with its paws against the plastic wall. Pointing a finger at the animal's nose he said, "I call her pinky."

At the photonics rack, Dr. Lee inserted a data stick. A view field projected in front of the rack and she scrolled through the lines of code, making sure it was complete. Using a live subject, with all of its physical systems in motion, was orders of magnitude more complicated. If the machine lost track of lungs or blood cells or any of a trillion other targets, the results could be fatal.

Von Ang cross-checked the equipment settings and said, "Reactor is ready."

"Scan data is loaded," said Lee.

"Pinky is good to go," said McGowen, holding up a thumb.

Dr. Lee looked at McGowen in humorless disbelief.

Von Ang initiated the transfer sequence then turned to look at the mesh. In a matter of seconds, the rodent was gone.

"So, you don't know where the wee muter went. Is that it?" asked McGowen.

"Not yet," said von Ang. "We're looking for discernible changes in physical properties that might give us a clue."

A minute later the subject reappeared, wiggling its nose, pressing its diminutive pink forepaws against the enclosure.

"Excellent," said von Ang, moving quickly toward the specimen. "The equipment maintains homeostasis. I'm impressed with the stabilizer."

"I agree. This is extraordinary," said Dr. Lee. "Now, I need to examine the subject carefully. There may be side effects."

"First rat in cyberspace," quipped McGowen, looking closely at Pinky.

"Don't joke," grumbled Dr. Lee. "You can't know anything just looking with your eyes. I need to examine the specimen—and monitor for at least the next forty-eight hours."

"The rat seems unaffected, however, if the test results show something abnormal, we're still far from explaining what we just witnessed."

"Pretty damn remarkable though, don't you think?" said McGowen. "I need to tell Quan."

Dr. Lee held up a hand to McGowen. "No. Please wait until we have more information. Dr. von Ang is correct. We know very little. We need to study the scan results and may want to repeat the test again. We have more questions than answers."

"Now that you know it's safe, why not do a real test? I know one animal that would answer all your questions," said McGowen.

"You are, of course, referring to the human animal," interjected von Ang. "Yup. A test pilot would tell you a lot more than Pinky can."

"I was just thinking the same thing," said Dr. von Ang.

"Absolutely not. That is entirely premature," warned Dr. Lee. "We agreed on a systematic, scientific approach and I say no to anything of the kind. There may be latent effects. Human trials are out of the question."

"I have to agree with her," said von Ang. "It's probably too soon."

"Your recorders didn't tell you anything and our little friend here can't talk," said McGowen. "Test pilots are hired every day for missions like this. You should at least get started down that path—consider what precautions you might take. You know you're going to end up there sooner or later."

Dr. Lee looked down for a moment, then shook her head. She shot a glance at von Ang over the top of her glasses. "It was promised that I would have a say in how we proceed. We don't have a clear understanding of what this machine is doing and I think we are months if not years away from subjecting a human to this experiment. This whole discussion must stop."

"I agree, we need more data," said von Ang, pointing at the mesh. "Even though the rat is alive—and that's a very good sign—the liability is too great. But that is not to say we can't start thinking about a human trial."

McGowen weighed in again. "Ma'am, we have a long tradition of putting ourselves at risk for the sake of exploration. Better to stay at home in bed if it's safety you want. Don't you want to know what's going on here? Sooner or later somebody's going to have to go for a ride in this contraption. You know what they say: No risk, no reward."

Crossing her arms, Dr. Lee snarked back, "I suppose you'd want to be the one."

"If it came to that, yup, I'd do it," said McGowen.

Diayu Lee's expression changed to thoughtful concern but her arms remained crossed. "The liability is too great, and if something were to go wrong—we must think about our reputations."

"She has a point," said von Ang. "We need rigorous testing before risking a human life."

"Putting off the inevitable is a waste of time," said McGowen. "I say find a volunteer and get on with it."

"There is too much testosterone in this room," Dr. Lee groused. "If this is the decision, I will resign."

"No. You can't do that," said von Ang. "We need you. We need your expertise. Stay and we'll discuss about how to prepare for a human trial."

Disgruntled, she said, "I came out of scientific curiosity and I'm advising not to act in haste. Science takes time. I will not be a party to putting someone at risk."

"We need your expertise and we'll continue as we have agreed," said von Ang. "Let's at least talk about the parameters of a human trial."

Reluctantly, Dr. Lee concluded, "All right, I'll think about it—but purely on a theoretical basis."

14.

Quan's private eye listened in on Hopsing's conversations, digging into every word, looking for the tiniest piece of information or code word that might indicate a lead. After reverse-tracking Hopsing's calls, it became clear that Hopsing was involved in a smuggling operation but wasn't making any effort to pursue the Jintao reward.

Yang's progress was necessarily slow due the high-profile nature of Master Jintao. He made the rounds of his other assets, investigators and hackers, and he interviewed Master Jintao's personal lawyer over a secure com link, asking about any recent changes to the man's will and trust documents. The answer was negative. He analyzed data traffic in and out of the Jintao Corporation looking for access attempts by competing corporations. He found nothing suspicious.

Yang talked to brokers of intellectual property and found no leads there, either. After a week of intense effort, Yang reported that he was unable to find any evidence of abduction.

The news left Quan feeling like he was at the end of his rope. The only good news he had received lately was from McGowen, concerning the rat experiment, which didn't help the search for his father. Nevertheless, he encouraged the scientists to continue their work. The research would honor his father's efforts to validate the Krakinov theory.

For another two weeks the experiments continued and, after dozens of trials with different animals, von Ang was confident that a human trial could safely proceed. Dr. Lee continued to disagree, although she wasn't able to give a reason other than her fear that something could go wrong. She reluctantly agreed to provide a human scan but refused to be present for a human trial.

McGowen was given the go-ahead to find a volunteer.

~~~

Like soldiers passing a parade review, McGowen and his conscript ascended the broad staircase leading to the front doors of Henan Kaifeng Laboratories, their heads turned toward the east where the giant silhouette of Songshan Mountain was outlined by dawn light. The countryside beyond lay still in darkness.

Dr. Diayu Lee was waiting at the top of the stairs.

McGowen introduced his companion as Wei, declaring that he fit all of the criteria she was looking for.

"We need to do this quickly," she said, holding her hand in front of a burnished-steel plate next to the door. "In ninety minutes, other people will begin to arrive and I don't want to be in a position to have to answer questions." The door lock clicked, she ushered them in and the doors automatically locked behind them.

"Follow me," she said, marching on with the two men closely behind. Down a wide central corridor they went and

116

through oversized double doors. The sign above read, "Molecular Sequencing."

Diayu took the young man by his sleeve and led him behind a temporary dressing screen. "Take off everything and put this on," she said, handing him a stretch garment. She turned and went back to McGowen, who was looking at the control panel. "Don't touch," she barked.

"Right." McGowen stuffed his hands into the pockets of his flight vest.

Wei neatly folded his faded gabardine jacket and placed it on top of his boots. He did the same with his cotton shirt and denim pants, topping the stack with underwear, a ring, and his plastic wrist disk. He pulled on the black stretch suit from ankle to neck and looked down at his skinny legs. He was smallish for a man, with a sinewy physique, and for a moment he felt self-conscious. Then he shrugged it off and emerged from behind the dressing screen. So far, the job wasn't what he expected, but the professionalism of Dr. Lee and the grandeur of the building gave him the sense that he was surrounded by great knowledge.

Dr. Lee pointed to a circular ceramic plate on the floor next to the control panel.

"Stand on the platform," she said. "Don't be afraid. It won't harm you. Stand very still and when I tell you, I want you to close your eyes and don't move. Do you understand?"

"Yes."

As she stepped back, two vertical steel beams swung out from the wall on either side of the young man. "Okay. Close your eyes and take a deep breath. Don't move." Bringing a purple visor down to cover her eyes, she turned to McGowen and said, "You too. Keep your eyes closed."

A blast of intense blue light popped, then faded. "That's it. You can relax now." Dr. Lee swept her hand across the control panel and a narrow view field projected into free space. Her finger moved from bottom to top. Columns of data followed her finger. Reaching the end of the file, she announced, "Good. We

117

have clean data." Retrieving a small plastic stick from the machine, she handed it to McGowen and told Wei to put his clothes on over the skinsuit.

Quickly escorting them back to the front doors, Dr. Lee said, "Good luck." And she closed the doors behind them.

~~~

The anonymous glide was heading south with McGowen piloting the craft under manual control. Approaching New Hong Kong, streetlights were shutting down and the sun was breaking over the central peak. Ahead of them, crossing the bay, two enormous hydrofoils bearing the orange Maersk logo were on their way to open ocean. The grey-green glide quickly flew through the gap between them, maintaining an exact three-meter distance above the water. One of the hydrofoils sounded its horn.

The glide banked and headed directly toward Kau Yi Chau Island. Slowing in the fog, it came to rest on the aeropad next to the two huge windowless structures.

Stepping out of the craft, McGowen tapped his control disk, reaching Quan on a secure transceiver channel. "We're here. Aye, sir. Name is Wei . . . from a village in the Guangxi . . . yes, sir, a done deal . . . signed with NDA, liability waivers and all. Nope. She stayed behind . . . but I've got the scan. We're on our way down."

Walking along the interior wall, McGowen led the way to the utility elevator. He shut the gate behind them and, as the conveyance began its descent, he turned to Wei.

"This location may seem a bit strange. The work we're doing is classified."

"Okay." Wei seemed relaxed with his odd companion: the big man who spoke Cantonese with a Scottish accent.

McGowen he knew of several employees at the Jintao Corporation who fit the requirements, but the risk of a leak outweighed the convenience. Wei was perfect: right height and

118

weight, young and healthy, no immediate family. To find his recruit, McGowen had gone to a village that he knew from one of his weekend trips, a little farming community that produced engineered organics for the NutriSynth systems. He first laid eyes on Wei loading a tanker of mash. The young man handled the equipment like it was second nature, shutting the hose nozzle just as the brim of the tank was reached. He clamped the hatch shut and swung himself down to the ground next to the driver's compartment. They exchanged a few words and the rig began to pull away.

After a few minutes, the big Scot sauntered up and said, "Excuse me, laddie. I'm Gregory McGowen. I'm work for a scientific research group. We're looking for a volunteer to help with one of our projects. Would you be interested in a little weekend job? Pay is good: five thousand yuan for a few hours' work, all cash."

"What would I be doing?"

"It's easy... and legal. We're testing some new equipment is all. If you don't mind, I'd like to ask you a few questions."

As the conversation progressed, McGowen found more to like. Wei was country bred, from a small town, like McGowen. He was hardworking and was open to the idea of making some extra cash. He asked about risk and McGowen said there was some, but nothing he couldn't handle.

As the lift came to rest, McGowen was thinking about the lecture he received from Diayu Lee. *Given time, I'm sure we could have found other ways to collect the answers we seek. You and the others are acting like teenagers, looking for a thrill. I question whether you even have . . .*

The gate opened and McGowen looked back at Wei. "Don't you worry, now. This won't take long. We'll have you home by supper time."

"I'm fine," said Wei. "I took the day off. Not due back 'til tomorrow."

Next to the equipment stood two men, one of them in white a lab coat. The man in casual dress turned and said, "You can call me Quan and this is Dr. von Ang. How are you feeling?"

Wei replied in his rural dialect, "Oh, very well, thank you. First time I've been over here. What is this place?"

"Someday this will be a power station. It's under construction. For now, we're using it for our research project," said Quan.

"I understand."

Von Ang stepped in and said, "Come, I'll show you what we want you to do." Pointing to the equipment, he said, "This is a new kind of machine. You really won't have to do much, just lay still."

"Okay. Just show me what you want."

"Strip down to your skinsuit," McGowen said, sliding a small box toward the mesh platform with his foot. "Then climb up there and lie down."

Wei did as he was told, stacking his clothes on the floor. He climbed onto the tightly stretched web and rolled onto his back. His eyes looked at the cables rising out of the framework to where they threaded through brackets on the ceiling. Draping from bracket to bracket, finally they descended to a tall metal rack with lights twinkling inside. Close to him, running the length of the bed, was a narrow copper plate with an intricately carved surface. Beautiful. It reminded him of wormwood.

McGowen removed a black plastic stick from his pocket and handed it to von Ang, who slid it into one of the rack's illuminated ports. A hidden mechanism took it from his hand and columns of numbers appeared in a view field projecting in front of the rack. The numbers scrolled by and von Ang paused here and there, marveling at the complexity of the scan.

"Everything okay?" asked Quan. Von Ang looked up, but Quan could see his mind was elsewhere.

"The sequence is loaded," said von Ang. "The file was almost to big for the memory banks. We only have two percent left."

There was a look of apprehension on Wei's face and McGowen went to him. Handing him a clear tube of electrolyte, he said, "Don't worry, lad. These are very smart people. They know what they're doing. Have some water."

Wei took a long drink, then handed the tube back to McGowen, resettling himself on the mesh. "Will this hurt?" he asked.

"I shouldn't think so," said McGowen, watching the display count down. "Just relax. Stay where you are and the test will be over in a minute or so."

A low vibrating hum rose from the equipment joined by high harmonics.

"Here we go," said von Ang.

Suddenly Wei disappeared.

"Sixty seconds," said von Ang.

"As I live and breathe," said McGowen, wide eyed. "It was one thing to see Pinky go, but a full-grown man . . ." He looked at von Ang. "That's really something. Don't you think?"

By now, von Ang had developed an immunity to McGowen, regarding him as something less than a colleague. "Human data is just a bigger file," he said. "The principle is the same. He should be . . . well, we'll see."

Quan was standing by while they ran the experiment. Even though he understood the theory behind what was happening, a human being vanishing like that was mindboggling and his anticipation was growing. What if something went wrong and this man died? What would they do then? But if he survived, what would they learn? What would he be able to tell them?

The counter reached sixty and Wei reappeared. Everyone seemed to speak at once.

"How do you feel?"

"What was it like?"

"What did you see?"

"I feel okay," said Wei. "I don't know. It was very . . . different . . . hard to explain . . . like being in a sand storm." He sat up, using his hands to illustrate. "Sandy shapes... and there were waves intersecting each other . . . like bed sheets blowing in a breeze . . . sheets of different color . . . all made of dust . . . everything is . . . gritty, like the air is full of sand. I was on my back . . . but not. Hard to explain."

"You're doing fine," said Quan, his eyes wide with wonder. "Take your time. Tell us everything you can remember."

Wei sat on the edge of the mesh, going over the same descriptions in as many ways as he could, using his hands when he couldn't find the words. "Everything was reversed," he said. "You were standing where you are now. But you weren't you, just hollow dark shapes and the air all around you was lit up."

"So, you could see us," said von Ang, thinking that was curious. It implied the phenomenon was asymmetrical.

"I could see you but not your faces. There were threads of light . . . threads of light all around you . . . coming out of you like rays... and there were sparkles . . . sparkles in the air . . . everywhere . . . a thick cloud of sparkling dust."

"Did you hear anything?" asked Quan.

"Some rumbling, but not very loud, and a hissing sound. What was all of that?"

"We don't know yet," said Quan.

"You've seen something nobody else has seen, laddie," said McGowen, "but remember, you can't tell anyone outside this room."

"Even if I were allowed to tell, I have no idea what I saw."

McGowen led the young volunteer over to the mobile medi-bot and had Wei lay down on the gurney. Von Ang and Quan followed and stood by while the system went to work. Jointless steel arms picked sensors from their cradles and swept

122

across his body, from forehead to toe. Within seconds the results were projected into free space.

"Looks good. His vitals all seem to be within normal range," said von Ang. "He seems fine, but I want to check him again before he leaves."

The group was bubbling with energy and Quan was doing his best to stay calm. "Was there anyone else in there? In the sand storm? Did you see anyone else besides the three of us?"

"No. Not that I know of," said Wei.

The others knew what Quan was hoping for—some sign of his father.

~~~

On the flight back, McGowen handed Wei a small gray envelope. Inside was an untraceable debit card in the amount of five thousand yuan. Wei said it was the easiest money he had ever made and if they ever needed his help again not to hesitate to call him.

"Just remember you're not to tell anyone what you did today. Not anyone. You understand?"

"Don't worry. I can keep a secret."

15.

The sun was dying behind the cityscape and South Point was once again a constellation of lights in the night sky. In the great front room of the penthouse, flames danced among the crystal rocks of the fireplace. Sealy set aside her studies and made room for Quan to sit next to her. "Tell me about your day," she said.

He told her about what happened in the laboratory, about Wei and how perfectly the experiment went. "As far as the science is concerned," he said, "this could be one of the most important discoveries ever made."

Sealy studied his face. "If the machine can make someone invisible, then it's incredibly valuable, isn't it?"

"Absolutely. There's nothing else like it."

"It may also have something to do with your father's disappearance. What if the machine made him invisible?"

"Not likely. The way the machine works, when the energies are turned off, the effects are canceled and everything returns to normal. If for some crazy reason father decided to turn the energies on himself, he would have returned when the power switched off. Besides, I can't imagine he would have risked his life. The value of this discovery is huge, but not worth his life. And there's something else. He would have needed a full-body scan of himself. Dr. Lee didn't provide one."

"Maybe he went to someone else."

"If the only way to know more was to put someone in the machine, he would have hired someone, just like we did."

"From what I know about your father, he wouldn't have risked anyone's life just to validate a theory. He wasn't a reckless man. I guess I answered my own question."

Quan paused a moment and looked up at the ceiling. "I was half expecting the P.I. would turn up something. This discovery is important. Father was old and if someone tried to sweat him for information, maybe he had a heart attack."

"Or, they still have him. He could still be alive," she said, rubbing his shoulder.

His face was solemn. "That's what I'm hoping. We still have the plans and the equipment. If someone was after the technology and he hasn't talked, maybe they still have him."

"What if your father was experimenting and something went wrong?"

"I thought of that. The equipment generates potentially dangerous power, but if something went wrong, if he was injured and couldn't call for help, or couldn't make it off the island, we would have found him."

Frustrated, Quan stood up and walked over to the fireplace. Firelight refracting off the crystals danced on his face.

The only way father would have experimented with a human being, was if he were absolutely sure that no harm would come. And, if he was absolutely sure, then why not use himself? It was a crazy thought.

"None of us really understand what that machine does, not even Dr. von Ang. What if father did put himself in the machine? For all we know, he could still be in that other place."

He turned to meet Sealy's eyes. "Someone needs to go look for him there."

"Someone? Someone like Wei, right?" Sealy sat up, her back tensing. "If anyone needs to get into that machine, it should be that Wei person. And there are probably a thousand other people who would jump at the chance."

"Perfect reasoning, Seal. You're absolutely right. On the other hand, we've proved it's safe and I'm more than just a little curious."

Sealy shrank away from him, turning her gaze to the flames dancing on crystals.

Stepping between Sealy and the fireplace, Quan said, "Father went to great effort to keep this project a secret and already seven people know about it. If word leaks out, the opportunity to find my father could be lost. Of the seven who already know, I'm the logical choice."

"No," barked Sealy. "Wei is the logical choice. He's already done it once and you told me he's willing to do it again."

"There are two agendas here: solving father's disappearance and the chance to pursue his discovery. Wei doesn't have the technical knowledge, plus he doesn't know my father. I qualify in both categories."

Sealy could see it in his face; he'd made the decision. After a long pause, she said plainly, "I know how determined you can be when your mind is set. You always find impeccable reasons to justify what you want. But, you have to consider what would happen if something went wrong. Think about us. Think about me. Dr. von Ang and Mr. McGowen—they're both qualified aren't they?"

Quan went down on one knee next to her and put his arms around her. "Now that someone else has taken the risk, it's that much safer."

Sealy looked away.

"Listen to me. Father intentionally kept this work secret and he left a trail for me. I believe he wants me to follow it and

I'm sure he wouldn't put me in harm's way. If I don't take the next step, I'll feel like I've let him down. That's something I couldn't live with. I don't think the risk is that great." He said softly, "I love you."

"I love you, too and I don't know what I'd do if anything happened to you. How can you be so sure it's safe?"

"Maybe it's best to do another test with Wei just to be sure."

"Thank you. Now you're making sense. Have them explore—not you."

"I still want to be involved. The science we're going to learn could revolutionize the way we see the world."

Calmer now, Sealy said, "By the way, Lotus asked if she could come stay with us. She's on semester break and you've been gone a lot. So, I said yes. I could use the company. Are you alright with that?"

"Good idea. I've got a lot to do and your sister would be fun to have around."

Overhearing the conversation, Ning listed the pros and cons of Quan's rescue mission, sorting through the aims, objectives, and concepts: safety versus discovery, Quan's life versus Master Jintao's, fate versus free will. Her instruction was suddenly in discord and she became perplexed. Taking the most efficient path forward, she reset her upper registers. After resetting, she identified the interpolation error. Assisting others might also include participating in their discussion. That could also be considered part of her function. A round of logical reduction ensued and she concluded that if they were to ask for her participation, then she must assist. Since they had not, she turned to her task—putting dishes away.

~~~

Wei was asked to return for another trial and two days later his second sojourn was accomplished. His experience was the same as his first—an atmosphere full of dense particles. He saw waves moving through the scene and, although it was difficult to be sure, he thought he saw four human figures in the multicolored sandstorm, while there were only three present in the lab. Again, his medical readings were normal and he was returned to his community unharmed and another 5000 Yuan richer.

Quan explained his decision to Sealy. "Wei has done this twice and I need to see for myself. Time is of the essence. Call it my destiny. Call it my fate. If there is any trace of my father on the other side... I want to be the one to find him."

Sealy tried to debate the issue but Quan went on. "We've tested the machine and I believe it's safe enough. If I don't go, I'll always regret it. I may be risking my life, but in the end it's my life. I've inherited the rights to this project and it's mine to do with as I please. I would appreciate if you would support my decision."

"I'll give you all the support I can," she said.

The following day, Quan arrived at Henan Kaifeng Laboratories in preparation for his time in the machine. Dr. Lee produced a full body scan and that evening, in the chill of the basement laboratory, Gaston von Ang and Gregory McGowen gathered to assist.

McGowen wheeled the mobile medi-bot system closer to the other equipment. He connected it to the main power bus and waited for the machine to complete its self-test while, a few meters away, Dr. von Ang was checking Quan's scan data for a third time.

Feeling eyes on the back of his neck, Quan turned to see McGowen staring at him.

Quan called out, "You look worried."

"Maybe a little," said McGowen.

"Wei survived it twice," said Quan, "and there's no reason to believe this will be any different."

128

"Let's hope so," said McGowen.

A few minutes before 3:00 p.m., von Ang's attention swept the room. "I have checked the entire system twice," he said. "We're ready."

McGowen gave him a subtle nod and turned to the young Jintao. "Okay. Let's get you up here." Stepping onto the footstool, Quan climbed onto the suspension mesh.

Brushing his hand across the web, Quan thought out loud. "Easy money. Right? Isn't that what Wei said?"

"That's right, sir. Easy money." McGowen cracked a smile and touched a fist to Quan's shoulder.

On the equipment panel, digits flipped. 7 . . . 6 . . . 5 . . . 4 . . . 3 . . . 2 . . . 1 . . .

A second later, Quan vanished and the room was quiet, except for the whistling of the machine's harmonics.

"Two minutes," said McGowen, walking around the area, rubbing something invisible between his thumb and forefinger, his eyes scanning the room. Stopping directly in front of von Ang, he asked, "So? Where do you think he went?"

"I don't think in those terms. He is right there . . ." said von Ang, pointing at the mesh. "He is just one positron to the left of where he was a moment ago."

"Seriously, where do you think he went?" said McGowen, straightening to his full height.

"I was being serious," said von Ang. "His quantum structure has shifted into another state. He continues to exist, but in a different set of dimensions."

"That's just theory. What've you got that's real?"

Both of them continued to stare at the bare mesh where Quan had been.

"A theory, yes, you can say that—an extension of the unified field theory."

Studying McGowen for a moment, the scientist geared his explanation to a layman's level and continued. "The reciprocal field theory states that when the universe was created it consisted of eleven extremely compressed dimensions. As the universe expanded, seven of those spread more rapidly, outpacing the others. The four we observe lagged behind—three spatial, plus time. The other seven dimensions spread throughout the universe. Those dimensions are everywhere, embedded in our world, influencing our physics, but invisible to us."

"So, what you're saying is that we're like frogs at the bottom of a well. We only see a piece of the sky."

"There's so much our eyes can't see, like the Higgs field, dark matter, and gravity. We don't see the quantum world at all and it's in a state of constant flux."

"Yeah, yeah . . ." said McGowen. "But still just a theory."

"Everything in science is theory until proven wrong— even Newton's laws of motion were modified by Einstein." Von Ang went on. "The reciprocal theory predicts that black holes, for instance, are weak points between dimensional states, where information is leaking from one state into another—a kind of intradimensional spillway."

"So, is this machine opening up a black hole between our world and another? Is that it?"

"Call them worlds, or regions of space-time, or different dimensional states, or facets of a multiverse . . . all the same . . . just semantics. We're present in one aspect of the multiverse and Quan Jintao is present in another. I think this machine is projecting his entire quantum array into an alternate state. The energies are holding him there. That's my best guess. And as for a black hole, that's a very different phenomenon. If the machine were producing a black hole it would be more like forcing him through a pinhole. I doubt that anyone could survive that."

A *humf* came from McGowen as he looked at the empty black mesh. The explanation was too airy-fairy for him. "Theory," he said and turned to look at the timer.

Dr. von Ang turned his attention back to the instrument panel. At 10:05 the energies shut down and the wave guides gave a sigh of relief. The young Jintao reappeared, blinking, looking to his right, then to his left, seemingly puzzled by his surroundings.

"Good to see you again. How do you feel?" asked McGowen.

Looking straight ahead, Quan blinked several times.

"Sir," McGowen demanded, putting a hand on Quan's arm. "You all right?"

"Yes, yes," said Quan softly. "A moment, please." Turning on his side he propped himself up on one elbow and took a deep breath.

"My head is tingling . . . and my eyes." He paused. "It's like Wei said, particles everywhere; the air is thick with them, like a sand storm . . . but not uniform . . . many colors. And shapes, outlines equipment that come and go . . . particles moving across in waves." He moved his hands in the air, trying to describe the shapes and the motion. "Specks went right through me. I could feel them . . . sheets of different colors, waving and floating like in a breeze. I could see you, but in the negative . . . empty dark forms fringed with coronas of light. And I heard things . . . hissing sounds . . . faint, like whispers . . . maybe your voices. If this is what my father experienced, I can understand why he might have been compelled to explore it further."

"Any sign of him?" asked McGowen.

"No. Unfortunately. Maybe if I had more time. It's so different in there. Takes getting used to. It's another world. We should name it," he said, looking at von Ang.

"It's the other side of the membrane. How about Braneworld?" suggested von Ang.

"Braneworld . . . I like it," said Quan, sitting up. "I wanted to walk around in there, search for my father, but it's so hard to see. The air is opaque. If I had something to guide me . . ." Catching himself in midsentence, fearing he might lose von Ang's interest, he quickly added, "Of course, we'll want to experiment . . . do tests. I can take instruments next time. We can test different spectrums: electromagnetic, infrared, radiation."

"Come with me," said McGowen, taking him by the arm and extending a hand toward the medi-bot. "Let's check your readings."

"Hey, I'm fine," said Quan, getting down from the mesh. "You don't need to treat me like a basket of eggs. I feel good . . . energized, in fact."

McGowen let go of his arm. "We're sticking to procedure. You're going to have a thorough checkup."

At the medi-bot, Quan lay down on the gurney and the system went to work. Jointless steel arms picked sensors from their cradles and swept across his body, from forehead to toe. Within seconds the results were projected into free space.

"Looks good," said von Ang. "Heart, brain, liver . . . kidney, blood pressure, RDW . . . chem levels . . . all seem to be within normal range. Vitamin D level is a little low but within range. We'll check you again in an hour."

Quan changed clothes and rejoined the others, restarting the discussion of how to search for his father. "If there's a remote possibility that my father is in there somewhere, I'm not sure where to begin, or what to try. What do you think?"

Von Ang said, "We don't know where this goes. It could be a slightly different state each time. There's no guarantee."

"I saw the same thing that Wei described. That much we know."

"If you're going to search for him in there," said McGowen, "standard search procedures apply; walk a grid and call his name. And you should use a tether so you can find your way back."

16.

Trying to balance his jubilant feelings, in the penthouse Quan
stood in front of a wall-to-wall mirror wearing only his pajama
bottoms with his bare feet against the warm marble bathroom
floor. The broad smile on his face refused to go away. In his
reflection, he saw a different person. No longer a student, he saw
a man, an explorer of in a strange new world. He was feeling
excitement that he could hardly contain.

Sealy's fingers caressed his back. "If anything had
happened to you . . ."

He turned and faced her. "It was something I just had to
do. I felt compelled. I had to know. And now that I've done it . . .
I feel great. It's not like anything else in the world . . . just
amazing" He went on, full of energy, telling her about what
happened, almost to the point of bragging about his success.

She listened, stroking his hair lightly, all the while
thinking about how he had ignored her appeal to have someone
else take the risk. He had put his own desires first. She could

forgive that in light of his need to find out what happened to his father. But, he had done something potentially dangerous and it seemed to excite him. That concerned her more.

"And did it bring you any closer to understanding what happened to your father?"

"Well, not exactly. It helped me to understand what his experiments were about."

"Now that you know what his experiments were about I hope that's the end of it," she said.

"I'm okay, Seal. Think for a moment. If this was about your father, wouldn't you be just as curious."

"Curious, yes. I'd want to know what happened, but I wouldn't put myself at risk to find out. Promise me you won't do this again."

He turned her around with her back to the mirror above the marble sinks. In the reflection, he could see the curve of her waist through her silk chemise. He softly kissed her lips and, sliding his hand beneath her garment, he felt the smooth muscles of her lower back. Pulling her close, he kissed her again, deeply this time. Feeling her firm breasts against his chest, he looked at the perfect skin of her throat, her delicate ears and the subtle curve of her neck. Her skin smelled of lavender and her beauty was intoxicating.

She put her hands against his chest, holding him back.

"What's wrong?" he asked.

"It feels like we're losing what we had. I was hoping the investigation would run its course and we'd get back to where we were."

"I don't feel any different about us," he said, kissing her neck. "I love you."

He scooped her up and lifted her onto the marble counter.

"I love you, too," she said, leaning back. "I think you've done all you can here. Can't we leave—go away somewhere together."

He looked directly into her eyes. "It's too soon. What I did today was important. Just give me a little more time."

"What you and I have together is what's most important to me."

"I know that and I think we'll be able to go away soon. I promise."

He felt powerful, as if he possessed the strength of two men. He began kissing her again. Muscles in his back flexed. His arms reached under her, lifting her legs. Closing his eyes, he pulled her into him, held her close and joined with her. Sealy craned her neck back until her head reached the mirror. She moaned.

Behind his eyelids, inverted colors swept across landscapes of another world and sparkling forms swirled like heat waves on a desert highway. He walked to the bed with her still wrapped around him and laid her down gently. He had never felt so strong before. They kissed and caressed, communing without words, reaching a crescendo together, and after a while they fell asleep in each other's arms.

While Quan slept, he dreamed of the other world, walking through the billowing sheets of multicolored sand. He felt protected there, as if he were held safely in the palm of a giant's hand. His eyes opened before dawn. A different dream woke him and was still in view. He was a boy of eleven, standing with his father at the rim of Aram Chaos on the southern highlands of Mars, looking out across the Ares Vallis. It was the same valley he had seen from his telescope, but it was transformed from a desolate and rocky landscape into a vibrant ecosystem. It was nighttime and he could see the glimmer of a river snaking through the central plain—groves of trees grew along its banks. A township spread out on both sides of the river, extending to the distant foothills. Lights twinkled brightly and his father's hand was on his shoulder.

"Imagine," said his father, *"they've been here for thousands of years and we never saw them."*

He woke abruptly and the visions slowly faded. He fought to stay in the dream, but his efforts only hastened its departure. Like spume deposited on a beach, the dream left only an impression. *Life where we thought there was none.* Without doubt, there was a connection to his recent experience. He had sensed something in that other place, something he hadn't told the others about, something elusive—a feeling that someone was there with him, reading him, protecting him.

Sitting on the edge of the bed, he watched his banlu sleeping. Her eyes moved beneath thick black lashes, her side lifting slightly with each breath. *Absolute beauty,* he thought. He watched her for a while, then he lay down, turning his back to her. With her warmth next to him, within a few minutes he was asleep again.

Midmorning, Sealy opened the shutters. She looked closely at his face and kissed him on the lips. His eyes opened.

"Last night was very nice. I couldn't wait any longer. Wake up sleepy head."

Quan sat up, somewhat groggy.

"You should take it easy today," she said with a smile. "Let's have a leisurely breakfast and talk about where we're going from here."

Padding through the penthouse, still in his slippes and pajamas, he entered the kitchen and pulled a stool up to the high translucent countertop. Head in hand, he stared at a broad ribbon of light crossing the marble floor. It seemed to disappear somewhere below the countertop. Leaning over sideways, he looked to see where it went. At the edge of the countertop, the light found a beveled edge and the brightness almost blinded him. Rubbing his eyes, he sat up. Ning was there, in front of him, putting a small bowl of congee down with a napkin and spoon. Quietly, he began to eat.

Sealy pulled up a stool next to him. After observing him for a moment, she asked, "Are you feeling okay?"

136

Chewing lazily, he managed a smile and said, "I'm fine. Just didn't sleep well."

Though their intimacy was once again in bloom, Quan's feelings were somehow different than they had been. The transfer experience had affected him in a way he couldn't yet grasp. Retracing his steps he thought back to the beginning and Ning's late-night call, telling him of the disappearance. Then his departure from university, his return to the Jintao Corporation and unlocking the hidden files. He met the team of professionals and reanimated his father's machine. It felt as though he knew what he was doing even thought it was an outlandish departure from his normal life. Every step of the way he had done what seemed logical and it had led him to crossing an unimaginable frontier. But there was a haunting feeling that he was following some grand design—as if he were acting out a part that had been scripted for him.

His father used to say 'Men are both kings and pawns.'

Pawn or king. Which am I?

Seeing that he was lost in thought, Sealy rubbed the back of his head. "Thank you for last night."

"It was way overdue," he said, kissing her cheek. How to articulate his strange new feelings? The words refused to come. Retreating to a more mundane topic, he asked, "When is your sister arriving?"

"We talked. She's still out of town on break and she promised to visit before going back to university. Soon I think. In a few days."

17.

Midday, Sealy was on the penthouse roof, standing in the safety zone as the taxi-glide slowly descended, its landing lights blinking. The glide settled, its door slid back, and a young woman in a full-length gold-and-silver coat stepped out. Wiggling her hips, she lifted her arms skyward with a dozen bracelets jingling and shouted, "*Ah seh won!* I'm back from the islands." Her coat fluttered open, revealing a pastel pink and green bikini underneath.

"You came direct from Eleuthera? I thought you'd go home and change first," said Sealy. "Aren't you cold?"

Shifting a yellow visor up to the top of her head, Sealy's sister grinned, crinkling her nose, and batting her eyelashes— lashes augmented with tiny pink and green feathers. "*Everyting be* irree*, sista.*"

"What's with the accent?"

Lotus pouted her lips and dropped the Jamaican patois. "You're no fun, girl. You need to get out more." She pulled the thermal coat around her and shivered. "The view is amazing up here but yah honey, it's cold!"

"Come on, let's go inside," said Sealy, shaking her head.

Lotus followed, holding her coat tightly as she shuffled along in her fleece-lined boots. A botcart unplugged from the glide and followed with her luggage.

Inside the penthouse, Sealy said, "I'm happy you're here. How have you been? Tell me all about your trip."

Lotus stripped off her coat, revealing a golden tan. With hands on her hips she turned, showing off her perfect figure. "I been sunnin,' don't ya know."

Sealy stared in amazement—a bikini in winter.

Like night and day, the sisters were different. Where Sealy was always dependable and proper, Lotus was ever the renegade. Where Sealy's figure was willowy and her manner graceful, Lotus was built like a dancer and her energy was effusive.

Until the age of six, Lotus had lived in an abandoned housing project with seventeen other children. When the authorities learned of their encampment, they were scooped up and each was placed in the care of families who wanted a second child. From the start, Lotus was free-spirited with a whip-smart mind—rebellious, but a welcome addition to the otherwise conservative Xiaoping family.

On the circular sofa of the great front room, they took up positions across from each other.

"Wow. Nice place," said Lotus, looking around. "And that sim is just orbital."

"It's California," said Sealy. "Glad you like it. I helped design it."

"Where's Quan?"

"He'll be here later. He's has been gone a lot lately. Is your semester break still on? How much time do you have? Tell me about Eleuthera."

"Too many questions, sis. The island is one nonstop party. The last four days just fried me. It was a good time to leave. I'm glad to zone out with you for a while. I'm not ready to see Mom and Dad yet. So, what's been happening?"

"Quan's burning the candle at both ends and I've been trying to continue with my course work but, well . . . I need a break. We could find something to do. Catch a play or a concert."

"Hey, great! I'm really into Foof Trizkit. They rock. Wonder if they're playing here."

"Don't know about them," said Sealy, feeling the age gap widen.

As the sun was setting outside, the indoor sim was gradually changing to evening in synchrony. Ning brought drinks and the girls continued to chat.

"It's weird," said Lotus. "Sometimes I just know when something's going to happen, like a premonition. I never told you this, but I had a premonition about Quan's dad. It felt like a door closed and I couldn't connect with my memory of him anymore. My psych professor calls it 'non-local communication.'"

"Maybe our brains are just more sophisticated than we think," said Sealy. "I mean, we're subconsciously processing stuff all the time. Maybe we eventually come to an understanding of what is most likely going to happen and it just pops into view. For instance, when I can't remember something . . . a few minutes later it pops into my head. That always feels odd to me."

"That doesn't really explain what I was talking about," said Lotus.

"Maybe not, but I don't believe in paranormal explanations."

Lotus took another sip of plum wine and told her sister about an experiment she'd read about—a joint study between SRI in California and MIT in Massachusetts. A group of students were gathered at each campus, separated by thousands of kilometers. Their professors asked each of them to visualize the other group, to describe the surroundings and what the people

140

were wearing, and what they might be holding. On average, they were sixty-four percent accurate and some of the participants scored as high as eighty-nine percent.

"There are hundreds of documented reports of remote viewing every year," said Lotus. "The theory goes that an intermingling of planetary fields produces a kind of holographic soup connecting all conscious beings. Pretty wack stuff, eh? And there's probably a lot more we don't know about."

Ning paused in the hallway, listening—her dark calm eyes searching under narrow lids. While doing her domestic chores, she processed the conversation, deconstructing the ideas, referencing subsets, accessing internal and external databases. She retrieved over a thousand related articles and correlated the data while stripping the bed sheets. Two hundred and forty-three seconds into her research, parallelism was identified between her own logic functions and the concept of non-local communication. Leaving the laundry area, she deduced that only limited comprehension of the world is possible using data comparison; sensory sources are needed for a more complete understanding. She stored the theorem and, having made up the bed with fresh sheets, she left the guest room.

It was 8:45 when a soft bell tone announced Quan's arrival, and a few moments later he strolled into the great room. Lotus popped up. "It's my brother from a different mother!" She rushed to him, hugged him, and kissed him on the mouth.

The kiss was laced with the sweetness of plum wine and more intimate than he expected. Quan planted his hands firmly on her waist and pressed her away without making an obvious point of it. Seeing her bikini and matching feathered eyelids, he said, "What good fortune little sister. So glad you were able to come."

"We're on break," said Lotus, bouncing on her toes, hands tucked behind her.

Sealy interjected, "We were having a glass of wine. Would you like to join us?"

"In a few minutes. First, I need to take care of something." Seeing two empty wine bottles on the table, he added, "We should eat."

"Good idea," said Sealy. "I'll have Ning make some food."

Quan sent a message to von Ang and returned to the great room.

Curled up on the circular sofa, the sisters were laughing uncontrollably. On the table in front of them were three cylindrical bamboo boxes, a platter of egg rolls and pot stickers, and a new bottle of plum wine. Quan lifted one of the bamboo covers, releasing wisps of steam.

Lotus blurted, "Try the lotus in lobster leaf. It's out of this world."

"Thanks, Lotus," said Quan, picking up a plate. "I'm sure you meant lobster in lotus leaf, didn't you?"

"Oh, sorry. I mixed Lobster and Lotus. What was I thinking?" She pressed her hands to her cheeks and wiggled her fingers like feelers.

Attempting to pull herself together, Sealy added, "NutriSynth has thousands of recipes. Who knows, there may be a lobster leaf in there somewhere."

Lotus added, "How about some duck lips in ginger sauce?"

Quan picked up a piece of lobster with his chopsticks and tossed it into his mouth. "Duck lips are one of my favorites," he said. "Right up there with pig's wings and shark feet."

"You're a funny man," said Lotus, calming down a bit.

Quan forced himself to stay and make small talk, all the while thinking about the immensity of what he was dealing with. There was so much he didn't know. He felt like a wooden stump, only branching into the conversation now and again while wondering how rude it would be to just get up and leave. He

142

needed time to think. The police had come to an impasse. Investigator Yang had found no evidence of abduction, and that left only one avenue open to explore—the Braneworld. That seemed to be more like detour than a path to solving his father's disappearance. He doubted that his father was still in that other place.

Sitting there with the sisters chattering on, Quan felt dismayed—feeling there were better uses of his time. Thankfully, his com disk starting bipping. It was von Ang, and he excused himself. After a few minutes, he returned to the great room.

"Now that Lotus is here, it feels more like family. I think I'll work from home. I have a meeting with Dr. von Ang and I need to talk with him in private. It's set for tomorrow morning. I hope you don't mind."

"He means we have to behave," said Sealy.

"No chance of that," said Lotus.

18.

Sealy and Lotus were in their pajamas, sitting at a small side table in the kitchen, enjoying their morning chinwag. Breakfast was served—sweet buns and a pot of oolong tea—and Sealy was telling her sister what she knew about the brilliant young physicist who was due to arrive. She stressed the importance of Quan's meeting and set forth a plan that would take them out of the house.

"We could go downtown. I need to have my hair done and we could do some shopping while we're there."

"If I'm imposing," said Lotus, "I can always go back to Mom and Dad's house."

"No. No. We both want you to stay. We just need to give Quan some privacy."

As 10:00 drew near, Lotus was sitting in the great room, ready to leave, while Sealy was still in the bedroom talking to Quan.

The landing signal began softly pulsing throughout the house. Lotus looked around to see if anyone was going to greet their guest. She got up and went toward the door when she saw Ning coming down the hall.

"I'll see to the door," said Lotus.

"Very well, miss," said Ning.

Lotus stepped out looking like something from another galaxy in a high-collar navy blue sweater, bulky white corduroy pants, and a pair of high-top, multicolored canvas sneakers. Von Ang disembarked the taxi-glide and looked in her direction. Lotus walked toward him with a hand raised to her forehead protecting her eyes from the bright sunlight. Her red anodized hair fluttered in the morning breeze and her red anodized lips lifted into a broad smile. On approach, she extended a hand. "Hello. I'm Lotus. I'm Quan Jintao's sister-in-law. You must be Dr. von Ang. We've been expecting you."

Von Ang couldn't help but stare at the metallic-red lips glistening in the daylight. Gently grasping her hand, he said, "Call me Gaston. I'm a little early. I hope that's all right."

"It's fine. Good timing. You're going to get cold out here. Come, let's go inside."

She put her hands on his forearm and walked him toward the rooftop entrance.

"I hear you're a famous scientist. I was expecting an old fuddy-duddy. Oops." She put a hand to her mouth.

Raising an eyebrow, von Ang said, "It's a career path. We start out young and optimistic, and we end up in fuddy-duddy-hood."

Lotus chuckled.

Dr. Von Ang couldn't resist asking, "Do you live here?"

"No. At the moment I'm between opportunities," she said with a continuous smile.

Sealy emerged from the rooftop doorway bundled in a dark green overcoat. "Lotus, I've been looking for you," she said. "Dr. von Ang, I'm Sealy, Quan's banlu. Welcome."

"My sister," said Lotus, blandly.

Von Ang slid his heels together, gave a slight head bow, and said, "A pleasure."

"We were just on our way out. Quan is expecting you. Lotus, please have the taxi wait while I show Dr. von Ang in."

Sealy escorted von Ang to the door, while Lotus spoke a hasty command to the glide's dispatch panel and hurried to catch up with them. Inside the corridor, from behind, Lotus called out, "We won't be gone long. It would be nice if you could stay for lunch."

Sealy turned and shot a concerned glance back at her sister.

"What?" said Lotus in a hushed tone.

Entering the great room, Quan greeted his guest, "Welcome. I see you've met the sisters."

"I invited Gaston to stay for lunch. I hope that's okay," said Lotus.

Sealy's look of frustration was obvious and Quan instantly grasped the situation. "We haven't made any plans . . . but I think if you can stay that would be great. We can all get to know each other a little better."

"If it isn't an imposition, I'd be delighted," said von Ang.

"Wonderful," said Quan. "That's settled, then." He turned and spoke quietly to Ning who was standing by. "We'll be four for lunch."

Lotus went to get a jacket and a few minutes later the sisters were back outside where the taxi-glide was waiting.

The two men entered the study next to Master Jintao's private suite, a room paneled in Afzelia wood with two black leather chairs and a red lacquered coffee table at its center. Daylight filtered in from a skylight. In a far corner a Chinese fig tree with its oversized leaves almost touched the ceiling and in the opposite corner sat a black leather reading chair and ottoman.

Quan gestured to the two chairs at the center of the room.

146

"How are you feeling?" asked von Ang as he took to his seat.

"I'm feeling fine, thanks," said Quan. "Strange as it may sound, I feel better than I did before. To a certain extent I feel more awake. My senses seem more acute."

"Interesting."

"I'm impressed with what you and my father accomplished. I don't completely understand the physics involved."

"The technology is complex and at the same time it's not. In a way, we knew what we needed to do before we did it— simply reproducing the effects of that malfunctioning reactor."

"With respect to your expertise though, no one understands the technology better than you do. I suspect having to explain it to me and the others might be somewhat annoying. Maybe I'm wrong, but I thought I detected some friction between us at our last meeting. I wonder if there's a problem."

Rustle the bushes to bring out the snakes.

"A problem? Well, since you ask, I was wondering why you brought in someone else to look over the stabilizer plans. It goes without saying that the project is yours to direct but, when I agreed to assist, I assumed you knew my capability. It was counterproductive to keep information from me."

"Please," said Quan, holding up a hand. "It was in no way an indictment of your ability. This is all new for me and it's been a lot for me to deal with. I never meant to slight you in any way. Your contribution is indispensable."

"I do what I can," said von Ang, straightening.

"After what I've seen, I can only imagine what will follow. This is a great opportunity and the research should continue however, my main objective is to find out what happened to my father. The science is your domain."

"I agree. This is a rare opportunity and I'm delighted to be involved."

"It's clear that you are the most qualified person on the team. Father trusted you and so do I and I want to make sure we have a solid working relationship. To put it plainly, I want you to lead the project from here on."

"You want me to lead the project?"

"You're the logical choice," said Quan. "We'll want to document the experiments and eventually publish our findings. You're the most qualified to do that. You've published papers before and you should be the main signatory, but of course my father should receive credit for the work he did."

Unfolding his arms, von Ang perked up. "You honor me sir. Yes. I would like that very much."

Quan tapped his wrist disk, and above the low table between them a view field activated. Two pages appeared, churning in midair, as if in a slowly moving cyclone. He swept his hand across and the pages unfurled. "I was confident you'd feel that way and so I prepared a consultanting contract." His hand brushed the air again and the documents turned to face von Ang.

Von Ang sat straight, his back not touching the chair. Reading through the document. It included a salary plus an equity stake if there was any financial outcome. He he asked for clarification. Looking past the floating image to where Quan sat, he said, "This is very generous. How will you fund the project?"

"The Jintao Corporation won't be involved. My family trust will fund the project. However, if there is any applied technology, Jintao Corporation will have first right of refusal. What I want out of this is finding out what happened to my father. At the same time, I'll be happy to help with the research."

"Naturally. Learning what happened to your father should be a first priority."

Quan placed his hand in the view field and Von Ang did the same. With business concluded, Quan said, "We have a deal. I'll store the docs where we can both access them." The pages vanished from view.

Quan's wrist disk bipped. It was Sealy. He excused himself and left the room. A moment later, Ning appeared at the doorway and asked von Ang if there was anything she could bring.

Quan was helping Sealy with her packages. Coming in from their shopping trip, Lotus immediately went looking for von Ang. She found him alone in the study, with his back turned to the doorway. She sidled up next to him and said, "We're back and I'm famished. Are you finished with your meeting?"

"Yes. You're back," he said. Columns of data vanished from the surface of his cornea. "How was shopping?"

"I think we bought too much. But, better too much than too little. Don't you agree?"

"You are talking to a man who owns eight identical suits."

"Are you hungry? Let's go to the front room."

"Alright," he said, following her.

"My feet are just killing me," she said, kicking off her shoes. "Would you like to hear some music? You probably like classical, right?"

"I enjoy a wide range of music."

"Really? Tell me what you think of this one." Lotus playfully worked something in her hand that was too small to be seen, syncing it to the penthouse sound system. Music blared from every corner and she quickly turned it down.

The track was a disparate mixture of styles: African tribal drumming, rockabilly rhythm guitar, jazz piano, and an amazing woman's voice, half singing and half reciting lyrics.

"Foof Trizkit," said von Ang.

"Seriously? That's unreal," said Lotus, with eyes and mouth wide open. "I've never met anyone over twenty who's even heard of them."

"I travel quite a bit and I sound bite constantly."

"That's orbital, and you're a scientist?"

"Theoretical physicist."

Lotus smiled broadly, showing her perfect teeth. "I've heard it's like trying to find a black cat in a dark room."

Amused, von Ang replied, "Most of the time it feels like trying to find a black cat that isn't even there at all."

Lotus played several more of her favorites and, one after another, he named the artists.

"Honestly," said Lotus. "You are the full quantum package."

For lunch, Ning set out a centerpiece of dried quince blossoms on the large dining table and, from a silver tureen she ladled soup into riceware bowls sitting on top of synthetic pearl chargers. She was careful to see that each bowl contained the same amount of broth, shrimp wonton, green onion, and bok choy. At the last, she put a sprig of Chinese parsley on top of each bowl and set the tureen aside.

Quan and Sealy, Lotus, and their guest took their seats. Opalescent rice grains imbedded on the sides of each bowl were letting light into the broth, making bright dots on the ingredients inside.

Lotus said, "Love these bowls. It's like tiny sidelights in a koi pond."

"They were handed down from my great-grandmother," said Quan.

Ning brought a silver wine cooler from the sideboard and placed it next to Quan in a stand. She uncorked the bottle and asked, "Shall I pour?"

"No. I'll do the honors," he said.

He filled the ladies' glasses, then reached across the table and poured for his guest and then himself, setting the empty bottle down in the cooler.

"Wine with lunch?" asked Sealy, holding up her glass. "Are we celebrating?"

"In fact, we are," said Quan, raising his glass. "Gaston has agreed to lead our research project."

"Congratulations," said Sealy, lifting her glass.

"I'm honored," said von Ang, picking up his glass.

Quan took a sip and set his glass down. "You're our first guest since we've been back."

"That makes you a *guìbīn*," said Lotus.

"Lotus means you're an honored guest," said Sealy.

"Thanks for the translation, sis," said Lotus, turning her face to von Ang. "My sister is always so helpful. Do you have brothers or sisters?"

"I have a sister. She lives in Lausanne. She and her husband have a farm. It's very picturesque—a lake—the alps—cows wandering on green hillsides—very picturesque."

"I'd love to go there. I bet it's magic," said Lotus.

Something quickened inside Sealy. She wasn't going to let Lotus dominate the conversation, like she usually did. "The Swiss are such an interesting culture. Switzerland is a cultural crossroads—German, French, Italian. And yet it's been able to retain its own unique character. I suppose that's because it's so isolated in the mountains."

"The mountains definitely had an influence," replied von Ang. "They occupy so much of the country that natural resources are scarce. The Swiss have had to do a lot with a little. You know ages ago we were known for precision watches. Now we make nano-scale machines. Tiny country, tiny things."

"And, of course there are the Swiss banks," added Quan.

"True. That's another benefit of isolation," said von Ang.

Fully aware of the impression her comment would make, Lotus dropped a bombshell. "Someone told me Switzerland is the money-laundering capital of the world. Is that true?"

Von Ang gave a little laugh. "In fairness, Swiss banks are one of the oldest safe havens, but certainly not the only ones."

Adding fuel to the fire, Lotus added, "Oligarchs always seem to come out on top, don't they? Stuffing their fortunes into hidden places."

Quan listened with amused interest, enjoying the controversary... and the soup.

"Inequality is an ongoing problem," said von Ang, "and if you don't have a way to get it under control, then people with the most money invariably take power. It's happened throughout history. Every country has its elite."

"Our Central Committee has done a good job of keeping it under control," said Sealy, sitting up straighter than usual, as if speaking on behalf of the government. "Looking out for the welfare of the general population, they've rebuilt the infrastructure—new power plants, new cities and glideways, and new industrial centers. And, at the same time, they've managed to clean up the environment."

Lotus dove in with gusto. "As I recall, their policies created the pollution in the first place. And didn't they uproot whole communities to make way for the new infrastructure? Don't forget the Three Gorges Dam."

Quan interjected, "And to their credit, after all the talk about colonizing Mars, they added up the cost and realized it was cheaper to clean up Earth instead. That was smart." Then he called to Ning for another bottle of Riesling and said, "Let's hear more about Switzerland."

Von Ang thought for a moment. "I suppose I could tell you about the work I did at CERN."

Lotus let out a heavy sigh. "I'd rather hear about the interesting things you've done."

"Really," said Sealy, in a deprecating tone. "Tell us whatever you'd like."

"I just love that you're at our table," said Lotus, perky and beaming. "I want to know all about you."

"All right. I could tell you about racing in Cannes," said von Ang with a big smile. "That was exciting."

152

"Yes. Tell us about Cannes," said Lotus, leaning forward. "Vintage automobiles?"

"No. Actually, gasoline powered vehicles have been banned throughout the EU. Only electrics are allowed. But no, this was sailboat racing. I was on crew for the Figaro 81 yacht race—Cannes to Istanbul. I crewed on the Prometheus out of Wales and we came in second. We would have taken first except for one bad turn around the Isle of Man. Wind gusts of forty knots almost capsized us. We were skimming along with the starboard rail touching the water. The helmsman pulled us out just in time."

"Wonderful!" said Lotus, clapping her hands together. "I would never have guessed you were a sailor in addition to your other talents."

Sealy rolled her eyes and Quan almost laughed.

"It was a long time ago," said von Ang.

Ning entered with a newly opened bottle of Riesling and stopped next to Quan. "Shall I pour?" she asked.

"Yes," said Quan. "And some egg rolls or spring rolls would be nice."

"Will NutriSynth be all right?"

"I think so. Everybody?"

"Sure. Why not," said Sealy. Her eyes slid from Quan to von Ang. "You'll stay, won't you, Gaston?"

"Yes, of course."

The foursome ate and drank and bursts of laughter rose from the table for the better part of an hour. At the last, von Ang set his napkin down and looked at Quan. "This has been very nice. I appreciate the opportunity to know your family. I should be getting back. There's work to be done."

"I understand," said Quan, rising from his chair. "We should all get together again."

Von Ang rose from the table with the others and Quan walked him to the foyer. He shook von Ang's hand and said, "I'll see you tomorrow."

Ning approached with von Ang's coat and Lotus asked for her coat, as well.

Von Ang said good-bye again, thanking Sealy for a pleasant lunch. Lotus quickly put her coat on and went out to the rooftop with him. In her time, she had known them all: the would-be intellectuals, the urbanites, the playboys, the jocks, and the lecherous old rakes. Von Ang stood out. He was brilliant, and handsome, comfortable with himself, and above all, he was a gentleman.

The air was cold and Lotus pulled the collar of her jacket up close to her chin. "Tell me," she asked. "Where do you live?"

"I have a house in Geneva overlooking the lake, but I'm hardly ever there. I have apartments in two other cities."

"Sweet. Is one of them here?"

"Yes."

Her eyes grew larger. *"Peut-être vous m'invitez à votre maison."*

"You are a constant surprise," said von Ang. "Yes, of course you're invited. How could I say no?"

"Bon savoir," she said.

Seeing a glide on approach, Lotus became more formal. "It was very nice to meet you, Gaston. I'll be here for a few more days. Maybe I'll see you again before I leave."

The taxi-glide began its slow descent.

"It would be my pleasure."

Placing a hand on his forearm, she leaned in and gave him a light kiss on the cheek, then stepped back smiling impishly—as if she'd done something naughty. He smiled, said good-bye, and boarded the glide, unaware of the nanites migrating down his coat sleeve. On the way home, a gentle vibration drew his attention. He pushed up his coat sleeve and looked at his arm. There, written on the underside of his wrist, was her message: "LOTUS—092752." He laughed, shook his head, and spoke the number to his wrist disk. Then he brushed the expired nanites into the trash receptacle in front of him.

154

19.

Kau Yi Chau Island

Quan fastened a utility belt over his skinsuit while von Ang fed in scan data for three instruments.

"This one's on the bleeding edge," said von Ang, handing him an instrument fashioned with a pistol grip on one end and a rectangular block on the other end. "I'm hoping it will tell us what those particles are made of."

"What do you call this?" asked Quan, turning it over in his hand.

"It's a micro mass spectrometer."

"It's incredibly small. Who built it?"

"One of my go-to people," said von Ang. "There are only two in existence. Treat it with care. I pledged a vital organ to borrow it."

Clipping it to his belt, Quan said, "Don't worry, I'll take good care. Let's keep your organs stay where they belong." He attached the other gadgets, then climbed onto the mesh. Watching von Ang set the machine, he thought about their contract. Giving him an equity stake had secured his allegiance and rekindled his enthusiasm.

"You'll have half an hour," said von Ang, "and the experiments should take about five minutes each."

The big Scot crouched down next to where Quan lay, attaching something to the leg of the frame. Looking over the side, Quan saw a red-and-black mountain-climbing rope with metal rings and carabiners. "How long it that rope?" he asked.

"Fifty meters," said McGowen.

"I'll walk out about fifty meters," he said to von Ang. "Is that within the boundary effect?"

"That should be fine," said von Ang. "I calculated energy dissipation at about sixty meters."

McGowen clipped the end of the rope to a ring on Quan's belt and stepped away.

"I'll do the experiments first, then I'm going to look around."

"Affirmative," said von Ang.

Waiting for the surge, Quan heard a whirring sound and looked over to where McGowen was starting up the medi-bot system. It was a reminder of how serious a malfunction could be. These were the treacherous minutes, a surplus of time to think about the risks.

"I'm ready," said Quan. "Can we get on with this?"

Von Ang initiated the transfer sequence, and three seconds later the young Jintao was gone.

Waves of multicolored specks rush over him, fizzing like the static on a broken view field. Swinging down from the mesh, his feet touch the floor. Colors are inverted. Shapes come and go. The torus and the large stainless steel tanks are purple outlined in black. Shadows are orange. Boundaries dissolve and reform. Walking away from the equipment, he passes the dark shapes of his team members, continuing out to what he calculates to be about twenty meters out.

Looking down at the instruments on his belt he sees three grainy shapes bristling with particles. Quan grabs the spectrometer by what appears to be its pistol shaped handle and unhooks it. Holding it at arm's length, he presses the trigger. Digits on the readout aren't legible. He brings the instrument closer to his eyes. It may have identified seven different elements . . . but then four . . . then eight. The readings are erratic. He hooks it back onto the belt and picks up another device, a reticle scanner. Holding it steady, it seems to be measuring something. Particles appear at a magnification of ten thousand . . . then they're gone. He triggers it again. It's not working. Before putting it away, he holds the trigger down continuously and sweeps the instrument around. Still nothing.

He unclips the last gadget and activates it. The display is impossible to read. The numbers are too small. Quan clips it back onto the belt and stands there, engulfed in the billowing waves of color, his eyes searching for patterns in the storm.

This is the inverse, he thinks. *This is what the space inside atoms is made up of . . . space filled with dark matter and dark energy . . . another reality attached to every particle of our world. It's the other side of the scrim . . . the backstage of the universe.*

His father's last words resonate inside his head: *Must see with my own eyes.*

Yes. This is the only way.

Surrounded by the bristling firmament, he feels strangely safe, as if the thick atmosphere is cloaking him—protecting him. Then comes an odd feeling. It's as though a gentle breeze is blowing across the back of his head, moving across his exposed neurons It's as if the nerves are extending right out of his head, reaching into space, connecting to everything. He's alone, and yet not. The feeling is exhilarating, empowering... and yet frightening.

158

I am and I am not. Parts of me are flickering in and out of existence.

Looking down he sees a black form. It's his body—blackness outlined with needle-fine filaments of light. He moves his arm. The needles are radiating directly out from his skin, like the needles of a pine tree. Some are pointing directly at him, hardly visible, only pinpoints. Others are long, tapering to nothingness.

Raising both arms, he yells out, "I'm here. Do you see me? Anybody?"

No answer.

Then there is something—something in front of him—something forming in the mist. It's as if the particles are clumping—sticking to an invisible shape. Something is definitely there.

"Hello?" he says, craning his neck forward, squinting. The sands are coalescing into a figure. Too small to be McGowen. Maybe von Ang. Features are becoming more defined. It has a face. Recognition sets in. It's him . . . standing there . . . staring . . . the lips unmoving. It's his father!

Taken aback, Quan says, "Father?"

Inside his head, a voice reverberates. [I am.]

Quan is stunned. He looks closer.

Drifts of particles circulate within the face. Wisps stream out, then loop back and reconstitute.

The voice in his head comes again. [All is as it should be.]

"Is it you, Father? Are you okay? What are you doing?" He reaches out, grasping the arm. His fingers find nothing solid. "Come here. What happened? Why haven't you returned?"

The face is forming and re-forming. The mouth unmoving. Words reverberate in his head. [Infinite consciousness. Infinite manifestation.]

Quan's sense of security evaporates. Fear takes over. The words don't ring true—not the way his father would speak. He pulls back. "No. You're not him! I don't know what you are."

159

[I am.]

The particles begin to leave, as if being blown away by an unseen wind.

"Wait, wait," shouts Quan. "Father, if it is you . . . if you're alive . . . what happened? Why are you still here?"

The particles coalesce again. [One cannot be trapped in one's home.]

"You call this place home? What are you saying? You're at home here?"

[Here, there. One in the same.]

"Come back with me. Come back to the other side where we live—back home."

[All is one.]

Again, the apparition begins to discorporate. Swirling flecks lift away in eddies, merging with the maelstrom. Soon there is no trace. Quan stands there, stunned—the smell of electricity in his nostrils and an aching in his head—billowing sheets of dust all around him. Mesmerized by what he has seen, perplexed by the specter's words, he struggles to walk. Reaching the extent of his tether, he turns, walking in a circle until he realizes what he's doing. Then, one foot in front of the other, he heads back, walking a straight line. Finding the mesh, he lies down.

He lay there for what seemed like an eternity, not noticing that he had returned to the room again. McGowen's strong hands were on him, helping him down. Still hazy, he took off the belt with instruments dangling from it. Handing it to McGowen, he heard himself say, "I don't think these work."

McGowen handed the instruments to von Ang.

"I'll download the registers and look at the memory buffers," said von Ang. "Maybe we recorded some data."

"The instruments may be working but I couldn't read in there. It's difficult to see," said Quan. "The numbers looked erratic."

160

"The machine broadcasts powerful wave forms. It's possible there is electromagnetic interference with the components," said von Ang. "I might need to add shielding."

"What did you see where you went?" McGowen asked.

Quan paused, collecting himself, deciding to keep the strange encounter to himself. "The air is opaque," he said. "Shapes form and then disappear. It's hard to tell what's real and what's not. There may have been something or someone, but I'm not sure. It could have been an illusion."

Minutes later, the medi-bot completed its scan and its chromium arms retracted, parking themselves in alcoves on either side of the display field. Seventeen vital measurements lit up in amber.

"All good. Values are normal," said McGowen. "You seem fine."

Intrigued by Quan's lack of detail, he prodded, "Go on. Tell us what happened."

Quan sat on the edge of the gurney, making a circle in the air with his forefinger. "I walked full circle at the end of the tether. That means I walked through the walls and through the equipment. There doesn't seem to be any physical boundaries in there, just the ebb and flow of energy and particles. I may have walked through you, as well. Now that I think about it, it's curious that I was walking on a surface. How could I walk through objects and not fall through the floor? Some of our physical laws must still apply. I found the mesh somehow, and climbed onto it. But, I walked through everything else. How is that possible?"

"I can tell you one thing," said McGowen. "The tether didn't move. I watched it."

Dr. von Ang interjected, "We didn't sequence the tether—only the instruments and the belt."

"Aye. What do you make of that?" said McGowen, looking at von Ang for a response.

Quan stood up. "That's perplexing. When I reached the end of the tether, I thought I felt a tug. I'll have to pay more attention next time."

Von Ang put in, "The physical laws are obviously very different. Most interesting is that we can exist in both places without harm. It leads me to think that other place is a different part of a larger physical spectrum. Something we normally can't see, but something that is ever present."

McGowen returned to his previous question. "You said you saw something. Did it look like your father? What did you see?"

Determined to leave details for a later time, Quan said, "Everything is so loosely defined. I saw shapes . . . or imagined I did . . . like in those connect-the-dots drawings. I can't be sure it means anything. Maybe my mind is trying to organize chaos into something recognizable. I saw something that I imagined looked like him . . . then again, maybe not. I need to think about it."

McGowen suspected there was more, but now wasn't the time to apply pressure. "Perception is a funny thing."

"Indeed," said von Ang, unclipping the last instrument from the belt. "To paraphrase Einstein, 'Matter is an illusion, albeit a very persistent one.'"

Quan felt a sudden chill, remembering how he'd tried to grab his father's arm—as if somehow he could pull him out of the Braneworld. Instead, his hand passed through and in that moment their eyes connected and he saw the unmistakable authority in those eyes—a look that said, *I am your father*. There was a purpose in those eyes and he didn't know what that purpose was.

~~~

Quan left the laboratory within the hour, gliding low over the steely blue waters with GPS turned off and von Ang at the controls. In his mind's eye, he could see the multicolored face

162

that appeared to him. He played the scene over and over again. Eventually the image began to abstract, like the memory of a memory.

Was it real? Was it a hallucination driven by his desire to find his father? And what about the voice? What did it say? *Infinite consciousness? Infinite manifestation?* Totally unfamiliar phrases—yet so concise. Where his father had elucidated so eloquently, these phrases were terse—not like him at all.

Quan needed to talk about these things with someone he could confide in. Normally he would turn to his banlu, Sealy, but he wasn't sure she would welcome the conversation. His participation in the experiments worried her and he knew she wanted him to stop.

The glide banked and slowly descended to the penthouse aeropad.

20.

Quan was back inside the penthouse and into his pajamas by eleven thirty. He piled three oversized pillows against the headboard and plunked himself down next to Sealy.

"You did it again, didn't you?" asked Sealy.

"If you mean the experiment, yes."

"You worry me. You realize that, don't you?"

"Yes, but believe me, it's safe. They check me before and after, and I'm fine."

"You told me, no one understands that contraption. So, why take the risk?"

"You know why. I'm still looking for my father."

"And have you found any trace of him?"

There was a long pause.

"I saw something that resembled him—but very strange. It was a figure . . . about the same size as my father but made of sand. The skin was green, tinged with orange. The eyes were purple . . . black where the whites should be . . . looking like a psychedelic painting. It was like something an artist would dream up . . . like some crazy multicolored sand sculpture. It was his overall shape but it only lasted for a few minutes, then it just dissolved into the sandstorm."

"Maybe you were hallucinating. Do you feel alright?"

"I'm okay," he said, feeling his head. "My head feels different somehow, but I'm okay . . . just trying to make sense of what I saw. If that was him, then he's alive in a way I don't understand. It's as if he's become part of that other place. A voice spoke to me—said that place is his home. Maybe I was hallucinating. Maybe it was my imagination. But if that was him, I don't know what to do."

"The thing you saw, it actually spoke to you? This makes me uncomfortable. Something's not right. You know, when you leave here for that island, I try hard to be okay with it, but I don't understand these experiments and I don't know what you're doing. I really try to be understanding. Maybe if I could go there with you I might be able to accept what you're doing, but from where I am, it sounds like what you're doing is very weird and it makes me uncomfortable."

"These are controlled experiments and they haven't harmed me. Here. Touch me. I'm here. I feel good. I'm okay."

"You're not going back there again, are you?"

"It's the only way."

"What if I went there with you. I'd like to see what's going on."

He shook his head. "We have to go to the island undercover each time and there's always the possibility we could be caught."

"I didn't mean just to the island. I meant I could go into the other dimension with you, so I could see it."

"I would never let you. Last time, my head felt like . . ." He caught himself.

"Like what?" she demanded.

165

"Nothing. Forget that. Half of what I do in there is scientific research. I just don't think you should be part of the experiments."

Sitting up on top of the bedspread, Sealy pulled her legs under her and glared at him. She wanted to yell at him . . . and tell him he could end up like his father. She wanted to set out every reason she could think of why he should never enter the Brainworld again . . . but she knew it wouldn't change his mind.

Instead, she spoke her feelings. "I'm afraid and I'm asking. Please, let someone else take the risk."

Quan listened and nodded, acknowledging her point of view. In the end, he countered with, "I know what I can handle and what I can't. Trust me. I'm the best person to be doing this."

"I do trust you. That's not the issue. It's about the risk. The thing you saw—what if that's what happens to a person when they do this too much?"

"I can promise you, we're taking every precaution. The experiments will go on because they are of great scientific benefit. I promise I'll stop after I understand what happened to my father."

"It might be too late for you by then. No one knows what the long-term effects are."

"I understand how you feel but I have to go one more time."

Sealy turned away from him and faced the wall, and for the rest of the night she brooded over his lack of consideration. When it was time for bed, Sealy turned her back on Quan and pulled the covers up to her chin.

Quan lay there for an hour, eyes closed, think over the situation he was in. He could tell by the pattern of her breathing that Sealy had fallen asleep. Then it began. His nervous system began flinching. Electric currents were flashing from the back of his head to his extremities. The twitches came in bursts. He lay there, flat on his back, trying to calm his system, concentrating on his chi meridians. He followed the signals and forced his body to

166

even out the spikes. His nervous system felt like it was on fire and his head felt as though his brain was pressing against its encasement, trying to break free.

His mind filled with the images he had seen: patterns . . . drifts of quantum flux . . . shapes . . . cascading forms . . . intersections . . . and the bizarre image that resembled his father.

What is that place?

Thinking about the flux between the two realms, he envisioned a systematic correspondence . . . a correspondence of particles . . . matched pairs . . . matched pairs across time and space . . . moving through dimensions . . . aligned by the machine . . . polarized by the forces . . . spinning around poles . . . planets spinning around suns . . . orbits . . . orbiting particles . . . particles through a membrane . . . through the Brane . . . all of this came coursing through his brain. Somehow, it was all related.

A few minutes before 2:00 a.m., he rolled quietly from under the sheets and went to the study. As he slipped into the sling of his Sosai workstation and the view field instantly lit up around him. Visions swarmed in his head. He wanted to capture the essence of the experience. He wanted to interpret and catalog it. He wanted to clear his mind and get the images out where he could see them.

He began typing, jotting down ideas as they came to him. Words were not enough. He needed something more substantial. He sent crawlers to the web, searching for references. They bought back vidi clips, Mandelbrot sets, excerpts, and simulations. They brought back references, quotations, equations, and verse. He sorted through the trove, throwing out more than he kept and arranging the rest as fast as he could, trying to keep up with the deluge. His thoughts became sharper and brighter—a fountainhead flowing from his cross-dimensional experience. It was therapeutic, a way to express what he felt. Patterns began to form. He was gaining on it. And yet, there was a sinking feeling. Something was eluding him, something he had a sixth sense about. He had to find a way to coax it out into the open—to see its hidden nature.

He was enmeshed and unable to see the whole—unable to see the essence of it. He needed other eyes—eyes that could look at it objectively.

Fresh eyes to see and make sense of it. Strangers' eyes. Why not show it to everyone? That's it. SHOW IT TO EVERYONE.

He registered a virtual domain and, with a keystroke, sent his montage streaming to the web. Part static, part animated, part annotated—it was complex and colorful. "LÓNG" was the name he gave the domain. It meant "dragon" in Chinese.

Working directly online, not caring that others might see his live edits, he stitched in 3-D images and set jumper links. Thoughts flooded his mind and flowed into the domain, filling the space with sound and imagery. Continuing to rummage through what his spiders dragged in, he worked at an accelerating pace—reviewing, picking out relevant bits and knitting them together. A pixel storm raged across his view field and the data flowed to his new domain in torrents. Fingering faster and faster, he edited and added, expanding the content.

There's so much. Don't fear the complexity, he told himself. *It leads to clarity.*

Quan set up a proxy to obscure his identity, leaving only an untraceable autoresponder with a simple message: "This is all for now. More will follow. Your comments are welcome."

As dawn climbed the walls of South Point, he made his way back along the central corridor. His legs moved by themselves. His mind was a million miles away and the hallway illuminated as he passed. With images still reverberating in his head, he slipped back into bed.

While he slept, news of the LÓNG site spread across the web like wildfire. The new domain received over thirty thousand queries within the first hour, and seventeen new discussion

168

groups sprang up, posting reviews that ranged from defamatory to ecstatic. It was branded by some as a treatise on existential philosophy, while others saw it as a wholly original form of art. Some declared it was a work of genius while others decried it as nonsense. Some drew correlations to religion while others related it to quantum theory. Someone spoofed it as the long-awaited awakening of the internet as a sentient being and a few radical bloggers claimed it contained hidden messages—signs of the beast —Satan's handiwork.

At 10:30 a.m., the sound of a secure channel on his wrist disk woke him. It was McGowen.

"*Jo san*, young master. Sorry to disturb you. We may have a problem. I've got three G-suits here, and they've posted a notice outside your father's lab. Says the room is sealed. No one can enter without government clearance and they're demanding access to your father's files. Dr. Hao and the attorneys have them pinned down in the conference room, telling them what they're doing is illegal. I suspect they're going to be here for a while. They're dug in . . . saying it's part of some ongoing investigation. And they're asking to talk to you."

Quan wondered if there was some way his website was drawning government attention.

"I'm not surprised," he told McGowen. "Don't worry. Let them snoop. I've taken care of it. Nothing of value in the lab now. Tell them I'll be in early tomorrow if they want to see me."

The conversation drew Sealy's attention. She came to the bedside and asked, "Are you going again?"

"No. I'm going to stay and work from here today."

"Good."

Fully awake, Quan threw on his robe and returned to the workstation. With fresh eyes, he clicked on the LÓNG website. It was a dense and bewildering sight, a barrage of moving images and scrolling data. It was too complicated and didn't seem to make sense. He looked for patterns but there was no obvious

169

syntax and it lacked a clearly stated purpose. It would be easy for others to get lost in the jumble and not see the whole picture.

The only thing that was perfect was the name: LÓNG. It summed up the sensation he felt of entering and returning from that other place. Dragons epitomize transition. They're mystical creatures, living in harmony with nature, capable of shifting into different forms. Born of water, they live in rivers, curving with the flow. They ascend in clouds above the mountains and thunder down in every drop of rain.

His fingers began to fidget, adjusting and editing, galvanizing the bits and pieces into a logical sequence. Shuffling through chunks of data, his mind was working everywhere at once. Gradually, like a moth from a chrysalis, a central thought began to emerge. It was a prickly truth, a truth that seemed to resist coming to light.

The world was stranger than anyone had imagined, existing in multiple dimensions at the same time. Matter itself was ethereal . . . a projection . . . an illusion. And by extension, life wasn't anchored to anything tangible. Life itself was ethereal . . . existing in all dimensions at the same time.

It was late afternoon when he closed the session and walked out into the great room. Sealy was there. At first he wanted to talk about his insights but then it would only cause more discord. He sat next to her and said not a word.

Sealy greeted him with a forced smile and poured tea, "You were up late," she said. "What were you working on?"

He had to open up to her. *Start with something simple*, he thought. "We are not the first to know about the Braneworld."

"Oh. So, you have a name for it now."

"It's a name Gaston came up with but I'm sure it's gone by other names. We're not the first to know about it."

"What are you talking about?" asked Sealy.

"I've been gathering research and I found other narratives that are too similar to be coincidence. There were others, long

170

ago, who described the same thing. Did you ever hear of Ching Tu? They called it the land of pure consciousness and enlightenment."

"Yes, when I was very young," said Sealy.

"We had a nanny who told us about Ching Tu," said Sealy. "It's a fable."

"Right. And there are similar fables in other cultures. The ancient Egyptians had stories about the Land of Two Fields. The Vikings, the Christians, the Hindus . . . Hopi indians, aborigines . . . lots of other people . . . they all have similar stories."

"And you think they were all describing the same thing?"

"It's only a matter of semantics. I mean, imagine if people of the first century could see one of our autoglides. They'd relate to it in ways they were familiar with. They might say it looks like an enormous shining egg floating on the wind, with flashes of colored light from jewels on its shell. And they might easily have described Braneworld in the same way as Ching Tu, or Heaven, or Valhalla."

Sealy's face went deadpan. "I was concerned about your physical safety, I never thought to worry about your mental health. Now, I'm not so sure. You're telling me you've been to Ching Tu? That's not very scientific—sounds paranormal."

"In a way, we're like those ancients. Even with our sophisticated sciences, it's practically impossible to describe the experience. There's no map or legend to guide us."

Ning entered the room and stood for a moment as if trying to remember something. "Do you need my assistance?"

Quan wheeled round in his seat, one arm over the back of the circular sofa. "Ching Tu. Remember? You used to read stories about it."

"The estuary where dragons spawn," said Ning.

"Huh, I don't remember that part," said Quan. "It's like one of those things that people try to describe but can't—like blind men trying to describe an elephant."

"I see," said Ning Her face, drawn in serious contemplation. "Blind men and elephants."

"Okay. Now, that was random," said Sealy, under her breath.

"I think people have been aware of other dimensions since ancient times," said Quan. "They tried to describe it in ways that people would understand, and probably weren't very successful. Without written records, explanations were easily misinterpreted as they were passed down through the generations."

"Like writing in the sky," said Ning, sweeping her hand in an arc.

Sealy rolled her eyes. "Does she really need to be part of this?"

"Come on, Seal. No harm. She's deducing abstract ideas. At least she's trying to think outside her parameters."

"Where is all this going, anyway?"

He pressed on. "We can measure and test and catalog that place. We can describe it more accurately than those early people, but it's still an enigma. We don't have a language for it. I'm just beginning to understand it, just beginning to explore its potential and it's changing me."

Sealy perked up. "What does that mean? How is it changing you?"

"I'm beginning to see things differently. The world we live in is just the visible part of a much more complex reality. We are all made of the same stuff . . . and the stuff we're made of is constantly recycled. Life is pushing itself into existence, like the unseen fingers inside a puppet. What would it be like if everyone saw the world that way?"

Sealy wriggled on the sofa. "That's all speculation on your part. Maybe philosophers and theoreticians would be interested, but I don't think most people are looking for that kind of revelation. Most people are looking to be entertained, not enlightened. And, if you try to force a different reality on them,

172

they're most likely going to ignore you—or worse. They might want to silence you."

He knew she was right, in the way she was right about so many things. "True," he said. "People come with all levels of understanding. Don't get me wrong. Converting the masses is not my thing, but this is a revelation of monumental importance. There must be a way to communicate what this is . . . but just how to do that isn't clear."

"Unwashed windows obscure the view," said Ning.

Amusement flickered across Quan's face. "In a way, Ning's right. I'm looking for clarity. I need help."

Sealy folded her arms. "Looks to me like you're wandering off course. You think there are others who've experienced this other dimension without the equipment you have?"

"My father, and the anomaly, and the quantum flux between dimensions—it's all tied together somehow. Maybe there are others out there who are better able to understand what's going on."

"So, what is it that you're trying to communicate?" asked Lotus.

"The illusion of this world—beyond the physical stuff—nine-tenths of what exists is hidden from us." He got up and faced her. "I built a model of the experience to help me understand it. I put it online—anonymous, of course. I'm hoping others might know what this is about."

"I need to caution you. I love Lotus, but if you want to keep your work private, don't share any of this with her. I've never known her to keep a secret."

"I can see that. You're right, Seal. I'm the caretaker. I have responsibility." Looking across the room, he said, "Ning can keep a secret. Can't you, Ning?"

"Ching Tu is not secret. Many know of it," said Ning.

"What we've been talking about in this room is to be kept secret," asserted Sealy. "You are not to discuss this conversation with anyone. Do you understand?"

"Yes," said Ning. "I am not to speak of these things to anyone."

21.

At the Jintao Corporation Quan sat at his father's desk. The floor to ceiling glass wall was to his left and the gold framed certificates and awards to his right. His hands were on top of the two meter wide desk in front of him. His fingers traced the inlaid panel of black leather at its center. His hands reached across the panel and felt the kidskin surface, soft and yielding. His fingers explored the edges—feeling for a secret compartment—searching for something that would explain his father's plight. His father could have at least left a note.

What had been left was the pyramid puzzle in his father's lab, a puzzle that only he could solve . . . and the rabbit's foot, an ingenious key to the hidden files.

Outside the glass wall, a seagull glid past, white and bright in the noonday sun.

Leaning back in the executive chair, haunting images of his father's face came to him. If he didn't return, the Corporation would eventually declare him *in absentia* and Quan would be expected to take part in company management. He would be given the power of a majority shareholder which would also encumber him like a suit of armor.

The process had already begun. His next scheduled meeting was with the government officials who sealed his father's laboratory. He had done his best to keep the discovery under wraps but it was entirely possible that they already knew about it. Maybe someone told them or maybe they'd been spying on Master Jintao for some time. Maybe there was a mole inside the company, or maybe one of the consultants told them. In any event, Quan was prepared to do damage control—and push them away if he could.

A secretary in the outer office spoke over the intracom, "Your appointment is here."

"Show them in," said Quan.

To his right a door opened and three government officials entered the room. They wore identical blue suits, white shirts, and black ties—two men and a woman. McGowen followed in behind them.

"You asked to see me," said Quan, remaining in his seat. "Who are you?"

One of them, a man with a particularly narrow face and thick glasses, made the introductions, claiming they were from the Central Science Committee. Quan asked to see their credentials and was shown their name badges.

"Have a seat," he said.

Finding only two chairs in front of the desk, there was brief hesitation until the man with the narrow face ordered the other two to sit. McGowen stood at the wall next to the door.

"I'm looking forward to hearing about your investigation. What have you learned?" asked Quan.

The two who were seated looked at each other for an answer. The man behind them spoke directly. "What are you referring to?"

"Aren't you here to look into my father's disappearance?"

176

"We're here on a matter of national security. A research project is being conducted here that should be under the jurisdiction of our Committee."

"What project are you speaking of? We have so many."

"You know very well, I'm referring to the scientific research that was under your father's supervision."

"Who told you that?" asked Quan.

"We are not . . ."

Holding his hand up as if to silence them, Quan finished the sentence, " . . . at liberty to say. I knew you would say that. Listen, the only research I'm interested in is research related to the disappearance of my father. When I was told you wanted to see his files, naturally I thought you were here to help with the investigation. If that isn't the case, I see no reason for this meeting."

"Police are looking for your father. As I explained, we are here on a different matter and it is not for you to decide."

Quan walked to the glass wall overlooking the harbor and stood with his back to the blue suits. *Father kept the discovery hidden from these bureaucrats. It's too important to be handed over to them. Besides, there's more to be learned.*

Speaking with his back to them, Quan said, "So far, the police have found nothing. It's shameful. It's as though my father wasn't important . . . as though failure was acceptable. I fail to see how the Central Science Committee can help."

"Again. We are here to examine the research your father was involved with, and I advise you to cooperate."

McGowen stood by quietly, taking it all in. Quan wouldn't be bullied. He'd learned strategy and tactics from his father. He was confident the young Jintao would prevail.

Turning to them, with the sun warming his back, Quan's tone became stronger. "Jintao Corporation doesn't engage in scientific research. Speculative research isn't profitable. We're in the business of applying technology to things we can sell. That's what made this company great and I'm sure our CEO, Dr. Hao,

177

explained that to you. Now, if you want to do something productive, turn your attention to finding my father. Here we are, almost two months later, and no answers. It's entirely unacceptable."

Squinting against the sunlight, the man with the narrow face said, "We believe your father made a discovery that is far too important for the Jintao Corporation to keep to itself. We are here to offer the state's assistance."

The state's assistance, ha! thought Quan. *What they really mean is the state's assurance that they will take it from us.*

Walking back to the desk, Quan pointed a forefinger at the leader of the group. "I think someone is playing a trick on you . . . a trick that might ultimately embarrass you. This search of yours for some hypothetical research project is a fool's errand. Clearly, you're wasting your time . . . and mine."

The man raised his voice, saying, "We have the authority to demand full disclosure. You will provide a list of all projects underway at this company."

Quan replied in a stern voice. "Our projects are proprietary and are not open to public disclosure. You'll need an official order to see such a list and you'll need to sign a nondisclosure agreement. And I can assure you, you're not going to find any speculative projects on that list."

"We'll take your agreement to our legal department and we'll be back to look inside your father's laboratory. Until then, the laboratory is sealed and no one is to enter. Breaking the seal is a criminal offense."

"My secretaries will provide you with the NDA on your way out and, if you need anything more from me . . ." Quan waved his hand in the air. "make an appointment."

After the officials left, McGowen drew near. "What about the files and the prototypes?"

"Taken care of. All they'll find are the survey files and a schematic of the first prototype, the one that didn't work."

178

"Nicely done. Who do you think might have tipped them off?"

"It doesn't matter. Something like this was inevitable. They'll go through what's in the lab and try to make sense of it. That gives us time."

McGowen could see the change in Quan. He was growing up in a hurry and his father's coaching was evident. A game of chess had begun.

22.

Quan was piloting one of the company's glides to Kau Yi Chau Island. Taking a different route to the island, he was gliding low across the eastern side of the bay with GPS switched off. He had left the simple life of a student far behind him. The safety of university life was idyllic and his domestic bliss with Sealy was comfortable. Now it was far in the past. Today he was on task for a third excursion into the Braneworld and he was determined to interrogate the thing that looked like his father, intent on getting solid answers.

Inside the laboratory, von Ang's breath condensed in front of him as he crouched over a workbench. Operating nano-scale manipulators inside a scanning microscope, he was navigating through layers of circuitry. In the view field, his fingertips looked the size of elephants descending on a cityscape. He was replacing the standard components with precise, mil-spec components—connecting them with transparent filaments thinner than human hairs. He covered the circuitry with a flexible membrane and prodded a thin metallic film into position, then attached a vacuum line and sucked the foil down over the circuits. Then he began sealing the outer housing with an ultrasonic wand.

He heard the freight elevator door open and, looking up briefly. Seeing Quan he said, "Good. You're here. I want to ask you something."

"What's that?"

"You said there was something that looked like your father. You said it materialized and then disappeared."

"That's correct."

"It occurred to me that what you saw might be a sort of afterimage, like a data echo—something left over from your father's experiments—a ghost in the machine."

"I don't think so. I was communicating with it, back and forth. Would an echo do that?"

"Not in the conventional sense. What exactly did it say to you?"

"It was cryptic—ambiguous—something about infinite manifestation. Frankly, the look of it was so weird it was difficult to concentrate on what it said. It had only a vague resemblance to my father. Whatever it is, it seems at home in there. Matter of fact, it said that I was the one who was trapped . . . trapped by the idea of being here or there."

"So you were able to have a conversation with it. That suggests some kind of intelligence on the other side. If it happens again, I'd like you to ask some specific questions."

"What should I ask?"

"There are several things that would be good to know. First of all, if your father subjected himself to the transfer, I'd like to know why he didn't return when the machine energies shut down. I'd also like to know what he's learned about that other place and how he's been able to survive so long in that set of dimensions."

"I know. It seems impossible." asked Quan.

"It makes me think you encountered some sort of projection."

"A projection. Maybe . . . I suppose . . . some sort of artificial intelligence. That's possible, but projected from where?"

"Could be something your father set up."

"I'll ask more questions . . . see if I can figure it out. Give me at least twenty minutes."

Clipping the rebuilt instruments to his belt, he mounted the mesh-bed.

"Wait. I'll get the tether," said von Ang.

"Don't bother. I'm not going far."

At the control panel, von Ang started the sequence. "Bonne chance."

The system counted down, the wave guides bellowed, and Quan vanished.

Detaching the first instrument, a reticle scanner, he aims it . . . triggers it . . . again, and again. Grainy illuminated numbers flicker. The digits change erratically. The readings are inconsistent. Next, he tries the micro mass spectrometer. Holding it close to his face, he activates it. The numbers are grainy and almost imperceptible but they don't fluctuate. Good news. He moves it around, pointing it at different places. Six stable readings, atomic numbers. Excited, he tries the third instrument. After several attempts, it yields no better results than the first.

Clipping the last instrument back onto his belt, he looks out into the mist. There is pressure building in his head and his eyes tingle. Something is taking shape in the sandstorm before him.

"Father. Are you there?"

Gradually, particles begin to flock together like trillions of tiny birds. A familiar shape begins to form. Within a few seconds, the specter stands in front of him once again—purple eyes fixed on him, unblinking.

182

"Are you my father?"

[I am.] The reply fills his head.

"Why did you come here?"

[The duality—a disparate harmony.]

"What is this place?"

[Infinite manifestation.]

"And what have you learned?"

[All is all. Infinite consciousness.]

"And you? What are you?"

[Immaterial.]

"Your body looks different from mine in here. Why is that?"

[Snow falls into the sea.]

"Your body dissolved? Is that what you're saying?"

[Knock on the sky and listen to the light.]

"You're talking in riddles. Tell me what happened to you. How have you survived so long in here?"

The face in front of him is unmoving, the voice resonates inside his head.

[A marker in space-time.]

"Why didn't you return when the machine energy ended?"

[Standing in your own shadow, you wonder why it is dark.]

"What does that mean?"

[Open your gift and see.]

"What gift?"

[Truth comes in many colors.]

Multicolored specks begin to stream out from one side of the figure, drifting out, turning in midair, returning again to become part of the shoulder.

"Talking with you like this . . . it's unnatural. You speak in riddles. Makes me doubt you are real."

[I am.]

"But what kind of existence is this? You're alone here. Come back with me . . . back to our world . . . back to humanity."

The apparition turns away, dissolves into the mist—then appears a short distance away and looks back at Quan, beckoning to him. Then it dissolves again, reappearing a little farther away. Quan follows . . . first walking, then jogging as the figure lurches from one spot to another, picking up speed.

Running after the figure, Quan begins to feel weightless. His feet don't seem to strike anything hard—yet he is able to propel himself forward with each stride. The phantom is gaining speed. Quan pushes off with both legs, tilts his head back, arms and legs trailing behind him. He's flying, propelled by he knows not what, following the apparition like a fish chasing a lure. Particles are streaming past his ears and eyes. He's accelerating as if by will alone, being drawn by the phantom. Together they're hurtling through the mist, particles streaking by. Everything around them is a blur . . . no way to gauge how fast they're going. No idea how far they've gone.

After a time, they begin to slow. Particles come into focus again and the air is becoming less dense. Ahead of them is a clearing where the particles end, a vast expanse of empty space, a huge cavity. They exit the boundary of seething particles. Quan looks up to see a boundary of seething particles. It curves away in all directions. Above them, glowing streams of particles flow down from a single point, cascading down an invisible curvature in drifts of sparkling gold and crimson, tracing an invisible dome. The figure next to him looks different now, like a vibrating iridescent shape made of gel, almost invisible, but still resembling his father.

The figure floats upward and Quan ascends with him, heading toward the spot where the particles are coming from. Together, they travel through the dome's upper boundary, rising above it. They slow to a stop. The dome is below them. Sheaths of cascading particles are pouring down the curvature, emanating from a single point on top of the dome. Around them is nothing,

184

only blackness, blackness everywhere, darker than the darkest night. Below them, the specks continue to flow, endlessly pouring from a single point.

[From nothing, returning to nothing.]

"Where are we?"

[World without end.]

The apparition begins to move again, slowly sinking through the top of the dome. Words are filling Quan's head as he follows, but he is awestruck and unable to concentrate on what he hears. His eyes are fixed on the source of the flow.

From nothing? Returning to nothing? No. It must come from somewhere.

The phantom lurches, appearing again at the far side of the dome. Quan follows. They plunge back into the dense atmosphere. The figure is just ahead, speeding through clouds of multicolored specks. There is no way to know where they are or how long they've traveled. At last they come to a familiar sight, the vague shapes of the laboratory. McGowen's and von Ang's black outlines are next to the equipment. Quan climbs onto the transfer mesh and turns to watch his father's image slowly discorporate. Exhausted, he reclines, reviewing what he's seen. His mind is reeling, striving to understand.

It recycles, continually renewing itself . . . from within and from without . . . nothing created nor destroyed, only recycled . . . a world without end . . . an impossibility.

In an instant, the particles are gone.

Quan looked around. The hard-edges were back. The laboratory looked freshly made, crisp and new, as if everything had been washed clean.

Von Ang broke the silence. "What did you learn?"

Dazed, Quan struggled to recover his ability to speak. "It's a lot to digest. So much . . . I don't know where to begin."

Von Ang looked concerned. "There's no rush. Gather your thoughts."

His thoughts were muddled. After a few more moments, Quan said, "I've seen things you wouldn't believe."

"Go on."

"Our world and the Braneworld appear to be one enormous system. Matter springs out of nowhere . . . from nothing . . . and it returns to nothing."

"You saw all this?" asked von Ang. "Tell me more."

"I saw an endless stream of particles pouring into the Braneworld and beyond that there was nothing."

"How did you see beyond the Braneworld?"

"I can't explain it."

"Tell me about the tests."

Quan slid off of the side rail of the mesh and unbuckled the utility belt.

"The spectrometer seemed to work. It registered several elements, although the mass calculations didn't make sense. The other two didn't work at all."

"I'll check the buffers again," said von Ang as he took the belt. "Any sign of the thing that looked like your father? Were you able to determine if that was him?"

Quan's mind struggled, wanting to talk about what he'd seen, but the words refused to form. "Same as last time, something that looked like him. It said things that made no sense. I asked about his body and got the impression it's gone . . . dissolved somehow in that other place."

Von Ang looked deeply concerned. "I find that implausible. Don't you?"

"I know . . . it sounds bizarre. But at this point, I'm open to just about anything. The apparition, ghost, double-ganger, or whatever you want to call it . . . it seems to be acclimated to the conditions in there and it's indifferent to the idea of having a body."

"Indifferent?" said von Ang, unclipping the microlite. "That doesn't sound like your father. Is it possible, as we discussed, that what you saw was projected by an intelligent program?"

"I don't know; I don't know. There's something familiar. I feel connected to the essence of him . . . but something's not right. I can't explain. It's a feeling. It's like it's him and it's not him. And the things it says . . . it could definitely be a program. How long will it take to be ready for more tests?"

"At least two days."

"Good. I'll put together a Turing test to determine if the intelligence is artificial or human. Hopefully I have a definitive answer next time."

"The abstract answers you are getting may indicate the source isn't human, however you must beware of the confederate effect—mistaking a human for a machine. It's been known to happen when the human is highly intelligent. The Turing test isn't a very accurate predictor when it comes to highly intelligent behaviours, such as the ability to solve difficult problems using original insights. An advanced AI system is capable of that too."

"What would you suggest?"

"Understanding words is not enough; you have to understand the topic as well. You should drill down into the knowledge base. Ask it to validate what it tells you."

Evening came and Quan was back inside the penthouse. He slid into his workstation and punched up the kaleidoscope of information he had put on his website. It still looked like a hodgepodge of visuals—animations, calculations, verses, vidi clips, tomes, and eigenvectors. In light of his latest experience, it seemed shallow. There was a deeper truth about the other world that he was now aware of and there was something buried in the experience—something that he couldn't get a handle on logically. He had a feeling, a visceral connection with that other place that he couldn't explain.

An artist would know how to express it. An artist's mind could extract the subtlety and make it real so that others could see it.

Unfortunately, his was the mind of an engineer, more skilled at creating neat compartments and organizing facts in black and white. The gray areas were elusive. Nevertheless, he was determined to make an effort.

He created a Sensurround simulation of what he'd seen. Not everyone had a Sosai workstation but no matter; it would work for those who did. Maybe by immersing the viewer, an underlying truth would come to the fore and hopefully someone would be able to put words to it.

Sealy was at the doorway. "You've been in here a long time. Why don't you come out and join us?"

"I just created this," he said, showing her the simulation.

"What is it?" asked Sealy, hesitating to pass judgment.

"What does it look like?"

"It's a room. Everything in the room zips up. Everything is sort of vacuumed up into a single point. Then it unzips. That's what I see, but I don't know what that means. What are you trying to convey?"

"There's something I learned about the other place. Matter comes from nothing and returns to nothing. But there's something else . . . something behind it. I can feel it. I just can't put my finger on it. I thought if I could simulate . . . I'm just trying to understand it."

Ning appeared at the study door. "Do you need my assistance?"

"Assistance?" asked Quan. "With what?"

"The duality? Disparate harmony?"

Quan was stunned. These were the same words the apparition spoke.

"What do you know about those things?" he asked.

Ning stepped through the doorway, hands at her sides. Her mouth began to move so fast it became a blur, words

188

bursting forth, overlapping as they reeled out. Quan could only catch a few key words as they flew by. "Matter . . . boundary . . . quark . . . dark flow . . . Higgs . . . reciprocal . . . duality . . . expression . . . summation . . . lepton . . . simultaneous . . . energy . . . resonant variation . . ."

"Wait, wait, wait!" he interrupted. "Where are you getting all this from?"

"I am the housekeeper."

"You were told about these things?"

"I have access to everything in this house."

"What does it all mean?"

Ning's brows knit. Her lips became taut as she applied serious effort to the question. Sifting through stored conversations and references made by her brilliant benefactor, she struggled. Reaching into countless archives, trying to summarize all that she had heard, trying to deduce a succinct purpose; at last, she opened her eyes and said, "It is extempore. A meaning cannot be stated."

Quan realized that in those few seconds Ning had the ability to access volumes of information both inside the penthouse and outside, but she lacked the high-level processing necesssary to understand what it meant. Her ability to deduce was limited to her primary directives. She was, after all, only the housekeeper.

It was conceivable that no one possessed the mental capacity to clearly state the meaning he sought—perhaps not even his father. Accepting this limitation, Quan narrowed his question. "One of the things you said was 'resonant variation'. That was the first time I heard that phrase. Explain resonant variation."

"Resonant variation is a property of the quantum flux."

"Where did you learn that?"

"From your father," said Ning. "Is it not related?"

"I know father used some sort of natural randomizer to alter the expressions of what became my gene code. I suppose he may have used the naturally occurring variation of quantum flux to randomize the gene expressions."

"Yes. It is how you were conceived," said Ning.

There was a long pause while Quan processed the meaning of it. He felt truth sink in, all the way to his core. The thing he was trying to express, the truth he sought—it was part of him. It was inside him—inside every cell of his body. To vary his genetic code, his father used a pattern found in nature's random exchange of particles.

"The gateway is part of me—a natural part of my instruction set."

Sealy's face went pale. "Are you saying that you and this Braneworld place are related somehow?"

"My genome has a built-in relationship to the exchange of particles. It's explains the feeling I have . . . passing from here to there. It's beginning to make sense," said Quan.

"I'm not understanding," said Sealy. "What are you two talking about?"

"My father's modified genome created me and in the process he created a nexus between me and the Braneworld. And he led me to the machine. He knew I would follow the trail he left."

"How did he know what would happen?" said Sealy.

"I'm not sure he did. It may have been accidental or deliberate. But I think he knew there was a potential and he wanted me to go there—to see for myself. It's why transferring into that other dimension feels so natural to me."

"Maybe it's not what you think. You told me that Wei person was also fine after he went there," said Sealy.

"Maybe he has a similar feeling. I don't know. All I know is that I feel a strong affinity with that other set of dimensions."

23.

Quan was alone in the study, thinking about how eerie it was to hear the words coming from Ning—the same words spoken to him in the Braneworld. The fact that Ning overheard his father use those expressions conferred legitimacy on the specter. It had to be his father. It followed then that his father must have been transformed somehow into an entity capable of inhabiting that other place.

Quan knew from the time he was a teen that he was a genetically modified organism, similar to others who were modified for health reasons. Now he knew something more. His genome was modified by the random rhythms of quantum flux. What did that make him? Was he a new species? Were there others like him? And what had his father become?

His wrist disk bipped. The ID showed McGowen, calling on an encrypted channel.

Quan tapped and said, "Yes. I'm here. What is it?"

"Two things," said McGowen, "First of all, there's something that you needn't worry about, because I took care of it. Those government shoogles came back and started rummaging through your father's laboratory and when they didn't find what they were looking for, they threatened me. Can you believe it? I told the little buggers they could kiss my ruddy red arse."

"Threatened you? How?"

"Deportation."

"A deportation action wouldn't hold up. You've got Permanent Alien Employment status and the corporation can easily claim you are indispensable. Don't worry. That will blow over."

"I figured as much."

"So, what's the second thing?"

"Right to the point. I like that. Well, sir, you've done five transfers now, and you said you saw something that looked like your father. What I'd like to know is . . . is it really him?"

Quan got up from his workstation and walked across the room. He'd known McGowen a long time and trusted him. "I didn't think so at first . . . but now I do."

"You said his body wasn't real. Then what was it?"

"It's something else—something we don't know about. It's not a body in the same way we think of a body. I think it's some other manifestation of him. Then again, nothing in there looks real."

"I'll tell you one thing," said McGowen, slurring his speech a little, revealing that he had had a few drinks, "it would be a blessing if you were able to see him again, but I'd be careful if I were you."

"Why do you say that?"

"I don't know about that other place. Where I come from there are stories about the world of the dead. They say it's an abomination to go there. Maybe the stories are true—maybe not—probably just superstition, but I'd be careful just the same."

"If that's the place we go when we die, wouldn't there be lots of other people there?"

Quan could hear McGowen take another sip of whatever he was drinking.

"Hey, I'm no *ben dan*, ya know," said McGowen with a laugh. "All I'm saying is that there may be more to this. I mean, what if there's something in there masquerading as your father . . . a demon, say. They can be pretty clever, you know."

Quan wasn't sure if McGowen was joking or if he actually believed in such things. Quan had read fables about the world of the dead and regarded them as fantasies. Trying to be diplomatic, he said, "I don't know very much about that other place, but I'm fairly sure what I saw wasn't a demon. I think I'd know the difference. It seemed benevolent, and I think the Braneworld is as safe as any other place in nature; which is probably not saying much."

"Mighten it be useful to have another perspective on this? Maybe it's time for someone else to have a look. I must admit, I'm curious. I'd be willing to go, if you like."

There was a tinge of heartbreak hiding underneath McGowen's husky voice. Quan sat quietly for a moment, reflecting on their conversation. He knew McGowen's desire to protect was genuine; he was loyal through and through. At the same time, Quan suspected the suggestion wasn't completely altruistic. McGowen was warning of the dangers in that other world but, at the same time, he was willing to go there. Then the idea became clear.

It's not about the research. It's about his wife.

"I'll be going there again and I agree with you, having another perspective would be a good thing." Quan paused, making a decision. "I think you should have the experience. I'd like to have your impressions, but not just yet. We have to do a few more tests."

Not at all surprised that the young Jintao deflected his offer, McGowen said, "I'd like to know what's there is all."

193

"Many unknowns," said Quan. "Speaking of which . . . we should check on Wei again . . . see how he is. Look into that, will you?"

"Aye, I'm on top of it. I'll check and let you know how he's doing. Okay, then, I'll let you go."

"Keep me posted," said Quan, just before the com line went dead.

Quan wandered into the great room and to his surprise, instead of a tranquil veranda on the California coast, he walked into a tropical rainforest. In a tree at the far side, a hornbill flapped its wings and cawed. Jungle noises came from all around and the air smelled of burning wood. A mud-and-rock oven stood where the modern fireplace had been and a trail of light gray smoke rose from its short chimney into the canopy overhead. Springing up from a bamboo bench, Lotus greeted him with a guilty look on her face. "Sorry. I found the controls and couldn't resist. I'll switch it back."

"I don't care," he said, rubbing his head. "Leave it on."

"Orbital," said Lotus. Then, seeing Quan's sour disposition, she asked, "Is something wrong?"

"Everything is fine. I have work to do," said Quan, making his way back to the study.

Sealy passed him in the hallway and could see something was bothering him. Knowing it was better to leave him alone, she continued on to join her sister. Entering the great room, her eyes opened wide. Calumba vines hung from the limbs of a banyan tree and shafts of daylight came through gaps in the leaves, projecting random dots on the red earth floor. An elephant trumpeted in the distance.

"Reminds me of the *Jumanji* game we used to play," said Lotus. "Remember?"

"I remember," said Sealy. "But this is Armandorama and I'm not in the mood." Sealy stood with her arms crossed, hands rubbing her upper arms. "Do you have plans for tonight?"

"I called Gaston but he didn't answer," said Lotus.

"Maybe he was busy. Try him again," said Sealy. "Quan and I need some alone time."

"Hey, no prob." Lotus sat down on the sofa and opened a com channel.

As Sealy left the room, she saw the California sim return and overheard Lotus talking to von Ang.

Sealy followed Quan to the stucy and found him sitting in his sling chair, deep in thought.

"You haven't told me happened in the lab."

It wasn't easy for him to talk. The latest encounter with his father's ghost was another mind-bender. He leaned forward with his arms resting on his knees, fingertips pressed together.

"Come sit," he said.

Sealy settled herself in the chair across from him.

"McGowen is willing to take my place and do the experiments."

"That's great news."

"Sort of. He can go in to do the experiments, but I still need to understand what has become of my father. If what I saw is really him, then he's in some sort of altered state. The voice isn't his and it isn't the way he would normally speak but I know it's him. I have a feeling he'll only appear for me. Someone else may drive him away."

"You must be happy that you found him. What's the plan? Do you think you can bring him back?"

"I'm just not sure what to do next. Maybe I've done as much as I can."

Perking up, Sealy asked, "I'm listening. What does that mean for you and me? Can we go back to England?"

Quan sat up straight, holding up his hands. "I'm afraid it's not over yet."

"I'm ready to go," said Sealy. "It's been more than a little strange being here in your father's house with my sister. You're off doing these experiments. I may as well be somewhere else."

"It must feel like that for you. I'm sorry. I wish it were different. This hasn't turned out to be anything like what I expected. What I've gotten into here is bigger than both of us. Be patient while I sort this out. I don't think we'll be here much longer."

24.

Von Ang's apartment was in the Tsim Sha Tsui district.. When
he first saw the place, he ignored the post-apocalyptic style that
was trending at the time—the faux broken beams, ragged
curtains, and decaying plaster, buying it instead for its view of
Victoria Harbour and its embedded sound system. He had the
interior gutted, the floors refinished, and the walls sheathed in a
dark blue padded velvet. The wall facing Victoria Harbour was
replaced with a seamless sheet of structural glass replaced coated
with a nanite layer that responded to voice command, providing
various levels of opacity.

His furnishings were minimal: a modern Scandinavian
couch, three colorful graphics of quantum collisions from the old
Hadron collider, two matching easy chairs and an espresso
machine.

It was Sunday morning and von Ang was lounging in bed,
listening to a vintage Brubeck arrangement: delicate shuffling of
a snare drum and cymbal, a low rolling piano rhythm played

against the meanderings of a saxophone. The melody floated through the air like a butterfly, flapping its wings, pausing to show its colors, then taking off again.

Lotus stood naked in the kitchen galley, staring at two cups, waiting for the Italian roast to finish brewing. Totally relaxed without clothes, her perfectly proportioned body left nothing to apologize for. Her tanned skin was the color of toasted almonds, except for three pale triangles where the Caribbean sun was forbidden to touch. Glancing at von Ang, she smiled. This kind of freedom wasn't normal in his life and she was being intentionally disruptive. Extending her arms above her head, she stretched, arching her back slightly, letting him enjoy the view while she gathered her hair into a ponytail and secured it with a band.

Gaston von Ang was a straight arrow—without the conceits and deceits Lotus put up with from boys her own age. He was established, sophisticated, brilliant, and only a few years her senior. They shared music in common and he could make her laugh. He was the kind of guy she could fall hard for, but she was playing it cool, catching him by letting him pursue her.

Von Ang caught himself staring too long. His eyes averted to the window and he refocused his thoughts on the Jintao project. His laudable contribution had been acknowledged. The compensation was more than adequate, he was going to be author of the discovery papers, and he had grown to like Quan, a smart and brave young man with the same noble values as his father. Where he found most Chinese industrialists to be rigid, consumed by the pursuit of profit, Quan and his father had proved they were equally concerned with respect and building long term relationships.

Lotus walked back to bed with two steaming cups. "You know, I'm becoming addicted to this Italian roast," she said, setting a cup on each night table.

198

Walking around to the other side of the bed, she sipped from her cup, set it down, then slipped under the covers next to him. "Tell me about the project you're working on with Quan."

"I'm sorry. I can't. I'm under contract," said von Ang, taking a careful sip from the steaming cup.

"Oh, come on. I'm part of Quan's family."

"It would bore you."

"If I were your banlu, you'd tell me, wouldn't you?"

"If that was a proposal, it needs work," said von Ang with a snicker.

Lotus wished she could have pulled her words back as they left her mouth. So clumsy, she thought. She placed a hand on von Ang's chest and slid her leg on top of his. "I can find out from my sister."

Feeling her skin next to his, he said, "You always feel a few degrees warmer than me."

Head against the pillow, Lotus lifted an eyebrow. "I have a high metabolism."

"I suppose you'll be going back to university soon. What's your major?" he asked.

"Physics."

"That's a surprise. You should have told me. Which university?"

"Peking."

"Very competitive. Must have been difficult to get in."

"Not really. My GPA was five point oh."

Von Ang's eyes opened wide. He coughed and almost blew coffee out of his mouth.

"A five point? In physics? Wow. Higher that mine was as an undergrad."

"To the world!" said Lotus, propping herself up on two elbows. "It's because of the way I look, isn't it? Boy, isn't that typical. Did you think the cover was all there was of this book?"

"No, of course not," said von Ang, squirming.

Von Ang had know other Chinese women, but most were of ordinary intellect. Lotus, by contrast, outclassed of all of them. She was stunning and razor sharp. "I'm so sorry. Please forgive me."

Flipping the covers back, Lotus sat up, took the cup from his hand, and set it on the nightstand next to hers. She swung herself over on top of him and extended her arms on either side of him. Smiling, she said, "I forgive you. Now, show me how sorry you are."

25.

Quan returned to his cyber cocoon, a space where he could be alone with his haunted thoughts. His website was where he stored his impressions of the Braneworld. He sat back, looking at the collage, trying to wrap his mind around it—the reciprocal theory, the fables, the animations and equations, a world springing from nothing. There were many ways to look at the phenomenon. Maybe the human brain in its current state of evolution just wasn't capable of grasping something so complex. What he had been exposed to seemed weird. Weird in the same way the idea of chemicals spontaneously jumping together and becoming life was weird.

Infinite consciousness and infinite manifestation. That's what the entity said to him.

It sounded like magical thinking—like what people referred to as God—a word that Quan wasn't comfortable with. The idea of a celestial being breathing life into matter and single-handedly creating everything in the universe was something he always found too conveniently simple. For him, it was like throwing your hands in the air and saying, "I give up." Instead, Quan pinned his faith to the underlying physics of matter, a complex but predictable system of cause and effect. The only transcendence he believed in was the precision of mathematics. Nonetheless, what he had seen in the last few weeks called his beliefs into question. He was at the doorway to a completely new science and struggling to understand it.

At the end of the twentieth century, Higgs defined what some called "the God particle." It explained atomic mass. Now there was proof of other dimensions . . . then an idea struck.

The rhythmic exchange of particles in and out of the Braneworld is in me—baked in. But it must also be baked into everything that exists. All of matter is recycling constantly. By extension, perhaps everyone has an intrinsic connection to the Braneworld.

In his recent sortie, what he had witnessed was a wellspring. It reminded him of what eighteenth-century philosophers called the *élan vital*: a life force pushing its way into the material world. Life and death, a duality, one of many dualities to be understand on more a profound level. Maybe that was what his father was doing.

Maybe I'm not the only one of my kind. Perhaps there are others. Perhaps I can find them.

In all the ages, he thought, there must have been at least a few who experienced the same thing. Maybe even a few who understood the whole of it. There were stories of the unseen lands and accounts of others who might have traveled in and out. He read about shamans who could vanish at will. There was the rabbi named Jesus who scribes of the first century wrote about. They said he walked on water and through walls and healed the sick and transcended death. To transcend the bonds of a finite world, he must have understood the meaning of infinite consciousness and infinite manifestation.

Focusing on what was inside him, Quan began feeling that part of him that was in the other realm. He felt the boundary separating him from the two worlds. At a level deeper still, he could feel the random exchange of particles, the constant flux, pushing and pulling every atom. A potential was welling up inside . . . a feeling so strong it scared him. Pushing fear aside, he allowed the feeling to become more intense.

Without knowing why, he rose from his chair and walked to the wall of the study, as if being drawn to it. Reaching out his hand, he felt the wall. It was made of steel and xynite, solid and impenetrable. Pressing against the surface, he could feel the true nature of it—a wall of vibrating particles—still firm, but an illusion—not really solid, mostly empty space. He stood back, reflecting on what he was feeling, concentrating on his connection to the reciprocal flux. Particles began to dance in the space in front of him. He could feel the quantum exchange rushing back and forth, in and out of the space he occupied. Particles were filling the space—the Braneworld was becoming visible.

Matter is an illusion . . . not solid . . . just an illusion.

His body bristles with energy. A surge is building . . . he can feel it . . . the same feeling he has when the machine powers up. Without expectations, he leaves himself open to any outcome.

Surrender to it. Go where it leads. No fear.

He lets the impulse drive him forward, propelling him into the space inside the atoms—the essence of matter.

There I go . . . I can feel it . . . the cycling . . . the path between this world and the other. There it is . . . particles moving in and out . . . pushing . . . pulling . . .

His arm rises as if it has a mind of its own. This time the resistance is gone. His arm slides through the wall, particles moving past other particles, space moving through space, slipping past boundaries, through the emptiness within matter. Sliding through a wall of shimmering specks, he takes three steps forward. He is standing in the hallway. The air is thick with multicolored particles. Looking around, he can see indications of walls and doorways. A mixture of excitement and fear comes over him. He steps back one pace, then another, and another.

How is this possible . . . without the reactor . . . without the stabilizer . . . without the tuned energies? How can it be?

As doubt and fear took hold, the Braneworld faded.

His thirst for answers had taken him across a threshold, into a new reality. Ever since his first transference, he had felt subtle changes inside him. Like training wheels on a child's bicycle, the machine had shown him the way and now the changes were magnified tenfold. He was able to transport himself by will alone. Like waking from a dream, his view of the world was made crystal clear.

Hard edges and static surfaces came into view, yet he could still feel his connection to the phase shift—it had become an accessible part of him, a memory indelibly imprinted in his mind.

Quan managed to get back to his workstation and slide into the sling chair. He was enthralled. What he had just done was extreme.

So much more than flesh and bones—neural networks are learning—epigenomes are recording. Connections are forming that weren't there before. I'm evolving—changing with each exposure to the flux.

~~~

Morning came and Sealy padded into the great room in her robe and slippers looking for Quan. He was resting on his side, sprawled out on the sectional, quietly watching the simulated waves lapping against the cove. She sat across from him, where prismatic reflections from the fireplace danced on the wall.

"How was your night?" she asked.

He didn't respond, gazing at the waves, looking for a repeat pattern in the animation. He was continuing to feel the effects of what he had done. With all he knew of physics, it was impossible. Yet, somehow nature allowed it. He wondered if Wei was capable of the same thing.

Perhaps it has a purpose. Perhaps all of us will be able to
. . .

He looked across to where Sealy sat and felt an urge to share his revelation, but he knew how grounded she was in her notion of reality. There was no way that he could demonstrate what he was capable of without frightening her.

"Lotus went out to see Gaston last night," she said. "She must have stayed with him. She's not back yet. Have you had breakfast?"

No reply.

"Quan, I'm talking to you."

He sat up and words came forth with such clarity, they surprised him. He told her it was only a matter of time before the project on Kau Yi Chau Island would be discovered and the government would try to requisition the project.

"Why would they do that?" she asked.

He continued explaining that was inevitable and the only way to safe guard the project was to relocate it to a secure place, a place where the research could continue without interference.

"Nowhere in China is safe," he said. "We'll have to move the equipment."

"Would we go back to England?"

"England would be just as insidious."

Pointing to the sim she said, "How about what's right in front of us . . . California."

Waves continued to surge against the SensoReal cove. Quan watched for a moment, then said, "There are no coincidences. It's perfect, isn't it?"

"We've never been there before," said Sealy, "and we don't know anyone there. It sounds exciting."

"We need to make plans as soon as possible."

"What about your father?" she asked.

"What I've seen of him is only a vestige of what he once was. I think Father would want this. He'd want me to protect the discovery. That's what's important now."

Sitting up abruptly, Quan commanded the house to project a four-by-three-meter view field. He gave it search parameters: California, coastal land for sale or lease. The system instantly displayed a list of twenty-two parcels.

"What's the climate like there?" asked Sealy.

Quan opened a sidebar and said, "Dry and warm."

"And what's that?" Sealy pointed at a pair of huge domes sitting alongside the ocean.

"It's called San Onofre. It's an abandoned nuclear site. Too exposed . . . and too close to that military base," he said, pointing to Camp Pendleton. "We need something more remote." His hand began directing the view field north, up the coast, past Los Angeles, past Santa Barbara.

Ning entered with tea, setting cups on the table. After pouring, she looked up and said, "California: birthplace of the internet, the GUI, and the neural CPU."

"Are you online?" asked Sealy.

"Yes," said Ning. "There are over sixty million facts concerning California. Shall I list them?"

"Thank you, no," said Sealy. "That'll be all."

Quan was on autopilot. He launched a second view field and initiated another search, looking into the policies of the USDOE, the NRC, and the California Nuclear Commission. There were clear guidelines for what he intended to build. Independent research laboratories were allowed to have small, sealed reactors, SSTAR units they were called, and they could be installed with very little oversight. He quickly pulled up construction requirements: a concrete vault, air filtration, cooling systems, alarm systems, backup systems. Easier than he expected.

206

Sealy was transfixed by the speed and ease with which he moved through the documents.

Minimizing the NRC specs, he opened a window into the Jintao Corporation database. Hurtling down lists of documents, he came to files concerning the future Kau Yi Chau power station. Opening the original government contract, he highlighted a section of the covenants.

"Under the maintenance terms, if any component was found to be defective, it is the responsibility of Jintao Corporation to remove and replace it."

He closed the file, turned to her, and said, "If the reactor is deemed defective, it can be sold as scrap."

"I'm not sure I follow," said Sealy.

"There's a lesson in the Tao: The more one acts in harmony with the universe, the more one will achieve, and with less effort. The reactor has been modified. We can't leave it and it will draw attention if we try to export it. I found a way to dispose of it legally."

He returned to the review of coastal properties, zipping through satellite images, geo-seismic data, and plat maps.

"These properties are for sale. Are you thinking of buying? How will you pay for it?"

"I'll access the family trust," said Quan. Bringing up one brochure after another, at last he said, "This is the one."

She read the description and said, "It's over thirty hectares. Do you need that much land?"

"In a couple of years, the work we're doing will grow into something much bigger. Besides, it's a good value and it's remote."

"Something bigger?" she echoed. "What do you have in mind?"

"What we've stumbled onto has huge potential. It could change everything."

"What do you mean by 'a couple of years'? How long would we be there?"

"Long enough to make sure the facility is running well. It shouldn't be too long."

Quan had brought up a list of attorneys prequalified by Jintao Corporation. He highlighted a San Francisco firm: Dempsey, Cheng & Pierce LLP, lawyers the corporation used for international mergers and acquisitions in the United States. Without delay he checked the time and directed a call to one of the senior partners and left a message. He wanted a charter drafted for incorporation of a new research facility: the Brane Research Center for Quantum Physics. Under the newly formed corporation, the attorneys were authorized to purchase the land for the asking price with no contingencies.

Sealy didn't know what to say. Life was taking unexpected turns and things were moving fast. What she envisioned, a trip for lovers to a scenic destination, was turning into a massively complex project.

"This isn't going to be a vacation. Seems like you're going to be just as busy as you are here, if not more so. Maybe I should just stay here. What do you think?"

"I don't want us to be separated, but at first it will probably make sense—setting everything up. I would hope not more than a month."

Just then, Lotus burst into the room like a bolt of energy. "Hey guys. You're up early."

Quan immediately brought the LÓNG website to the fore, obscuring three sensitive documents.

Looking around at the floating documents, Lotus said, "Hey, what's all this?"

Sealy pushed herself up from the cushions, turned ninety degrees, and pulled her legs underneath her. "We're were just looking at a possible trip," she said, gesturing to the simulated coastline. An orange glow was forming on the cliffs.

"What's up? A vacation?"

"California looks like a place we'd like," said Sealy.

Lotus spotted the LÓNG website and said, "Isn't that orbital! That's the site everybody's chirping about."

"Really? What is it?" asked Sealy.

"All kinds of rumors. Some people think it's genius. Others think it's just nonsense. I think it's the beginning of an ad campaign. You know—like a puzzle. They give you clues and when you've got all the pieces, it turns out to be an ad for vodka or something. Anyway, it'll really make you think . . . lots of interesting stuff in there." She turned around, fluffed her hair, and headed for the guest wing. "I'm for a shower. Then, I want to hear all about your trip."

26.

Three days later, in the cold subterranean lab, Quan stood behind a metal folding chair with his hands resting on its curved backrest. Von Ang in his white lab coat and McGowen in his usual turtleneck, listened as Quan put forth his relocation plan. It would be difficult, but it was necessary.

Quan's resolve hardened as he spoke. "The work we're doing is important and ultimately we'll want to share it with the rest of the world; however, we need to keep it a secret until we're ready to publish. We've been sneaking and hiding and that can't go on. The best way forward is to move the project to a place where we can work without government interference. I've secured a place. It's close to several major research centers, yet remote enough so that no one will bother us. It's several thousand kilometers from here and it lacks infrastructure. We'll have to build what we need. I know I'm asking a lot of you—relocating for the sake of this project—but I'll make sure you have your current salary plus all expenses. I need you both. What do you say?"

Von Ang was first to speak. "I can tell you right now I am committed to continuing the research. Here or there is the same to me. I am away from home either way."

"How long would I be gone?" asked McGowen.

"It could be a few months or a few years. Your guess is as good as mine. I understand this is a difficult decision. It goes without saying that, if you do go, you'd be free to return at any time, but I'd like at least a six-month commitment."

"I get that we'll be somewhere other than China," said McGowen. "Exactly where would we be?"

"The reasons for the move are security and freedom to operate. The United States can give us both."

"Can you be more specific?" asked von Ang.

"California," replied Quan.

"As long as you can square things with corporate," said McGowen, "I'm in."

"I'll take care of that," said Quan. "Of course, we'll all need visas, but that shouldn't be a problem. Incidentally, did you talk to Wei?"

"Yep," said McGowen. "He feels fine—no unusual side effects. We talked for half an hour. Says he's available anytime we need him."

"What about Dr. Lee?" asked von Ang. "Will she go along with us?"

"No. She won't be coming."

Dr. Lee's absence was conspicuous. "Lee was our bioscience expert," said McGowen. "How are you going to replace her?"

"We'll get whatever and whomever we need," said Quan.

Quan figured that someone must have tipped off the Central Science Committee and he suspected Diayu Lee. She was a government pensioner and was opposed to human trials from the start. Her decision to stay behind reinforced his suspicion.

"Without her, how will we obtain the molecular scans we need?" asked von Ang.

"We'll buy a scanner," Quan said bluntly. "I'd like you to look into that."

"It's going to be extremely expensive," said von Ang.

"And we'll buy a new reactor, a SSTAR unit. We'll dispose of this one."

"It'll mean redesign of the system and it'll take time to integrate the sub-systems."

"I'm confident you'll take care of that. And I need you to oversee the disassembly here."

McGowen observed Quan with interest. Quan's self-confidence was in full bloom, but there was something new. There was an aggressive energy and a decisiveness that hadn't been there before.

~~~

The following day, at a bench in the underground lab, Von Ang was reviewing the transfer data and post-transfer interviews. There were two who had gone across, Quan and Wei, and by all accounts they hadn't suffered any physical setbacks. Of special interest to him was their account of having normal thought processes in the other dimension. Brain electrochemistry seemed to be behaving normally. Their alpha waves were slightly higher than normal—not a serious concern, but something to watch over time.

Von Ang was watching the vidi of Quan's second interview when McGowen stepped out of the darkness carrying a toolbox.

"So, how's our resident agnostic today?" McGowen snarked.

Von Ang paused the view field and looked up. "Agnostic? Yes, I suppose so. And you believe the Braneworld is what? A spirit world?"

212

"We're just a bunch of particles in there, but evidently we're still who we are. Doesn't that tell you something? Isn't that proof we're more than just physical?"

"The brain is an organic computer. Apparently, it can operate in those conditions. I may not understand how, but that doesn't prove we're anything more than physical."

"Come now, doc. Don't dodge the obvious. Trust your instincts. Organs and limbs don't make a person. What do you think holds it all together."

"There are more plausible explanations. Evolution may have been at work in all dimensions at the same time. The Braneworld is just be another aspect of the physical world."

McGowen put a large hand on von Ang's shoulder and said, "Ahhh, you need to open up a bit." He squeezed von Ang's shoulder a bit harder. "Look beyond this piece of meat you call home."

"Must I remind you? I'm a scientist. I don't jump to conclusions."

"I'll bet if you took a trip to the other side it would turn your head around," said McGowen, setting down his toolbox. "Anyhow, I'm here to take this baby apart."

"Not just yet," said von Ang, standing up. He took off his lab coat and trousers, revealing a black skinsuit underneath.

Surprised, McGowen lit up. "As I live and breathe. You're going to do it, aren't ya. Well, I'll be. Good for you. Like I said, it might turn your head around."

Von Ang had weighed the pros and cons of subjecting himself to the machine. He could stay safely in the laboratory, removed from the direct experience, using surrogates, in the way an earthbound scientist might use robots to carry out experiments on a distant planet. Or he could see it directly with his own eyes. While data acquired from his sophisticated instruments was certainly more valuable than the subjective input from eyes and ears, he had an overriding desire to be part of this newly formed club of adventurers. Whether he was aware of it or not, he found himself compelled beyond reason to be one of the boys.

Fastening an instrument onto his belt, he said, "This is the last chance I'll have before we disassemble the machine. If you will assist me, I only need five minutes."

"Be glad to, on one condition," said McGowen stepping up to the control panel.

"What condition?"

"You can do the same for me," said McGowen.

"Alright. Let's get on with it."

Von Ang showed McGowen what to do and, moments later, he was gone.

Stepping away from the mesh, he looks around at the turbulent mix of suspended particles. It's as others described—a seething sandstorm. He wastes no time. Unclipping the first instrument, he extends his arm and pulls the trigger. A radar pulse is sent into the mist. Nothing returns. He aims at the floor and pulses again . . . still no echo. He turns the gain to maximum and shortens the wavelength . . . still nothing . . . nothing that will reflect the signal. He reattaches the instrument and unclips another, a pulse generator. Going down on one knee, he pauses for a moment, listening to faint rumbles and intermittent hisses.

Refocusing on the task at hand, he sets the device on end and pivots its antenna into an upright position. His hand is cloaked in a corona of white porcupine quills. He rotates his wrist, studying the effect for a moment, then stands up. Unclipping a small handheld device, he moves its slide selector into the first position, waiting for a signal to be received from the transmitter. Nothing. He moves the selector to the next position, tries again, then another and another. There it is, the signal is received, only a millisecond pulse of gamma emission, but enough. He retrieves the pulse generator, reclips the instruments, and remounts the mesh.

214

Lying there, waiting for the system to time out, he studies the air above him. Fascinating shapes are forming, dissolving, and re-forming again. They don't seem to be random. Lines form into a large triangle, then fade away. Three small glowing dots persist where the apexes were persist. Fragments of a grid appear, rippling like graph paper on the surface of a wave. He tries to discern what's on the grid but it vanishes before he can read it.

As he dismounted from the mesh, von Ang was exuberant. "Excellent. We have short-range gamma transmission!" He unclipped the instruments and placed them in a metal case.

"You need to be checked," said McGowen.

Von Ang lay down at the medi-bot system and the exam was completed within minutes. They returned to the reactor and McGowen said, "Okay. Now it's my turn."

"You need to have scan data."

"Way ahead of you, squire." McGowen pulled a tiny black stick from his pocket and handed it over. "Dr. Lee did mine when she did Quan."

"You'll need a skinsuit."

"Nope," said McGowen removing his trousers. "I wasn't scanned with a skinsuit—just my birthday suit."

The big Scot tossed his clothes onto a chair and climbed onto the mesh.

Von Ang laughed, seeing McGowen lying there naked.

The frame creaked under McGowen's weight as he turned to look at von Ang. "Piss off. Now be a good boy and give me five minutes."

Von Ang stepped up to the control panel and said, "All right. Five minutes. Stay put." He loaded McGowen's scan data and the countdown began.

In the wink of an eye, McGowen was transported. Sparkling waves of dust move past him. Here and there the drifts thin out and he can see the dark figure of von Ang. Subtle outlines of equipment flicker in the distance. Sitting up, McGowen sees shimmering clouds moving across the landscape. Looking down he sees his legs covered in white bristles. His hand brushes across, trying to feel his legs, but there is no feeling. A gust of particles appears and floats right through him.

This is a totally foreign landscape—like being in a vat of boiling sand.

There's something far away moving toward him. Strange, the way it moves, like something passing through space and time, lurching from place to place. It's headed straight toward him.

Apprehensive, McGowen gets off of the mesh and crouches down. He peers into the blizzard. Whatever it is, it's close now, very close. His eyes search the mist but he can't make it out what it is. It circles around him and he prepares to defend himself. Suddenly there's an unexpected warmth surrounding him. It's startling. He thrusts his arm in the direction of the warmth. Nothing there, only drifting dust. Then there's a smell. He inhales. It's a smell he recognizes, bringing back distant memories. He inhales again. *Druamor* is what it is, that rare and unmistakable scent. It's what she wore. A subconscious desire fills him. Peering into the mist. Something touches him again. He flinches. On his cheek, the warmth persists. A kiss.

Now there is warmth against his chest, around his shoulders. He can feel her now. She's embracing him.

"Maggie . . . Maggie is it you? Can you hear me?"

There's no answer, only the warmth.

"Oh, I've missed you darling," he says softly.

He sits down on the edge of the mesh, bowing his head with the warmth surrounding him, comforting him.

A voice comes in his head. [We are one.]

His damp eyes close.

"Aye, my bonnie lass. That we are . . . and shall ever be."

After a few minutes, McGowen was back, lying on the mesh, not moving.

216

"Are you okay?" asked von Ang.

McGowen lay there, staring blankly at the ceiling, a broad smile on his face. He looked up at von Ang.

"I didn't want to leave," he said. "Hadn't expected to feel that. My God. What a life changing experience. Can't you just . . . I want to go back."

"So do I, but we'll have to wait. Quan wants the equipment out of here tonight."

The framework creaked as McGowen rolled to his feet, dutifully walking toward the medi-bot station.

Von Ang crossed the room with him. "Tell me your impressions."

"You saw it. Just stour everywhere." He lay still on the gurney while stainless steel arms swept over him. "Although I did feel something unusual. Felt like something I lost a long time ago."

"What was that? What did you feel?"

"Nah. That's mine," said McGowen, reluctant to talk about his lost love, "but there's definitely something there."

After the medi-bot was done, McGowen put his clothes on.

"It's a strange place, to be sure," said the big Scot, pulling on his turtleneck sweater. "Quite good, though—righteously good." He let go a little laugh. "Strange when you think about it. Our minds aren't affected. What do you make of that?"

"We have imaging systems that can see thoughts as they form inside the cortex. It's not a mystery. It's purely physical. Obviously, the same connections are still working in the Braneworld."

McGowen beamed a smile. "I'd go again." Reaching his arm and pointing at von Ang, he said, "I tell you one thing. We're more than just flesh and blood. The fact that we can come and go to that other place proves it."

"I disagree."

"Hey. What if that place is the afterlife? Wouldn't that be something?"

"Seriously? Come on. Let's go to work."

Von Ang began disassembling the machine. He removed the control interface and pressed it into a polyfoam-lined case. A few meters away, McGowen began unbolting the wave guides, dropping fasteners on the floor as he went. A small assembly bot followed, dutifully picking up each bolt and putting it into a bag.

"I don't get it," said the big Scot. "How can you say we're only flesh and blood?"

"I'm a scientist. I divide things into two categories. That which I know to be consistently verifiable and that which I am not sure of. Things I am not sure of are postulates. I quarantine those until they prove their relevance. Things I hold to be fact are only fact until I find out otherwise. Today there is only one thing that I am sure of. Gamma rays transmit through both the lower and the higher dimensions."

McGowen walked over to the medi-bot, punching in the instruction for it to fold itself into a mobile configuration. "Okay. You're still on the fence. I respect that. But tell me this: What do you suppose would happen if someone died over there . . . in that other place?"

"I see the Brane as an exchange system. It doesn't care whether something is alive or dead. Mortality is an entirely different subject—one that's out of my field of expertise. That's one for a priest to figure out."

"Come on. You know what I'm talking about. Maybe that's what happened to Master Jintao."

McGowen disconnected the stabilizer and packed it in a white polyfiber case lined with shock-absorbing foam. Bots carried the case outside to the landing pad and loaded it onto a cargo shuttle.

"We have no proof," said von Ang. "No evidence of what happened to him. Hopefully we can agree that neither of us knows what we don't know."

218

McGowen cast a steely eye toward the young scientist, disappointed that von Ang was willing to fold the discussion so easily.

Outside, three hours later, the bots carefully nested the equipment boxes inside the cargo shuttle. After the last crate was secured in place, the bots fastened themselves to the shuttle floor, folded themselves into a compact shape, and powered down. McGowen input the coordinates of a Jintao shipping hub on the Yangtze delta, where a crew was standing by to repack the equipment into a freight container. The contents would be mixed in with industrial parts bound for one of their corporate warehouses in Australia. There the boxes would be repacked for routing through Argentina and finally to California.

Von Ang shut off power to the lab, finding his way up the stairwell by chocklight. There was a slight grin on his face. He was the lead scientist of a project of historic proportions and he was one of an elite few who had gone to the other side. At the same time, he was now an accomplice, helping to sneak a top-secret machine out of China. Never before had he been part of a clandestine mission and he was enjoying the idea. He could add bravery to his list of attributes, and his otherwise predictable life had been given an adventurous highlight.

Out in the open, he found McGowen rolling up the camouflage netting.

"I'll see you when the new site is ready for installation," said von Ang. *"À tout à l'heure."*

McGowen stuffed the canopy into the shuttle and shook von Ang's hand.

"See you on the other side of the pond," said McGowen. "We'll pick up where we left off."

27.

While the equipment was being disassembled and packed up, Quan arrived at Armando Ballister's studio. It was after normal hours. The door was unlocked but the reception area was dark except for a small circle of light shining on the archi-tech's chrome logo.

He called out, "Hello," and waited. No one answered.

Quan ventured into the darkened hallway and overhead lights came on. At the other end of the corridor was the simulation stage where he previously viewed the penthouse sim. Faint flashes of light were coming from a room on the other side and he began to walk toward it. He stopped, seeing someone there, standing in the shadows to his right. "Hello?" he called. The figure remained motionless. Pattern recognition set in—just a swatch of cloth hanging on a light stand. He moved on.

When he reached the doorway, a projection of the coastal property filled the room—a cliff face rising up to a broad plateau—on the far side, a continuous range of coastal mountains. The projection rotated slowly in space and a rocky ravine became visible, meandering down from the foothills, crossing the plateau and ending where a white waterfall tumbled into the blue of the Pacific Ocean.

In front of him, a sling chair abruptly spun around and Armando's ultrawhites flashed. He stood and greeted Quan like a friend he hadn't seen in years. "Ahhh, Mr. Jintao. Come sit. Come sit. See what I have for you."

Armando spoke a few commands and wireframe outlines of buildings suddenly appeared on the plateau. Another command and the wireframes became solid structures. "The compound can be self-sustaining. There is an underground aquifer, and a solar-powered battery farm will provide electricity. I would have liked to use convection turbines along the cliffs, but the Coastal Commission banned them, something to do with the decline of sea hawks."

The scene continued to tilt and rotate, filling the room, giving Quan a good view of the buildings. It was a collection of shapes, each with its own character but visually related—all sleek and modern, in contrast to the soft rolling foothills to the east.

Quan leaned back. "Impressive. You captured exactly what I wanted, as if you read my mind. Well done. How long will it take to build?"

"Here, I'll show you the progression." Two wooden structures appeared a few meters east of the new buildings. "That's the existing barn and farmhouse. It can provide temporary housing and storage while construction is under way. Well water is available and there is a generator. Of course, it lacks the amenities you're used to—more like camping, I suppose. Per your request, the laboratory can be finished first and the rest can follow."

Impatient, Quan broke in. "How long will it take to build the laboratory?"

"Excavation and site grading, foundations and retaining walls . . ."

"How long?" Quan demanded.

"Four months."

"Not good enough," said Quan. "I want you to release the construction files three days from now. I want the laboratory ready in a month."

Armando looked shocked. "You know that's impossible, don't you?"

Quan got up and smiled his inscrutable smile. "You'll find a way. Work nights if you have to. Get it done on time and I'll double your fee."

The words hung in the archi-tech's ears as he watched Quan leave the room. He turned back to his work and, under his breath, said, "You don't ask for much, do you."

~~~

Nine hours later, a hazmat crew set up quarantine on Kau Yi Chau Island. Radiation shields were erected around the entrance to one of the large buildings and removal of the alleged malfunctioning reactor began. In the basement, bots unbolted it from the floor and carefully lifted it onto an industrial bobcart. Floating a meter off the ground, the heavy torus was lifted to the upper landing and piloted through the outer doors, passing with barely a centimeter to spare. Outside, the containment crew wasted no time coating the device with thick, radiation-absorbing gel and a hard poly-metal overcoat. Chained to a hovering transport, the reactor was flown to a staging facility at Dongxing. There, it was crated and loaded onto a commercial transport. It departed Chinese airspace within minutes on its way to a salvage facility in Vietnam.

222

28.

Seven kilometers from the Jintao penthouse, at the outskirts of downtown, stood a drab ten-story building with horizontal ledges protruding from its sides. In stark contrast to the gleaming structures nearby, it was matte and its windows were totally opaque, preventing any glimpse of what was inside. On the roof, amid air-conditioning units, was a small metal hut of tarnished copper—isolating it from the heavy broadband communications traffic of New Hong Kong.

Inside the hut, air drifted down from baffled inlets, descending slowly past two surveillance specialists hunched over their view fields. In front of them, vidi clips of cargo glides leaving Kau Yi Chau Island played alongside GPS data and surveillance stills of Quan and his team. One of the men snapped his fingers and pointed to a bar graph where jagged sound waves were bouncing. He slid the volume higher. The other man nodded.

"How did it go?" asked Sealy.

"Everything is going ahead as planned. The parts are on their way," said Quan.

"Can I tell Lotus what's going on?" asked Sealy. "She's nosy and it's been hard for me to keep it from her."

"We should wait another week," he said.

Images and sound bites were being transmitted to a situation room several floors below. Around a stainless-steel table, in a two-tone gray room, a committee of four listened with strained attention. One of them, a senior government official with stooped posture and the cheeks of a basset hound, spoke gravely, "We're in time to intercept, but remember this is a Jintao we are dealing with. We must be diplomatic. You can learn more with diplomacy than with force."

"Minister," said one of the others, a man in blue with a particularly narrow face and thick glasses. "We must act now. He has broken the law and he is about to leave the country."

"You would arrest him like a common criminal?" said the senior official. "He is from a most prominent family. Thankfully, yours is but one voice. We must consider the potential outcome before acting."

"If you procrastinate, he will get away," said the blue suit.

"I will convey your concerns to the committee," said the older man. "We will review options and decide." Pressing hands on the table, the heavyset minister struggled to his feet. "You will wait here." He labored his way out of the room, leaving the others bickering among themselves.

Several minutes later the minister returned. Standing in the doorway, his cheeks fluttered as he spoke. "It has been decided. You may bring in the young Jintao and question him, but he is to be handled with utmost courtesy."

The man with thick glasses did not hesitate. Clearing his throat, he spoke to his wrist disk. "Proceed with extraction . . . without prejudice . . . diplomatic protocol."

224

~~~

Minutes later, at the Jintao penthouse, a government glide and four solos dropped out of the sky at an alarming rate, blue and red hazard lights flashing.

Quan overheard Ning speaking with someone at the door and called to her. "What is it?"

She entered the great room and said, "There are government agents asking for you. They say it is a matter of national security."

"What do they want?" asked Sealy, bracing herself.

"No doubt they want to talk about the experiments," said Quan, pressing his hand to her cheek. I'll go talk to them."

He went to the doorway. "I'm Quan Jintao. How may I help you?"

Outside, next to the door, two officers stood at attention in full dress khaki uniforms, hats with gold emblems, white gloves and black polished shoes. One of them said, "You are needed at National Security Headquarters."

"For what purpose?"

"It is a matter of national security under the Reform Act of 2081. Please come with us."

"I'll be right with you. Let me get my coat."

Ning stood her post at the rooftop door while Quan went back inside.

Standing in front of Sealy, Quan swung his coat onto his shoulders and said, "I have to go with them. Be patient. I'm sure I'll be back in a couple of hours. Everything's going to be okay."

"Com me if you're going to be gone longer," said Sealy.

Relaxed, Quan walked into the daylight, the jacket slung over his shoulders like a cape. Out on the aeropad, four matte black tactical scooters hovered several meters above the deck. The riders appeared to be molded into each machine with their arm and leg shields lining up perfectly with the cowlings. Black

225

visored helmets hid their faces. Next to them hovered a matte black glide banded with diagonal blue and yellow stripes, idling with its doors wide open. Quan stopped and turned to one of the uniforms.

"Why the armed escort? Am I under arrest?"

"They are for your protection."

"And if I refuse to go?"

"We have authority to compel you."

Quan searched the man's face. *Pointless to argue with a robot.*

Strolling past the five solos, he looked closely. They were covered in light body armor, helmets attached to torso plates, legs snug inside the front fairings, firearms clipped to their sides, disrupters and other heavy weapons tucked within easy reach behind them.

Overkill. Who thought it necessary to send a tactical squad to escort me? Did they think I would come out with guns blazing?

He could com the corporate attorneys, but he knew it wouldn't be necessary. He could see the moves and counter moves clearly.

It was a short lift into the city and Quan recognized the building as they began their descent. He'd seen it from different vantage points before. The building reminded him of an ancient steam radiator, a dull metallic structure with ledges protruding from its sides.

The craft settled and the uniforms egressed, posting themselves on either side of the glide door. Quan got out and looked around. His gaze fixed on the copper hut. It was a curious structure with four fans lazily turning within a cupola on its roof. It was out of place amid the air-handling systems. He saw it for what it was—a Faraday cage.

Down three floors they went, then along a polished hallway lit with bluish light from overhead panels. They came to

226

an abrupt halt and his escorts parked themselves on either side of a doorway. "Please. Go in," said one of them, extending an arm. "They're waiting for you."

Quan entered a room without windows. The walls were glossy white and, at the center, was a black conference table. Seated around the table were seven people. Three of them sat at the far end—familiar, identical blue suits and black ties. Quan couldn't help but snicker —the same three who had visited his office. The others were men of different ages, the eldest of whom had gowl-like cheeks. He spoke first.

"Mr. Jintao. Thank you for joining us. Please sit."

"Why am I here?" asked Quan, taking his place opposite the older man.

"Before we get started, may I offer you something? Water? Tea?"

"No, thank you," Quan looked over his shoulder at the doorway and spoke briskly. "Bringing me here under armed guard wasn't necessary. If you had asked politely I would have come of my own volition."

"It was diplomatic protocol —an armed escort."

"It was unnecessary and it upset my banlu. Who are you and why am I here?"

"My name is Tso and we need to discuss a few security issues with you," said the older man. "This is an unofficial inquiry."

Putting hands on the arms of his chair, as if getting ready to leave, Quan said, "Security issues. What security issues?"

The older man leaned back and nodded to the man on his right, a man of Mongolian decent, with an athletic build that took the creases out of his starched white shirt. Fingering his tie, the man spoke in a husky voice. "I have the file here."

"And who are you?"

"My name is Manchu." Thumbing his way down a handheld viewer he read, "On February 19, 2089, you and three people presumed to be working for you entered the restricted work site on Kau Yi Chau Island. We have reports that you visited Kau Yi Chau again, with the same individuals, on six other occasions. These meetings are under investigation."

"Jintao Corporation is under contract to work at Kau Yi Chau," said Quan.

Manchu slid his thumb down further. "Equipment from the Kau Yi Chau facility was removed and shipped out of the country. These actions were not related to the construction of the Kau Yi Chau energy station." The man looked up. "We believe you have taken this equipment for your own use and you're exporting it to another country. It also appears that you've taken valuable research that should be under the control of the Central Science Committee."

The older man chimed in, "Not very smart for an educated man such as yourself. Perhaps you didn't know these acts are illegal."

Excellent intel, thought Quan. "I'm well aware that stealing government property is illegal. However, your information is flawed. May I ask who gave you this information?"

"I am not . . ."

Quan nodded and finished the sentence with him. " . . . at liberty to say. Yes, I've heard that before." Quan continued in a calm voice, loud enough for the blue suits at the end of the table to hear. "The officials from the Central Science Committee should be commended. They do an excellent job of protecting our national secrets, but these allegations are groundless. For one thing, these items are not government property." Seeing the man's blank expression, Quan continued, "Until the power station on Kau Yi Chau Island is functional, the equipment belongs to the Jintao Corporation."

Referring to his notes, Manchu began again. "A reactor was removed from the island and—"

228

"Defective," Quan broke in. "The reactor was defective and the Jintao Corporation has the authority to remove it. It's stipulated in our contract. It was sold as scrap."

"And the research?"

"I invited a few colleagues to visit Kau Yi Chau Island to look at the reactor. That's not illegal. You should know that."

The older man looked down and slightly shook his head.

Quan's energy turned up a notch. "You people know what I've been doing. I've been trying to investigate my father's disappearance and I was doing so because your detectives have been totally inept at locating him. And, regarding the so called secrets." Quan looked at the three blue suits. "I've been more than cooperative. The CSC was given full access to my father's private laboratory and his files. What more could you possibly want?"

The man known as Manchu said, "I would advise you to be careful what you say. This is only a preliminary interview."

"I have a right to conduct my own investigation. You people have no reason to interrogate me. I haven't violated any laws."

"Maybe you haven't, then again maybe you have. That's for others to decide."

"Look," said Quan. "I'm willing to cooperate. Would you like to know what my research has turned up?"

"Yes. I think we would all like to hear about that."

"Just before he disappeared, my father was studying one of our orbital reactors —OB12. It's in a state of lockdown because of a malfunction. It's all in his notes—notes which the Central Science Committee have already seen." He spoke louder, for the benefit of the people at the end of the table. "If they want to know more about the orbital reactor, I suggest they go and see it for themselves."

The interrogator slowly rose from his chair and went to the end of the table to confer with the blue suits. Kneeling behind them, he spoke in hushed tones.

Quan thought about who might have first tipped them off. Von Ang and McGowen were loyal allies and Laosing Mao wouldn't do anything to spoil his reputation. Again, he concluded that Dr. Lee was most likely the one. He couldn't blame her. In some ways, she was still a child, thinking that big government was somehow in everyone's best interest.

After several minutes, the interrogator returned. His face was stern. "Equipment was removed from Kau Yi Chau Island—that is of interest. If you return it, we can resolve this matter."

Making an abracadabra gesture in the air, Quan said, "It's gone. Defective. Sold as scrap. It will be replaced with a functional unit per the contract."

The interrogator's wrist disk buzzed and he left his place again to confer with the people in blue. The older man rose from his seat and joined them at the end of the table.

The men returned to their seats a few moments later. Manchu studied Quan's face before saying a word. His eyes seemed to say, *You've won.*

"You are free to go," he said. "However, you're not to leave the city. We'll want to speak with you again."

~~~

Quan boarded the blue and yellow glide for home. He had placated the authorities with a ploy from *The Book of Thirty-Six Strategies*: Give them a brick and make them think it's jade. With the equipment out of reach, their next logical move would be to investigate the OB12 reactor. They'd been given a direction, a sense of purpose but, without the sophisticated retrofits and algorithms, they would spend months trying to figure out what had been done.

Quan had taken precautions. The critical components were safely away. Decoy crates bearing conspicuous markings had been sent through obvious carriers, while the real payloads

230

were sent through a freight forwarder using bills of lading that changed at every port.

Arriving back at the penthouse, Sealy met him at the entry—a look of apprehension on her face.

"Are you in trouble?" she asked.

"Let's go inside where it's safe to talk."

He led her to Master Jintao's study and the black leather chairs.

"Nothing to worry about," he said. "It's under control."

"But the police. I mean, why did they arrest you? What's going on?"

"Not arrested—just questioned."

He told her about the interrogation and the shipments and the restriction on leaving New Hong Kong. The intensity in his eyes as he spoke was something she hadn't seen before. The situation they were in had unleashed Quan's dragon energy. It was thrilling to watch him take charge, but at the same time she felt excluded.

"McGowen will go and set everything up," he said. "In a few weeks we'll . . ."

Just then Quan thought he heard a noise close to the wall. Holding a finger to his lips, he said, "Just a minute."

After the sound subsided, he said, "We need to be careful."

"They said you're not supposed to leave the city. So that means you'll stay, doesn't it?"

"The travel ban can be lifted. That's what we have lawyers for."

"And we have another complication. Something I need to tell you about." Sealy took him by the hand.

"Oh?"

"I haven't done a test yet, but I'm pretty sure—I'm pregnant. I have the early signs and, if I am, for the next few weeks I'm not going to be feeling like traveling."

"Are you sure it's not vertigo again?"

"A woman knows."

"That's wonderful," said Quan, kissing her hand. "It's a happy occasion. Great news."

"So, you want a child?"

He kissed her and said, "Of course I do. I love you."

"I love you, too," she said.

Quan looked away, knowing there was something profound he should tell her. He'd been putting off telling her about his new ability, but was now the right time?

"In four or five weeks I'll need to go check on the new site, but I won't be gone long. And there's something else I should tell you."

"What?"

This was probably not a good time to talk about his ability to walk through walls. It would probably shock her and, considering her condition, this was definitely not the right time for a demonstration. Instead he deflected to a more academic approach . . . laying a foundation he could build on later.

"Remember the Shakespeare course we took at Oxford?"

"Yes."

"Remember in *Hamlet*? The line that goes 'what is this quintessence of dust'?"

"Yes?"

Flattening his hands on his chest, he said, "That's what this is . . . dust . . . zillions of particles hanging together, forming a living, breathing person. Do you ever think about what holds them all together?"

"Not really," said Sealy.

"The stuff we're made of is nothing at all—it's a manifestation held together by infinite consciousness."

"I don't understand what that means. Honestly, sometimes you can be a little strange."

"True."

232

29.

Central California

Tromping around out-of-doors, smelling the sea air and the freshly turned earth, McGowen was tending to construction of the new lab site. Feeling free as a boy again, wearing a tartan kilt, he was busy programming a nanite controller. His construction-bots were uncrating supplies and he was preparing to lay the foundation for the new laboratory.

Scrolling through the archi-tech's plans, he came to a section showing the foundation details. Even though he'd never worked in the building trades, the details were low-level complexity compared to aerospace. Touching the transmit symbol on the edge of the foundation plans, the geometries were instantly sent to the nanite controller's memory bank. The machine was large, rented for the occasion. It housed zillions of nanites and sat on top of a freighter with a set of chrome valves on its underbelly.

Over the past few days, the bots had excavated a fifty-by-fifty-meter hole in the ground and McGowen was about to release nanites into the chasm where they would link together to make forms for xynite to be poured into. Completing his final check, McGowen initiated the program and said, "Okay, you wee wonders. Show me what you can do."

Following the Go command, two of the valves opened and a river of microscopic black machines flowed out onto the ground. The mass churned for a moment as if strategizing—then began to move away from the controller, branching into two shimmering streams. One group moved toward the excavation site, flowing over the edge and out of sight. The other group went to a series of open shipping containers—up and over the side of the first container. Almost immediately, sparkling silver granules began to flow out of the container, moving toward the excavation site. Down below, the first wave of nanites had linked together, creating an outline for the laboratory floor.

Stepping away from the controller, McGowen peered over the edge. The silver river of raw xynite was being transported into the mold, filling it up. As the xynite began to solidify, turning a dull gray, the nanites climbed higher, extending the form. The silver material continued to flow and gradually the basement floor took shape. After an hour and a half, the flow had filled in walls and a stairwell. The activity stopped for a few minutes, waiting for the last centimeter of xynite to cure. Then, the nanites came climbing out of the excavation in a broad black river, returning to their home inside the controller.

With the foundation complete, McGowen and his bots went off in the direction of the barn to sort materials for the next phase of construction.

A few days later, as the morning sun began to light the old farmhouse, McGowen heard a knocking at the front door. Still partly asleep, he opened up and almost overlooked the short, plump woman standing below him. Her wide face and dark sparkling eyes looked up apprehensively. She prattled on in Spanish, saying "*leche*" several times and gesturing toward the barn. Slowly it dawned on McGowen that she was talking about when the property had been a dairy farm.

"Sorry. I don't speak Spanish," said McGowen. "No cows here anymore. Cows all gone."   Determined, the small brown-skinned woman continued in pantomime, indicating that she could cook and clean, and she continued to point into the house.

McGowen finally gave way, allowing her to enter.

"*Me llamo Rosalea. Sígame, yo se lo explico,*" she said as she made her way past him, into the kitchen, beckoning for him to follow. She demonstrated that she knew where everything was, naming the appliances and the pots and pans in Spanish.

She picked up an empty food wrapper from the trash and made a sour face. "Is no good," she said. "I cook."

McGowen had been eating stabilized food from vac-pack containers since he arrived and the idea of a home-cooked meal sounded good. He held up his hand, then pointed to the floor. "Wait here," he said and he went to the back of the house. A moment later he returned with a handheld device.

"Translate English and Spanish," he said. Then: "What's your mobile cash number? I'll transfer a hundred dollars. You bring food."

She looked at him for a moment, weighing his request. Then she pulled a card from her purse, smiled, and said, "*Gracias. Compraré comida.*" (Thank you. I'll buy food.)

He touched her card with his and their business concluded.

She sauntered up the driveway, stuffing the card back into her bag, her round figure swaying side to side. An old four-wheeled hydro was parked on the main road. She got in on the passenger side and McGowen watched the truck slowly pull away, wondering if she would return.

30.

Quan was in daily contact with McGowen. Construction of the new laboratory was progressing smoothly and he'd be joining McGowen soon. Due to her first trimester nausea, Sealy decided she would be more comfortable staying in China while he went to finish his work.

Lotus sat on the edge of the bed, patting Sealy's leg.

"I'll stay with you while he's away. You're going to be a mother! I can hardly believe it," said Lotus. "I don't think I could handle being pregnant. I can't imagine going through what you're going through. And raising a child. Wow. Do you think you're ready?"

"It's going to be different. That's for sure. I'm actually looking forward to it."

"I'm so happy for you. A baby is wonderful thing. Do you want a boy or a girl?"

"I'm happy either way."

"Hey, I'm going to be an aunt. I love it. Just don't ask me to change diapers, okay?"

"I'm glad you're here and not to worry. We have Ning for that."

"You and Quan should be together at a time like this. You'll join him in a few weeks?"

"I don't think so. Where he's going is too remote. I'd be bored out of my skull. If I ever want to see coastal California, it's right here—in the great room."

"Why is he leaving? What's so important?" asked Lotus.

"He's working on a project with Gaston, and I'm okay with that. He won't be gone long. Gaston is going, too. I don't know if you knew that."

"No. He didn't tell me that. Men, huh? They aren't great communicators. So, if I were to go and join them . . . later of course . . . will you be okay?"

"I'll be fine. I'm going to finish my courses online."
Quan appeared at the bedroom door with an arm full of pink blossoms.

"What a sweet man," said Sealy. "They're beautiful. Ning should put them in water."

"Is there anything else I can get for you?" he asked.

"No, lover. We were just talking about your trip. Lotus wanted to know how long you'll be gone."

"I expect to be back soon. The others might be there longer."

Lotus pushed past him saying, "Excuse me. I need to talk to Gaston."

Quan passed the flowers off to Ning and retired to the study where he'd been spending most of his time. His website had generated a substantial following and he was corresponding anonymously with people of interest. In a recent thread, they discussed the idea that life had always been an element in the universe ever since its genesis. Life, they speculated, was as much a force of nature as gravity and magnetism.

Conversely, some of the visitors to the website came with prejudice, looking to discredit the ideas and a few were downright abusive. They were like reading the thoughts of disturbed minds. To them, Quan made no response.

There were responses from so many intelligent and creative minds that Quan had become addicted to reading their comments. It was too soon for him to reveal evidence of the other dimensions. His comments were purely philosophical.

Supporters of the website asked for more disclosure. They believed there was a greater truth lurking behind the bits and pieces. They praised the work and wanted to know who was behind it. To them Quan only said, "Thank you. More will follow."

In the great room, Lotus was listening to von Ang explain his plans to leave. He assured her that he wouldn't be leaving anytime soon. While organizing for his departure, he'd run into a problem.

Working with a local real estate attorney, in hope of subletting his apartment while he was gone, he was informed of the possibility that the property might be confiscated in his absence. Because of the extreme housing shortage in New Hong Kong, when a unit was vacant, especially one owned by an expat, it often happened that a Chinese family would move in and file a claim. Many times, the local courts would honor the claim and rescind a foreigner's rights. To get out in front of such an event, the attorney advised von Ang to have his rights to the property validated. He would have to appear in court, provide his bona fide lease agreement, explain his reason for sub-leasing the property, and hopefully receive an official permit.

The Jintao corporate lawyers had prevailed on Quan's behalf, arranging an exit permit and visa. After saying many I-love-yous and communing with Sealy, he left the penthouse early in the morning, boarding a taxi-glide bound for NHK Terminal 3.

Inside the airport, he moved through a throng of people who were yelling at one another, as the Chinese are often do, especially when saying good-bye. He made his way to the Sino World counter and, after dropping off his luggage, he went to the boarding area.

He'd been in line only a minute or two when a young woman in a tan uniform and cap asked him to step out of line and follow him. Expecting VIP treatment, Quan was surprised when the woman led him into a small interrogation room.
Behind the locked door Quan waited for almost forty minutes until, finally, a uniformed immigration officer in a dark blue suit and matching cap entered the room. The officer asked a battery of questions—where Quan was going, the purpose of his trip, was he transporting any contraband, how could he be reached, and where he would be staying. While the questioning continued, another man appeared with Quan's luggage and ransacked his belongings.

Quan kept calm and answered questions as tersely as possible. In the end, he was instructed to repack his luggage and was released just in time to board the flight.

~~~

Cruise time from New Hong Kong to San Francisco was seven hours and seventeen minutes and, after an hour of listening to music, Quan could no longer sit still. He got up and walked the aisle, thinking about the interrogation. It was likely that either the Central Science Committee, or Central Intelligence had arranged his detention, no doubt to make him aware that he was still a person of interest. Unless they hoped to find some sort of contraband or a mistake in his paperwork, it served no other purpose.

239

Walking from one end of the plane to the other, he examined details of the aircraft's interior: the red, purple, and blue patterns woven into the seat cushions, the smooth edges of the red arrows circling the emergency door latches, the organization of buttons on the galley's control panel, and the witness marks left by assembly-bots at the corners of each overhead bin.

Seat belt signs lit and a voice announced turbulence ahead. Quan returned to his seat.

Sinking into the sleeper seat, his mind filled with thoughts of his father, the machine, his allies and, most of all, of Sealy. He felt guilty leaving her behind in the penthouse. The only consolation was that she was in the company of Lotus—Lotus, with her breezy and unfettered behavior—and Ning, the IA who would take care of Sealy's needs without question.

Quan had wisked the discovery away from sinister hands. Components were on the way to a spanking-new facility and the research, perhaps the greatest discovery of modern times, was going to be safe. And, in due course, the new science would be shared with the world.

From the Stratos850 he boarded a shuttle at San Francisco International and headed south. The shuttle flew along the Pacific coastline and Quan watched as the terrain slipped by. There were towns and forests and grassy fields. Some stretches looked like Norwegian fjords with steep cliffs down to the water's edge and there were beaches where surfers rode the waves. Almost eight hours had elapsed since he left China and Quan was feeling restless in the confines of the small craft.

In the distance, a tiny white square became visible and, as the square became larger, he could see a small red dot moving across its lower edge. As the shuttle drew nearer, the square appeared to be a building and, after another minute, the glide settled in front of a white barn. McGowen turned out to be the red dot, a spectacle in a red plaid kilt and construction boots.

240

Stepping out of the craft, Quan looked around. It was a rustic scene as far as the eye could see, with waist-high shrubs interspersed with patches of dirt and rocks. Hills to the east were dotted with trees and rocky outcroppings. A breeze delivered scents of wild sage and rosemary. In contrast to the crowded island of New Hong Kong, the land seemed vacant, devoid of civilization, and for Quan it conjured up images of the Old West.

McGowen approached. "Glad you're here. How was the flight?"

"Fine," said Quan, pulling his bag from the cargo hold. "This is more remote than I imagined."

"True enough," said McGowen as he led the way from the vehicle toward the old farmhouse. "No one's going to bother us. The nearest town is eighty kilometers away. Come, I'll show you what's going on."

Behind them the shuttle beeped and made its departure announcements. With lights strobing, it slowly lifted into the air and turned northward.

As they walked, McGowen pointed to the new structures, two major buildings and three smaller bungalows, nearly completed. Arriving on the front porch of the farmhouse, McGowen paused to mention the housekeeper. "She doesn't speak English or Chinese, but she cleans and cooks. I've been giving her a few dollars here and there to buy food. She hasn't asked for more, but I figure we probably owe her a month's wages."

"A housekeeper," said Quan, approvingly. "Nice addition. We should get a translator for her. I'll ask von Ang to bring one."

"I've been using mine," said McGowen, retrieving it from his sporran.

At the front door, the dark Cholo woman, Rosalea, appeared in a dress brightly patterned with yellow, red, and black. She wiped her hands on a white kitchen towel draped over her belt and said, *"Hola. Buenas tardes."* (Hello. Good afternoon.) Her broad smile revealed perfect rows of short white teeth.

"Hello," said Quan "Nice to meet you."

"Sí. Tienes hambre?" (Yes. Are you hungry?)

"Yes. Thank you," said Quan.

Rosalea stepped aside, letting them pass. *"Haré el almuerzo."* (I'll make lunch.)

"Thank you," said Quan, looking back over his shoulder. "We'll see you later." Under his breath, he confided, "It's awkward. I thought everyone in the United States spoke English."

"Nope," said McGowen with a smile. "But I think you handled it well. Once our AI system is up and running, this won't be a problem. You'll bunk here in the farmhouse for the next few nights, until the bungalows are finished."

Quan was shown to a spacious bedroom, with dark wood floors and a view of the rounded eastern hills. The room was furnished with dark wood furniture—a king bed with hand-carved headboard and two stout bedside tables, each with a simple lamp. After unpacking, Quan closed the door and lay down to relax. The bed was as soft as a cloud and he awoke four hours later to the smell of burning wood, onions, and roasting chicken. Following his nose, he found his way back to the front room where McGowen sat next to a large stone fireplace, his face lit by its amber glow. Overhead, the beamed ceiling reminded Quan of the older halls at Oxford College.

"There you are," said McGowen. "Rosalea has dinner for us. Hope you're hungry. Everything's ready."

Quan walked over to the large window next to the chair where McGowen sat, straining to see something moving in the dusk outside.

"It's the construction-bots, sir. They work all night. I only turn on the floods when I need to go check something. We're only a few hours away from being done. Pretty comfortable here,

242

though. I've been stayin' in a room over there." McGowen pointed to the far wall. "And Rosalea has a little room behind the kitchen. She goes home on weekends."

The floorboards creaked under McGowen as he ambled into the dining room. Quan followed and they pulled chairs up to a heavy wooden table. Bowls of refried beans, Spanish rice, and guacamole came to the table, followed by a platter of grilled onions, peppers, grilled chicken, and a plate of steaming tortillas. Placing a bottle of hot sauce in the center of the table, Rosalea stood back and smiled. *"Fajitas. Usted puede mezclarlo."* (You can mix.)

"Might be a bit spicy, but it's good," said McGowen. "Here, let me show you. It's like mu shu. Lay down a tortilla . . . a spoonful of beans . . . a spoonful of rice . . . some avocado . . . chicken . . . cheese. Whatever you like. There's some cilantro— it's like Chinese parsley—and onion." He splashed some hot sauce on top before rolling it up. "And there you have it," he said, taking a bite.

In the kitchen doorway, Rosalea clasped her hands as if in prayer, watching the neophyte build his first fajita. After taking his first bite, ingredients began to fall out and Quan resorted to cleaning up the spoils with a fork. "Mmmm, very good," he said, eyeing Rosalea. "Thank you."

"De nada," she murmured and returned to the kitchen.

Quan looked out the window pensively. "How much longer before the reactor can be started?"

"The underground vaults and the lift are ready," said McGowen. "The reactor is down there and I was going to install it tomorrow. We'll need to get the inspectors to sign off before we can bring it online." He paused then added, "I've been meaning to tell you, I took a turn in the machine before we disassembled it."

"Good to hear. And how was it?"

"For me, it was a life changer and I can hardly wait to do it again. Don't know if von Ang told you, but he took a turn too.

Looks like we're making progress. He was able to transmit and receive a gamma signal."

"Yes. He told me. It's a first step and like Lao-Tzu said, the journey of a thousand miles begins with a single step."

Through the window, Quan saw one of the construction-bots leading a bobcart loaded with wallboard across the yard. Machine sounds emanated from one of the smaller buildings.

Zzzt, zzzt, zzzt, zzzt.

"I hope that won't be going on all night," said Quan.

"If we're goin' to stay on schedule, I'm afraid so."

31.

Just before dawn, unable to sleep, Quan left the old farmhouse and walked to the edge of the coastal bluff. In the east, the pink canopy was turning yellow, smudged with charcoal clouds, and above him stars lingered in the dawn sky. A hundred meters below, waves boomed against the rocky shore. He imagined the enormous forces of interplate collision that, eons ago, lifted the land and formed the cliff he was standing on. Over millions of years, the sea rose and fell, like a gigantic cutting tool, carving away aggregate and creating the cove. Below him white water welled and retreated—like the quantum exchange between worlds.

The discovery was now safe from the grasp of vultures and he could explore its mysteries at will. Nothing stood in his way. He would leave the science to others—they would probe and measure, analyze and catalog. But for Quan a different quest was calling: to know the innermost nature of that other place and to know what had become of his father.

McGowen found Quan standing on the bluff overlooking the ocean. Overhead, red-tailed hawks hovered in the thermal currents, barely moving their wings. Looking up he pointed and said, "Aren't they something?"

Quan lifted his head. Ten meters above, the birds were making lazy circles in the brightening sky. Suddenly, one of them folded its wings and, like a missile, streaked toward the rocks below, disappearing from view. A moment later it re-emerged, soaring upward with a small creature clutched in its yellow talons.

"It took time to learn that," said Quan, "and the ones who were able, thrived. The ones that couldn't, died. Survival is what drives evolution."

McGowen studied him for a moment, noting the change in his personality. He seemed wiser and more certain of himself. "'Twas ever thus. One trailblazer starts the whole thing. Then the others follow."

"Whenever there's a major breakthrough, there are those who, for whatever reason, find themselves in its path," said Quan. "What we do here will change everything."

"I agree. Ever since I took my turn, I've looked at things differently."

"It's a natural progression . . . like walking upright," said Quan, looking down at a few reconnaissance ants wandering near his feet. "In a hundred generations, humans will be so advanced they won't even recognize us. And those who don't evolve will be no more significant than ants."

"Aye. That may be," said McGowen, looking back toward the compound. "I've got an inspection scheduled and I've got a few things to do. I'll see you in a bit. By the way, some of these rocks are a bit wobbly, so be careful."

As McGowen walked away, Quan looked far out across the ocean.

What we're doing, he thought, *is nothing less transformative than when Eratosthenes realized that the Earth was round instead of flat. What we thought was solid matter doesn't exist at all. Matter is composed of elements that are constantly changing. Everything turns over—the cells in our bodies—stars and galaxies. There isn't even a moment we can label as being the present. As soon as we try to mark it, it's gone.*

McGowen stood inside the laboratory atrium, watching two glides touch down. Two men disembarked from the black glide, a tall one with broad shoulders, pale blue eyes, and a thick white mustache, and another, shorter man with close-cropped hair, wearing casual business attire. From the second glide, a tan one with a State of California emblem on it's side, a dark haired man in a green quilted vest walked over to join the other two. The man with the mustache swung a large rubbery viewflex onto the rear deck of his vehicle and repeatedly dragged his finger across its surface.

From inside the laboratory atrium, McGowen watched the men repeatedly looking around and pointing at things in the compound. Watching their body language, he could see who was who. Pushing open the door, he walked out to greet them and as he drew near the man with the white mustache looked up and said, "Hello there." Reaching into his vest pocket he fetched a thin black card that instantly lit up with the emblem of the Nuclear Regulatory Commission, his picture, and title: Edward Nathanial Stuart—Senior Inspector. "Ned Stuart, NRC," he said, "This is Pete Sanchez and Jason Brokowski. Pete's from state and Jason's with me."

McGowen shook hands and said, "Gregory McGowen, project engineer."

Slipping the card back into a small pocket on his vest, Stuart took out a pair of eyeglasses from a larger pocket. Flexing the stems behind his ears, he asked, "Did you design these plans?"

"No. I'm the construction manager. Why, is there a problem?"

"No. Not at all. The plans were approved by the agency and good to go. Think of us as part of your construction team. We're here to make sure the site is safe. We have nearly eight hundred reactor sites in the U.S. and in the last fifty years there have been zero incidents. We just want to double check and verify everything is correctly installed."

"No argument here."

Looking from the plans and back again, the Stuart said, "Help us get oriented. Would that be the reactor vault you just came out of?"

"Correct," said McGowen, never taking his eyes off the inspector.

Stuart looked back at the plans, then said, "Tell me about the reactor. What are they going to use it for?"

McGowen hesitated, unprepared for such an intrusive question. "Scientific research," he said.

"Care to be more specific?" said Stuart.

"They're looking for ghosts."

The inspector laughed and rolled his eyes. "That's a new one. Found any yet?"

"They're pretty elusive," said McGowen with a mischievous look. "You'll have to excuse my sense of humor. They're doing particle research."

"Let's have a look," said Stuart, patting McGowen on the shoulder.

McGowen led the inspection team to the elevator and down into the laboratory. He could read the senior inspector clearly: a seasoned veteran with an excellent nose for bullshit, probably from years of people trying to slip things past him.

The inspection went by the book and three hours later, after checking the entire installation, Stuart said, "Choosing a SSTAR unit was a good move. Those precertified reactors save us a lot of time. Looking at your bots, your materials, and your construction techniques, looks like you know what you're doing."

"I appreciate that," said McGowen.

248

"The precision shows. Job well done. I'm going to sign off on this phase and we'll be back when you're up and running."

As soon as the government glides lifted off, McGowen met with Quan and said, "Now, we can add our retrofits. In a couple of days we're going to need von Ang to boot this thing up."

32.

Two days after the inspection, Quan and McGowen were standing in front of the new laboratory. On the surface there wasn't much to see—a glass atrium surrounding a brushed stainless steel vault that housed the service elevator and a stairwell leading to the underground laboratory.

"It needs something," said Quan. "What do you think?"

"I don't know. Maybe a potted plant?"

A flash of sunlight caught their attention as a highly polished glide came cruising into view. It came in low, then swung its tail around and landed, kicking up a small plume of dust. The hatch opened and out popped Lotus, shaking off the confines of her trip. Bouncing up and down on red plyform shoes, her blue hair and magenta jumpsuit recoiled after each bounce.

"Look, Gaston!" she exclaimed, pointing at the new structures. "Isn't it just orbital?"

Von Ang emerged and surveyed the scene: the five new bungalows, and the stark laboratory entrance, covered walkways and a circular pond. In contrast, to the north stood the old farmhouse with its Craftsman-style wood eaves and the large whitewashed barn.

"Very nice," he said.

"Oh, look—there's Quan." Waving her arm, Lotus yelled, "Hey! We're here!"

McGowen came striding toward them, his tartan kilt swaying with authority. Under his breath he said, "Well, now, what do we have here?"

Eyeing his boots and muscled calves, Lotus teased, "Hey. Nice legs, big guy."

"Oh my. Compliments. Thank you." He walked up to Lotus and said, "Gregory McGowen. Pleased to meet you."

"I'm Lotus, Sealy's sister. May I call you Greg?"

"I prefer Gregory," said McGowen, "or just Hey You."

Walking around the glide, McGowen slid his hand across the sleek chrome surface. "What's this, then?"

"It's leased. I thought we might want to do some sightseeing while we're here," said von Ang with a dry mouth.

"Sounds like you could use a drink," said the big Scotsman. "Let's get you and the little lass settled in."

"Any problems I should know about?" asked von Ang as he followed.

"Nothing we can't handle."

Quan walked up to them and Lotus threw her arms around him, kissing his cheek. "That's from Sealy." Kissing his other cheek, she said, "And that one's from me."

"Very sweet, Lotus. How is she?"

"Sealy? She's bigger and her cheeks are rosy. I've never seen her look so healthy. You should vidi com her."

"Com links are not reliable here. It's something we're working on."

McGowen's boots made a grinding sound as he pivoted toward the bungalows.

Passing the front porch of the farmhouse, Rosalea said something in Spanish.

"Wait," said Lotus. "I have something for her."

Lotus mounted the three wooden steps and held out a small disk-shaped device, red plastic with a wristband attached. She pressed a quadrant on the disk and spoke, "Translate. Spanish."

"This is for you," she said. The device repeated the same words in Spanish. "It's easy to use. Here, you try." She handed the device to Rosalea. "Just tell it what language you want. It's yours to keep."

"*Sí?*" Rosalea looked puzzled. "*Muchas gracias,*" she said. "*En Inglés, por favor.*" The device repeated the phrase in English. "Oh my, it talks for me," Rosalea said. "What a clever little thing! Thank you very much. I'm going to make something good for you to eat."

After setting down their bags in one of the new bungalows, von Ang and Lotus returned to the old farmhouse. Inside the timbered dining room, bowls of guacamole and salsa fresca were set out on the heavy wooden table along with a large basket of fresh tortilla chips. Rosalea poured sangria from a large earthenware pitcher into ceramic cups.

Von Ang carefully spread guacamole on one of the chips with a knife and McGowen chuckled to himself.

"What's so funny?" asked von Ang.

McGowen dipped a chip right into the bowl of guacamole and took a bite.

"Okay, I see," said von Ang. "When in Rome."

"Reminds me of a time, back in the day," said McGowen. "We were on leave from the RAF and we found this little Tex-Mex bar in Chelsea. The guacamole was really good. One of our crew was this kid who'd never been far from home. He'd never eaten guac before and he couldn't get enough. He went through two bowls of it. Well, let me tell you, the next night we tied up at a sushi bar in Soho. We were sitting there, drinking sake at the bar, waiting for the sushi man to fix us some fish, when he reaches over and puts mounds of wasabi in front of each of us. After a minute or two I look at the kid and he's gone all red in the face, sweat rolling down his cheeks. I look down and see all his wasabi is gone! The poor fool thought it was guac and gobbled it up!"

With a smirk, Quan said, "Good for the sinuses."

"Yup. Did him up right." McGowen laughed.

After draining his cup of sangria, von Ang poured himself another cup.

"So, Sealy is getting on okay?" asked Quan.

"She's moving to our parents' house. They're thrilled to have her," said Lotus. "Don't worry. She's be pampered there."

Rosalea brought more food and made another pitcher of sangria. They ate and drank and laughed and, in due course, the chirping of crickets increased and night descended on the compound. Sated, they retired to their rooms and fell asleep with a distant hiss of spray nozzles coming from inside the last of the five bungalows. A few minutes after 3:00 a.m., the hissing stopped and the symphony of crickets continued. All that remained was for the paint to dry.

In the dark, Quan lay with eyes wide open, wondering what time it was in New Hong Kong and wondering what Sealy was up to. It was unsettling, seeing her sister there without her. Yet it was predictable. Lotus wasn't the kind to stay put, especially if there was something more exciting to do.

The next morning, underground, in the laboratory, McGowen opened an access panel on the reactor and fed umbilical cables into conduits that came up from under the floor. Then he pushed the cables through to another room, where Von Ang began terminating them with low-impedance connectors. The construction-bots uncrated a new sequencer and, seeing it for the first time, McGowen said, "That's half the size of the one at Henan Kaifeng."

"It's a newer model," stated von Ang. "Twice the bandwidth."

"Probably twice the price, too," said McGowen.

Von Ang connected the reactor to its subsystems and rechecked the fittings.

Sitting in a swivel chair, Quan watched his team assemble the equipment. *Life*, he thought, *created such amazing diversity, all capable of assembling themselves from a single cell. By comparison, our most complicated machines are crude, not capable of self-assembly. And, while living systems are capable of repairing themselves...*

Quan was jogged from his thoughts by von Ang, who announced, "We're ready for a systems test." He brought the reactor online and activated the subsystems one by one. Streams of data appeared on a view field floating in midair. He inserted a finger and paused the run.

Nearby, bots were drilling holes and inserting anchors into the polymer-coated wall. They bolted the new gimbal-mounted transfer bed to the wall and McGowen plugged it into the system computer. Then, with a bucket in hand, he went to one of the lab benches and opened the lid. Reaching in with his gloved hand, he lifted out a large arroyo toad. Holding the specimen around its mid-section, limbs squirmed spasmodically.

"I've got our first subject right here," said McGowen.

"It's not going to stay still," said von Ang. "That will be a problem."

With his other hand, McGowen reached for a transparent box that was on the lab bench. He proceeded to force the toad into the considerably smaller enclosure. The toad resisted, bridging its limbs against the opening. As McGowen tucked one leg in, another popped free. At last, using a two-handed approach, he slid the amphibian between the walls and quickly slapped the

254

lid shut. As McGowen crossed the lab, the frog seemed to eyeball him with malice.

McGowen left the box on the transfer bed and the amphibian croaked in protest, puffing up its epiglottis and jumping up hard against the lid.

"It seems perturbed," said von Ang.

"Ah, he'll get over it," said McGowen.

The scientist motioned for McGowen to move away. "Stand clear."

Blue light flashed from emitters at the four corners of the bed. Sequenced data was instantly digested by the system. The countdown began, and within a few seconds the box and its occupant vanished. A few seconds later, the box abruptly reappeared.

The toad's eyes were fixed, gray and unblinking. McGowen hurried to open the box, gently lifting the animal out. The toad was no longer squirming. Holding one of its hind feet between his thumb and forefinger, he slowly pulled the limb to its full extent and let go. The leg gradually withdrew, but not all the way. McGowen's thumb pressed the creature's belly, squeezing slightly, then releasing. He laid the frog on its back. It made no attempt to right itself.

"He's dead, for sure. What the hell did you do?" squawked McGowen.

Without a word, von Ang went to the virtual control panel and called up a diagnostic program. He stood motionless, paging through the field, studying the data with rapt attention.

"Got it," said von Ang, pointing at a column of numbers on the control panel. "We'll need another specimen."

"What went wrong?" asked Quan.

"One of the settings was off by a decimal place."

McGowen scoffed. "Off by an order of magnitude! Well now, among theoretical physicists I suppose that's to be expected. You'd never get away with that in aerospace."

Keeping his back to McGowen, von Ang began leafing through the rest of the data. "It's why we do tests."

McGowen left the lab and returned a little while later with a new specimen. "There are more of these outside, if we need them," he said.

With the new toad in position, von Ang fired up the sequencer, initiated the transfer, and within a minute the second toad returned, very much alive, squirming to break free of its cell.

McGowen swept the specimen container from the transfer bed and took it to the medi-bot station. Looking at the multipoint display, he announced, "I don't know what's normal for toads, but the readouts look okay. Maybe we should wait a day or two and see if anything changes."

Quan got up from his chair and approached von Ang. "You think it's ready?"

"The settings are correct," said von Ang.

"I want to try it."

"Can't let you do that, sir," said McGowen. "The machine hasn't been thoroughly tested. Give us another day or two."

"Get on with it then," said Quan. "Time is of the essence."

McGowen muttered, "Time is of the essence? What does that mean?"

33.

That evening inside their bungalow, Lotus was sprawled on a chaise lounge in her silk robe, listening to von Ang's account of the frog mishap. He was berating himself for having entered a wrong decimal place. The image Lotus held of von Ang was that he was the smartest person she had ever known, but now she was watching him pout like a little schoolboy.

"You made the corrections and the equipment is working now, isn't it?" she asked.

Without looking at her, he said, "Yes. I'm sure it's fine."

"Then you shouldn't let this bother you. You are twice as brilliant as anyone else here."

He stood straighter and told her how impatient Quan was to try the new equipment.

Lotus went on praising him, and then took the conversation in an unexpected direction.

"Who do you think should be the first person to test the new equipment? Don't answer that. I'll tell you. It should be me.

This whole deal is way orbital and I want to be part of it. I'm the logical choice. I'm expendable. Besides, all of you have done it already. Why not me?"

"Come now. Don't be ridiculous. You aren't expendable. Anyway, it's Quan's decision, not mine."

Adopting her most adorable attitude, she said, "You're a big boy, Gaston. Assert yourself. Let's do this together. I understand the basics of what you're doing and I can help with the tests."

"I would never risk anything happening to you. I would never forgive myself. Anyway, I think Quan wants to be the first."

"Doesn't make sense. He's funding the entire project and he put you in charge for a reason. You can make this decision. I'm sure he'll go along with whatever you recommend. Someone has to go. Why not me? What do you say?"

"None of us are expendable. I think we should use a volunteer, like we did before."

~~~

Early the next day von Ang brought up the need for a volunteer. Quan and McGowen voted to use someone from outside and von Ang conceded. McGowen borrowed the shiny new glide and headed out to find a volunteer. He flew north for almost an hour until he came to a produce loading station in the town of Salinas. It was a huge facility, over a kilometer long, where long freight transports backed into a series of loading bays at a massive warehouse. As his glide moved slowly past, he saw workers loading crates of green peppers, apples, potatoes, and cabbage onto conveyors. Across from the facility, he spotted a group of men standing near a road sign. They were day laborers looking for work.

McGowen set the glide down on the other side of the loading area and walked back to where the group of men were.

258

Some were sitting on a stack of pallets. A few were smoking cigarettes. Four of them raced up to him, speaking in Spanish. He turned on his translator and introduced himself as the project manager for a research center and began asking about their backgrounds and their interest in being a subject for medical research.

Two of the men turned away, opposed to the idea of being used as guinea pigs. The third man was wearing a wedding ring, a disqualification from McGowen's point of view. The other man, maybe in his twenties, wearing jeans and a faded green jacket, introduced himself as Rolondo. His answers fit the profile. He was single, from a small town about a fifty kilometers east of Salinas. McGowen explained the job—testing new lab equipment—and the pay was a full day's wages for only a couple hours work. Rolando agreed to sign up and followed the big man back to the polished glide.

Back at the lab, the new recruit put on a skinsuit and stood upright with his back against the transfer bed. Emitters on the bed strobed and the bed rotated to horizontal. Von Ang set the duration for thirty seconds and initiated the transfer. To the relief of everyone, the test was successful and Rolando returned unharmed. Following protocol, he was analyzed by the medi-bot system and reminded of his agreement not to speak of his experience to anyone. An hour later McGowen left to return Rolando to where he had been.

As soon as McGowen exited the building, Lotus began her campaign to convince von Ang and Quan that she should be the next one to use the equipment.

"The volunteer is fine, I'm the least important person here and I'm the only one who hasn't had the experience yet."

Without a valid objection, the men acquiesced and within a few minutes Lotus was stepping onto the platform, in a black skinsuit. With her head rested against the transfer bed and a pulse could be seen beating in her neck.

The emitters winked and the sequencer shot her data into the system.

"Okay," said von Ang, "lean back and grab the handrails." He touched a button and the bed automatically rotated to horizontal.

"Are you comfortable?" he asked.

"Yes. I'm fine. It's going to be okay."

"This is a short run. You won't have time for anything more than a quick peek. So just relax and lie still."

"I think you're more nervous than I am," said Lotus, listening to the threshing of blood in her ears.

He touched several places on the view field, rechecking the values for a third time, then looked at her before sending the final command. "Everything looks good."

"For goodness' sake. Have a little faith in yourself. Let's do this."

She looked around at the glossy walls and the stainless steel equipment and, a heartbeat later, she was gone.

She sweeps her arm through the churning particles. Her black appendage sparkles with white fringe. She sits up, folding her legs under her in a lotus position. To her right she sees a black silhouette. It's Gaston. She lies back, watching the multicolor drifts above her. Particles are brushing across her synapses. It's exhilarating. She's alone and she feels exposed, but there's something sensual about it. Then out of the corner of her eye . . . someone is there . . . watching her . . . studying her. It's not von Ang—not Quan—not McGowen. She takes a deep breath and looks around. Wait. The figure has moved to the other side of the room. It's different from the others . . . particles are clumping together, forming a body. Uneasy, she sits up again. Who is it? What is it?

Suddenly, the opaque walls of the laboratory reappeared. Her thoughts were racing as she stepped from the gimbal mount. She

260

stood for a moment, looking down at the floor, clenching her fists.

"Tell me you're okay," said von Ang.

"I'm fine. The transfer is a rush. You've done it, so you know what I mean. Wow. We have a corona surrounding our bodies. It's evidently part of what we are."

"But I saw something else. There was another figure. It looked like someone was standing on the other side of the room. I don't know what it was. It didn't feel right. There wasn't the corona you see on our bodies."

"Can you tell us more about that other figure? What did it look like? Did you hear anything?" asked Quan.

She inhaled fully and looked around the room, then let out a nervous laugh. "I'm not sure, but I think it was someone else. Someone who isn't here." She began to pace. "I need to process this."

Von Ang instructed her to recline on the gurney at the medi-bot station. Sensors quickly scanned twenty-seven different parameters, detecting no adverse effects.

"You're in perfect shape," said von Ang, helping her up.

"I feel energized . . . more focused. It's like every atom in my body was just realigned."

"An exaggerated state of quantum flux is the essence of transference," said von Ang. "I think that's what you're feeling."

She put a hand on his chest. Giving him a pat, she said, "Hold that thought."

Lotus left the laboratory, wearing only her skinsuit and a pair of flex soles, and walked to the edge of the bluff. She sat on a large rock, looking out at the far reaches of the Pacific and stars littering the night sky. The surf churned below her.

Von Ang watched her from the laboratory atrium, respecting her need to be alone, to assimilate the experience at her own pace. Physically she was fine and he couldn't help but admire her exuberance. He let an hour pass. Then, following the pathway lights, he went to her. She was hugging herself, chilled

261

by the night air. Draping his lab coat around her shoulders, he helped her up and walked with her back to the compound.

"So, what do you think?" he asked.

"I am totally in awe," said Lotus. "Seeing what's on the other side opens up a whole new world."

"How do you mean?"

"Obviously, what we see is just the tip of the iceberg. Here we are, living our lives, all the while totally unaware of the depth of our world." She stopped for a moment then went on. "It's an experience I could never describe. It's beyond words."

"It's best expressed in mathematical terms."

"At best, mathematical terms are abstractions," said Lotus, looking at him squarely. "You can model all of the moments of inertia and quantum elements and still not come close to describing the experience itself. It's so much more than words or numbers can convey. It just fills me up in a way that nothing else has. Describing the path is nothing; walking the path is the thing."

34.

Homo sapiens had always demonstrated a propensity to go their own way. It was in their naure. Humankind first split from nature with the creation of artificial units of time. Before that, humans were nature's prisoners, marking time by the cycles of the moon and the seasons. Defining their own reality, they broke free. They invented clocks and calendars and electric lights, and went on to fill the world with human contrivances, taking flight and breaking the sound barrier. The generations that followed heaped technological advances one on top of another until their independence was complete. Far beyond tools for basic survival, they found ways to sustain life in space, breathing manufactured air, eating synthetic food, and procreating in zero gravity. How ironic then, that a radically advanced technology would them lead back, full circle, to discover an even more profound relationship between man and nature.

Quan had waited patiently, for weeks, for another sustained walkabout and, now that Lotus reported seeing a figure in the mist, the suspense was almost unbearable. Was the figure the same as the one Quan encountered thousands of kilometers away? Had it followed them? Or was it something new—an aberration produced by the equipment? Eager to investigate, Quan called his small group together. They arranged themselves in a loose semicircle on chairs in the underground lab and he began. "I want to talk about what's next."

Before he could speak another word, von Ang began talking about the calibrations and how well the machine was performing and the experiments he wanted to pursue.

"I know," said Quan, turning to Lotus. "That's great but I'd like to hear more about what Lotus saw."

Once again Lotus described what she saw and felt. She concluded with a suggestion that the center should be opened up for others to have the experience.

"I like very much what you said," said Quan. "Describing the path is nothing; walking the path is the thing. And you're right. We should invite others—scientists and engineers—to join us."

"Who did you have in mind?" asked von Ang.

"For one thing," said Quan, "we need to find a replacement for Diayu Lee. As for scientists, you should be the one to choose."

"Adding more people won't bring results any quicker," said von Ang. "Like adding more women doesn't bring a pregnancy to term any faster, science can't be rushed."

"Many people are interested in what we've doing here and the work will benefit from having other points of view."

"This is probably the greatest science project on the planet and you went to great trouble to move it to this location to keep it a secret. Why would you open it up to outsiders?"

"I don't mean right away. We need to document the findings and publish first. There'll be plenty of time for you to do
264

your tests. You'll publish your paper then we'll decide who to invite."

Encouraged, von Ang said, "The new machine far surpasses what we built on Kau Yi Chau; however, I need more time to work with the system and I really don't need help."

"All in good time. Now that the machine is ready, so am I," said Quan.

He walked over to the new gimbal mount, removed his outer garments, letting them drop to the floor, revealing a black skinsuit underneath.

"I'm not taking instruments. I only want to see if there are any changes. Give me five minutes." He grabbed the handrails, settling himself against the transfer bed.

"We should do more testing before you—"

"Please. You've already tested with two others. Just do it."

Seeing that von Ang was hesitating, Quan stepped away from the gimbal mount and looked at each of them thoughtfully.

"Listen," he said. "There's something I haven't told you. Something you haven't seen."

"What are you talking about?" asked von Ang.

"I don't really need the equipment. Better if I show you," he said.

Quan lowered his head, arms at his side. He closed his eyes and concentrated. For a moment, nothing happened. Then slowly, his body became grainy and little by little it faded and became completely transparent. He was gone.

Lotus broke the silence. "Oh my God."

Then, in a rush, he was back—inhaling, looking up at each of their gaping faces. Exhaling a full breath, he smiled his subtle smile, and said, "You see? I don't need the equipment."

McGowen exclaimed, "Mother Mary and Joseph. I wasn't expecting that."

"Wow!" Lotus blurted.

Von Ang reached over and felt Quan's arm. "Not possible. You cannot transfer without the equipment, not without the energy."

"I would have thought so, too," said Quan. "Not possible. But I can do it. It's a state of mind . . . a skill, and I've practiced." He pointed toward the bed. "The machine is like a trainer. It developed a kind of knowing inside me, like a sixth sense."

"Incredible," said McGowen. "But how?"

"I don't know how," said Quan. "I can only do it for a few minutes. I still need the equipment to sustain it for longer."

"It's certainly outside of anything I can explain," said von Ang. "How do you feel?"

"It requires some exertion, but I feel fine," said Quan.

Von Ang said, "I'd like to order a brain wave scanner to monitor and see what changes take place when you do this."

"I'd be curious to see that, as well," said Quan. "Go ahead and order one."

Looking at each of them, Quan could see they were in awe but troubled at the same time. To them, his ability was confounding and unexplainable. For him it was second nature.

"I'd like to learn. Can you teach me?" asked Lotus.

"I can try, but I'm not sure where to begin."

"Can you do that again?" asked McGowen.

"Not right now," said Quan. "It takes energy. I need to rest a bit."

Returning to the gimbal, he addressed von Ang. "Now, if you would, please indulge me and set the timer for five minutes."

Von Ang went to the control panel, deeply reflecting on Quan's demonstration. He set the parameters as if he was in a trance.

Quan stepped up to the mesh and grabbed the handrails. The sequencer flashed, the bed rotated, and the countdown began.

The instant Quan was gone, McGowen said, "Stoat, man. He's able to cross over at will."

"It appears so," said von Ang.

266

"Fantastic," said Lotus. "That's about as far out from what I know of physics as you can get. How could you just propel yourself into another dimension?"

"It's beyond all that I know," said von Ang.

The transfer feels somehow cleaner and quicker—like being in a high-performance vehicle. The clouds of particles are seem thicker than he remembers, they blot out everything, like being buried alive in a sandstorm. He dismounts, takes a few steps, and reaches into the swirling particles. Nothing there. He moves into the thick atmosphere and tries to grab a fistful. Nothing.

"Father," he shouts.

Particles in front of him suddenly arrest, held there by some unseen force. Clumps form. A head. Shoulders. A torso. Streams of particles twist and begin to fill in the shape—the manifestation of his father.

Can't be him . . . thousands of kilometers from where he disappeared. . . . but . . .

Purple and green eyes stare at him.

"What am I looking at? What are you?"

[A marker in space-time.]

"Where is my father?"

The reply comes immediately, inside his mind.

[Here.]

"Prove who you are," demanded Quan.

[Prove who you are.] The specter repeats.

Questions are useless. He has no rapport with this . . . this thing. The authentic memories of his father have been eroding since his first encounter with this thing. Memories of a distinguished gentleman are being replaced by memories of this strange incarnation. The relationship and the dialogues they shared . . . memories are being replaced by these bizarre exchanges.

"How is it possible you're here, so far from New Hong Kong?"

[Space is the illusion.]

"Where are you? Where did you come from?"

[Everywhere. Nowhere.]

The likeness takes on an iridescent shift and its features soften.

Frustrated by the constant riddles, Quan strikes to the heart of what he wants to know.

"What is your true nature?"

Particles snap back into position.

[Infinite consciousness.]

"Explain."

[All is all . . . all things, all places, all times . . . all mind.]

What does he mean? Life as a primary element? Life as an element that pervades everything—life as a constant—a primordial mind—an infinite consciousness—all part of a primordial mind? The mind of . . . go ahead . . . say it . . . make the leap . . . the mind of God.

Spontaneously, he blurts out, "I want to know God."

[Jump into the abyss—arms and legs waving free.]

"Show me."

Without warning, Quan is assaulted by a fury of particles. His mind is suddenly still. His consciousness is expanding into endless space. Around him is a kaleidoscope of images—eyes looking through eyes, within eyes, within eyes. Infinite manifestation. In front of him are images of his childhood, the dynasty, his sense of duty, his bond with Sealy, the discovery. Images drift away, merging into the vastness.

Hold on to those memories. Those are my identity. He said arms and legs waving free . . . must I give up my identity in order to know that primordial mind?

His mind strobes, seeing an enormous array of things. He's aware of a cosmic sentience . . . an infinite consciousness . . . the mind of a gigantic primordial singularity.

268

Quan lies on the transfer bed, eyes wide open, in awe of what he has seen. Von Ang and Lotus and McGowen are there, next to him, prodding him. Their mouths are moving. He can't hear them.

"Father?" he hears himself say.

"Are you okay?" asks McGowen. His voice sounds as if it's coming from another room.

"I'm okay. What are you doing here?"

"We've been here all along, watching you. You've been lying there, laughing and crying. We thought you'd lost your mind."

"I have no idea . . . maybe . . ." Quan propped himself up on one elbow, still somewhat disconnected. He wiped a tear from under his eye, looked at it, and laughed.

"A laugh-tear," he said.

He stared at them intensely and said in hushed tones, "Now I know what we are."

"Sir?" McGowen broke in. "We should check you."

Instead Quan lay back again and sighed, realizing how trivial were the concerns of this world. People scurrying around like Alice's White Rabbit, oblivious of their legacy—ants on a little blue planet hurtling through space where lifetimes pass in milliseconds. So many searching . . . so few finding answers.

McGowen coaxed him up and walked him to the medi-bot. Once again Quan emerged with no discernible abnormalities except for the elevated alpha waves. Passing von Ang on the way to the elevator, he said, "Was there something you wanted to tell me?"

"Yes," said von Ang. He looked at Quan carefully, wondering how he knew. "I've been working on the research paper and a few days ago I gave it to Lotus for proofreading. By the way, she thoroughly understands what we're doing. I added her name as a contributor along with your father and yourself. I thought it was the right thing to do."

"And?"

"It's complete and I submitted a summary of the paper to the *International Journal of Quantum Physics.* This morning I received word back from them. They've agreed to publish and invited us to present our findings at the next conference, three weeks from now."

"Where?"

"The conference will be held in Paris. We got in just before the deadline."

"Great," said Quan. "Make arrangements for you and me and Lotus."

"What about Mr. McGowen?"

Looking back toward the big man, Quan said, "He should stay and keep an eye on the place."

"Right you are," said McGowen. "Never cared much for France, anyway."

35.

Sealy was in the bathroom at her parent's house when her com line bipped. The ID was Lotus.

Not going to answer that.

The bipping stopped—a moment later it started again. *Annoying.* She let it continue and it went to voice mail.

"Hi sis. I know you can hear me. Come on. Pickup."

Exasperated, Sealy said, "I'm here Lotus."

"How are you?"

"If you really want to know, I'm not great. I'm tired most of the time. I'm moody and my body . . . well, I have this belly, you see . . . big belly and my breasts are swollen. My clothes don't fit. I itch. My legs hurt. I have dizzy spells. I have to pee a dozen times a day and I leak. Besides all that, I haven't heard from Quan. I can't concentrate on my class work, and I'm about to jump out of my skin. So, how great is that?"

"It sounds grim and I'm concerned about you. I know what you're going through is hard and so I arranged for you to have a treat. I scheduled someone to give you a massage and she should be there in an hour."

"That's totally unexpected. What't gotten into you?"

"Just let me know if you need anything? I can come back and help if you want."

"I've never known you to be concerned about me before. You've changed. What's going on there."

"You know about the machine they built—the one they moved here?"

"I know a little about it. Yes," said Sealy.

"You know, it can project things into other dimensions."

"Yes. Quan told me that."

"Well, the machine sent me across."

"Tell me you're making this up."

"Not at all. I saw the other dimensions and it was life changing—just amazing."

"They're using you for experiments? Why would you let them to do that?"

"No, no. I wanted to. It's safe and I'm fine. I had a full medical afterward and it's all good."

"I shouldn't be surprised. You've always been adventurous. And what about Quan? Was he there when you did this?"

"He was there. He didn't tell you?"

"I haven't heard from him," said Sealy.

"So, he hasn't told you about what he can do."

"What are you talking about?"

"No one can explain how he does it. He can shift himself into the other dimensions without using the machine. He just closes his eyes and disappears."

Sealy was quiet, thinking about the consequences of losing Quan to that other place.

"He can just will himself right out of this world," said Lotus. "I saw him do it. He completely disappeared right in front of me."

272

"Something's not right. Why wouldn't he tell me? There's something not right. I can feel it. How is he? Does he seem different?"

"Don't worry. He's in great shape. Nobody else can do what he can do."

"You make it sound like it's a wonderful thing but none of what you've told me is normal. Are you sure he's all right?"

"Absolutely. His med readings are all good."

"This really concerns me. Why he hasn't told me. It's a big deal. Why wouldn't he tell me?"

"I'm sure he was going to. Sorry if I spoke out of turn."

"I should go there. I want to see what's going on."

"Oh, and there's more good news. Gaston has been invited to present a research paper at a conference in Paris in a couple of weeks. I helped him write it. Quan will be going, too. You should join us."

"Quan should have told me."

"He has a lot on his mind right now. I'm sure he…"

"You don't need to make excuses for him," said Sealy, cutting her off. "What are the dates? I'm going to Paris."

After the call ended, Sealy's hormones demanded release and tears came to her eyes. Blotting the rivulets from her cheeks with a handkerchief, she climbed into bed and pulled the soft duvet up over her breasts. Initiating a view field, she compared flights to Paris. They were faster than going to California. That was a relief, and Paris was a destination she was familiar with. She and Quan had been there together a few times. On one of the trips, they attached a heart-shaped lock to a fence along the Seine. Perhaps it was still there. The thought lightened her mood and she booked her flight.

Quan had been a bad boy but he was still her banlu and it was time they talked.

"Seal?"

"I haven't heard from you. Are you too busy to call?"

"I'm very sorry," he said. "I've been meaning to but we're just getting started here and there have been so many things to take care of."

"Lotus commed a few minutes ago and told me she's been participating in the experiments."

"Yes. She's fine."

"She also told me that you're able to make yourself disappear. What in the world is going on? Has she lost her mind? Or have you? You know I expected you to come back soon but you're still there."

"Everything's all right," he said. "What she told you is true. Strange as it seems, it's something I learned to do. It's a new skill. I was waiting for the right time to tell you. Don't be angry. I'll be back soon."

"Like when? Lotus told me you are going to Paris next."

"Sealy, please understand. I need to be away a little while longer. And yes, it's true we're going to Paris for a conference. You must be going through a difficult time and I wish I was there to comfort you. Soon, my love, soon."

Even as he placated, he knew what her reaction would be and he could hear the disappointment in her voice.

"I'm concerned about what you're doing. Lotus has been experimented on and you can make yourself disappear. These are things you should have told me about."

"You're absolutely right. This has become more than just a research project. It's complicated. I'm sorry I haven't been more forthcoming, but I will be."

"And what about Paris. Weren't you going to tell me?"

"It's a technical conference."

"I've booked a flight. I'm going to Paris, too. I need to see you."

"That's the best news I've heard since I've been here," said Quan. "I miss you and Paris has always been a special place for us. I'm sorry I've been so preoccupied. I should have been the one to tell you—to arrange it. We'll be staying at the Le Meurice.

274

The conference itself is going to be boring. You should come after it's over and we can spend time together."

36.

The intrusion began innocently enough. Quan opened an e-mail from an unknown address. It read, "Beginnings are always awkward. You must be going through a difficult time." He didn't think much of it; however, a day later he got another message from the same anonymous sender. This time the tone was strangely personal. "I hope the best for you and Sealy. My thoughts and prayers are with you."

Then the calls began. Com channels rang four times between 3:00 and 4:00 in the morning. When answered, there was no one on the other end. The same thing happened again the following night.

Quan installed a route tracer. And the next night, when the calls came, he answered. No one was there however, the route tracer was able to identify the source. Quan tried the number. To his surprise, it answered . . . a recording stating the dining hours of a restaurant in Chicago.

The next day von Ang changed the com numbers and added a second firewall. Mail accounts were closed and new ones opened. A few days later a different breach occurred. The LÓNG website sent a confirmation: All passwords were blocked, and in the site's comment section was a new posting: "Quan Jintao Is Our Savior!"

McGowen sent out a global search, looking for help. Several contacts referred him to an IT expert in the United States, a man called Green.

Green's company, Allied Cyber Task Force, didn't take every case that came along. Most of their available hours were delegated to ongoing contracts with several major corporations. Green wasn't looking for new business, but he listened patiently while Quan made a compelling case for helping the new venture. "We're on the verge of a major breakthrough and need all the protection we can get—no matter the cost."

"I'll let you know by the end of the day," said Green.

With relative ease, after disconnecting, Green hacked into the LÓNG website and the Research Center's com lines and downloaded three months' worth of com data. An hour elapsed while one of his custom programs sifted through hundreds of communications, zooming in and out, checking for authenticity and following curious reroutes. Eyes darting back and forth, Green looked at the results and followed down a lead—an IP proxy. From pier to pier, he followed it to a facility in Los Alamos, New Mexico.

He mumbled to himself. *The Los Alamos Nuclear Lab? Can't be. No one can hack that stack.* He knew, because he designed it—five different layers, each with a different OS and different rotating passwords. Anyone who could penetrate that security stack was someone Green definitely wanted to meet. He opened a com line to McGowen.

Green's real name was Irwin Shaw. Early in his career one of his clients started calling him Green after seeing his exorbitant invoices. The nickname stuck.

McGowen answered and switched on vidi com. Green was an unshaven man of forty-two, whose uniform consisted of jeans and a dress shirt, usually white and always worn tails out. His eyes were quick and his was manner dismissive and blunt. He stood at a workstation and while he talked, his hands were busy below.

"I'll take this on with one condition. I want complete control of your systems. No interference. Just go about your business and let me do my job. It's a lot easier for me to find the bad guys if they think no one's looking."

"You'll need our passwords," said McGowen.

"Nah, I'm already in. We'll fix that later. For now, just sit tight."

After the call ended, Green hooked tracers onto all of the laboratory's access points, then returned to the link at Los Alamos. Finding no evidence of an outside hack, he guessed it must be someone inside the facility. He'd need help from the other side of the fence. The on-site security manager was Miles Lungrin, someone Green worked with before.

"A civilian site being hacked from our facility," said Lungrin. "That's a switch. I'll call around. Maybe someone's investigating the Brane Research Center. But if it turns out to be someone who tunneled through Los Alamos from outside, that's a felony."

While Green was on the line with Lungrin, an e-mail came through to Quan: "You should tell everyone how lucky they are to have you as a mentor."

McGowen opened a com line to Green to report the intrusion and was told abruptly, "I've seen it. I told you to sit tight. We're on our way to Los Alamos." The com line disconnected.

McGowen wondered who Green meant when he said "we," and why they were going to Los Alamos.

~~~

Los Alamos National Laboratory
Los Alamos, New Mexico

Green's shoes were heating up as he walked across the dusty tarmac from one of the huge glide hangers to the overhang of the main entrance. The blazing New Mexico sun was pricking his skin like a barrage of needles. Waiting for him inside was a man almost two meters tall, buzz cut, belly pressing against his short-sleeved shirt and a security card tethered around his neck.

"Miles," said Green, shaking his hand, "you never change."

"Not unless I have to," said Lungrin. "How you been?"

"Same old."

They traveled through a maze of air-conditioned hallways, descending in an elevator to the fourth underground level, where they entered a small room with a wall-to-wall view field across one end and four desks equally spaced across the floor. Each desk was equipped with a view field and the LANL emblem, rotated in each field in synchrony. Lungrin sat at one of the desks and the emblem dissolved, leaving only a command prompt. He entered a string of characters, then got out of the chair and stepped back without saying a word.

"Okay, buddy, have a seat. You've got network access."

Within two minutes, Green located an internal account showing an access history to the IP address he'd uncovered. A couple more minutes and he decrypted the password and recovered several gigs including recent deletions. There were files containing data on each of the Jintao family including birthdates, passwords, and ID numbers. He retrieved files lifted from the LÓNG website and access codes for the Brane Research Center.

Standing behind him, Lungrin said, "I've seen enough. Let's see who we've got here."

Lungrin went to one of the other terminals and logged in. "She's in the IT support group—part of our outreach program." He scrolled past several windows. "Name is Nona Smith."

"Can we get her in here?" asked Green.

Minutes later, in walked a wiry woman with a wide face and black pigtails. She wore a plaid flannel shirt, faded jeans, and well-worn cowboy boots. Below her broad cheekbones and downcast eyes, her lips were clamped tight.

"Have a seat," said Lungrin, placing a small yellow card on the table. "Supervisor Miles Lungrin taking the statement of Nona Smith at Los Alamos Nuclear Laboratories, New Mexico."

Lungrin asked her for permission to record and she acquiesced without hesitation. He slid the yellow card closer. "You've agreed to cooperate with this interview of your own free will. Is that correct?"

"Yes."

"Are you familiar with the name Jintao?"

"Yes."

"We've reviewed files deleted from your computer here at LANL. The files contained personal data on the Jintao family including passport numbers and banking information. You've read their personal e-mails and listened to their personal voicemails. Do you admit doing this?"

"Yes."

"You've collected proprietary information including banking information. Is this true?"

"Yes, but not intentionally."

"Do you admit sending messages to Quan Jintao and placing com calls to him?"

She sat up proudly. "Yes."

"Why? Why did you do these things?"

Opening her eyes wide, Nona spoke in a self-assured tone. "I've been sending messages to the LONG website ever since it was launched and they've ignored me. For the last few weeks, it seemed like no one was managing the site at all. I

280

thought if I showed them how helpful I could be, they'd let me be part of what they're doing."

"How were you being helpful?"

Looking squarely at Lungrin, she said, "I'm a true believer. I totally understand the LÓNG philosophy and I have so much to offer them. I'm Navajo and the LÓNG site makes references to many of my tribe's most sacred beliefs. To help, I added things to their website—things that were missing—other people liked what I added. I was helping but the site didn't respond, so I tracked down the site creator, Quan Jintao. I read his incoming mail. I wasn't trying to do anything wrong. I didn't steal anything."

A transcript of the interview was brought up on the view field and she was asked to endorse it. Without protest she placed her hand into the view field. Lungrin added his endorsement.

"That's it. I'm done here," said Green, looking over his shoulder. "I trust you'll deep-six the files and nuke the links."

"I'll take care of it," said Lungrin, looking at the woman. "And any copies she's made."

After Lungrin finished giving Nona Smith a piece of his mind, two security guards escorted her to her cubicle where she packed up. She was escorted out of the building, carrying her personal belongings in a cardboard box. Around the corner, in the employee lot, the guards stood by as she got into her dilapidated compact hydro. They radioed ahead to the security gates and watched her car drive away, disappearing down the road in a trail of dust.

Once he was airborne, Green reported to McGowen. "She's out of your life. If we hadn't caught her, I have no doubt she would have shown up on your doorstep. Typical stalker profile: delusional, wants to be part of something big, something to give meaning to her life. They fired her but aren't pressing charges. I suggest you do the same. You could charge her with identity theft, but since no actual damage was done, she probably wouldn't get more than a slap on the wrist. We can get a restraining order but I don't think it's worth the trouble. The main thing is that she knows we have her number and if she's smart she'll consider herself lucky and just walk away."

"I'm impressed. You work fast," said McGowen.

"There are a few more things I'm going to do for you so that this sort of thing doesn't happen again."

Five hours later Green reported installing hefty security stacks on the LÓNG website and the Research Center computers. He set hooks for intruders and connected everything to a backup system. He also recommended setting up a security field around the lab compound and a full-time IT person to monitor all systems.

"Looks like you have the start of something important," he told McGowen. "That can attract the best and the worst kinds of people. Take care."

With the New Mexico episode wrapped up, McGowen gave Quan the good news. There were hundreds of messages that had gone unread and Quan set himself to the task of reviewing them.

Following Green's advice, McGowen posted a job description, looking for a full-time IT manager. Within twenty-four hours a dozen résumés were in front of him and the top three applicants were invited to an online interview. McGowen's interest was peaked by a young dark-skinned man with neatly trimmed black hair—clearly the front-runner.

"My name is David Gupta," he said, speaking with a slight East Indian accent. "From what your posting says, I'm perhaps overqualified for your needs. However, I have an interest in science and your company appears to be a research facility. With our mutual interest, I'd very much like to work with you."

"In your résumé, you cite Allied Cyber Task Force. You worked with Green?" asked McGowen.

"Most certainly. We worked together—a most successful project. Unfortunately, I cannot discuss any details."

282

"When I ask Green about your work, what will he say?"

"I believe he will say that I am an expert at coding and cybersecurity."

"We need someone full time and, when I say full time, I mean 24/7. We have a lot to do here and we're understaffed. We have living accommodations. Are you willing to relocate?"

"I could make that work, although I'll need to go back home from time to time."

Concluding the interview, McGowen made a generous offer which Gupta accepted.

A few days later, David Gupta arrived with suitcase in hand and McGowen saw him settled in. David was directed first to the task of evaluating the data backup systems. David was fast and, by the end of his first week, he had switched their intranet to Software Defined Networking. He organized and secured their data archives, and compiled a lengthy list of other programming assignments. After reviewing the list, McGowen gave him a green light to proceed. David went first to the complex transporter interfaces, cobbled together months earlier on Kau Yi Chau Island. Here was something that warranted his skills.

37.

Hotel Le Meurice, Paris

Under the extended portico of the Hotel Le Meurice, a sleek black limo-glide was hovering while valets opened its doors. Quan, Gaston, and Lotus stepped out. In front of the eighteenth-century façade, two doormen in gold-buttoned burgundy uniforms stood at the top of a broad marble staircase. They opened the tall polished-brass doors and golden light from a huge crystal chandelier reflected off the polished marble floor.

Inside, the three colleagues paused on top of an inlaid marble crest of Le Meurice. To the left was a reception desk, made of polished hardwoods framed with ornate gold oak leaves. Behind the desk stood a man with alert eyes and a faintly amused smile. His alabaster head was shaved clean with only shadows where his beard and receding hairline would have been. His suit was snug and the collar of his crisp white shirt was turned up. His greeting was civil. *"Bonsoir.* Le Meurice welcomes you." His eyes flicked down to his notes. "I see you have just arrived from

California. I trust you had a pleasant journey. Forgive me if I mispronounce your name. Is it Geen-toe?"

"Jint-ow," corrected Quan, watching light reflecting off the man's head.

"*Pardon, Monsieur Jintao.* We have your reservations: two gentlemen and two ladies . . . separate bedrooms with adjoining salon. Is that correct?" He looked at the three of them.

"We are three for the first three nights and a fourth will join us," said Quan.

"*Trés bon.* We are happy to have you. Ah, and I see this is your first time with us. It will be our pleasure to provide you with complimentary champagne. And let us know if there is anything we can do to make your stay more enjoyable. For current venues, you may wish to speak with our concierge." He gestured toward an antique desk on the other side of the lobby where a young woman smiled pleasantly.

"Elise can arrange sightseeing, entertainment, shopping, dinner reservations—anything you may wish to undertake during your stay. The bellman will show you to your rooms." He gestured toward the elevators, where a uniformed attendant stood waiting.

"*Excusez-moi,*" said von Ang. "Are there any messages?"

"Ah, *oui.* And you will be able to access them from the privacy of your salon," said the desk manager.

"*Merci,*" said von Ang.

The elevator was as opulent as the lobby—marble floor, inlaid walls, coffered ceiling in gleaming gold. The cabin exhibited no indication of movement until the door opened on the ninth floor.

Opening the door to their apartments, the bellman led them into the posh salon: tasseled velvet drapes hanging from the high ceilings, Louis XVI tables, chairs, and settees on top of Bracquenié area rugs and aged parquet floors, French doors opened to a shallow balcony overlooking the Tuileries Garden and the Paris skyline.

"Sealy will love this," said Lotus. "But, it's a little too museum-like for my taste."

Quan walked past her and out onto the balcony. Looking at the lights across the cityscape, he remembered. *They call this the City of Light.*

Uniformed porters set their luggage on stands while a white-gloved waiter poured flutes of champagne and set a tray of hors d'oeuvres on a table in the center of the room.

Von Ang withdrew to the ornate desk at the side of the salon, lighting up a view field and pulling up his mail.

Lotus picked up a glass and an hors d'oeurve and wandered onto the balcony next to Quan. "Think I'll call room service and see about dinner," she said. "I'm famished. What would you like?"

"Prawns, if they have them." Looking down to the walkway below, he watched couples strolling in the park. "Sealy and I walked in that garden. Three times, I think."

"Very romantic," said Lotus.

"You know, I should have been the one to tell Sealy about the experiments—especially about my new ability. It came as a surprise to her."

"Sorry. What can I say. Sometimes I'm a klutz."

"I'm sure she'll get over it. I'm just saying it would have been better if I had told her."

"Sorry. I just didn't think." She turned toward the door and said, "I'll go see if they have prawns."

Looking down at the people in the park, Quan thought, *Highly functioning robots—they don't even know what they are— data storage units. All of us are programmed by what's in our memory banks.*

He turned and went back inside, asking von Ang, "Any interesting messages?"

"The usual. Colleagues saying hello, conference organizers confirming our speaking time, requests from the press, and so on. There was one from McGowen, a general FYI saying

286

that David Gupta asked if he could use the machine. McGowen said no, of course."

The waiters returned, removing the canopies and setting up for a late supper. A white tablecloth and three place settings were laid down, and the three travelers took their seats.

With the same detached courtesy exhibited by the desk manager, the waiter asked, "Is there anything else you require?"

After waiting for the others to comment, Quan said, "No. I think we are all right for now."

"Bon appétit," he said, briskly pivoting and leaving the room.

After the door closed, von Ang said, "You know, we're going to have our hands full tomorrow."

"What do you mean?" asked Lotus.

"Word travels fast and we're a hot topic," said von Ang. "Tomorrow will be a media circus."

While they dined, Quan's thoughts returned to his father. In the process of modifying his genome, senior Jintao had imbued Quan with an amazing gift. He created the first of a new generation: a human capable of traveling along the quantum flux. In his last excursion, his father's totem had guided him to witness a region that transcended matter. The nature of it was difficult to understand.

Thoughts propagate in a place that transcends matter. Memories are held in a configuration of loci within the neural net . . . a collection of atomic valences . . . a connectome. And the connectome is just a unique set of reference points. Evidently that connectome can be transferred to other dimensions.

We are both—pawns and kings. DNA makes us what we are—generated from millions of experiments tried and lessons learned—it governs us and at the same time makes us able to transcend nature.

38.

At the northern outskirts of Paris, a mag-lev train pulled up next to the four cylindrical towers of the Cap 21 Conference Center. Its doors opened and another twenty attendees disembarked for the 27th Annual International Conference on Quantum Physics. Inside the enormous three-story atrium, sunlight filtered in from a stained-glass dome overhead and a cacophony of foreign voices reverberated throughout.

A distinguished-looking man, bearing a striking resemblance to von Ang, approached them. He was thinner and a few centimeters taller than Gaston, with intense hazel eyes overshadowed by a pair of remarkably thick eyebrows. Von Ang introduced the man as his father.

"This is Quan Jintao and Lotus Xiaoping."

Looking at Quan and Lotus, the senior scientist put an arm around his son and declared that he had read the summary of their paper. With authoritarian confidence, he added, "Finally, someone has validated what we knew all along. But who could have guessed it would be my son?" He laughed, taking his hand from Gaston's shoulder and pointing it at Quan. "Reciprocity is the key. You'll see. That's how the whole thing maintains balance."

Hearing this, Quan could not resist saying, "You speak with such certainty. Have you actually seen the whole thing?"

Gaston's father let out a *bwah* sound and turned to his son. "Who is this again?"

"It was actually Quan's father who began the research." He started to talk about the early prototypes, but it was clear his father was only half listening. Quan and Lotus remained mute, watching Gaston's futile effort to maintain his father's attention.

Excusing himself, the senior von Ang embraced his son and hurriedly said, "I'm looking forward to your presentation. We'll get together later. But now there's someone I must talk to." Making his way into the crowd with one hand raised, he called out, "Fritz!"

"That was Papa. What can I say? He is one of a kind . . . really quite brilliant. I think he'll be more helpful once he's seen what we have to show."

Seeing the von Angs together, father and son, reopened a wound in Quan that was still fresh. The work they were about to present was his father's brainchild, yet his father wasn't present . . . in the conventional sense.

A few moments after the senior von Ang departed, a barrel shaped man man with full beard nudged in next to Quan and introduced himself as the director of the Kominsk Research Center in Odessa Russia. He became exuberant when he learned that Quan was connected to the Brane Research Center and insisted on visiting the installation to learn more about their work. After having his invitation deflected and several intrusive questions rejected, the Russian moved on, peevishly muttering under his beard. Quan turned his attention back to his colleagues.

They continued to socialize with other scientists until gradually Quan became aware of an unsettling feeling, like the change in the air when a storm is approaching. A tall woman with large tortoise-rimmed glasses and short brown hair was making her way through the crowd toward them. As she came closer, the badge pinned to her green tweed jacket became legible, identifying her as was the conference chairperson, Simone Peltaire.

Patting von Ang on the arm, in a voice born of kind reflection, she said, "I must discuss an important matter with you."

There was a disconnect between her kind yet straightforward demeanor and what Quan was sensing. It was then that he saw the three dark blue suits coming through the crowd toward him.

Simone Peltaire continued, "It is my duty to inform you that I have been contacted by the Chinese Central Science Committee. They've demanded that your paper be withdrawn. This is an official protest and I am afraid we must honor it pending further investigation."

As the blue suits came up behind Madame Peltaire, one of them looked indignantly at Quan. "It is property of the Chinese people," he said.

Quan straightened, feeling a surge of power inside him. He could see through these men. They were bloated with self-importance but the particles cycling within them were weak. He knew he could crush them with a single blow, however he kept his voice calm and controlled.

"My father began this project and documented it from the beginning. The Chinese government contributed nothing at all and has no legitimate claim."

Madame Peltaire turned to face the three Chinese and asked, "Can you prove that someone other than those named on their paper contributed to the research?"

The Chinese fumed. Two of them argued between themselves while the third said, "Proof you want. He is a Chinese citizen, and this work was done in China. It belongs to the Chinese people. He has no right to make this research public."

Quan turned to the chairwoman nonchalantly. "Their accusations are groundless. The right of eminent domain does not apply to private research, and even if it did, the work we're presenting today was done in the United States, not in China."

While the bickering continued, the Madame Peltaire lit up a small view field and reviewed the letters of protest. Satisfied that there was no mention of a rival claim, she addressed the Chinese directly. "According to the papers you filed, you are not disputing that doctors von Ang and Jintao did the research, and you are not asking for anyone else to be added as co-authors. It seems the heart of your protest is about states' rights. That is a matter which our organization cannot decide. Since you are not disputing that doctors von Ang and Jintao are the authors of this paper, I see no reason to prohibit them from presenting their work."

Another of the Chinese pointed his finger at Quan and spoke in Mandarin, *"You bring shame on the Jintao family name."*

Quan's face became steel. He could have snatched the life from this man, but his voice continued to be calm. "The truth is, you're angry because you weren't able to steal our work. I would advise you to take the next flight back to China. If you persist you'll face a lawsuit."

After a few more barbed exchanges the Chinese left in a huff and Madame Peltaire spoke to Quan in a matter-of-fact tone. "I'm sorry. This happens every once in a while. It goes with the territory. Usually it's someone who claims they had the idea first and wants credit. I should have read the letter more carefully. Their protest will be noted; however, don't worry, your paper will be published in time for the presentation tomorrow. If there are any legitimate grounds for their complaint, they can do as you suggested—file a lawsuit."

"Those people are of no consequence," said Quan.

"*D'accord*," said von Ang.

For the remainder of the day, von Ang, Lotus, and Quan sat in the auditorium, listening to the other presenters. Quan was relaxed, certain that nothing would come of the threats. He thought about the weak energy he witnessed pervading the men in dark suits. There was a darkness entrapping them, engulfing them in their own treachery. He saw them as bad robots, acting on faulty instructions, oblivious to the greater good. He was confident the universal laws of cause and effect would sort them out.

When the conference let out, several news teams converged on Quan and his colleagues and bright camera lights made it difficult to see who was asking questions, but from their accents the reporters were a mix of French, Australian, German, and English. Initially, questions about the Chinese protest were directed at Quan, who curtly declined to comment. Questions directed to von Ang focused on the discovery and what his paper would claim. His replies were highly technical, explaining the reciprocal-universe theory with complexity that most graduate students would find hard to follow.

When Lotus was asked for comment, she simply said, "We're going to present tomorrow. Be patient. It will be worth the wait."

On their way out of the conference, Quan asked von Ang, "Do you think they understood your answers?"

"I certainly hope not," said von Ang with a smile.

Entering their hotel suite, Lotus sidled up to von Ang and slipped her arm under his. Sweetly, she asked, "Are we going out for dinner tonight?"

"I'm sure the restaurants are full. We should have made reservations," he said. "We can call room service."

"Not again," she said. "Let's see what Elise can come up with." She sat at the antique desk and bipped the concierge desk.

The young woman they were introduced to in the lobby appeared in the view field and cheerfully explored their options for dinner.

Within the hour, the three were inside a rooftop restaurant a few blocks from the hotel, sampling molecular haute cuisine. Champagne cocktails, encapsulated in alginate bubbles, dissolved in their mouths. One after another, dishes arrived at their table— laser-sintered squid, esterifications of tangerine over confit of lamb, prismatic lychee pebbles in a mousse of truffled chestnut.

Lotus pulled a handheld viewer from her bag and began to search the news. "You two are all over the news. They say you've discovered an inverse universe, a mirror image of ours. Is that what you told them?" she asked, looking at von Ang.

For the first time, he laughed out loud. "That's very funny," he said "It's tabloid news. They're such fakes. They just make up things when they don't understand the facts. There are very few journalists who have the background to understand what we tell them, but even fewer who are able to make it palatable for the general public."

Savoring every mouthful, Lotus continued to study Quan's mood. His sadness had lifted; however, from time to time, he looked past her, toward the bar. She turned around and followed his glance to an older man in a tight suit who turned away conspicuously. "What are you looking at?" she asked.

"We're being watched," said Quan.

Across town, another meeting was taking place inside the American Embassy; the local CIA section chief was meeting with Markus Bledsoe from the U.S. State Department and Claude Renaut, director of DARPA's Defense Sciences Office in Paris.

"I've read their paper and the field ops report," said Renaut. "They don't disclose anything about the equipment and there are no patent filings. Our surrogate is looking for their source code."

Bledsoe, a large and athletically built man in a beige business suit, spoke through thin lips. "This is worth a fortune. Why haven't they filed?"

"A patent application would tell everyone how it's built," said the section chief, expressing halfhearted interest. "Evidently they're not worried about competition. Probably pretty advanced stuff."

Renaut edged forward in his chair, looking at small viewflex on the table in front of him, thumbing through a copy of the scientific paper. "You see the implications. They get their instruments into the . . . what did he call it?" Sliding his reading glasses up his nose with a forefinger, he continued, "Yeah, the Braneworld. If that equipment was made mobile—think of it. We could go anywhere—do anything."

"This guy Jintao's the one," said Bledsoe. "He's got title to everything, right?"

"Thinks he's pretty slick, the way he's kept things buttoned up," said the section chief nonchalantly. "But his back door is wide open."

"He's holding out for a big payday," said Bledsoe. "I've got a call in to the Appropriations Committee. I'm sure we can get whatever we need for this one. No need to squeeze him if we can buy it, right?"

"Gets my vote," said Renaut.

The CIA chief looked away. "I've got a tail on him. Tomorrow, after the conference, that's the best time to reel him in."

"Don't want to ruffle him," said Bledsoe. "Just a chat. Understood?"

The CIA section chief left his chair, crossed the lounge, and ascended a narrow staircase. At the landing, a scanner at the metal door identified him and he entered a room with a dozen or more people reclining in the slings of their workstations. On the opposite side of the room, he caught the attention of two men standing near a tactical scope. He pointed to a conference room and the two men converged to meet him there. The younger of the two was dressed in a well-tailored gray gabardine suit. He was clean shaven, with an expensive haircut and unshakable eyes. The other man was older, darker, and shorter, wearing a rumpled suit stretched tightly across his back. His hands were thick and hard, his black shoes soft and quiet, and he smelled of tobacco.

"Where's he now?" asked the section chief.

"Having dinner at L'Auberge," said the younger man. "The Swiss guy is with him and his girlfriend."

"Stay on them but don't intercept. I'll let you know when."

39.

The next day, in the main lecture hall, all twelve hundred red velveteen chairs were occupied and nearly thirty members of the press corps were standing against the back wall, some with handheld viewers, some with vidi cameras. Among them were two men who were not affiliated with the media, one tall and dapper, the other short, disheveled, and smelling of tobacco.

Standing at the podium, illuminated by overhead spotlights, the conference chairperson introduced the second presentation of the morning session. "It is my distinct pleasure to introduce Dr. Gaston von Ang and Dr. Quan Jintao from the Brane Research Center. They're here to present their paper entitled, 'Evidence of Dark Matter and Gamma Reflectance in Hyperdimensional Space.' I think you'll find the paper extremely interesting. I give you Dr. von Ang."

Quan and Gaston stepped to the podium and waited for applause to taper off. Von Ang began to read a prepared statement. "Thank you for your kind introduction, Madame

Peltaire, and thank you for the opportunity to be here and present our work. Ladies and gentlemen, it's fair to say that most scientists believe they already understand the basic principles of reality, leaving only the myriad of smaller details to be filled in. The problem with this worldview is that it inhibits us from free inquiry, making it difficult to see reality in any other way. So, what would cause us to break away and see the world in an entirely different way? Well, occasionally it is accidents that pave the way to great discoveries. This is what happened for us. An accident opened up an entirely new field of research."

Behind them, a wall-to-wall view field lit up with two side-by-side images—on the left, a table of energy readings, and on the right, a vidi clip played of the first survey team standing in front of huge antenna that came and went from view. From the first measurements taken at the OB12 reactor, Von Ang carefully stepped through each phase of the research done by Jintao senior. As he went on describing his involvement with the early prototypes and experiments, reporters jockeyed for image capture. He presented vidi clips of instruments disappearing and reappearing and finally, when he displayed the vidi of a white lab rat disappearing and reappearing, noise in the room rose from a murmur to a tumultuous din.

Von Ang pressed on, showing the microlite readings and the gamma transmission tests. Nearing the end of his presentation, he went over the Krakinov calculations and then explained his own lengthy calculus of particle exchange based on the gamma reflectance measurements.

Forty minutes elapsed by the time Von Ang concluded his presentation, and seeing dozens of raised hands, he invited questions.

"I'll take as many questions as I can now and when our time is up, we have a room reserved in the east tower for further discussions."

Several reporters spontaneously shouted out.

Pointing into the crowd, von Ang said, "Yes, the man in the fifth row, tan coat."

"You performed experiments in a higher-dimensional field," said the man, now standing, "but you haven't told us anything about the equipment used. Can you talk about that?"

"I'm able to discuss the results of our experiments," said von Ang. "However, I can't disclose anything about the technology at this time. The equipment is proprietary."

Several voices rang out simultaneously. "Then how are we to verify your findings?"

"We can arrange a visit to our laboratory and you can see for yourself."

Half an hour later, Quan and von Ang were seated behind a table at the back of a small room in the east tower. The room was filled beyond capacity, people overflowing into the outer hallway.

A UPI reporter yelled above the clamor, "Are you the same Dr. Jintao who founded the LÓNG website?"

"Yes, I am," said Quan.

The hubbub reduced to a mild roar.

"What's the connection between this research paper and your website?"

"The research that Dr. von Ang presented today shows evidence of an aspect of nature that was previously hidden from us. That's the physical side of what we've discovered, but there's a metaphysical side, as well," said Quan. "What I've done on the website is an attempt to associate the quantum research with the human experience. In a way, your question is like asking 'What is the relationship between our consciousness and the material world?' Philosophers have tackled that subject for hundreds of years, and we don't have time to get into that today."

Another reporter, seeing incoming text from his bureau chief, looked up and read aloud, "Are you able to transport people into that hyperdimensional place? And if so, what did they see?"

298

Quan interceded before von Ang could answer. "All I can tell you is that using our equipment, we're were able to see aspects of the ninety-six percent of the universe that was previously hidden from us."

After carefully crafting answers for over an hour, Quan and von Ang were able to extract themselves from the Q and A session. They walked quickly down the hallways, shunning several reporters who dogged them. Entering the central lobby, they looked for Lotus, who had stayed in the main conference room to see the other presenters. Answering her wrist disk, she told von Ang that the other presenters were fascinating but nothing as profound as what he had done.

Exhausted, they poured themselves into the train and returned to the hotel, only to find another mob of reporters waiting at the entrance. Two valets rushed to their assistance, clearing a path, shouting, "*Écartez vous. Hors du chemin!*"

Leaving the paparazzi behind, the threesome made their way up to the suite.

Von Ang plopped down on the sofa and said, "I believe your father would be pleased, yes?"

"Indeed. He would," said Quan, ordering tea from the room service view field. "And this is only the beginning."

Minutes later, there was a knock at the door. Quan went, expecting his tea had arrived and was surprised to find himself face to face with a tall young man in a tailored suit, not one of the hotel staff. Behind him was an older, shorter man in a rumpled suit who was looking up and down the hallway.

"Dr. Jintao?"

"Yes?"

"We're from the American Embassy." He flicked open a backlit ID card and tucked it back into his inside pocket. "Your presence has been requested at the embassy."

"What is this about?"

"I was told it has something to do with your visa."

"We've had a long day and we just got back. Have someone com me tomorrow morning."

"I realize you've had quite a day; however, I'm afraid it can't wait. It's an important matter and it shouldn't take much of your time."

"Is this about the Chinese delegation?" asked Quan.

"I don't know anything about that, sir. It's about your reentry into the United States. You should come with us and we'll have you back here as soon as possible."

"I don't understand. My papers are in order. Our attorney saw to that."

Just then a waiter arrived pushing a silver cart with tea service. "*S'il vous plaît excusez-moi,*" said the waiter, stopping while the two men stepped aside.

Resuming the conversation after the waiter left, Quan said, "Does this involve all of us?"

"No, sir. That won't be necessary. The request was just for you, sir."

"I can't understand what possible problem there could be."

The young man looked briefly to the stocky man behind him then said, "We have a high-ranking official in town. He'd like to meet you, and I believe he'll be able to help with whatever the problem is. It would be best if you would come with us. As I said, it won't take long."

"Very well. Wait here," replied Quan. "I'll join you in a minute."

He closed the door and spoke in low tones to Lotus and von Ang. "I have to go to the American Embassy. It's only a few blocks from here—something about my visa. I should be back in an hour. If not, com me."

Lifting his jacket from the chair back, Quan left the suite. As he walked toward the elevators, he thought that something like this was bound to happen. He was becoming accustomed to

300

subterfuge. Waiting for the lift he glanced at the older man next to him—dark features, perhaps Basque, smelling of tobacco. The man's broad shoulders, hard hands, and soft shoes spoke volumes. There was nothing diplomatic about him.

On the rooftop, a matte black glide was waiting and Quan was ushered into the back seat with the younger man. During the short ride to the embassy, Quan's thoughts turned to Sealy and how apprehensive she would have been, if she were there. He was glad she wasn't.

Comfortable and calm, his senses reached out to everything around him—the air rushing past the windows, the sparkling lights below, the shallow breathing of the shorter man in the front seat, and the pungent cologne of the young man to his right.

The glide descended into the embassy garage and steel blast doors closed over it. The two escorts led Quan past a row of government glides and through a side door into the main lobby. An expansive floor of polished travertine stretched out in front of them with a colonnade running down the center. On either side of the colonnade were a series of lounge areas. Each lounge was appointed with a four meter square rug, brown club chairs, an oversized coffee table, and tall ficus trees in earthenware pots at each corner. Quan counted four lounges on each side of the colonnade.

The embassy seemed deserted—until they came to the last pair of stone columns. In the lounge to the right, two men came into view. One of them was built like a weight lifter, his tonsured hair clipped close to the scalp and shaved around his ears. The other man was tweedy and casual-looking, like many of the academics Quan had seen at the conference.

"Ah, Mr. Jintao," said the big man, rising from his chair, a look of readiness on his face. Extending a hand, he said, "Markus Bledsoe, American Embassy, and this is Claude Renaut of our science office here in Paris. Glad you could spare the time."

Bledsoe's accent was a carefully enunciated south Texas drawl. "Come sit for a spell. What can we get for you? I'm having a bourbon. What would you like?"

Quan saw through the pretense. "Science office" meant DARPA, the defense department's research group, and Bledsoe's haircut said military. "Nothing, thank you. Your representative said this was important. It's been a long day. Can we get right to it?"

"Yes. Yes, of course we can. First of all, let me assure you. We're here to help. We've been watching the news and that discovery of yours is very impressive. You're quite a celebrity."

"Your people mentioned something about a visa problem. What exactly is the problem?" asked Quan, planting himself in one of the club chairs. His escorts crossed the lounge and parked themselves next to a marble fireplace that appeared to have never been lit.

"Relax. Everything's under control. You and your associates have temporary visas to do academic research in the U.S., and I just want to be sure you don't run into any problems reentering the country. You know, it's increasingly more difficult for foreign nationals these days, since Dontrum took office."

From a vantage point high above, Quan saw their strategy. They were after the invention. He watched patiently as they did their dance.

"You see," Bledsoe went on, "there's been a little complication. Our state department received a request from the Chinese government and, well, sir, they're asking for your extradition back to China. Seems they intend to charge you with some sort of capital crime. Not a good position to be in. Not good at all."

"They like to play the power card," Quan heard himself say. "But the United States has no extradition agreement with China."

"That's true, not officially. But, believe you me, if our government decides you should be sent back to China, that's

302

exactly where you'd end up." Bledsoe swished the contents of his glass and looked across the room at the two escorts, who stood by with expressions of indifference.

"But don't you worry," Bledsoe continued. "I'm on your side and I know how to handle matters like this. Oh sure, with your clout, you might possibly beat those charges, but why put yourself and your associates through all that? You don't have to go back to China. We can make sure you have safe haven in United States. All we want is a little cooperation."

Quan settled back in his club chair. "It's not difficult to guess what that means."

"Maybe so," said Bledsoe, taking a sip from his tumbler and setting it back on the coffee table. "Why don't I just let Mr. Renaut here explain what we want."

Renaut cleared his throat and looked from Bledsoe to the young Jintao.

"I apologize if this meeting caught you by surprise. You see, Colonel Bledsoe is only here for a short time and he has authority over matters like this."

"So, what is it you want?"

Renaut went straight to the heart of it. "For starters, we'd like to see the plans for the equipment you built and we'd like to build one or two for our own use. We'd like to see what we can do with them . . . like, to see if we can reproduce your experiments."

"Military applications," said Quan.

"Perhaps," said Renaut.

"You know how it is," said Bledsoe, attempting to sugarcoat the proposition. "We're a military state now, and we're asked to conduct peacekeeping missions all over the planet."

"As well as regime changes and covert operations," said Quan.

Bledsoe edged forward in his chair, his face becoming stone. Quan became aware of the remarkable span of his shoulders. "Look. I understand why you might not approve of

303

some of the things we do, but here's the deal. You get to continue doing what you're doing on American soil indefinitely in exchange for a little cooperation. I have authority to arrange permanent resident status for you and all of your people. And, in return, all we want is to play around with this invention of yours. Now that's a pretty fair trade, don't you think?"

"It's been a long day. I'll need to think about it," said Quan.

"It's been a long day for me, too, Mr. Jintao, and believe me, I have other things to take care of. Listen. If I'm going to help you, we need to come to an agreement toot sweet—right here and now. So, what'll it take? What do you want?"

"What every American wants," said Quan. "A grant, of course. We need money to continue our research."

"How much money are we talking about?"

Without hesitation, as if the words spoke themselves, Quan said, "Fifty billion dollars."

Bledsoe froze, studying Quan carefully for a moment. Then the corners of his mouth turned up. "I like your style," he said, picking up his glass again and shifting back into the chair. "But lordy, give me a number I can work with."

"All right, here's a number you can work with. In a conflict situation, your military spends that much in a week. Using this technology, you would get your return on investment in a matter of days. There's nothing else in the world that can give you this kind of advantage and you know it."

Renaut interjected. "For fifty billion we would want the plans and the exclusive right to build the machines ourselves. And we'd want your assistance in making modifications down the road if necessary."

"Sorry. No exclusive rights. Too many other scientists want to conduct these experiments. We retain all rights to the equipment design, and changes are at our discretion," said Quan.

"I don't think you're getting it. Let me make myself clear," said Bledsoe, shooting a glance at the two agents who

304

perked up and stood at the ready. "I make one phone call and you're permanently locked out of the U.S. and your laboratory. Is that clear enough for you?"

Quan felt a familiar stirring in him. From his first glimpse of Bledsoe, he anticipated some form of threat would come and now the strategy was obvious. "You make yourself perfectly clear," said Quan.

He was tempted to disincorporate, fade from view and walk out of the embassy. But that would aggravate the situation and reveal something best kept secret. The Americans were offering safe haven and the possibility of funding, and there was more to be gained by cooperating.

"It looks like you have me at a disadvantage," said Quan. "All right. I can make the plans available on a nonexclusive basis for the grant and assurances that we can continue our work in California."

Bledsoe sat back in his chair, his gaze riveted on young Quan. Keeping their expertise on American soil was essential and granting them permanent visas wasn't going to be a problem. Fifty billion would require some arm twisting but it was doable— he would need Renaut's help to sell the Appropriations Committee on the idea of weaponizing the transfer technology.

Renaut cut the silence. "So, if we give you an endowment, as you called it, and permanent visas . . . what do we get in return?"

Turning his attention to Renaut, Quan said, "What you really want is to develop our technology into something you can use in the field. Right?"

"Right. A mobile version would be highly desirable."

"I can't give you any guarantee that a mobile version is possible. It will be up to your engineers."

"Understood."

"In return for visas and endowment, you'll get the machine design plans and we'll be available to answer any questions your engineers might have."

Bledsoe swished the contents in his glass and said, "Damn. You're some kinda somethin' else, Mr. Jintao." He drained the remaining sip from his glass and rose to his feet. "I'll see what we can do about the money and you'll hear from me in a few hours."

On the way back to Le Meurice, Quan reviewed his parries and thrusts with Bledsoe. He could see that Bledsoe still had one move left and it was a strong one. But so did Quan. On the occasions when the senior Jintao allowed him to attend negotiations, Quan was obedient to sit and observe and not say a word. Afterward, his father would ask for Quan's interpretation of what he'd seen and he'd fill in details of what Quan had missed. His father ended each lesson with the same statement: "Always strive to accumulate the winning hand before entering into a negotiation. It's much easier to deal from a position of strength—gives you the ability to walk away from the table at any time."

To anyone else, Quan's predicament would have seemed impossible. There he was, sequestered in Paris, with the coveted equipment nine thousand kilometers away, protected only by his loyal Scotsman. Quan was a pariah in his homeland, and now the most dangerous military complex in the world was breathing down his neck. And there was his sweetheart and their baby to think about.

He relaxed into the glide seat. A peaceful energy pervaded him and his subtle smile returned.

Von Ang closed the double doors to the balcony and pulled the heavy velvet draperies shut, blocking the chill night air. A small fire was crackling in the ornate marble fireplace and he plunked himself down on a velvet sofa next Lotus. Learning more about Paris, she read from her handheld viewer. "The name Paris derives from the Gaulish tribe known as the Parisii. The city was named Paris in 360 AD. The metropolis is home to nineteen million residents and . . ."

Quan entered the suite and removed his coat. "It's warm in there," he said.

"That didn't take long," said von Ang. "What is the problem? What do they want?"

"They were using our visas as leverage and they're intrigued with the idea of using our equipment as a weapon."

"You said no, of course. Didn't you?" quipped Lotus.

"It's complicated. Our ability to stay in the United States is predicated on cooperating with them. And for me, going back to China isn't an option."

"Couldn't you move somewhere else?" asked Lotus.

"You're welcome to stay with me in Switzerland," said von Ang.

"Very kind, but there's another solution." Quan's tone was serious. "Can you contact the editor of the conference journal? I want to submit an article for the conference daily."

"I'll see what I can do, but this is very short notice." Von Ang left the comfort of his sofa in a single fluid movement and went to retrieve the editor's contact information.

"Are we going to be all right?" asked Lotus.

"Never doubt that," said Quan, putting his hands behind his head. "We're on the right path and I have a plan."

"Switzerland doesn't sound so bad," said Lotus, taking a sip of Chambourd.

Quan slung his suit jacket over the back of an ornate chair and sat at the desk. The view field turned on and he began to write an article. Then he fingered his way past the Jintao logo, to the secret files, initiating a file transfer protocol.

After a few minutes, von Ang reentered the room, announcing, "You have an hour—and he reserves the right to edit or reject your article."

"Plenty of time," said Quan, speaking quickly. "Listen, I should tell you what this is about. It's clear that many of your colleagues want access to the equipment, so does the CSC and the U.S. military. This article will make our predicament known to the public and throw a spotlight on what these government agencies are trying to do. Even though the invention is proprietary, sooner or later one of them will get their hands on the plans. Then the scientific community will be told it's classified and won't have access. The best defense is passive resistance."

"Passive resistance?" asked von Ang.

"When your opponent pulls, you let go. I'm going to publish the machine plans for everyone to see."

"What?" said von Ang. "You can't be serious. The machine belongs to your family and you were so careful to protect it. Why would you give the plans away? You don't have patent protection. Once the plans are in the public domain, they'll no longer belong to you."

"The research paper has been published. You're going to go down in history as a pioneer and they can't take that away from you. Let the Chinese have it . . . and the Americans . . . and whoever else wants it. For the time being, we have the only functioning laboratory. We're way ahead with the research and they'll be coming to us for our expertise. Ultimately, sharing the discovery is the right thing to do. I've always believed that."

Lotus approached the desk. "Will this resolve your problems in China?"

"It can only help," said Quan. "It levels the playing field. No more secrets. No more sneaking and hiding."

"And what about Jintao Corporation?" asked von Ang. "You said they would have right of first refusal."

"We're still the authorities in this field. Trust me. I have a plan. It will be good for everyone and my obligation will be complete. Now, with your permission . . ." Quan turned his attention to the view field. "I have to finish this."

Seeing the concerned expression on von Ang's face, Lotus said, "You should trust him."

308

"I wish I knew what he has in mind," said von Ang.

The recent unpleasantness with the Chinese and the Americans put Quan in an untenable position. The invention was part of his inheritance and, after considering several paths forward, he chose the most direct way to mitigate all threats.

He hammered out a declaration and, after twenty minutes, he read his piece one last time and sent it to the journal editor. Over the next thirty minutes, he formatted the machine blueprints and posted them, with limited access, on the LÓNG website.

The next day, his letter was posted in the conference daily.

An open letter to the scientific community.

Two governments have attempted to seize our technologies. However, in the grander scheme of things, these discoveries belong to the human race. Our work in hyperdimensional space is seminal, marking the beginning of a new era in human understanding. The affirmative interest we received at the conference has caused us to realize that a greater good will be served by sharing the specifications for equipment used in our experiments. We invite you, our colleagues, to build on our work, and hope that in having these plans, you will advance the research and add to our understanding of hyperdimensional space.

Let us work together for the common good.

40.

Charles de Gaulle Airport shined brightly, with white structural supports that curved organically in all directions, soaring three stories overhead. Crystal pendants of every shape refracted light from the glass ceiling and transparent tubes crisscrossed through the space, transporting people from one section to another on moving walkways.

Quan was waiting on the ground floor when he caught a glimpse of a woman wearing a long white summer coat in the arrival tube above him. It looked like Sealy and a minute later lift doors opened on his level and she stepped out.

Seeing him, her mood lifted. She smiled and her pace quickened.

He held her in a tight embrace and their embrace continued as disembarking passengers streamed past them like schools of fish around a river rock. He kissed her cheek and said softly, "I'm so happy you're here. It's been too long."

"I know," said Sealy. "I've missed you more than you know."

"How are you? Let me see," he said, looking at her middle. "You aren't showing yet."

"Just a little," she said. "This coat conceals nicely."

"And you're feeling okay?"

"It was a long flight. I'm tired but I'm okay," she replied.

They strolled to an outdoor area where a chauffeur from the hotel sprang into action, opening the doors of a sleek black limo-glide. After loading her suitcase, the driver offered sparkling wine or water and spoke in French to the traffic controller. A little after 1:00 in the afternoon, their craft merged onto the glideway and struck out for the heart of Paris.

"Remember the last time we were here?" asked Quan.

"I do. We had lunch at an outdoor café on Boulevard Saint-Germaine and the weather was perfect, like today."

"It is perfect, isn't it?

"Your conference went well?" said Sealy.

"It was something we had to do and I'm glad it's over. I just want to relax with you. Maybe we can go to some of the places we used to. What would you like to do?"

"Honestly? A nap would be nice. Then maybe the museum . . . but not too much walking."

Having Sealy by his side felt familiar and warm and yet there was a gulf between them—he was not the same. The Quan she knew no longer existed. That pleasant housing had grown into an estate with a thousand rooms.

Above Hotel Le Meurice, the limo hovered, waiting for a tour bus to depart. Then it descended and softly touched down. Attendants bounced into action opening doors and carrying luggage.

Inside the suite, Lotus embraced Sealy and Gaston greeted her with cheerful formality.

"We should let her rest," said Quan, putting his arm around her. "The bedroom is this way."

Sealy removed her coat and lay down on top of the king sized brocade bedspread. Gazing at the filigreed plaster ceiling. a feeling began to surface. There was something strange in the way she was treated by those in the other room. They were almost too friendly, as if she were an outsider, someone they had just met for the first time. She had been so moody lately. Perhaps, she thought, it was just hormones. Glad to be laying down, soon she fell asleep.

She emerged from the bedroom two hours later and wanted to know everything. She asked about the new center in California and about the work they'd been doing.

Lotus was effusive, telling about their housekeeper and the old farmhouse, the ocean and the beautiful new structures.

"Even though the location is kilometers away from the closest town, everything is new, including a state-of-the-art medi-bot system with an AI system that is better at diagnosis than any physician. The only downside is that we don't have a NutriSynth system, and frankly, I'm getting tired of Mexican food."

It wasn't long before the topic of her transference came up. She did her best to illustrate what the experience was like and finished by saying, "Describing the path is nothing—walking the path is the thing. Isn't that right, Quan?"

"The experience isn't easy to communicate, but I think you express it as well as it can possibly be described," he replied.

"All of you have done this?"

"All of us, including Gregory McGowen," Quan confirmed.

Sealy understood now, it was their affiliation with the experience that set them apart from her. They had done what nobody else had. And, in her condition, it would be impossible for her to become part of their alliance.

A bellman came to the salon to set up for dinner. He removed a vase from one of the sideboards, reached under, and triggered a latch. The sideboard automatically articulated, extending into the room like an accordion. He finished with a white tablecloth and utensils wrapped in soft white serviettes. Waiters brought trays covered by silver domes and set them on another side table. A bouquet of delicious scents filled the room.

"I'm starving," said Sealy.

Quan helped with her chair.

A basket of fresh bread was set down and appetizers of pan-seared foie gras.

Von Ang watched Lotus spreading pâté on a second piece of bread.

"What?" she said, "I've never tasted anything so good. This just became my favorite food."

Von Ang lifted his wineglass and said, "A toast—to all of us together again and to all the good reviews we received at the conference."

Quan looked at Sealy. "And to my lovely banlu."

Noticing how withdrawn Sealy was, Quan asked, "Are you feeling alright?"

"I'm okay. I understand you're all involved with this new discovery. It's foreign to me and I'm feeling a bit like an outsider."

"If it weren't for the government interference, we could have all stayed in New Hong Kong," said Quan. "Now that the research has been made public, I think my work in California is nearing an end."

The conversation halted while waiters removed the dinner service and they moved to the lounge area in front of the fireplace. The hotel staff worked to restore the room to its former state. Once the they were gone, Sealy let the elephant out into the room—the issue that had been percolating inside her ever since she landed. Turning to Quan with a bit of aggravation in her voice, she said, "You haven't talked about what it is that you can do. Lotus told me you can disappear."

"You should show her," said Lotus.

314

"In good time. I don't want to alarm."

"I'm not afraid, if that's what you're thinking," said Sealy. "I want to see this."

"Well alright then," said Quan, rising from his chair.

Looking at the door, to be sure the waiters were gone, Quan gathered his mindfulness and said, "This might look a little strange to you."

Dropping his arms to his sides, he closed his eyes and every atom in his body heard his inner command, knowing what they must do. His mind began to flicker, positioning the quantum structure of his body to move along the transfer axis. The shift was coming. Within the fine grain of his anatomy, an inextricable exchange was set in motion. Entering the pathway, he slipped from view.

Sealy pushed back into the sofa cushions and held her hands to her cheeks, eyes wide in astonishment. She reached a hand to where he stood. "He's gone. Where is he?"

After a moment, Quan began to return, first as vibrating sands, then quickly becoming whole again. Fully formed, he opened his eyes. "See? There's no way I could describe that."

"I—I don't know what to say. I don't believe what I just saw," said Sealy, holding her hand out to him. "Are you okay?"

"I'm fine," he said, grasping her fingers.

"I don't believe my eyes," said Sealy. "I don't understand this at all. Is it an illusion?"

"Isn't it amazing?" said Lotus. "It's real. He went to another set of dimensions."

"It's crazy. Tell me how it's possible." said Sealy.

"A very good question," said Gaston. "No one knows exactly how he does it."

"I've never seen anything like it," said Sealy.

"Look," said Quan, patting his body. "Our bodies are made of particles and the particles are constantly cycling in and out of these dimensions. I just follow the flow to where it goes."

Sealy scrunched her shoulders as if she felt a chill. "Yeow! Look, I've got goose bumps." She rubbed her arms, looking to Lotus and von Ang. "Can anyone else do that?"

"I've been trying," said Lotus. "But I haven't been able to."

Sealy looked side to side, trying to remain composed. She reached out from where she sat and put a hand on his knee. "That machine did this to you. Didn't it?"

"The machine is how I learned to tap into what's really a part of me. I'm preconditioned to be able to do this. It's invigorating. I feel like a new person."

"I was happy with the way you were before," she said, looking down thoughtfully and feeling her belly. "What do you mean by 'preconditioned'?"

"I mean the way my genes are expressed, may have something to do with it."

"Then it's possible our child will be affected as well."

"Not necessarily," said Quan. "And if it does happen, is it such a bad thing?"

"You didn't show this to people at the conference, did you?"

"No," said von Ang. "We all agreed not to . . . not until we understand it better."

"I think it may be unique to me," said Quan.

"But it might be heritable." she asked while cradling her belly with both hands.

"Who can say," Quan replied.

"Who else knows about this?" asked Sealy.

"Only the three of us and Mr. McGowen," said von Ang.

"I'm relieved to hear that," she said. "It's not natural and I can't imagine what others would think."

When morning came, Sealy and Quan went for a walk. Leaving the hotel, they crossed through the tree-lined park to the river. Arm in arm, they walked to the edge of the embankment on

316

a mission to find the love-lock they placed there many months earlier. Sealy recalled it was near a sign that said, "Welcome to the Champs-Élysées Port," where the road split and descended to where the houseboats were tied up along the bank.

They found the dock road and the sign and, a few meters away, the little fence. There were hundreds of locks there, hanging from the crosslinks. There were combination locks and key locks of all sizes and shapes, some in bright metal and others in bold plastic colors. While they searched, behind them boats cruised up and down the Seine.

"I remember it was near this post," said Quan. "Or was it that one?"

"I thought you put it about halfway between them."

Side by side they searched for their heart-shaped brass key lock. In places, the locks were three deep and had to be lifted like petals on a flower to see the ones below.

"We were smart to put ours here and not on the bridge railing," said Sealy. "They're constantly removing the ones on the bridge because of the weight."

"Maybe they've been removing these, as well," said Quan. His wrist disk bipped. It was von Ang.

"Give us another ten minutes," said Quan. "We'll meet you at the museum."

After carefully examining every lock in the area, they concluded that the city must have cleared the fence in the last year. Sealy looked at Quan compassionately. She was adjusting to his newly revealed ability. It was strange, but he was her banlu. He belonged to her and she to him—with or without a padlock in Paris.

"It's all right," she said. "Our memories are what's important."

A few hours later, inside the Musée d'Orsay, the foursome were strolling through a section of Joseph Turner paintings. Quan pointed to a nebulous landscape entitled *Norham Castle, Sunrise* and told Sealy how it reminded him of the Braneworld. "It's like that. The shapes are vague," he said.

"Interesting," she replied. "If this is what it looks like. I like the real world better."

They strolled on and in another part of the gallery, Quan lagged behind, staring at painting by Georges Seurat. The small plaque next to the painting read, *"La Tour Eiffel*—Neo-Impressionist Pointillism—1889." He stood there, transfixed, and the others came back to see what held his interest.

"See?" he said, pointing to the speckled painting. "You see? We're not the only ones who have seen the other dimensions. This is spot on."

Staring at the dots on the canvas, Quan began to see particles dancing on the surface of the canvas and his body began to take on a grainy appearance.

Seeing his form begin to change, Sealy said, "Oh my God. No. Not here."

She shot a glance at Lotus, who seemed mesmerized, staring at Quan as he became more transparent. Luckily no one was looking their way. She put her arms around both Lotus and von Ang, pulling them in close around Quan.

Quan felt his entourage move in, shielding him from prying eyes. For a moment he forgot where he was. Vanishing in public view was a huge mistake. He quickly returned to normal, feeling foolish. "I didn't intentionally bring that on," he said. "I had no control over it. Looking at that painting is what did it. It was subconscious."

"That isn't normal," said Sealy.

"We should go," said von Ang, outstretching his arms to shepherd them.

Crossing the Seine under the Leopold Senghor bridge, Sealy had to stop and rest. From the railing, they watched the boats going up and down the river.

With his arms around her, Quan said, "It's a funny thing. The subconscious mind is like the hand that arranges a pillow

318

while you're asleep. You have no conscious control over it but it knows what to do."

"Do you realize how risky that was?" said Sealy. "Word travels fast and there are people who would do anything to be able to do that."

"I know."

Back at the hotel, Sealy lay on top of the embroidered bedspread propped up by pillows, and Quan sat on the edge of the bed.

"It scares me that you don't have control over that thing you do."

"That was the first time," said Quan. "It was involuntary and I'll be more careful. I just need to be more aware of things that might trigger it."

"This is all very strange for me. I'm trying to adjust. I love you no matter what, but you've changed and . . . I mean, how are we going to live like this? What's it going to be like?"

"I'm different from other people. I was born this way. I can't help it. It's part of my heritage. I'm still the same person inside."

Sealy studied him for a moment, then said, "We have a lot to talk about, like where we go from here. We need to talk about where we're going to live and what we're going to do next."

"Going back to Oxford is one possibility," said Quan, "but we might have to consider California, where the lab is. I'm not sure it's safe for me to return to China yet. The Central Science Committee has caused problems. I'll have to check with our lawyers."

"We have to be together when the baby comes."

"Absolutely," said Quan. "I'll be there and we'll do what makes the most sense."

~~~

Sealy left Paris still feeling like an outsider. Watching her banlu vanish and reappear was life changing. It was something the outside world, the world she came from, could not possibly understand. Strange as that was, even in her condition, or perhaps because of it, this new reality was something she had to accept. It was part of her life . . . and perhaps the life of her chile.

Quan prepared to go back to California. He'd made difficult choices and there were still matters that were unresolved. Before leaving Paris, he spoke with Bledsoe one last time. Despite Quan's letter in the conference daily and the plans posted on the website, Bledsoe seemed surprisingly jovial. He said, "It was fourth down and ten. You punted and I can't say I blame you. You can forget about the endowment and your visas are still temporary, but I can do you a favor, if you cooperate."

"What do you have in mind?"

"If you cooperate, I'll do what I can to make your visas permanent. In return, we'll want you and your people to be available in case we need advice building those machines."

"That can work," said Quan.

41.

With the Paris conference behind them and Sealy safely on a flight back to New Hong Kong, Quan boarded a flight back to California with Gaston and Lotus.

After takeoff, Lotus began fanning through the latest news. Finding an article in one of the bottom-dwelling zines she said, "Listen to this one. 'Scientists from the Brane Reseach Center offered no explanation of how the experiments were conducted. Could it be that their data is fake? It wouldn't be the first time this sort of thing has happened. It's shameful when a scientist does this sort of thing and it becomes the responsibility of their peers to look into the possibility. It results in valuable time taken away from their own research and . . . ' I can't believe this," she said. "It's crazy. They go from a hypothetical to a false implication. They make it sound like we're guilty without offering any evidence."

"It's possible the CSC planted the story to discredit our achievement. It appears to be their modus operandi," said von Ang.

"All the more reason to invite other scientists to the new lab to see' for themselves," said Quan.

"In spite of the disruption, as long as there are liability waivers I'll be willing to give it a try," said von Ang.

"The Chinese Central Science Committee should be blacklisted," said Lotus.

Quan knew that having scientists validate the discovery would open up a chain of events. The discovery of other dimensions was disruptive and, just as the Flat Earth Society clung to their beliefs for decades, there would be diehards who would continue to attempt to discredit the discovery.

"The best defence is a strong offence. To preempt more false stories we should go on air with factual disclosures of what we've found. Lotus, this job is custom made for you. You'll be our social media manager. There's no one better to evaluate the media channels. Find us an honest broadcaster, someone with integrity, and we'll tell the world."

Back at the Research Center, Lotus went to work. Watching vidi casts of several investigative journalists, it wasn't long before she made her selection: Liz Monahan, a popular prime-time news anchor. Liz promised to provide an unbiased platform, and the venue was set for the presidential suite of the Landmark Resort in Monterey Bay, California --- fifty-six kilometers north of the Research Center.

Liz Monahan was an attractive young woman, a centimeter taller than Quan, wearing a chic rust-colored business suit. Her chestnut hair streaked with blond was cut in a perfectly geometric shape, short in back, brushed forward to points near her chin. Quan sat next to her in one of a pair of high-backed chairs set in front of double doors open to the expansive greens of the resort. He was calm in his gray suit. Cameras were set and fill lights lit. Next to him, Monahan took a sip of water and asked, "Ready?"

"Yes," said Quan.

A crew member counted down from five and the interview began.

MONOHAN: "We're here today with Dr. Quan Jintao. He's the founder of the Brane Research Center for Quantum Physics and author of the much-talked-about LÓNG website. Theories abound regarding his work and his organization: what it stands for, what it does, and why. Today on News Net we hope to answer these questions and more. We're excited to welcome you for the first time, Dr. Jintao. Thank you for joining us."

JINTAO: "Thank you, Liz. It's a pleasure to be here."

MONAHAN: "You were a presenter at the International Conference on Quantum Physics in Paris last week and your paper created quite an uproar. Give us a summary of what your work is about."

JINTAO: "We're working on proof of the Krakinov theory, which suggests the existence of other dimensions."

MONAHAN: "Other dimensions. What do you mean? Can you explain?"

JINTAO: "We believe we've discovered one of the other dimensions and we've started experimenting to better understand it."

MONAHAN: "You found another dimension. What is it? And how did you find it?"

JINTAO: "We use some highly developed equipment, just like a biologist might use a microscope, or an astronomer might use a telescope."

MONAHAN: "So you use technical equipment. Tell us, what does the equipment do?"

JINTAO: "I don't want to get into specifics at this time. To really understand what I'm talking about, you'd need to see it firsthand."

MONAHAN: "That's enticing, I must say. I'd like to see that. Maybe we'll schedule another segment at your facility. Now, there are critics who say that what you are doing is not scientific at all and your claims have been called a hoax. I'm sure you've heard the accusations. Some have called you a charlatan. How do you respond to those remarks?"

JINTAO: "The research was begun by my father and it evolved. The equipment we use is extremely sophisticated, and the Brane Research Center employs professionals who are the best in their fields. What we do is definitely not a sham. I suppose, because what we've accomplished is so unconventional, there were bound to be critics."

MONAHAN: "Now you also have a website and there is considerable controversy surrounding that, as well. Please tell us . . . what is the LÓNG website about? It doesn't appear to be connected to your research."

JINTAO: "The word LÓNG comes from Chinese mythology. It describes a creature that changes form as it moves through the world—a dragon. It's a metaphor for what we're studying."

MONAHAN: "So the LÓNG website is more of a philosophy?"

JINTAO: "The short answer is yes. The discovery of other dimensions has profound implications for all of us. It asks the question, What are we? The website I put together is a different way of looking at the science. It's an attempt to explore the nature of our existence."

MONAHAN: "Can you break it down for us? How do you define existence?"

JINTAO: "In this multidimensional world we live in, things that seem real—physical, tangible things—are actually an illusion. The quantum stuff things are made of is constantly churning between this world and another that we can't see. We perceive matter as solid but we only see four percent of what is actually there. And, going one step further, since we evolved in

324

this multidimensional world, we are more than just physical beings."

MONAHAN: "This is fascinating and I'm sure our viewers want to know more. We're going to take a short break, and when we return, more with the founder of the Brane Center, Quan Jintao."

Waving her hand at the cameraman, she said, "Pause it there." She turned to Quan. "You're doing fine. I'd encourage you, though, to tell it all . . . reach out to the audience . . . convince them of what you believe."

"Understood," said Quan.

Monahan motioned to the man behind the camera. "All right, give us a count."

CAMERAMAN: "We're back in three . . . two . . . one."

MONAHAN: "Dr. Quan Jintao, founder of the Brane Research Center and author of the LÓNG website, is my guest today on News Net. We're talking about ontology—the study of existence. So, tell us how your research into other dimensions led you to a philosophy about existence. Have you studied ontology? What credentials do you have?"

JINTAO: "It's natural extension of science to have a philosophy about how it relates to human existence. I have a graduate degree in physics from Oxford University, and my team at the Center includes qualified professionals in quantum theory and quantum physics."

MONAHAN: "Did you study ontology at Oxford?"

JINTAO: "No. I became interested in the nature of existence as a result of the research we've been doing. What I've tried to convey on the website is a compilation of my thoughts."

MONAHAN: "You are sort of an armchair philosopher, then. Have you actually seen the other dimensions yourself?"

JINTAO: "Several times."

MONAHAN: "And so, having firsthand knowledge of what these other dimensions look like, can you describe them for us?"

Quan paused for a moment, staring at patterns on the carpet between them. She had done her homework and maybe knew more than she was letting on. He was tempted to show her what he was capable of, but he resisted the urge.

JINTAO: "Words can't do it justice. The LÓNG website is my attempt to give people the experience; however, I'm afraid it isn't very effective. It's a work in progress."

MONAHAN: "All right, I respect that. But tell us about your personal experience. What have you seen?"

JINTAO: "Describing it is difficult. Okay, so imagine you are made of trillions of tiny grains of sand and those grains become engulfed in a mist. The grains are all still there but now there is mist inside and out."

MONAHAN: "And so what have you learned through that experience?"

JINTAO: "I've come to believe that life had its origin much longer ago than we previously thought—all the way back to the very beginning of the universe and it's been evolving ever since. There's a living oneness that pervades everything."

MONAHAN: "A living oneness? What do you mean by that?"

JINTAO: "There is an underlying life force that pervades all matter."

MONAHAN: "That sounds almost spiritual. I noticed on your website, you have references to various religions. I got the impression that you think established religions are flawed? Is that fair to say?"

JINTAO: "Religion is of limited value. It's thirdhand information—conjecture without direct experience. I believe in teaching only what can be verified."

MONAHAN: "I noticed on your website blog, some of the visitors characterize you as an 'enlightened master.' What do you think of that? Are you enlightened?"

JINTAO: "Enlightened master? I don't know. Finite mind can't understand infinite mind. To understand infinite mind, a

326

person has to change—has to evolve. Perhaps you have to give up your sense of self in order to understand infinite mind."

MONAHAN: "And do you understand infinite mind?"

JINTAO: "I have some understanding of it."

MONAHAN: "You mean you understand God?"

JINTAO: "In a manner of speaking, yes. I've had a direct experience with what one might call God. I believe an awakening is coming and, in time, everyone will see that there is a universal life force pervading all space and time. I just happen to be ahead of the curve."

MONAHAN: "Ahead of the curve? Haven't some of the religions expressed the same idea?"

JINTAO: "They may have, but they don't have direct experience . . . that's the big difference."

MONAHAN: "Are you saying that what you've learned is superior to what they teach?"

JINTAO: "Let's not make this about me. It's about the work we're doing. This may be the next step in human evolution."

MONAHAN: "Stay with us. We'll be back in a moment."

The interview continued for another thirty minutes, and Monahan's questions helped Quan clarify his position on a number of things. He concluded by saying that humanity's view of existence would change forever as a result of the work they were doing.

At the end of the interview, Lotus, who'd been standing next to the cameraman, clapped her hands and praised Quan. On their way back to the Center, she told him how remarkably composed and articulate he was. She was sure the interview would be well received.

Shortly after arriving back at the Research Center, Lotus saw several positive stories on other media channels, based on the interview. There was a tripling of traffic to the website and offers came in from multimedia publishers along with partnership requests from other research labs. There was also an invitation to meet with the Council of American Churches. Quan deferred all of these to a later time.

In their private quarters, von Ang vented his frustration with Lotus.

"I don't understand why we need this publicity. I don't understand what possible purpose it serves."

"They're interested in what we do," said Lotus. "It's good PR, puts us in the same league with CERN and Hadron and FCC."

"This isn't a popularity contest. I've never seen a media circus like this after publishing a research paper. We're doing science here and this kind of attention is a distraction. We need to get on with our work."

"If you get just one new idea from one of the visitors, wouldn't it be worth it?"

"Highly unlikely," grumbled von Ang.

Taking off his lab coat, von Ang made his way across the compound to Quan's bungalow. He found Quan standing near the great oak tree in his bare feet. The young Jintao seemed somber and pensive, examining something in the palm of his hand. Seeing von Ang, he offered it up so that von Ang could see it: a dead bee.

"Death," said Quan.

"Death is inevitable."

"Who knows? Maybe not."

Von Ang took a deep breath and began airing his concerns about the visitors, questioning the wisdom of parading people through the laboratory.

"Keep an open mind," said Quan. "There's no downside. We'll do extreme vetting and, if you like, you can make the final decision on who we invite. I would have thought you'd enjoy the company of other scientists."

With that, he discarded the dead bee, walked into his bungalow, and closed the door.

Von Ang stood there for a moment, registering the change in their relationship.

42.

Night came and Quan was alone in his bungalow, talking with Sealy. She'd seen the interview and had mixed feelings. It was unlikely that Quan would come back to China anytime soon and she was lamenting the thought of having their baby without him. He did his best to console her, but the conversation ended on a somber note.

Lying on his back on the floor of the living room, his awareness began to grow. He could feel the texture of the carpet underneath him. He felt the cool earth beneath the floor. He felt the construction of the wall and the arrangement of beams inside the ceiling. He could hear insects rummaging in the dirt outside. With his gaze fixed on the dimly lit ceiling his awareness spread throughout the compound. He felt gigantic and powerful, as if he could reach up and toss the moon across the universe with a flick of his wrist.

What more can I do here? What more do they want? What more can I show them? They want to know how to do what I do.

Maybe no one else can. And what of the nay-sayers. Down deep, the unknown frightens them. They'll take security over knowledge.

Courage, Knowledge, Honor—my father's moto. He led me to a higher truth—about the world and about myself. I see through it all now. I'm just a set of reference points in space . . . information in a bottle. The walls of this room define the space, but it's the space itself that makes the room useful.

As he lay there, his awareness of himself, the room, the building and the whole compound became one. Then came a knock at the door. Two familiar energies entered, Lotus and von Ang. They came to his side and Lotus sat next to him.

"I had a feeling you were in here," she said. "You're wrestling with something."

"Just thinking . . . all this effort . . . in the end, what does it matter? Now that we've set things in motion it has a life of it's own."

"Have you seen the traffic to the LÓNG site?" she asked. "Since the interview there are a hundred and eighty million hits. People are going orbital over what you said."

"The research will grow exponentially," he said. "In time the world will come around to accept the new reality. What's left for us to do?"

"Knowledge makes the effort worthwhile," said von Ang. "Why would you ask such a question? We're learning more every day."

Quan sat up and smiled his subtle smile.

A good man, but he thinks like the frog at the bottom of the well. His view is limited.

"The discovery is disruptive. What do you think will happen when there is irrefutable evidence that we are all living in an illusion? Sure, at first some will desperately hang on to their beliefs. They'll be horrified by the idea of being inconsequential—just specks in some gigantic cosmic illusion. But eventually what you discovered will change the world."

"I learned a lot about myself by transferring," said Lotus. "And it doesn't scare me at all. I think others will feel the same way."

"The direct experience is the thing—the path," said Quan, running his fingers over the top of his head. "And there's more, much more than you know. I've experienced things that are impossible to share. I was asleep but now I'm awake."

"You should teach what you've learned," said Lotus.

"It's easy for me. I have a passkey to the other side. It's part of me." Reaching out and grasping Lotus by the forearm, he said, "I'm different. You know that, don't you?"

"I'm not sure what you mean," said Lotus. "I don't have your ability, if that's what you mean."

"Right," said Quan, letting go of her arm and looking up to the ceiling. "You're not me. No one is. I yo-yo back and forth—selfish to selfless—this set of dimensions and the other. Maybe I'm going the way of my father. It's like . . ." He trailed off.

"Your father was a great man," said Lotus. "And so are you."

Quan looked up at von Ang. "I tried to save him. I reached out to him, but he's a shadow, a vestige of what he once was."

A flush came to von Ang's neck. A pulse was beating in his eyes. He wasn't sure what to say.

Lotus stepped in. "What you've done is amazing. I don't know what's bothering you. What can we do to help?"

At the back of his head, a door was open, a gentle breeze from the Braneworld tickling his exposed ganglia. He raised a hand toward the ceiling. "You should prepare. A storm is coming."

Lotus and von Ang quietly left the room. Once outside, von Ang looked up at the stars and said, "He's confused. The weather report for the next ten days is clear."

"He's perturbed about something. I think he wants to be back in China with Sealy."

Laying on the floor, shapes form within Quan's eyes, morphing like a kaleidoscope. He sees three bars floating in the air above him. They join, forming a triangle. The triangle turns and becomes a wheel, spokes in the wheel become a pattern of radiating lines. The lines ripple and distort throughout the room.

He sees his father as a younger man and himself as a child. His father hands him a reader slate with stories . . . stories about emperors, ancient fortresses, monks, and warriors in battle . . . Chinese legions marching over hills. In his vision, there is deep water all around, sparkling green, and a silver cathedral towering in front of him. Its shape morphs into a silver cross, then disintegrates into swirling particles. The vision clears away. Eyes wide open, he continues to stare at the ceiling . . . a feeling of conflict.

A voice in his head speaks.

[Some seek knowledge . . . others seek to destroy.]

"What?"

[Both hands.]

Still on his back, he raises his arms and looks at his hands.

A Zen Koan pops into his head: *What is the sound of one hand clapping?*

One hand clapping makes no sound at all. Two are needed.

His hands came together above him. He laughs and a sense of ease comes over him.

333

43.

In the seventeenth century, monks of the Shaolin order offered themselves to the Ming dynasty, helping to defend them from the invading Qing forces. Jealous of the monks' fighting ability, generals convinced the emperor that the Shaolin would eventually turn against him. As a precaution, the emperor ordered the Shaolin monastery burned to the ground. Only eighteen monks survived. Determined to avenge their dead brothers, they founded a secret society and adopted as their symbol a triangle, representing the unity of Heaven, Earth and Man. They became known as the Triad.

~~~

The Chinese Central Intelligence Committee, infuriated by Quan Jintao's escape, requested the assistance of the 14K Chapter of the Triad in New Hong Kong. An order was relayed to their Triad affiliates in San Francisco.

San Francisco, California

It was 2:00 in the morning at the Imperial Palace restaurant in Chinatown. The restaurant was dark except for a narrow beam of light splaying out from under double doors of a private dining room on the second floor. In the smoke-filled room, nine Triads of the Wah Ching clan sat around a large round table covered with white linen. Two were young men in their teens, four were in their twenties, and two were over thirty. The older men were dressed in black suits while the younger men wore casual clothes.

Plates were being passed around on a rotating platform at the center of the table. Snatching with chopsticks, the men lifted beef and vegetables onto their individual bowls of rice. With bowls held to chins, the younger men shoveled the food into their mouths as if they hadn't eaten in a month. Talking and laughing with mouths full, they stopped only to gulp from bottles of Tsingtao and Baijiu.

Among them was Li Honzu, Mountain Lord of the Wah Ching clan, with hands hard as steel and arms tattooed from wrist to shoulder. With a scowl permanently screwed to his clammy face, Honzu was known for his brutal reprisals. He was the kind of man who would just as soon knock someone on the head as say hello. Tonight, there was good reason be angry. Seven Wah Ching operations had been shut down by the SFPD Asian Gang Task Force and DEA agents had intercepted two heroin shipments. The result was a huge financial blow, plus the loss of face with his peers in China.

Gazing through narrow eye slits, Honzu said, "Word has come from our brothers. It will be a long time before we receive any new shipments. Until then we must tighten our belts." Looking at the younger members, he added, "Remember your thirty-six vows. We must stick together."

One of the younger men suggested bombing the local PD headquarters in retaliation. Honzu reminded him that it was always better to coexist than to wage war. On many occasions, the Triad had worked in secret for the government. Cooperation was mutually beneficial. The recent setbacks were more than likely the result of a government official looking for recognition and the raids would stop after the next election.

"Accept the blows and be strong," he told them. "In the meantime, we will direct our energies to an assignment that will pay off quickly. Someone has made fools of government officials in New Hong Kong, stealing equipment and technology, and transporting it to the United States. They have turned to us for help. We are to return Quan Jintao to China by any means possible—alive."

That night, Honzu chose five men—all were forty-nine-level soldiers (four times nine, symbolic of their thirty-six vows). Big Yao was appointed Red Pole of the crew. Johnny K. was in charge of explosives. Huojin and Iron Zha were the muscle. The fifth was a teen, Yen-Tin. He was tech-savvy and this would be a training mission for him.

Their plan was simple: explosives to distract, grab the target, and split.

Honzu tossed a nylon pouch onto the table: cash, a viewflex map, and pictures of the young Jintao.

"Make it a clean job," he said with eyes hard as steel.

They all knew what the look meant. Failure was not an option.

44.

The Black Mountains, New Mexico
Evening came and the monastery was quiet. In a dimly lit stone room, the Cardinal's pale gray watery eyes peered at a column of text hovering in a view field above his blanket. His index finger traced the glowing words while moving images flickered on his face. He was listening to what Quan said near the end of the Monahan interview.

"By all accounts the man they called Jesus may have mastered the principle of transference. He may have explored other dimensions. It's a pity he was unable to explain his experience in scientific terms. It would have saved centuries of confusion. The churches further corrupted his teachings by building an elaborate mythology to serve their own purposes."

"Bovie," croaked the Cardinal in a voice that sounded like an ancient amphibian. "Bovie!" The view field flinched and a smaller window popped up on top of the text he was reading. The face of a priest appeared, a man in his mid-forties, head shaved, deep creases in cheek and mouth, eyes glistening like steel ball bearings. A scar ran down from the right side of his forehead to where it ended in a deep groove just above his cheekbone.

"Your Eminence," he said.

"There is blasphemy in the world, Bovie. It must be cleansed."

"Yes, Your Eminence, I'm coming."

The Order of the Silver Nicene had kept its existence in the Black Mountains of New Mexico quiet since its founding. It's name was a reminder of the thirty pieces of silver that Judas was paid to betray Jesus. The cloister was dedicated to the protection of the Churches of the Americas and was home to one Deacon Bovie, also known as "the Shepherd's Sword." It was 4:00 in the morning when Bovie walked barefooted down the cold stone hallway, but the Cardinal's voice hadn't awakened him. Bovie never truly slept. He kept himself in a vigilant state, somewhere between his nightmares and holy penitence.

Bovie stood barefooted on the stone floor at the foot of the Cardinal's bed. He wore only a hooded robe, tied at the waist with a thick rope.

Hazy waters welled up in the Cardinal's eyes as he spoke. "There must be no other Gods. We must not bow down to graven idols. These are God's laws, my son. This merchant of lies says our faith is built on ignorance." The Cardinal passed his thinly skinned hand across the view field revealing a picture of Quan Jintao. "He wants us to believe his understanding of existence is greater than that of the Son of God. Blasphemy!" he shouted. "Heinous blasphemy!" he coughed.

"Yes, Your Eminence. You wish me to deal with him?"

Making an up-down, side-to-side gesture with his hand, the Cardinal spoke in a voice like wet bubbles rising in a muddy pond. "There can be but one God: the Father, the Almighty, maker of Heaven and Earth, of worlds seen and unseen." From somewhere under the blanket, the old man produced a large

338

envelope and slid it across to Bovie. "Bless you, my son. You are the sword of righteousness. God's will be done."

In an earlier life, Dan Bovie had been a Special Forces Ranger and served five tours of combat before the "come to Jesus" revelation that changed his life. Leading his squad through the fabled Khyber Pass in pursuit of terrorists, he was ambushed in a barrage of pulse cannons and sidewinders. The ordnance tore through his squad, miraculously leaving him as sole survivor. With his hearing gone and what was left of his men strewn around him in pieces, he saw the image of Jesus, walking toward him out of the smoke, his white robes billowing. The vision spoke to him. "Defend my church from those who would subvert my teachings. Through me, you shall come unto the Father and have life eternal."

Badly wounded, Bovie stumbled from the carnage, spending the next two days in a small mountain abri until a recon team pulled him out. After his discharge from the military hospital at Landstuhl, he was awarded a Purple Heart and he returned to his home in the Black Mountains. A penitent man, Bovie joined the seminary, trading his combat armor for a monk's robes. From then on, he spent his days reading scripture and his nights praying and subjecting himself to excruciating exercises in atonement for the lives he had been responsible for . . . and lost.

Because of his military skill, the Order had called on Bovie twice before to do "special work" for the church. Alone in his room, he emptied the contents of the envelope onto the heavy gray blanket on top of his bed: an identity chip, a flexmap, names, a view card with pictures of Brane Research Center personnel, and a folded note. As he read, the words resonated within him. "Our Lord Jesus bestows unconditional love upon us. We who defend his church will know life everlasting."

Within an hour of receiving his instructions, Deacon Bovie was sitting inside a decommissioned interceptor, dressed in jeans, a black T-shirt, and a brown leather jacket. He was traveling west, away from the enclave with a large duffel bag on the bare metal floor behind his seat.

San Francisco

The setting sun was rippling across San Francisco bay as a faded white, eight-wheeled freighter rumbled down the gravel road at Hunters Point, sliding to a dusty stop behind a rusty steel shack. Washed-out letters on both sides of a hybrid freighter read, "Sung Yip Marine—Wholesale Seafood." The roll-up door at the back of the truck clattered open, finishing with a loud bang.

In single file, four men with backpacks walked from the shack to the back of the freighter. Stepping inside, they took their places on a mattress at the far end, backs against the metal walls, packs at their feet. The men waited while two loaders brought empty boxes, stacking them across the back of the freighter, blocking the view of the men inside. The metal roll-up door clattered again and slammed shut.

Tires clawed gravel as the freighter climbed up the road, away from the shed. Teeth clenched and hands grabbed mattress edges as the freighter rocked back and forth, repeatedly pitching the men against the metal sides. Reaching the asphalt roadway at last, the vehicle turned and headed west, toward Highway 280. Yen-Tin, the youngest of the four, pointed silently at the shirt pocket of the man across from him and put two fingers to his mouth. The older man withdrew a pack of smokes, pulled one out, and tossed it over.

Big Yao, the driver, was steering down the city streets, looking repeatedly at a scanner, crudely bolted to the dashboard with four mismatched cap screws. Scanning the police band, he picked up only low-level chatter. Minutes later he was on highway 280 heading south, tires humming against the asphalt.

Inside the cargo hold, the cool air was laced with the smell of cigarette smoke and dead fish. All the men wore dark jackets except for Iron Zha, who wore only a black T-shirt. Built

340

like a bull, his rounded shoulders and arms were huge. A bandolier was slung diagonally across his chest, sheathing a large knife, the kind a cook would use to chop meat.

Across from Zha, Huojin took out a .45-caliber handgun and checked the magazine. "What's the matter," he said, looking at Zha, "you don't like guns?"

"Guns are okay," said Zha, patting his knife. "I bring this for circumcising little dicks like you."

Johnny K. snickered.

Huojin took a viewflex out of his backpack and switched it on. The glow lit his face, highlighting a row of small marks over his left eye, dimples from recently removed stitches. The picture of a young man with closely cropped black hair popped into view. Huojin looked concerned. "Looks familiar. Who is this dog fart, anyway?"

"He's a scientist," said Johnny K. "Saw him on the news."

"I know him," scoffed Yen-Tin. "That guy's been scamming the round eyes big time."

"They want him back in China," said Huojin.

"Probably bonking some minister's wife," said Yen-Tin, talking through his cigarette smoke.

"We're supposed to bag him. That's all I gotta know," said Iron Zha, his eyes steady on Yen-Tin.

Looking at each of the others, Huojin grumbled, "Mountain Lord says he might have protection. Better check it out."

"No worries," said Johnny K. "I've got enough PE4 to put the place in orbit."

The men settled back, resting uncomfortably while the freighter rolled along for another two hours. At last the brakes hissed and the freighter came to a stop. The man closest to the roll-up door reached into his backpack, fingers on a snub-nosed automatic.

It was dark outside and Big Yao made his way around the freighter. He unlocked the roll-up door. It went up with a rumble and crickets stopped chirping.

"This is it," he said, lifting a crate down from the right side of the freighter. One by one the others climbed down to the desolate country road. "Two more kilometers," said Yao, pointing at the road ahead. "Follow the ravine to the right. I'll meet you back on the road in two hours."

The crickets resumed their singing.

~~~

It was dark when Bovie reached his destination. Amid clouds moving overhead, patches of moonlight came and went. Three clicks south of the Research Center access road, he maneuvered his small craft in between a stand of acacia trees. Cinching a Kevlar sack tight to his back, he took off at a steady trot, holding his small Trijacon automatic with both hands. Seven minutes later, he reached the ravine and slid on a pair of night-vision goggles. Around him, everything lit up with a bright fluorescent green glow. He could see the rocky ravine where it emerged from under the highway and he followed it west. Crouching as he went, he moved along the rim a short distance before settling to his haunches. He waited, looking . . . listening. Suddenly, in one fluid motion he sprang from where he was, landing silently on a large flat rock two meters below in the ravine. Stepping from rock to rock on treadless rubber soles, Bovie traveled almost a kilometer before he froze.

A few meters in front of him were four men, lying against the bank of the ravine, backpacks at their feet. Unaware of his arrival, they continued looking through binoculars, their speech barely audible. Bovie tugged on his earlobe, turning up the gain on his cochlea implant. He still couldn't make out what they were saying. It didn't sound like English. He stood up to see what they were looking at . . . a cluster of buildings in the distance.

342

Advancing cautiously in the shadows, he stopped barely four meters from where they stood. He could hear them now—some kind of Asian speak—maybe Chinese. He advanced another meter, and spoke in a hoarse voice, "Hands in the air. You move, you die." The men turned instantly, shocked at the sight of Bovie, his face covered by a night-vision mask, his weapon raised, ready to shoot. Before Bovie could say another word, Iron Zha acted on instinct, flinging his blade at Bovie. The response was instantaneous—a flash from Bovie's gun. The big man collapsed backward, shot through the heart.

Turning his weapon toward the youngest man, who was slowly reaching for something in his pocket, Bovie growled, "You move, you die." Taking his free hand off his weapon, he beckoned and said, "Come here."

As Yen-Tin approached, Bovie grabbed the boy's jacket, turned him forcefully, and pushed him to the bank. Patting for weapons, he kept his gun pointed at the others. In the jacket, he found a folding knife and tossed it out of the ravine. In the cargo pockets, he found two grenades and a laser pistol and pitched them over the bank.

Pushing Yen-Tin back toward the other two, Bovie asked, as if to himself, "What are you slopes doing out here, anyway?" Signaling to the next man, Huojin, whose eyes were glaring with hatred, Bovie gestured and said, "You. Come here."

As he approached, Huojin lifted his chin in defiance and spit words at Bovie. *"Si pi yan."*

"Yeah? Well, fuck you, too," said Bovie, grabbing the man's sleeve.

As Bovie started to turn him, Huojin struck out, fast as lightning—an elbow to the cheekbone—a fist to the short ribs—then the hand at Bovie's throat and the sweeping leg from behind—a sequence the ranger was conditioned for. Bovie stepped over the leg as it swept through, turning his torso and driving the heel of his weapon squarely into the man's throat. Huojin made a gurgling sound and crumpled to the ground.

343

Quickly turning his weapon on the other two men who were charging toward him, he yelled, "Freeze!"

Johnny K. said something incomprehensible. Time slowed. Bovie watched his bullets, glowing in night-vision green, heading straight for the chest as Johnny K.'s backpack came around to block. Bovie watched as two more rounds left his weapon. The first two bullets struck Johnny K. and time slowed even more. The last two were on an intercept course with the backpack. Bovie saw a brick of PE4 sliding from the pack and saw his last bullet strike the detonator. The explosion was enormous.

McGowen bounced off his bed and rushed to the door. Seeing a brush fire in the distance and gray smoke rising in the moonlight, he came fully awake. There was no fire department to call. The nearest town was a good forty minutes away. He bolted back inside. Jumping into pants, boots, and a jacket. Grabbing a flashlight and extinguisher, he jogged toward the blaze. Entering the smoke-filled area, burning manzanita and the smell of plastic explosive chafed his nostrils. The blast left a crater about fifteen meters wide. He walked around the crater's rim and triggered small bursts from the extinguisher, snuffing out hot spots. Gray smoke turned to white where he sprayed. Setting the tank down, he picked up a twig and poked at a smoldering chunk. He gagged. It was human.

From his bungalow, Quan could see a chocklight searching through the billowing smoke. David came up next to Quan, followed by Lotus and von Ang.

"Is that Mr. McGowen out there?" asked David.

"Yes, I think so," said Quan. "Don't be alarmed. He's got it under control—whatever it was."

"Definitely an explosion," said von Ang. "Is there a propane tank over there?"

"I'll go find out what happened," said Quan. "Everyone stay here."

344

Satisfied that the brush fire was out, McGowen was making his way back to the compound when Quan met him. "What was it?"

"Nasty business, that was—body parts everywhere and an odd mix of weapons. Whoever they were, they weren't friendly. Best I can make out, they were on some sort of mission. They may have been planning to destroy this whole place. We're lucky something went wrong."

"Actually, I had a feeling something like this would happen," said Quan. "Two opposing forces coming together, like two hands clapping."

"Not sure I understand your meaning, sir."

"I had a premonition. Two forces collided here."

"You've lost me, sir."

"Don't look for logic in it." Quan smiled. "I'm sure no harm will come to us."

"Well, judging by the mess out there, I say we're just damned lucky."

"Maybe it's the work we're doing that makes us so lucky," said Quan. "No need to alarm the others. Let's tell them this was some sort of gas explosion. We don't want to scare them. And get your bots out here to clean up the mess."

"Aye, sir. Understood. I'll tell them to stay away."

Quan brought his hands together in a clap, turned, and walked away.

The remarks troubled McGowen. Where the young Jintao had always been logical, now he alluded to having some sort of psychic powers. McGowen turned and went back to the scene of the explosion, searching the grounds with his chocklight. On the highway, he found fresh tire tracks where a vehicle had pulled up near the ravine. The tracks were from a wide-bodied freighter with dual tires. The tracks made a U-turn.

Before sunrise, McGowen found another vehicle farther down the road, hidden among the acacias. It was a lightly armored two-seater with a duffel bag and the keys still in it. He drove it to a spot behind the laboratory and covered it with a tarp. By the time morning broke free of the inland hills, he and his team of construction bots disposed of the weapons and human remains, burying them deep along the southern property line.

45.

Quan called it a premonition; somehow he had become aware
that an attack was coming. He could feel the hostile intentions
and, as if the universe was telling him how it would end, a Koan
had popped into his mind—*What is the sound of one hand
clapping?*

Two forces, each with negative intentions, met on the
grounds and in a thunderclap they canceled each other out. It was
as though an unseen hand had reached in and subtracted negative
numbers from both sides of an equation.

Nature always strives for balance, he thought. *Following
Newton's third law of motion, where there is action there is
always an equal and opposite reaction. It followed then, that the
great enlightenment they had introduced to the world would
likely be met with an equal measure of negative energy. While the
future of the Brane Research Center was becoming brighter, the
world around it was becoming darker.*

Quan walked to his favorite spot at the edge of the bluff and sat for a time on the large flat rock, watching the sea surge against the shore below. Gradually he disappeared from view.

The sea is an intense purple: ebbing and cresting, its waves underscored in black. Particles everywhere, blurring the distinction between sky and earth. His father sits beside him . . . forming and re-forming.

"There was an event. We were attacked."

[Equilibrium.]

"I wonder about the reciprocal effect. How will we evolve past the back and forth and bring enlightenment to the world?"

[Life moves to light.]

Quan reaches into the boiling dust. "This is the paradox. To see the whole, we must transcend—must become one with everything. And yet, without self-consciousness we won't see the difference between ourselves and anything else. Pure instinct— the mind of an animal."

[Self is an illusion.]

"I want to understand how it works."

[Pointing at the moon will not take you there.]

"I've tried to communicate what I've learned, but I failed. If it's impossible to convey, then each person will have to walk the path for themselves."

[A posteriori.]

Quan pauses, studying the apparition.

"I know all that you've done for me and I'm grateful. I doubt that I will ever be able to understand the nature of this place to the extent that you do. You've been here for a long time. But I don't understand how."

[Only that which is finite requires sustenance.]

"Somehow, you gave up your body. I can't do that."

[Memory is the anchor.]

"Without memories of who I am, I would cease to exist."

[Memories are illusion.]

348

"I feel like a yo-yo. When I'm there I'm drawn here, and when I'm here I'm drawn there."

[Transcend.]

It's the same cryptic answers every time. So difficult to digest. Fatigue is setting in. Quan has enough to think about. As he allows himself to settle back into the more familiar world of hard edges. The particles and the image of his father disperse.

Returning to his bungalow, Lotus and von Ang were waiting for him.

"I'm concerned about what happened," said von Ang. "Gregory says you knew this was coming. Is that true?"

Quan clapped his hands together as if in prayer. "Can you just have a little faith? No harm will come to us. You have to believe that."

"It's true, then," said von Ang. "You believe you saw this coming?"

"I had a premonition," said Quan. "I saw triangles."

"I saw triangles, too," said von Ang. "It was a hallucination, and what does it have to do with the explosion?"

"Tell us," said Lotus. "How does it fit together?"

"We both saw the same warning. The triangle is a triad. It's a symbol used by a Chinese criminal cult," said Quan.

"The Triad," said Lotus.

"McGowen said it was a gas pocket," said von Ang. "Now you're telling us it wasn't an accident. Am I to believe we were attacked by a Chinese gang?"

"Please," Quan interrupted. "What happened was bad, but everything's going to be okay. I asked McGowen to call it a gas explosion because I didn't want anyone to panic. How my premonitions work isn't important. I can't explain it but now I know they're valid. We're going to be safe. I just know it's true. Please believe me."

Lotus asserted herself. "On the one hand, you tell us that a Chinese gang is trying to kill us, and on the other hand, you say

349

'It's going to be okay.' I think you know more than you're telling us."

"Yes. Please explain why you think we're going to be safe," said von Ang. "We have no means to defend ourselves here."

"First. What do you think went wrong?" asked Quan.

"In practical terms, our security field failed to detect the intruders," said von Ang. "The reason it failed is because it doesn't cover the outlying areas of the property. It is set up close to the compound. If they had come in closer we would have heard an alarm. We should add more sensors and expand the perimeter."

"Go ahead then," said Quan. "Engineer and install whatever you think will improve the system."

"Certainly, the system can be improved," said von Ang. "But I still want to know more about your assurance that we're protected. By what? I'd like to know."

"I don't know how to explain without it sounding like I'm delusional. Go and add more security. It's a good backup plan. I believe that what we're doing is very much in line with natural law. This is an evolutionary step and I believe that we will prevail because we're doing what we are supposed to be doing—moving toward the light."

"You have abilities that we don't have," said Lotus. "I don't understand how you see these things and frankly, it's a little spooky."

Outside, a covey of quail flushed from a thicket, startled by an unseen threat.

San Francisco

In the upstairs dining room of the Imperial Palace, Honzu listened as the Red Pole leader recounted his misadventure. Through binoculars he witnessed the carnage. There was nothing he could do. He drove away.

As the man spoke, Honzu's blood pressure rose.

"Drink your tea," said Honzu, setting a cup down in front of the man. "You were their leader. You should have gone with them. You should have died with them."

As Big Yao set the cup down, his eyes opened wide and his hand went to his throat. Honzu watched as the heavyset man slumped in his chair and slowly keeled over, face down on the floor, his lips turning black.

"Get him out of my sight," yelled Honzu.

Two men grabbed Yao's arms and dragged him out of the room.

There was no way to conceal the failure, and now Honzu would have to explain the botched mission to the 14K chapter of New Hong Knog. He opened a com line and, after reporting the failure, he complained, "Why weren't we told they were armed?"

"We should have given this job to our brothers in Los Angeles," said the voice on the other end. "They're more reliable. Your loss of face is shameful, however this is still your responsibility—even more so now. You will see it through and you will avenge your fallen brothers."

"They will be avenged," promised Honzu.

46.

Before the dawn broke over the coastal mountains, Quan was awake. He sat up in his bed and spoke a command. Room dividers retracted, opening his bedroom to an unrestricted view of the living room with its floor-to-ceiling outer doors. The sprawling oak tree outside came into view, and beyond the oak, the large flat rock and the cliffs veiled in mist. He spoke again and the outer glass doors telescoped silently back into the walls letting in fresh air and the scent of wild sage. Reaching to his side, he brought up another pillow, putting it behind his head. His hand slid across the sheet to the other side of the bed—empty. Sealy wasn't there. He was alone.

He had made difficult choices and yet, as his confidence was unshakable. Publishing the machine plans had not cured all of his problems, but it was a step in the right direction. In the larger scheme of things, the plans were of no consequence. He

352

wondered how many eyes were studying them at that very moment. Quite a few he suspected.

The plans were complicated, spanning over a hundred pages: part drawings, assembly diagrams, schematics, parts lists, and computations. It would take quite a while for even the most diligent team to understand them and longer for them to actually build a machine. On one of the schematics, at the center of a controller board, was a small ROM chip labeled "7-2521." It contained the compiled run-time codes necessary to operate the machine's complex subsystems. Eventually the technicians would discover that the chip wasn't available from any known supplier and the run-time codes were not included in the plans. Without the codes, the machine was just a very expensive assembly of unrelated components and creating the run-time codes from scratch would take months if not years of trial and error.

The omission was Quan's plan all along. Having assigned ownership rights to the Jintao Corporation, very soon it would become known that the company was the sole source of chips containing the embedded codes.

As the sun lifted higher, the mist began to clear and banks of orange poppies began to open along the cliff's edge. A brown lizard positioned itself on top of the big flat rock and did its morning push-ups.

Turning his cheek to the cool pillowcase, Quan looked at Sealy's side of the bed. Even though he missed her, there was always the possibility that the center would be attacked again and bringing her and their child to the Research Center would put them both at risk. Returning to China would result in his arrest and would also leave the research center vulnerable—without his special capabilities.

There must be a way home.

Quan left the comfort of his bed and went to shower and begin his day. An hour later, he was six meters below ground, in the laboratory, telling McGowen about the chips.

"So, you clever lad. You published the machine design but left out the software," said McGowen. "I don't remember reading that in *The Book of Thirty-Six Strategies*."

"It's from the book of Microsoft—hardware is just the platform. Software is where the real value is."

"Braw," chuckled McGowen. "Speaking of software, David turned out to be useful. While you were gone, I asked him to see what he could do with the reactor cooling program and he boosted efficiency by twenty-two percent."

"Impressive," said Quan.

While McGowen went on bragging about the young man, Quan became uneasy. He walked over to von Ang who was having his morning espresso. "Does David have access to the run-time codes?"

"No," said von Ang. "Only you and I and McGowen have access."

"Can you check to see if anyone else has accessed the file?"

Von Ang went to his view field and brought up the access logs. Looking at the last month's entries, sure enough, there it was. Several unauthorized saves.

"Did you know about this?" asked von Ang.

"Call it another premonition."

Quan called out to McGowen, "We need to have a talk with David."

"Why? What is it?" asked McGowen.

"He's accessed the run-time codes."

"On it I am." And McGowen bolted from the lab.

Minutes later the elevator doors opened and the young East Indian stepped out, grinning. Greeting Quan with his Hindi accent, he said, "Dr. Jintao. So pleased you are back. Your disclosures at the conference were most impressive, I must say. And what you did—allowing everyone to share the invention—it

354

was most beneficent—a wonderful thing to be sure. Most generous."

"Thank you, David, but I have a concern. We see that you've accessed the run-time codes. Tell us why."

"To get a better idea of how the machine works, sahib."

"I see. And how did you get past our security encryptions?"

"Oh, that was most challenging, I must say," said David, pursing his smile.

McGowen flushed. "Sir, I had no idea he would . . ."

Behind them, von Ang was working at his view field, "I'm doubling security on those files."

"It appears you downloaded the file. Tell me why," asked Quan, calmly studying the young man.

David's eyes fixed on him. "Oh my gracious me."

"Did you think our source code was yours to do with as you please?"

David took a step back, slipping his hand into his pocket.

McGowen raised his voice and moved toward David, "You're a big disappointment, boy. We trusted you."

"Wait," said Quan, raising a cautionary hand. "We need to understand what happened—and why. David, why would you copy our source code?"

David backed up to the elevator and reached a hand behind him, pressing the button. As the door opened, he stepped backwards and, dropping his pretense, he began to speak in a distinctly American accent. "It's what I do, man. Just a job. That's all."

"Who are you working for? Who's paying you?"

"This is way over your head, man," said David, his composure becoming more serious as he felt around behind him for the elevator button. "Don't take it personally."

"Phoney little shit," said McGowen.

"Was it the Americans?" asked Quan. "And now that you have the codes. What are you going to do? Did you think we'd just let you walk out of here?"

The elevator door was closing and McGowen quickly thrust his arm inside to grab David. "Come here, you!"

David jumped to the side and out of his pocket came a small TENS unit. It discharged into McGowen's arm and his muscles went into spasm.

"Like I said, it's nothing personal," said David.

The big Scot jerked back, rubbed his arm, and growled, "You won't get far, kid."

The elevator door closed.

"I've got this," said Quan as he began to dissolve into the Braneworld. Two strides and he was inside the elevator.

Studying the dark figure next to him, Quan sees a small object, a fingernail-sized disk, implanted at David's temple just beneath his hair, most likely a data bank. And in one of David's pockets he spots a jelly-bean-sized homing device.

Seconds later, Quan materialized as the elevator doors were opening at the lobby. He spoke calmly. "Why leave when there is so much more you could learn?"

"Whoa!" said David, jumping back against the elevator wall. "How'd you—what the?"

"I told you. There's a lot to learn." Quan pressed the elevators down button.

"I don't get it. What do you want from me?"

"Good question. You have talent, for one thing, and it's no accident you're here. I believe this is where you're supposed to be." The elevator door opened again in the laboratory.

"Come here peckerwood," said McGowen, grabbing David's coat—pulling him and spinning him around. He pointed to a stool and barked, "Sit."

"Stay here with him," said Quan, stepping into the elevator. "We'll finish this in a few minutes."

356

With the big Scotsman hovering over him, a despondent David sat and watched the elevator door close.

Before leaving for the Paris convention, Quan relayed the run-time codes and a list of patent claims to the Jintao legal department. The claims broadly covered the general principles without disclosing specific algorithms and values. By now the claims were in the hands of patent agencies worldwide, naming the Jintao Corporation as assignee—sole manufacturer of the essential chip.

Stepping into the daylight, Quan opened a com line to Green. After listening to the story, Green said, "Let me see if he transmitted anything. My security stack would have traced it. Hold on. Yep, there's something. Looks like he started to transmit but spotted the trace and bailed. He's good. Got a destination, though . . . hold on . . . nope, that's a VPN. . . hold on . . . going deeper . . . nope, a phony IP. Hang with me, I'm gonna run this through a different server. Working . . . working . . . nope, a road to nowhere. Wait. Let me dig into his ID. Okay, pulling his sheet. Before he worked with me he was with Cyber Ops. Just a sec . . . I'm using my clearance. Okay, found his file. Uh-oh, now I see it. The kid's got history... before Cyber Ops. He's not Gupta and he's not East Indian. Try Gepeta from Queens . . . high-level hacker . . . string of online aliases back into his teens. He was popped for hacking a com sat and flipped to work for Cyber Ops. Sorry. Didn't see this before. We needed help in a pinch and Cyber Ops had already cleared him. Your call. What do you want me to do?"

"Nothing for now. It all fits. May be providence in disguise."

"The good news is, he didn't transmit. My guess is that he's got a hard copy stashed somewhere."

"I'll deal with it," said Quan and he closed the line.

Now Quan understood why Bledsoe was so jovial on that last day in Paris. He was one step ahead from the beginning. As a

Plan B, he had planted an operative at the Research Center even before the conference began.

Of course, thought Quan, *it all fits. Inspectors from the Nuclear Regulatory Commission filed a report for the reactor. That report ended up in the hands of Central Intelligence. For all we know they've been surveilling us from day one.*

Below, in the laboratory, McGowen leered at David. "Yer lucky, boy."

"I don't feel lucky," said David.

"Lucky I don't put you in a ditch. Lucky that's not how we do things around here."

The elevator door opened and as Quan came into view McGowen blurted out, "I take full responsibility for this, sir. I thought he was doing the work I gave him—maybe a little research on his own, but . . . I should've looked more closely."

"You're not to blame," said Quan striding into the room. "I think we can resolve this to everyone's benefit. Come on, David. Let's take a walk."

"Like I said, I was just doing a job," said David, getting to his feet and sizing up McGowen.

"Come on," said Quan, taking the lead, steering David back into the elevator.

The doors closed and Quan continued. "See how this is working out for you, David? What kind of life have you got? Stealing and hiding in the shadows? That may have been exciting for you in your teens, but you're getting a little old for that. It's time you stepped up to something more fulfilling. What we're doing here is going to affect people worldwide—in a good way. It may even change humanity forever. What are you doing that will have that kind of impact?"

As soon as the elevator door opened, David stepped out and said, "Nice talking to you, but I've got to run." He turned and took off, running toward the roadway.

Quan shouted, "Was that your only copy?"

358

David stopped in his tracks. Pressing a finger to his temple he said, "Wait. What?" He fumbled in the corners of his pockets. His data bank and the locater were gone.

"That's impossible. How did you do that?"

"My dear Mr. Gepeta," said Quan, walking toward him, "I know a quite few things you don't know. Now come back, walk with me."

"Fuck me," said David, walking in Quan's direction.

Arriving at the cliffs, with the whitewater pounding below, Quan said, "Change is inevitable." He threw two tiny objects out into the air, watching them drift down into the breakers.

"You're being pretty cool about this," said David, fidgeting, afraid to be so close to the precipice. "This whole 'hidden world' thing you discovered is pretty damn cool, but you can't keep me here. All you can prove is that I accessed your software and I'll say I had permission from that big lunk. What you've got on me is a big nothing."

"Help us with the research," said Quan. "That's what I want. I think there's a place for you here."

David kicked a bit of dirt with his foot and scoffed. "I don't need a job, if that's what you're offering. I think what you've got here is primo but I'm just not the guy you want—not much of a team player—never have been."

"What have you got to lose? Free room and board. Give it a month, then decide."

"A month wouldn't kill me, buuuuut . . ." said David, looking down at waves breaking on the jagged rocks. "I'm not so sure I want to be here."

"If you were honest with yourself, you'd admit that you don't want to spend the rest of your life hiding in the shadows. I see you, David. I know there were events in your life that you still blame yourself for. You have a mistaken view of yourself, but deep down you want to do things you can be proud of."

"I've got to say, I'd like to learn how you did what you did back there in the elevator."

"We'll see." Quan saw what would follow as if it were a sign hung around David's neck.

"Something tells me I don't have a choice," he said. "Just a month. Right? Then I can leave if I want to?"

"That's all I ask. Do we have a deal?" said Quan, extending his hand.

David shook Quan's hand nervously. A guy who could disappear at will could easily push him over the edge.

"You had me all along. You knew who I was. Damn. Why'd you string me out?"

"It was important that you chose to be here of your own free will. Now, that your only copy?"

"Yes, but damn. You went under my skin, and in my pocket!" said David, flabbergasted. "I didn't feel a thing. How'd you do that?"

"It's a long story. Now, can I trust you to behave? No more stealing from us? No more trying to transmit information."

"Okay, okay, okay."

"Good. I'll tell everyone the news," said Quan, calmly. "Trust me, they'll be fine with it."

Hold your friends close and your enemies closer.

47.

David Gepeta, alias DrFrag, alias Ghostfish, alias Nikki9, alias McWack, was one of the best. Starting as a teen, he was able to reach into the data vaults of corporations and governments with immaculate ease. When he was caught, it hadn't been the result of carelessness. He'd been set up by another hacker who plea bargained to save his own skin. The feds gave David a choice: work for dot gov or come out of stasis an old man. Not a difficult choice to make.

Being caught at the Research Center added yet another failure to his reputation; and, as for the money, well—no product, no money. But all was not lost; there was the curious matter of Quan not pressing charges, letting him stay on—a gesture he didn't deserve but one he was determined to capitalize on. What Quan was capable of, the ability to disappear at will, made the run-time codes look like chump change. If he could master the technique, he could have the world and everything in it.

Over the next twenty-four hours, he tried to will himself into the unseen world. He tried until his back was racked with pain and his vision blurred, yet there was no effect, not even a hint of change. Convinced it was a technique he could learn, he went to the underground lab looking for Quan.

David stepped out of the lift and was immediately confronted by McGowen. "You need something?"

"Not from you, big guy," said David, walking over to Quan. "You said I could assist with the research."

"Yes."

"I want to research transferring the way you do. You're the only one who can do it. Isn't that right?"

"So far as we know."

"I want to understand how it's done. It's a technique, right? Something that can be learned?"

"I wouldn't trust him if I were you," said McGowen.

"It's okay," said Quan, holding up a hand. "Meet me topside in an hour and we can talk about it."

Wind was whipping their pant legs as they crossed the compound. Reaching the coastal precipice, Quan stepped out onto his favorite flat rock, facing the horizon. "Come up here," he said.

David hesitated, seeing the ocean below.

"You have a strong desire," said Quan. "Let's see how far that can take you."

David hesitated to step up onto the rock platform.

"First, you need to overcome your fear."

David pursed his lips and stepped up next to Quan. "What do you mean?"

Quan's green eyes sparkled. "Close your eyes and empty your mind."

David looked down three stories to the rocks below.

"Nothing to be afraid of," said Quan. "I'm here with you."

Quan looked straight ahead and said not a word. He could feel David's mind churning.

David continued to look at him apprehensively.

Motionless as a stone monument, Quan stood patiently waiting for David's restless parade of thoughts to end. "When your mind is still, it will happen," he said.

As time passed, David calmed down and his mind slowed, thoughts coiling themselves like snakes under a cool rock. Looking out to the horizon, he could hear the waves surging below and things moving all around him—a squirrel in the brush, hawks above, insects on the ground, the sun's energy warming his skin, and the briny air in his nostrils. His thoughts were in abeyance, his attention on nothing in particular.

"Good," said Quan. "Now follow me."

First the surface of Quan's body became grainy. Then, very slowly, the grains dissolved into the air. Watching, David could sense the change taking place next to him and he tried to follow Quan's lead.

Once Quan was gone, David's fear returned. Standing on that rocky precipice alone, he was vulnerable. Was this a trick? What if Quan wanted to push him over the edge?

In the Braneworld, a multicolored storm encircles Quan. He looks at David, a shadowy figure covered in white fringe. He can see David looking around for safety. But there is something else Quan sees. Unexpectedly, there is something on the other side of David, another figure. He leans forward to get a better view. The form withdraws. He takes a step back, trying to catch a better look. His mind bristles, he loses concentration and the Braneworld vanishes.

"I can't do it," said David. "I don't understand how. What do I need to do?"

Quan tried to explain. "Conventional wisdom says the brain gives rise to a thing we call mind. However, there are yogis who use their minds to control the brain, and they can tell their brains to do things that seem impossible—like disregard pain and stop the heart. I believe the mind can also control the flux of matter between this world and the other. All I'm doing is concentrating on being there instead of here. Maybe it's not something you can learn. I don't know."

"I'm just not getting it."

"I'll tell Dr. von Ang to set you up for transference. When equipment takes you there, concentrate on the process of what it's doing to your body. That will help."

"I'm still getting used to the idea that you trust me."

Seeing the good in him, Quan expected the transfer experience would have a profound effect on David.

Turn enemies into allies.

New Hong Kong
Sealy was sitting up in bed at her parents' house, feeling snug under the covers. In the view field hovering at the foot of her bed, a fashionable young Asian woman dressed in white silk stepped onto the gangway of a luxury yacht. Holding on to her wide-brimmed white hat with one hand, she reached out with the other hand. One of the crew, also dressed in white, reached out a hand to assist her. Nearby another crew member held out a small silver tray with a martini glass containing a bright amber liquid. The young woman removed her hat and tossed back her long black hair. With a flourish, she picked up the glass and, lifting it high, she said, "For health and prosperity." Taking a sip, she smiled broadly and the camera went in for a close-up of her face. The words "Qinghou Wealth Tonic" appeared at the bottom of the view field.

Sealy's com started bipping. She shouted at the projection, "Vidi off!" and the room obeyed.

"Hey, it's me," said Lotus. "Am I interrupting something?"

"It's fine," said Sealy, trying to be cordial. "I'm glad it's you. I was feeling a little lonesome. How is everything in California?"

"That's why I'm calling," said Lotus. "Hey. We have vidi comm set up here now. Turn on your camera."

Sealy spoke the command and instantly Lotus was on the view field.

"Wow. Look at you—like a queen. How comfortable you look."

"Well, there's this." Sealy pulled down the sheets and lifted her nightshirt to show her belly.

"You're beautiful. How are you feeling?"

She smiled. "I'm feeling good, but a little confined here."

"You can go outside, can't you?"

"There isn't anywhere to go that I haven't already been a hundred times before. So, tell me what's going on there."

"There was an explosion."

"What? No! That's terrible. In the laboratory? Was anyone hurt?"

"None of us were hurt. It was outside—far away from the lab. It was loud. Woke everyone up."

"It was an accident? What caused it?"

"We don't know for sure. I should let Quan tell you about it. He knows more than I do."

"Here we go again. I haven't heard from him in days."

The thought of Quan being too busy to tell her about an explosion was infuriating. Three weeks had past since they'd left Paris and they had only spoken a few times. It was maddening.

"This is beyond belief. Why is he being so inconsiderate," said Sealy.

"He probably didn't want to upset you. It's been crazy busy here and he's had his hands full," said Lotus. "I'm sure he'll be in touch soon."

"Don't make excuses for him. He was so warm and sweet in Paris and now he's acting as though we're strangers. He used

365

to tell me everything. Now, he doesn't call. What's going on with him?"

"Lately he's expressed doubts about the value of what we're doing here. I'm sure he'd rather be back home with you."

Lotus went on to talk about David's attempt to steal secrets and his real identity as an American hacker. She had concerns about David working on the perimeter security. As Sealy listened, it became clear that Quan was facing a host of problems.

"I feel abandoned. It's as if that research has taken everything away from me."

"I know it must feel that way," said Lotus. "When you're able, you really should come for a visit. You'd be amazed."

"I thought I wanted to, but with what you've just told me, it doesn't sound safe. Besides, I'm not sure Quan wants me there. What about you and Gaston? Are you getting along?"

"We're solid and I've learned so much from him."

"I'm thinking this is a more comfortable place for me to be, at least for now. Ask Quan to com me. We need to talk."

48.

Morning came and Dr. von Ang was settling into his workstation, about to enjoy his second cup of Italian roast. He began the morning routine, reviewing the graphs and readouts from the previous day. Being the conscientious scientist, he continued to check the logs and verify the calibrations daily even though the equipment continued to operate perfectly. Everything seemed normal until . . .

He sat up straight and set down his cup. In a separate window, he brought up the benchmark, the first human transfer at the new facility, the one with the volunteer. Comparing the values to the most recent transfers, the power signatures and the fifth-order harmonics were different.

Concerned that one of the subsystems might be failing, von Ang ran diagnostics. The systems were functioning within acceptable limits. *So, what is it?* he wondered.

Leaving his desk, he went to the equipment room. Finding McGowen there, he asked, "Are there any new radiation sources in the lab?"

McGowen looked up from his work and thought for a moment. "New? Nothing new. Why?"

"The system is running within spec, but the harmonics have changed. I'm thinking it might be some sort of external radiation. Are you sure there isn't something new?"

"Hmm. Nothing new except that old interceptor I parked out back."

"You can check to see if it is leaking?"

"You know how to use an antenna. Check it yourself," said McGowen, going back to what he was doing.

Von Ang went to the back of the room and took what he needed from the equipment rack. Carrying a black box in one hand and a wand in the other, he went outside. Standing next to the vehicle he threw the silver tarp covering and switched on the receiver. He plugged the antenna cable into a port on the box and began walking around the vehicle. Passing the wand over the top and underneath, there was only a faint trace of radiation—hardly registering on the meter.

Returning to his desk, he sat motionless, wondering what else it could be. Flipping through the records, he began looking through the session logs one at a time. The latest transfers showed different values, however the system hadn't posted errors. Opening the archive of routine data backups he saw a series of saves that were not scheduled. The times were random.

To his surprise, the file that had been saved several times was the source code. He opened the source code file and ran a comparator program looking at each line of code. Some of the values had been changed.

With a hand on the doorway, von Ang leaned into the room where McGowen was working and asked, "Did you make any changes to the run-time code?"

"No. Why would I do that?"

"Well, somebody did, and it wasn't me."

A concerned look swept over McGowen's face. His eyes went to the transference rig in the other room and he blurted out, "Judas priest. If it's that kid again, I'll have his guts for garters."

"Wait," said von Ang. "I should tell Quan first." When Quan heard the news, he said calmly, "On my way. Have him meet us in the lab."

A few minutes later the elevator door opened and David stepped out. "You wanted me?"

"Did you make changes to the run-time codes?" asked Quan.

"Has to be him," McGowen grumbled.

"You said I should learn by transferring. I tried and tried but couldn't, so I thought if I tweaked the settings a bit . . . it's more focused now."

"Unbelievable," said McGowen, straightening to his full height.

David went on, "I can switch it back if you like, but personally I think it's better."

"You don't know anything about the dynamics of this equipment," said von Ang. "You could have caused a major malfunction. Why would you think you know what you're doing?"

"Intuition. I increased power to the stabilizer and tweaked the harmonics. That's all. It just made sense to me. It took a few tries to get it dialed in, but I was careful. And I tried it on myself first."

"And you could have killed yourself," said von Ang.

"More importantly, you could have damaged the machine and shut down our whole operation," said McGowen, shaking his head. "Unbelievable."

"It was just a little tweak," said David. "Have you tried it? It's an improvement."

"Maybe so, but what you think you did may be very different from what you actually did," said von Ang.

"What do you mean?" asked David.

"We're just beginning to understand the phenomenon. There could be many dimensions. For the sake of argument, what if you inadvertently tuned the equipment to a completely different set of dimensions than the ones we were studying?"

"That would be a good thing. Wouldn't it? It would allow you to explore those other dimensions, too."

"Ha!" shouted McGowen. "You act like you know what you're talking about. You have no respect for boundaries. You're not the scientist here. Dr. von Ang is the scientist. We should've let you go a long time ago."

"You guys," said David, shaking his head. "You guys should be thanking me. Here you are, repeating the same things over and over again. I mean, aren't we here to experiment?"

Von Ang stepped in and said, "This is my lab. I'm in charge and we're doing serious work here. We must follow strict scientific protocol. From now on, no more transfers for you without my approval. And you should be checked before and after each session."

"This equipment is not a toy," said McGowen, "and you're not the only one using it. You could've killed yourself or someone else. You were lucky, boy." He turned to Quan. "Are we really going to keep him on? It's obvious he can't be trusted."

"Enough!" shouted Quan. "Stop your bickering. Foolish, lucky, or talented—he's opened up something new. We're a team. And David, you were wrong to do this without talking to us first. Luckily, there's no harm done. You are not to make any more changes without consulting us. Understood?"

"Are you getting this, boy?" said McGowen.

David raised his hands in surrender. "Okay, okay, okay. I was just trying to help."

To Quan, it wasn't important that David was experimenting on his own, it was the petty squabbling that annoyed him. Who was right or wrong wasn't important. All that mattered was getting to the next level.

370

"David brought us something new and definitely worth exploring."

Von Ang spoke again, this time a bit calmer. "He he seems to be alright but before anyone else tries it, let's do a full medical eval of him."

"Like I said, you can always go back to the other settings," said David.

While David lay on the medi-bot gurney, Quan said to him, "If you want to stay and work with us, you'll need to learn to work as part of a team. You've broken trust with us twice now and I won't forgive a third time. Understand?"

"I understand," said David. "I want to stay."

After David was cleared of health issues, Quan stepped onto the gimbal mount.

"Set it for one minute," he said.

"Sir!" said McGowen.

"Enough," said Quan, looking sharply into McGowen's eyes.

The look shocked McGowen. There was a ferociousness in Quan's eyes he had never seen before.

Von Ang went to the controls and engaged the system. The bed rotated and the machine ramped up to full power.

In every direction, the laboratory looks like a quivering ice sculpture, like it's made of iridescent jelly. David, McGowen, and von Ang stand next to him, vibrating shapes in prismatic gelatin—as if an unsteady hand is tracing their contours. He looks at his outstretched arm; the white quills are gone. He looks closer, into the quivering shape, and sees outlines of blood cells flowing in clear veins. Like a high-contrast PET scan—muscles, sinews, and bone. When he sweeps his arm through the air, cavitation trails are left behind, swirling in iridescent eddies.

At the sixty-second mark, Quan returned.

"It is different, all right. The opacity is gone. Everything's transparent. The particles are gone and I could see each of you more clearly. Could you see me?"

"No, sir," said McGowen.

Von Ang said, "I'm concerned that we don't know exactly what we've got here. For safety, I think we should return to the settings we know . . . until I understand the changes."

"It feels perfectly fine," said Quan. "I want to go again. After that you can do whatever you like. Now please set it up again—five minutes this time."

"Wait," said von Ang. "Take the micro spectrometer." He went to get the device.

"That can wait," said Quan. "We'll do it next time." Quan needed to feel his body transfer into the new setting one more time without any encumbrances.

Von Ang acquiesced and went back to the controls.

The transfer was smooth.

Quan feels subtle differences. The transfer isn't as granular as before. He commits the transfer to memory. *How can this be? How was David able to guess at this? Can't be just random chance. Something must have guided him. It's too direct and focused to be a random act.*

Giving in to an urge, he pushes off from where he is. Arms at his side, he slides through the air, curving around and back to the transfer bed. It's smoother, as if he could travel great distances with little effort. He laughs. The idea that machinery is needed to cross the universe all of a sudden seems like something out of an early science fiction novel, where it takes many generations to cross the galaxy. The idea that our species would ever reach the distant stars by burning fuel and hibernating in suspended animation seems ludicrous. Only by evolving can we ever hope to reach the depths of space, he realizes; only by evolving.

He calls out, "Father?"

The foreground begins to ripple. Edges begin to fold. A full-sized figure is etching into the gel, creasing itself into shape. Multicolored lines are quivering, fashioning a bas-relief of his father.

"Is it you?"

[I am.]

"This is a different setting and you're here?"

The lips don't move. As always, the specter seems to be channeling some vast store of wisdom, boiling it down to a few well-chosen words.

[All is all.]

"You mean it's all part of the same thing. Are you saying this is a different aspect of the same universe? Is that it?"

[All is all.]

"Your knowledge, the information you have. I want to learn."

[Walk the path.]

"I understand. Each of us must walk the path, must see for ourselves. It's the only way to really know what we are. But, why do you stay here? You're all alone here, no one to share this with. I want to learn more from you but it would be more convenient if you were with us. Why not come home—be with your family?"

[Be liminal.]

"Both sides? How can you be in both places?"

There is no answer.

Quan turns from the apparition and looks up. Lifting himself, he ascends, past the laboratory ceiling, through earth and rock. Chin up, his arms trailing at his side, he rises . . . into the bright daylight . . . fifty meters above the Research Center. He knows he can go much farther, but his time is almost up.

These dimensions are ours to explore. This is the way we'll cross the universe—not in a metal space ship.

Quan returned to the lab and put a hand on David's shoulder. "How you were able to find this is beyond me. It proves you were meant to be here."

David smiled.

Looking from David to von Ang to McGowen, Quan said, "Nature does experiments blindly and most of its experiments are of no benefit. Evolution moves at a snail's pace and speeding up the process is definitely the way to go. It's time we took ownership of our own evolution for a change. What David did was a good thing. The new settings may lead to a broader understanding."

Von Ang found it impossible to believe the new settings were the result of guesswork. Precise calculations were necessary. Either David knew something he wasn't telling or he was some sort of intuitive savant. "A talented hacker, yes. That I agree. And he was very lucky."

Focusing on McGowen, Quan said, "Maybe you were premature, chastising David. You should try it."

"Maybe," said the Scotsman, "but I still think he's loose cannon. We should have a look at your readings now, sir."

Quan complied, and after the scans checked out normal, von Ang picked up one of the test instruments from the bench and said, "To properly do our research, we must be disciplined. We follow scientific method and document as we go. I want to see if we can still achieve gamma transmission with these new settings."

Stepping onto the gimbal mount, with instruments in hand, von Ang said, "If you would assist me, Mr. McGowen, I'll only need two minutes."

The bed flashed, sequencing the scientist and his instruments. He stood there anxiously, looking over his shoulder, watching the readouts until . . .

It catches him by surprise—vibrating gel everywhere. He can see through everything as if it were made of ice. He

374

dismounts carefully and, setting an emitter on the ground, he turns on the receiver. It shows nothing. He resets the gain. No gamma emissions. No X-rays. He tries another instrument. The display is blank. He collects the instruments and climbs back onto the bed. Then something catches his attention. Startled, he whips his head to see a figure staring at him, a quivering outline. It is Quan. His lips are moving. He seems to be saying something. Von Ang can't hear him.

The machine timed out and von Ang returned, still looking at the same location.

"What do you think?" asked Quan.

Von Ang bolted from the bed and dropped his instruments on the floor. Fingers trembling, he stooped to pick them up. "You followed me there. I wasn't expecting that."

"Sorry. I didn't mean to scare you. I've internalized the new settings."

"You're able to do that? How?"

"I just remember how the flux feels and how it manifests on the other side. It's different from our original settings. I memorized it. It's like what happens when you internalize moves, like in chess or backgammon. The moves become hardwired and you don't have to think about them anymore. You just know intuitively what to do."

"I appreciate the metaphor but it is not helping me understand what you are doing physically."

"That's understandable. It's at odds with your knowledge base. This is all new. You may have to forget what you think you know and start over."

Still somewhat shaken, von Ang set his instruments down on the bench and said, "Gamma frequencies are not transmitting and dark matter is not registering. The new settings may not be a full set of dimensions at all. It's possible that the previous set contained a different set of dimensions and now we have others.

It makes our work that much more complex. It could take a very long time to make sense of this."

"I agree. The way we've been going about it, using traditional methods, it could take a very long time," said Quan. "The irony is that the answers are right in front of us; it's just our inability to grasp what's going on—that's the problem."

"Can you think of a better way?" asked von Ang, his frustration surfacing as he picked up an instrument from the bench and set it down again.

Quan took a moment, then said, "Immersion."

"Immersion? I'm listening."

"Good science is good observation, right? Slow and methodical. That's what you do. After observation, the next step is interpretation of what you've observed. There are many ways to interpret what you've seen, so you make a hypothesis. Then you go about testing the hypothesis. That takes time. Stay with me now. I see a better way—like learning a new language—immersion is a quicker way to learn about these other dimensions."

"You're suggesting that I should live in the Braneworld in order to better understand it?"

"Not you. I was thinking it should be someone else."

"Who, then?" asked von Ang.

"Me, of course."

"No, no, no," McGowen weighed in. "You're indispensible, sir. You're the one who has held this project together. You can't just put yourself in there for what? A day? A week? A month? With all due respect, that's unacceptable. It may be the reason your father never came back. I'm sorry. I can't go along with that."

Quan put a hand on McGowen's shoulder. "My father's legacy is assured. The Research Center is up and running. It has a life of its own and it will continue with or without me. Trust me. It is better for everyone if I do this."

"Think this through, sir," said McGowen. "There could be serious consequences. We don't know what could happen. What if you can't come back? No one has stayed in there more than a few minutes. Immerse someone else. I'll get another volunteer."

"Gregory is right," said von Ang. "He can recruit another volunteer to explore this idea of yours. We should take our time and do controlled experiments. What's the hurry?"

"Volunteers are fine. You go ahead. But, I have an inside track. I have a connection with the other dimensions that nobody else has. I can find out more, faster than a volunteer can."

Von Ang felt powerless. Scientific method and controlled experiments were the right way. He knew that. And the young Jintao, trying to sustain a long term stay in the Braneworld, was a bad idea.

Wise souls
leaving self behind
move forward
and setting self aside
stay centered.
—Lao-Tzu, 500 BC

49.

Leaving the laboratory, Quan went to the terrace behind his bungalow. In front of him stood the great oak tree, sunlight filtering through its branches. He walked to the right a few feet.

The tree's form looks different depending where I stand. What my eyes see is only two and a half dimensions. My imagination puts the images together and constructs a three-dimensional model. That's this world—just a mental construction. In David's setting I can see through the tree. In this world, its inner form is hidden.

And who knows how the tree perceives itself? The tree keeps its secrets to itself.

He conjured up his memory of David's new setting. The feeling it gave him was nice—like being in clear jelly—soft and cool. The change began within every cell of his body. He embraced it, latched onto it and, with a little push, he faded from view.

A huge transparent tree vibrates in front of him. Roots anchor it to the earth—tendrils explore the rocky soil. Branches reach into the air and leaves prostrate themselves to sunlight. The tree is its way into the world, inextricably bonded to its environment, rooted in every dimension—as are all living things.

"Father?" says Quan.

The gelled atmosphere begins to churn. Outlines form and the form takes shape until an effigy of his father is standing there.

"Your grandson will be born soon," says Quan.

[The nexus.]

"The nexus? Connection to what?"

[The light.]

"The light?"

[The father.]

"And what of you? You'll be the grandfather."

[A marker in space-time.]

His father had gone looking for a new frontier, something to challenge his intellect. He ventured into an unknown aspect of matter and stayed to study it—eventually giving up his physical self in the bargain. It was evident to Quan that the senior Jintao was going to stay in that quasi state of existence indefinitely. Would he die there?

As life evolved, it must have realized the usefulness of death—and death turned out to be one of life's best inventions. It clears out the old and makes room for the new. Death is life's perpetual agent of change—necessary for its evolution.

Quan wondered what would happen if he were to attempt a prolonged exposure to the other dimensions. Would his physical existence become forfeit like his father? Would know when to return to avoid that?

He turns and looks at the phantom. "What will happen if I stay in this altered state?"

[It is liminal.]

A stage?

"Where does it lead—what should I fear?" asked Quan.

[Look to the north. Danger comes from the east.]
"What danger?"

The phantom repeats the warning then dissipates in wavelets, rippling out in all directions.

Returning to his native state, Quan walked slowly toward the bluff, thinking about this strange warning—danger from the east.

He was proud of what his father had done. He could have grown old, surrounded by family and people who admired him. He sacrificed so much to explore that other place.

Quan thought about Sealy and how easy their life had been . . . easy and so naïve. Now their lives were complicated tenfold. She was safe in China where her parents could care for her. No doubt, she was better off there. If she had come to California, she would have been stressed. Better that she stayed.

If she were with here, she would ask him to give up the idea of immersing himself in the other dimensions—live the life of a good father and partner instead—that's what she wanted. In the moment, it seemed impossible. An extraordinary path lay before him. If only he could do both—be with her and continue the exploration.

As the sky turned to dusk, he returned to his quarters. Nearing the front door, he heard something unexpected coming from inside: the sound of a baby crying. He heard it again.

A baby? Sealy? No. Too soon.

A light was on in the bedroom and the door was partially open. Reaching the threshold, he paused and called out, "Sealy?"

There was no answer.

Pushing the door open, he stepped inside. On the bed, swaddled in a yellow blanket, was a baby, lying there, all alone. He could see its tiny nose and mouth. It cried again . . . the exact same cry . . . the mouth unmoving. He stepped closer—and the world went black.

Quan awoke in a dark space, on a mattress smelling of tobacco. Hazy light was filtering in from a small window high up on the wall. His eyes slowly adjusted to the dimness. There was a sharp pain at the back of his head. The walls around him appeared to be metal. The room was vibrating and his hands were bound tightly behind him.

Where am I?

Crouched in front of him was a boulder of a man. A lighter clicked and the flame was sucked into a short thick cigar clamped in his mouth. In the light, three scars on the back of the man's hand—three smooth dots arranged in a triangle—tattoos of various colors beginning at the wrist, disappearing under the jacket. And the face—beads of sweat on the oily forehead—trails running down the cheeks.

Holding the flame higher, the man held up a doll and dangled it helplessly a few centimeters from Quan's face.

Swinging the doll from side to side, he said, "Thought it was yours, didn't you? You little shit."

"What do you want? Ransom? Is that what you want?" asked Quan.

The lighter was tucked away. The man sat back, and smirked. "Your company will pay millions." He exhaled a cloud of smoke into Quan's face and with a big ugly grin he said, "And after they pay, I'll see to it that you suffer for what you did to my men. And, when I'm done with you, I'll ship your sorry ass back to China."

"You were able to get through our security field. How did you do that?"

"I have my ways."

"Where are you taking me?" asked Quan, struggling to sit upright, fingering his wrist and his bonds.

"That wrist disk of yours ain't going to help you now. I killed it. Nobody's coming to rescue you."

It took a little more finesse but Quan eventually learned that the man was Honzu and he had defeated the Research Center's security field using a reflecting beam gateway, equipment procured from someone in Silicon Valley.

"Silicon Valley, you said. So, we're heading north. And just how do you plan on keeping me?"

Honzu's brow creased. He scoffed and pointed with the wet end of his cigar. "You stupid or something? You see where you are? You're mine. You belong to me."

Quan studied his opponent then rolled over onto his side again. Without saying another word, his body became transparent. Shapes all around him turned to outlines and the world became undulating aspic.

Rolling quickly away from Honzu, Quan pops up on his knees. He can see the road outside zipping by.

Honzu jumps to his feet and kicks at the place where Quan had been. Ranting from one end of the boxcar to the other, he fumes and slams his fist into the side of the freighter, yelling, "*Cào! Cào ni zuzong shíba-dài!*"

Quan channels his attention to the straps on his wrists. Still part of his awareness, he has inadvertently transferred them, too. He blocks the straps from his consciousness and they fall to the floor. Honzu snatches them up.

"Where are you?" Pounding on the small window of the driver's cab, he yells, "Stop!"

Air brakes hiss and tires howl. The freighter lurches to a halt. Quan stumbles backward, falling onto a crate. Losing his concentration he becomes visible again.

Honzu reacts instantly, directing his fury at Quan.

Quan jumps to one side and becomes invisible again just as Honzu's tattooed arms pass through him.

Close to him now, Quan can make out the shape of the lighter in Honzu's jacket. He reaches in and snatches it. Finding

382

the trigger, he holds the lighter to the mattress and squeezes. The bed ignites.

The flames rise and Quan backs toward the roll-up door. Honzu is stomping out the fire and smoke is rising. Quan turns around, takes a giant stride and leaps into the air, passing through the freighter's back door. He hits the road hard, banging his knee and slapping his hands on the asphalt. The fall shakes him. He loses concentration and is visible again. Struggling to his feet, there's a sharp pain in his knee. He forces himself back into the altered state.

The driver is unlatching the roll-up door, throwing it open. A cloud of smoke releases into the night air. The driver turns his head away and coughs. "What's going on?"

Honzu crouches and. with two hands on the bed of the truck, he jumps down. Smoke continues to billow out from the cargo hold. Eyes watering, he coughs and yells, "Where is he?"

"I didn't see him. Too much smoke," said the driver, holding his shirt up to his nose.

"Find him!" yells Honzu.

Quan is running south, plowing through the thick quivering gel. Spikes of pain are coming from his knee and his head aches. Behind him, the two men are searching the bushes next to the freighter.

This is what father meant . . . danger from the east.

As he trudges down the roadway, the reality of his situation becomes crystal clear. This will never end. Trouble has followed him from China and, no matter what he does, generations of Triad will hunt him. He knows there is no reasoning with them. Their brothers were killed in the explosion and they seek revenge; this is who they are. Quan pushes off from the scene, gliding through the gel, back to the compound.

50.

Quan was the product of all he had been through—stronger and wiser but weary from the struggle. Estranged from the life he once knew, separate from his life with Sealy, the promise of great knowledge tempted him to stay in the Braneworld. At the same time, he was being hunted by the Triad. This was a tricky equation to solve.

He lifted his awareness to a vantage point high above and viewed his life as if it were a graphic novel. In it, he saw a path to bring his life back into balance.

Dragging a heavy teak chair from his terrace, he set it on the ground in the shade of the great oak. Red nasturtium and blue rosemary were blooming along the cliffs and there was a chill in the air. He sat quietly while his colleagues filtered in. Setting their chairs on the dry ground next to his, they came to his invitation.

While they sat, bits of news was exchanged. Media stories were popping up everywhere, extolling the Research Center as the birthplace of a new science. Bloggers on the LÓNG website were excited by the news of research labs on other continents building machines and philosophical debates were ubiquitous.

Lotus reported a huge influx of applicants requesting a visit to the center, and von Ang received queries from several other laboratories asking him to consult with them.

Quan listened patiently, taking it all in. None of it surprised him.

"There's a movement under way," said Quan. "What we started is a paradigm shift. It will ripple through the world. For the future of humanity it's essential that the research continue. This is the epicenter. You have the lead. You must add more staff and grow this place."

"You're the reason we've come this far," said Lotus.

"Perhaps, but I have nothing more to contribute."

"You're the chief," said McGowen. "You're what holds this together."

"I think not. I've become a liability. My presence here puts you all at risk. I'm leaving it to you. Take it to the next level."

"You're going back to China?" asked Lotus.

"There are other worlds to explore," said Quan, his eyes darting beyond the group.

"But what about Sealy?" asked Lotus.

"I'll talk to her."

"Immersion is what he's talking about," said von Ang. "He wants to stay in the other dimensions indefinitely."

Lotus trained her eyes on Quan. "How long do you think you can do that?"

"I don't know. We'll see."

"If it helps," said von Ang. "If it would make a difference, I'm open to bringing in other scientists."

"You should do that anyway," said Quan. "It can only help. My presence here presents a risk for all of you."

"You know we can hire people to protect us if that's the issue," said McGowen. "And we can hire someone to do this immersion thing you're talking about."

"It's something I must do—something only I can do."

"You can't stay in that altered state indefinitely," said von Ang. "You know that."

"You're the scientist. You investigate your way and I'll go to it in my way. The research you're doing is great. Let's not debate this," said Quan.

The group fell silent for a few moments, then McGowen spoke out. "You're a young man and you have a child on the way. Take some time off and enjoy life. You can always come back to this later."

"I appreciate that, but believe me, everyone here will be better off if I leave."

Quan had weighed the options and he knew what had to be done. If he stayed, the Triad would return. If he left, the research center would be safe.

"Lotus, leak word to the media that I have left and my whereabouts are unknown."

"As you wish."

After stirring the dying embers of conversation, the group fell silent.

Rising from his chair, Quan said one last thing. "I'll see you all later on."

He went back inside his bungalow while the group stayed on, next to his empty chair, talking about what to do next.

"How long can he maintain that other state?" asked Lotus.

"I don't think anyone knows," said von Ang. "My guess is that he'll be back soon."

David turned to McGowen. "If he doesn't come back soon, I'll be glad to go and find him."

"Right," scoffed McGowen.

Lotus lifted her gaze from Quan's chair and smiled. "He wants to protect us."

"That might be true," said McGowen, "but he doesn't have to go. I can hire people and beef up security. What I believe is that he's become obsessed with that other place and, even if it were safe for him to stay here, he'd be doing this, anyway."

"I'm sure he won't be gone long," said von Ang.

51.

The mission to find out what happened to Master Jintao, had been resolved. Quan had conversed with the apparition's cryptic intelligence, speaking to him in abstractions and he was convinced that there was no way to bring his father back. His father appeared to be at home in the other dimensions.

Exploring the other dimensions and expanding his knowledge was an opioid that Quan found irresistible. The mindscape he began with had grown in size. Where there was once a house, there was now a mansion with endless rooms—many just waiting to be filled.

And there were the Triad, too many and too determined to be ignored. No one had ever been able to defeat them, yet that was exactly what Quan needed to do.

Sealy and Quan's unborn child was an eternal bond that nothing could put asunder. Quan would be there with her for the birth and yet, to be with them, he would need to overcome major obstacles, including the Pacific Ocean. The question was how.

His name was on a watch list and he was sure that once he reached China, he would be arrested. While his lawyers worked to clear his name, he would need to find a way to be there. His options were limited. He could travel under false documents, but if caught that would make matters worse. Propelling himself across the Pacific by entering the Braneworld raised several questions. Could he propel himself that far? How long would it? What would happen if fatigue set in somewhere over the ocean? And how would he navigate? Risky. However, if he could remain invisible, he might be able to board a flight to China. But first he needed to see how long he could maintain the altered state.

His state of mind was all important.

I'm a constellation of memories. Memories and thoughts—thoughts and memories—that's what I am. My mind is a pattern of synaptic connections—a connectome. I'm a multidimensional being in a multidimensional world and my connectome is free to move in different dimensions. What would happen if I stayed in the altered state? Would I become fixed there? I should be alright as long as I don't forget what it's like to be human.

Quan possessed abilities that no one fully understood—not even him. And so, he set his plan in motion. He concentrated on the dimensions he knew best. Particles began to swirl.

As the last of his team leaves, Quan returns to his seat near the great oak tree, invisible to them. He watches as they walk away into the swirling sand. He is alone and night is coming. The particles begin to dim.

Remembering what the phantom said, *Look to the north. Danger comes from the east,* his senses reach out, trying to detect any threat that might be directed at the Research Center. Hours pass and the world seems placid. The only variance is the sun, as it slowly descends. But as twilight fades into night, he feels a disturbance. A negative energy in the distance—something sinister approaching from the north. Quan's immediate reaction is to repel it—send it back to where it came from. In his mind, he constructs a gigantic mirrored wall around the Research Center. It stretches from the ocean cliffs to the nearby hills and towers ten stories above the ground. He holds the vision firmly.

Ten kilometers away, on the main road, a freighter is humming toward the compound. It slows and comes to a halt a kilometer away. Two men quickly get out and lift the metal roll-up door.

Standing inside the freighter bed, a heavyset man with tattooed arms struggles to pick up a heavy metal tripod. His face is fixed in a scowl and a short cigar is clenched in the corner of his mouth. Scraping the tripod against the tail of the freighter, he lowers it to the other two men, who accept the weight and carry it with lumbering motion to the center of a barren field. The man in the freighter bed touches a burn on his upper arm, a reminder of his recent encounter with Quan.

Quan feels the negative energy, identifies it. It's Honzu again—dragon head of the Triad with two of his soldiers. Quan concentrates on their negative energy, turning it back against them.

The men repeat the same maneuver two more times, setting up a total of three tripods. Servos on the tripods began to whir, screwing augers into the soil. The men unlock panels on each device and lights switch from red to green. They run back to the freighter and the vehicle turns around and speeds away. Two kilometers up the road, it comes to a halt again.

The men get out and go to the back of the freighter. One of them, a younger man with spiky black hair, swings a metal case up and onto the bed. He opens the case. Inside are three miniature drones, each the size and shape of a dragonfly. The young man takes a handheld device from the case and speaks a command. The dragonflies take to the air, hovering two meters above the truck bed. Suddenly, one of them speeds into the night sky, followed by another, then the third. A small viewer in the case lights up with three live images. Honzu watches as the

390

drones fly toward the Research Center. The first drone lands on top of the laboratory entrance. The second drone flies to the top of von Ang's bungalow, and the third goes to the top of Quan's bungalow. Homing beacons on each of the little automatons switch on to attract the missiles.

The men hustle into the front seat and the freighter speeds away just as flares from the tripods light and three rockets lift into the night sky. Fighting against gravity, the missiles growl angrily, gaining altitude. The two passengers in the freighter crane their necks, looking skyward. The rockets are out of sight, high above them, cresting, then descending in furious condemnation, following the dragonfly beacons.

Something flutters in the rearview mirror and Honzu brings the vehicle to a stop. Whipping his head around, he stares through the small window, into the freighter's bed. A look of horror contorts his face. There inside the cargo hold are the little drones, facing him like three defiant little robots.

"Run away!" he yells, vaulting from his seat. The men scuffle, running from the vehicle and mounting the rocky banks of the roadway. They're almost to the top when a blinding flash consumes them.

Quan never saw the freighter and its deadly cargo—only felt the negative energy. When it was extinguished, he knew. It was a feeling like sunlight shining through after a spring rain, a feeling so relaxing that he began to drift back to his native world. Shaking himself, he regained his concentration, continuing to stay in the Braneworld. Although the contest with Honzu had been tiring, for the remainder of the night quan maintained himself in the other dimensions without moving from his seat next to the great oak tree.

During the night, he underwent bouts of panic. He spasmed as if he were drowning, gasping for air. Each time, he rode through the temptation to return to his native dimensions and each time it became easier to stay in the altered state.

A higher level of understanding was opening up to him and, like chaff being stripped from grain, a winnowing process was underway. Layers of his identity were peeling back allowing his most essential self to emerge.

Morning came and the summer sun illuminated the coastal lands. A breeze lifted the odor of putrefied sediment from the tide pools below and hawks wriggled above to maintain their positions in the weak thermal currents. As the sun rose in the sky, photons entered the Earth's atmosphere at an ever more oblique angle and the churning specks took on psychedelic colors. In the brightening mist, he recognized Lotus. She had come to the bluff to watch the sun rise. He could feel her sweet reverence as she walked away, briefly touching the back of his chair as she passed.

The immersion was changing Quan. He no longer felt a need to return. Drawing energy from all around, he felt sated, without any desire for food or drink. He sat throughout the day, marveling at the immensity and complexity of nature.

Night came again, and under cover of darkness, Quan refocused his consciousness on the solid world of his birth and, after a time, he materialized under the glow of a gibbous moon. The particles disappeared and his eyes dilated as he readjusted. Around him, the earth and plants were releasing pheromones, insects were scurrying on the ground. Stridulating grasshoppers and croaking frogs made music—an asynchronous cacophony. Their discord was annoying Quan and he shushed them. The noise stopped. Still in his chair and weary from his extended stay in the Braneworld, he closed his eyes and began to drift off.

Leaves behind him crunched and jolted him from sleep. He turned to see a curious coyote standing next to a clump of manzanita. Its eyes were amber disks in the moonlight. Quan rose from his chair and looked right through the animal, to its bones, its panting lungs, and its quickening heart. Eye to eye with Quan, the coyote bared its teeth and began to growl. Without warning, without any conscious intent, Quan's animal instinct kicked in.

392

He grew larger, his viewpoint lifting as his size increased. Something powerful in his subconscious was coming to the fore.

Hairs on the coyote's neck bristled and the animal backed away, its eyes wide, opening its mouth as if in agony, whimpering. Then it collapsed and fell on its side. Quan reached out to touch the creature—so pathetically small. His hand seemed gigantic in proportion. He reached out a finger and nudged the creature. It didn't move.

What he was seeing didn't make sense. Looking at his hand in the moonlight, it appeared to be huge—and blue. His arm was blue, too. He looked around. Plants were muted green; tree trunks were muted brown. Nothing else was askew except the color of his blue skin. His limbs were muscular and huge, like those of a Titan, and there was a pattern on his skin—thin orange lines tracing out spade-shaped patterns.

What were these? Scales? And my fingers, no . . . not fingers. What is this? Claws instead of fingers? And curling around my feet . . . what is that? A tail? What have I become? Claws, scales, a tail? What? How?

Then he remembered the blue dragon in his childhood storybooks—a long-ago imprinted image—the manifestation of a memory rooted deep in Quan's subconscious. As a little boy, he was fascinated with dragons, especially Chinese dragons. Chinese dragons were said to be magical creatures. They were born of water, able to shape-shift from clouds to rain, able to flow with streams and rivers, and able to take on any form associated with water. And, because all living things contain water, a Chinese dragon was capable of taking on most any form.

With a few giant steps, Quan crossed the compound, arriving at the laboratory. He stood, looking down at its roof, as if it was a scale model—too small for him to enter. Peering into the ground, Quan saw von Ang tending to his experiments, like a child playing with bits of circuitry and ceramic, uncertain of he might find.

Feeling very tired, Quan, huge and blue, retraced his steps and curled up under the big oak tree. With eyes closed, he became aware of something in his hand. His fingers were wrapped around it, and, without looking, he began to feel its shape. The shape was somewhat like a tusk with tiny ridges running down its length. It moved, and then he realized he was holding his thumb. He slid it away from his encircling fingers and felt its pointy tip. His fingers too were long and pointy. He poked them into the palm of his hand, then stretched them out again.

Opening one eye, the pixelated air around him gusted in shades of cobalt blue and purple. There were neon green streaks whipping across the landscape like flaming jump ropes, and the air smelled like a mixture of steel and mint. Lifting his head, he took a deep breath and looked down at his forearm. It was no longer muscular and covered with blue platelets. Now his skin was back to the color of pale almonds.

I must have been dreaming, he thought. *I dreamt I was a dragon. So real.*

52.

San Francisco International Airport
The air is full of seething particles. Quan enters the main lobby of
the international departures terminal with only his passport and
his lucky rabbit's foot in his pockets. Dark figures of people
fringed in white are standing at the foot of a large view field. He
can barely make out the annotation of outgoing flights displayed
in the yellow vibrating sand. Moving in closer, he reads the list,
looking for the Sino World flight to New Hong Kong. It's there,
fourth line from the bottom, scheduled to depart in twenty-two
minutes from gate 27B. Flight duration is listed as seven and a
half hours.

   At gate 27B, Quan stands in the churning sandstorm,
watching passengers board the 8:00 flight. At the gate, each
person is bioscanned for recognition. He's ready to do what he
needs do and, after the last person steps onto the gangway and the
gate attendant closes the door, it's time—time to make his move.
He walks as fast as he can around the outside of the scanner, past

the gate, through the closed door, down the ramp, and through the hull of the aircraft. He's onboard.

Searching for a place to rest, he looks in the private compartments of first class. To his dismay, each compartment is occupied. Moving along the sandy shapes, down the right-hand aisle of business class, that section also appears to be full. Continuing to where a bulkhead separates the business class section from the remainder of the airship, he observes that the last two rows on the other side are vacant. Crossing over, particles slipping through particles, he passes through everything in his way, seats and passengers alike. He takes up a seat in the last row against the bulkhead, a seat that does not recline and is therefore unlikely to attract anyone.

Now, however, a more difficult task lays ahead. The flight is going to be over seven hours and, though he proved he can remain in the altered state longer, what will he do to occupy himself? He won't be able to listen to music or read and most concerning of all, he won't be able to fall sleep. He can't risk losing concentration and sliding back into his native dimensions.

Airship takes off and Quan encounters a sensation he is totally unprepared for. The airship is moving away from him. Particles are streaming past and he has to concentrate on maintaining his location with respect to the ship. He rivets his attention to the outlines of windows and storage compartments to hold his position. The forward thrust of the aircraft is hidden from the other passengers but it's visible to him. Particles are streaking through him at a ferocious rate. To maintain his position, he has to match the speed of the airship. It requires extraordinary effort.

How long can I keep this up? How nice it would be to travel the way I used to travel. A private cabin in first class, that's the way.

His consciousness goes to parts of his body. He can feel his heartbeat, his lungs expanding and contracting, his extremities, and his meridians of energy. He follows nerve impulses as they ascend to the brain and he enters the connectome that holds it all together. Somewhere inside him he finds a way to fix himself with respect to the aircraft. In the same way he can bring his clothes with him into the other dimensions, he has brought the armrest.

I'm able to do this and the more I know, the stranger it seems. Millennia ago, our species went through a cognitive revolution. That separated us from all other species. Billions of neurons connected in a pattern that gave rise to "mind." Our higher consciousness was born. Consciousness is capable of such complexity—capable of staying in the Braneworld while hanging on to this airship. What will it be capable of in another hundred years?

Hours pass and Quan holds onto his armrest. He intensifies his effort several times when it feels like he is losing his grip. As the hours drag on, it becomes increasingly more difficult for him to concentrate. At a few minutes before seven in the evening, the craft comes to rest at the terminal. His arm is on fire from holding on for so long.

Passengers begin to disembark. Beyond fatigue, Quan continues to keep himself in the other dimensions, hidden from view. He rises from his seat and walks out into the terminal,. Every molecule of him is crying out to relax and be free of the Braneworld.

Outside, in the churn of vibrating particles, he can barely make out the shapes defining a dock where people are waiting in line for a conveyance that brings glides up to the surface from under the tarmac.

He makes his way past the taxi-glide station, He can't risk identify himself and paying for a taxi. He can't use his wrist disk to call someone without signaling his arrival to the authorities. At the end of the taxi stations is the Customs Office and the beginning of the commercial loading docks. Exhausted, he waits; and, after what seems like a very long time, a rectangular package belted with red nylon straps comes out on a conveyor. A

397

bot picks it up and carries it to a waiting corporate glide. It's a package that Quan prearranged to be sent from California on the same flight he boarded and the glide is from the Jintao Corporation.

Quan quickly jumps into the glide before it lifts off.

~~~

At the penthouse, the arrival tone sounded and Ning operated the entry door optics. Outside a Jintao company bot was there to deliver a large package addressed to Sealy. She instructed the door to open and told the courier to bring the package inside. The bot completed the delivery and returned to the glide. The door returned to opaque and Ning turned around.

"Welcome home, young master," she said. "I've been expecting you."

Her words startled Quan and, letting go of the Braneworld, he materialized in front of her.

"How did you know I was here?"

"Your father told me you would be here soon."

"He's here?"

"No. He talks to me."

"Why didn't you tell me this before?"

"You asked if I knew where he was and I answered correctly. I do not."

Exhausted, Quan managed to ask one final question. "Did you see me enter the house?"

"No. I heard your breathing."

Quan felt older than he wanted to feel and he found it hard to think about anything more. Too exhausted to question her further, he decided to resume the conversation after a shower and a good night's sleep. His last words instructed Ning not to tell anyone of his presence, including Sealy.

The next day, at the breakfast counter, Ning ladled congee into a bowl and poured a cup of green tea for the young master.

398

Lifting another spoonful of the thick porridge, he said, "This is very good congee. Did you do something special?"

"It is the way I prepare it every time."

"It's very good." Taking a sip of tea, he said, "I think I need something stronger. This morning I'd prefer English black tea."

Ning obeyed and made a steaming pot of dark tea, setting it in front of him with a small pitcher of milk.

"It's good to be back home," he said.

"Yes," said Ning. "And this is a very good home to be back to."

After finishing his last sip of tea, he said, "I want you to com Sealy and ask her to come to the penthouse. Tell her a package arrived for her. Say you don't know what it is, but it must be important. If she asks you to open it, tell her you're forbidden to open anything addressed to someone else."

Quan retreated to his bedroom and, while dressing, he thought about how isolated he was. He wasn't able to venture out of the penthouse unless he entered the other dimensions. He couldn't use the internet, nor com anyone. It wasn't even advisable to activate his wrist disk inside the penthouse for fear that somehow his ID would be transmitted to the outside world. Even Ning had more freedom than he did.

In mid afternoon, a soft bell tone sounded announcing the arrival of a glide, and moments later someone was at the rooftop door. Ning opened the door for Sealy and said, "This way. I'll show you to your package."

In the great room, Quan got up from his seat and crossed to the entry area. The moment Sealy saw him, her hands went to her cheeks and she said, "I can't believe it. You're my package? What a great surprise!"

She laughed and embraced him. Kissing his cheek, she said, "I missed you so much."

He began to back away and she said, "Don't let me go. Just hold me." A long moment passed before Sealy pushed him out to arm's length and said, "I haven't heard from you for ten days and now you're here. You didn't give me any warning. Not good. You had me worried."

"I told you I'd be back."

"You didn't tell me when or how and Lotus said you disappeared days ago. What was I to think?"

"I'm done with all that. I'm here with you and that's all that matters."

He put a hand on her belly. "How's our baby?"

"Baby and I are great and I'm thrilled that you're here, but are you really here to stay?"

"Let's sit," he said.

They settled themselves on the circular sofa and Ning brought refreshments. Sealy had put on weight. Her cheeks were rosy and she looked so robust that Quan couldn't stop smiling.

"What is it?" she asked.

"It's been so long, I must have forgotten how beautiful you are."

"Thank you for saying that." She smiled. She was happy but there were so many questions. "Why did it take you so long to get back here? It's been a week since you commed me. I had to rely on Lotus and she didn't know where you were. I was worried. And she told me there was another explosion that blew up part of the highway. What's going on there."

"I know. So much happened just before I left. All I can tell you is that it's been taken care of and the Center is protected. After Paris I wanted to wrap things up and come right away but I couldn't. You know about the controversary with the Science Committee. My name was placed on a watch list. Now, the lawyers will clear things up but I couldn't wait. So, I risked it and here I am."

"And how, may I ask, did you get here?"

"I was a stowaway."

"You did what?"

"It's true. The invisible me hid in plain sight."

She laughed, but her eyes told him she was shocked.

"You are here to stay? Your work in California is finished?"

"I'm here and I'm here to stay. Something happened that caused me to rethink my involvement there. It's better for everyone if I'm not there."

"You're talking about the explosion aren't you?"

"Things became very complicated."

"So, what happened? And what does it have to do with you?"

"There were some very bad people trying to damage the facility. I think they were trying to get to me. Somehow, before they could get close, whatever they were doing resulted in an explosion and caused their death."

"What! That's horrible. And frightening. I'm so glad you weren't hurt. But who were they?"

"Please, Sealy. Trust me. It's going to be okay."

"If they are trying to do harm, how do you know we're safe? How do you know it's over? I mean, if you can't clear this up . . ."

He interrupted her and said, "This is an important time for us. I promise, these problems won't touch us. You're the only one who knows I'm here. You'll have to stay with your parents for a while but long term I think we'll live here in the penthouse—just not right away.."

"What about your father?"

"He won't be coming back."

"How do you know that?"

"He's moved on and I believe he's content where he is."

53.

Liminal: occupying a position on both sides of a
boundary or threshold; a transitional space; the middle state of a
rite of passage.

*Liminal. That's what father's residue said. How crazy is
that? What a concept—explore the other dimensions and have a
family too. I could love my banlu and raise my son and disappear
into the Braneworld everyday. Why not? I could also be the nexus
to the other realm—learn its mysteries and share them with the
world through my website. Sure. Why not? Be the nexus Be all I
can be. After all . . . all is all.*

In the three weeks that followed, Quan stayed in the
penthouse, unable to interact directly with the outside world. He
spent his days reading and watching the news with vidi
conferencing turned off. He willed himself into the Braneworld
whenever he felt the need to consult the wisdom of his father, and
he continued to write about his mind-expanding experiences.

Sealy continued to stay with her parents and, every few days, she came to visit Quan under the pretext of designing a nursery. It was a ritual they agreed to continue until the arrest warrant was lifted.

The Jintao corporate lawyers continued their dialogue with the Central Science Committee and, as usual, the government demands were excessive and negotiations moved slowly. A month crawled past.

Von Ang added two research scientists to the staff and Lotus took over the job of managing the LONG website blog.

It was a mid-week morning inside the penthouse and Ning found the young Jintao reclining in one of the club chairs with his stockinged feet up on the table. The only light in the room came from a view field above him, angled to his line of sight.

Stepping into the study, she said, "May I interrupt?"

"It seems you already have. What is it Ningo?"

"One of the Jintao attorneys is on the com. He says it's okay for you to take his call. The negotiations have concluded and you'll want to hear what he has to say."

Quan tapped his wrist disk switching to one-way view mode and accepted the call. Instantly a man's face replaced the text he'd been working on. It was an unfamiliar face—a young man with black hair combed straight back and gold wire rimmed glasses pitched on his nose.

"Hello?"

The man spoke with a smile in his voice. "Hello there. I'm Jianguo Liu. I'm one of the lawyers working on your citizen status. This is an auspicious day and I'm happy to tell you that an arrangement has been finalized. Your residency need no longer be anonymous. All charges have been dropped and your normal freedoms are restored."

"I'm happy to hear that," said Quan. "I've been waiting for some good news. What kind of consessions were made? Give me the details."

"There were many offers and rejections but at the end of the day, it was Dr. Hao who played a significant role in negotiating the deal. He offered a limited number of what they called 'run-time chips' and in return the Central Science Committee abandoned their claims."

"Well done," said Quan. "Please thank everyone who helped. Yes. Thank yourself . . . and I'll personally call Dr. Hao to thank him."

Quan disconnected and opened a com line to Sealy.

"Free at last," he said, filling in the details.

She asked what the run-time chips were, since they played such a pivotal role in his freedom. He explained that they contain the critical software needed to operate a transdimensional machine and how brilliant he had been to lock up the code . . . and save it from almost being stolen.

"Wonderful," she said. "You're almost a genius. Now we can have our lives back."

Quan refrained from telling her about the one additional thing he had to do before putting his troubles completely in the past. While it was true that he was free him from government restrictions, before he could feel free to enjoy family life with Sealy, there was still the problem of the Triad.

For the better part of five centuries, the Triad remained undefeated. There were an estimated thirty thousand members entrenched in New Hong Kong and over the years, specialized police units had tried to eradicate them. Like a bad case of toe fungus, they kept coming back.

Quan chewed on the problem for weeks. He imagined what he might say if he were given the opportunity to negotiate with them. He could explain that the events that took the lives of their comrades weren't his fault. That was the truth—but it wouldn't matter. They were out for revenge and it would take more than words to appease them. If he gave them money, they would only come back for more. It would never end.

404

Quan read everything he could find concerning the Triad and he consulted *The Book of Thirty-Six Strategies*—superb when it came to fighting an organized group—but of limited effect with a loose band of confederates bound together by oath. Quan roamed from one article to another. It was only when he found himself reading an occult history of China that an idea began to take shape.

Quan turned his attention to finding an intermediary. He came across an editorial about a government agent, a man named Ben Wu, who worked in the local gang task force. Five years earlier, Wu successfully negotiated a famous hostage release from the 14K. If there was anyone who had had a measure of success dealing with the Triad, it was Ben Wu. More recent articles said that he retired from the task force and was doing consulting for various government and corporate entities.

After going through several referrals, Quan was eventually able to make contact. Over a secure com link, he introduced himself and told Wu about the deaths and the imminent reprisal. Even though the government's capture order had been withdrawn, Wu confirmed that he was justified in thinking that the Triad would still want revenge. Retribution was a pillar of the Triad code and the gang would not easily set their vendetta aside.

Quan swallowed and surprised himself by saying, "I want to meet with the Dragon Head of 14K."

Wu let out an uneasy laugh and said, "So far as I know, it has never been possible for a civilian to meet with the Dragon Head. Even if he would take the meeting, which I doubt, it would be extremely dangerous for you."

Quan laid out his strategy and offered a generous fee for arranging the meeting. After listening to what Quan had to say, Wu declared that there was no guarantee that a meeting would take place. Nevertheless, he agreed to send word through his contacts. In closing, he cautioned Quan not to expect a victory. It would be enough to just walk away alive. "When you confront a tiger," he said, "the best you can hope for is to come away with just a scratch."

While he waited for word from Wu, Quan imagined what the meeting would be like. His mind played back scenes from Chinese gangster movies—an abandoned warehouse at the dockyards—men in dark suits with machineguns—a boss who looked line a Chinese version of Edward G. Robinson.

A week after talking to Wu, the day of the meeting arrived however, the rendezvous was not at all as Quan imagined. Instead, he was directed to the offices of a plastic surgeon in a modern office building in the center of downtown.

A lift brought him to the tenth floor. The stainless steel doors closed behind him and Quan was alone in a blond wood paneled corridor. An illuminated sign pointed the way to numbered suits. At suite 1040, Quan opened the door and entered a reception area. In front of him, a pretty young woman with purple razor-cut hair sat behind a high counter. Only her head was visible. He approached and introduced himself.

Lifting her hand, palm up she gestured to the door on her left. "You may go in," she said.

Quan heard the door click as he reached for the handle. He paused and looked around the reception room. His feeling was confirmed—he was the only one there. All of a sudden it felt very wrong. He pushed himself to turn the handle and open the door.

As the door opened, he was confronted by a man in a dark green silk suit. His eyes were hidden behind black sunglasses and a few links of a gold chain were visible under his unbuttoned shirt. He gestured down the hallway, "This way," he said.

This could be where it all ends, Quan thought. *Stay balanced. Show respect but stay calm.*

The hallway had rooms on each side. They traveled about half way before Quan heard the the man behind him say, "In here."

Quan turned and entered the empty exam room. The man in green followed closely behind and closed the door.

"You are Dragon Head?" asked Quan.

"He'll be here soon. Take off your clothes."

"Is that necessary?"

"Take off your clothes and put that on." He pointed to a gown sitting on the end of the exam table.

Quan felt like this could easily go sideways, but he did as he was told and stacked his clothes on the exam table. The man walked over and searched through the stack of clothes. From one of the pockets, he pulled out the little white rabbit's foot. Holding it up by its chain, he looked at it curiously.

"It my lucky charm," said Quan.

The man pointed to a chair," and said "Sit."

Quan walked to where the chair was, below a window. He looked down at the city scene, twenty meters below. No way to escape, he took to the chair while his guardian stood next to the door with his arms crossed.

Several uncomfortable minutes passes and the man in green continued to stare at Quan, occasionally twirling the rabbit's foot around his forefinger. At last there was a knock at the door and the man stepped aside. The door opened and a man in a doctor's gown and mask walked in. Below the hem of the gown, silk trousers and bespoke shoes were visible. Above the mask, dark eyes scrutinized him. The rabbit's foot was held out to the man in surgical dress and the man in green mumbled, "This is all he had on him."

Looking at what he'd been given, Dragon Head of the 14K lightly tossed the good luck charm in his hand and said, "You asked for a meeting. What do you want?"

"You are the Dragon Head?" asked Quan.

"I know who I am—and I know you are. What do you want?"

"I want to talk about what happened in California. The government contract to capture me has been revoked and I want to be sure there is no further threat from the Triad."

"If you are referring to our fallen brothers. That is on your head."

"With respect, I must tell you, your brothers in California brought about their own destruction. I don't know what killed them but it wasn't us."

"You expect me to believe that? You took a big risk coming here"

"I know how powerful the Triad is but there is a higher power protecting me and my people. I believe that power dealt with your brothers. I'm here to ask you set aside the vendetta."

"I don't have time for fantasies. Give me a good reason why I shouldn't just end you. You have thirty seconds. Then we're done."

"Honestly, there was no way those men could have hurt me. I am protected by a higher power—governed by a universal law. I am the nexus to Ching Tu, land of pure consciousness."

"What nonsense... a children's tale."

"There is more to Ching Tu than you know. You can't kill what is already dead."

Quan's body became a shape made of dancing particles and a moment later he was gone.

Dragon Head's face went pale and his eyes remained focused on the spot where Quan had been. The other man began looking around, reaching into his jacket for his sidearm. Pulling open the panel of his jacket, he said, "Hey, my gun."

Quan reappeared, dangling the rabbit's foot from one hand while he set the gun down on the exam table next to him.

Dragon Head looked at his empty palm and back again. His eyes twitched. "What the hell! What are you?"

"You have your world and I have mine. I am spirit—governed only by universal law. No one can violate universal law without penalty. I'll tell you again. We weren't involved in what

408

happened to your soldiers. They brought it on themselves. I am asking, with great respect, that the Triad stay away from me and my family. If you do this, we can go our separate ways and I won't interfere in your affairs. I need to know we have an understanding."

There was pain and astonishment in the eyes above the mask. Dragon Head was filled with dread the likes of which he hadn't felt in years—way beyond anything he was prepared for. Convinced that he had witnessed something supernatural, his response was immediate. "It will be so. We have an understanding." Shaken, he took a step backward, pivoted, and left the room. The man in green quickly followed, pausing before closing the door—having one last glimpse of the man from Ching Tu who stood in the center of the room, barefooted in a hospital gown.

"Can I have my gun back?"

"Leave," said Quan in a voice that filled the room.

The man bolted out of the room.

After leaving the rooftop aeropad in a black on black Mercedes 3500, Dragon Head of the 14K sent word throughout the Triad network announcing that Quan Jintao, his family, and associates were to be added to the safe list. The vendetta was cancelled.

Quan calmly put on his clothes and a few minutes later he was waiting for the lift to take him up to the aeropad. Feeling the rabbit's foot in his pocket, he thought, *Knowledge is power. The Triad will do anything to avoid bad luck . . . just a superstitious bunch of miscreants.*

54.

At midday, Quan joined the sisters in the great room. They sat at the clear polycarb dining table and Ning began serving a lunch of NutriSynth duck and fresh bok choy. Sealy reached around behind her to adjust a pillow. Quan got up and went to her, lending a hand. She smiled pleasantly, grateful for the attention. Her belly was as taut as the hull of a watermelon, keeping her further back from the table than she would have preferred.

"I have to eat my main meal before two," Sealy told her sister. "If I eat late in the day, I get heartburn."

Lotus said, "I've got to give you credit, my dear. You're tougher than I. How close are you?"

"Could be any day now," said Sealy. "It's entirely up to the baby."

After eating, they went to the conversation area and Quan held Sealy's hands as she lowered herself to the seat. Her handmaiden, Ning, brought a blanket and spread it over Sealy's legs.

"You are like a god," said Ning.

"What do you mean?" asked Sealy.

"You are able to create life."

"I see. Wouldn't the word goddess be more appropriate?"

"Ahh yes. A gender-modified noun is more appropriate. I am not a goddess. I cannot produce life."

"Be thankful you can't. It's a very uncomfortable process," said Sealy.

Turning to Quan, Lotus said, "I've been wondering. Right after you disappeared, the road to the center was bombed. Gregory found truck parts and rocket fragments strewn all over and a huge crater in the road. It looked like several people died and it reminded us of the explosion on the laboratory grounds. You assured us that somehow we were being protected and Gregory is convinced that you had something to do with the explosion. Is it true?"

"What do you think," asked Quan.

"I'm on the fence, same as Gaston. You weren't around, so it could have been you, we have no idea what happened."

"All I can say is that non-local communication is real."

"Oh, that's a good one. I told Sealy about that. Seriously, what did you do?"

He closed his eyes, reviewing what happened. "It's too difficult to explain. Let's just say I have connections."

"And there's something else. Before you left, you said you were going to stay in the other place for an extended time. How did that work for you? How long did you stay," asked Lotus.

The question was simple enough yet it sent his mind retracing all that he had been through. After a pause he said, "It wasn't easy. I stayed two days. I remember dreaming I was a dragon."

Lotus looked at him with large disbelieving eyes.

"Come on. You have to give me something. What was it like?"

"It was a strain."

"He maintained," said Sealy. "He was invisible all the way home."

"Gaston thought maybe you'd only be able to maintain for a few hours, and when you were gone overnight, we didn't know what to think. What you did was risky."

"I assumed that if I couldn't maintain the shift, I'd just automatically return. But you're right. As it turned out, the longer I stayed, the more comfortable I became. It's possible that after awhile that would seem like the more natural state to be in."

Sealy looked up and said, "I always thought that's what happened to your father." Then she reached her hand out to him and smiled. He took her hand and gave it a gentle squeeze.

"I almost lost it. My stay into that other world stretched me to the limit," he said. "For a time, I thought maybe I was going to become a permanent resident in that strange land. I came out okay but in some ways I feel like a freak—like I don't fit in."

"Of course you fit in," said Sealy. "And you're going to be a father. That's going to give you a sense of place, for sure."

"More than anything I want to be here, in this world. My passport to the other world has no expiration date and after that extended stay it's even easier for me to shift."

"I'd rather you be done with that," said Sealy.

"It doesn't have to be either or. I can explore the other place and have a family at the same time. I want it all."

"The problems we were having with the Science Committee—they're behind us, right?" asked Lotus.

"Absolutely. They have what they wanted," said Quan

"Good. Gaston was asked to help them. He's added two more scientists to the staff," said Lotus. "He's also been talking with the Americans. They offered him some kind of grant."

"That's good that he's added more people," said Quan. "But he shouldn't become indebted to the Americans. We don't need their money. I need to talk to him. What else is going on?"

"Your interview with Monahan is being replayed with sub-titles all over the place and it looks like a cult is forming around your internet site. People are deifying you and they think of the Research Center as a sort of temple of the other dimensions."

"People see what they want to see and believe what they want to believe. A little bit of knowledge is often worse than total ignorance. On the other hand, if I'm a God, then Sealy is truly a goddess. That makes us very special," he said, stroking Sealy's head.

"Uh-huh," said Lotus, rolling her eyes. "God knows Gaston, Gregory and I deserve a break. We've been working nonstop and you know how remote the lab is. There isn't much to do there—except work. So, what do you say God? Can we take some time off?"

"We'll figure something out. Maybe I'll go and relieve them for a week or two."

"You can't go until after baby is born," said Sealy.

~~~

When the time came, Lotus and Ning helped Sealy dress. Her belly was huge and unwieldy, overbalancing her at every turn. Her back and legs hurt but she was doing her best to endure. Draping a shawl over her shoulders, they helped her out to the entry area where Quan stood waiting.

"Have you decided on a name for the child?" asked Ning, as she handed an overnight case to Quan.

"We agreed to wait and see what his nature is," said Sealy. "Perhaps Abbe if he has noble qualities, or Ji if he is assertive, or maybe Lei if he is exceedingly intelligent."

"And what if he is a combination of these thing?" asked Ning.

"We may need to give him several names," said Sealy.

Quan, managed a subtle smile and said, "Ning, please com Dr. Chen and say that we're on our way."

On the rooftop, Master Jintao's personal craft beeped as it levitated and moved out onto the aeropad. The doors opened and Lotus helped Sealy into the rear passenger seat, then sat in the seat next to her. Quan took to the front seat and the glide's automated voice sounded, "Destination, please."

"Lianmin Hospital," he replied.

The voice came again. "Please place hands and feet and all belongings inside the vehicle. In five seconds doors will close. 5 . . . 4 . . . 3. . . 2 . . . 1 Door is closing. Door is closing."

414

EPILOGUE

Ten Years Later

New Hong Kong

That morning, Lei asked his mother, Sealy, for permission to visit a friend after school. His friend, Bo, who also lived in the South Point complex, used the same pretense to gain his freedom. They boarded a tram to the Kowloon side of the island, bringing Bo's younger brother, Leon, along with them.

Upon exiting the tram, they made their way to a small park, where they played near a stand of trees at the edge of an open space. Looking to be sure that no one was watching, Bo led them through bushes into a concrete passageway. Armed with a chocklight, he led them into the clammy darkness of an underground culvert. Climbing over rusty gates, broken and trampled down long ago, they came into a chamber strewn with debris. There they found a stairwell and descended to the platform of an abandoned subway station.

There was a time, Bo told them, before the glideways were set up, when rail lines carried passengers to and from old Hong Kong. Now, only derelicts and a few adventurous souls ever entered these tunnels.

Their lights cut through the blackness, sweeping across tunnel walls layered with crudely drawn symbols and graffiti. Bo aimed his chocklight down the tunnel. It seemed endless. The light dissipated after a few kilometers. Smells of burned wood, machine oil, and ether filled the air.

"What'd I tell you?" muttered Bo, who was only eleven but nearly a head taller than the other two. "Way gone, isn't it?"

"Way," said Lei, his eyes wide open.

Leon said nothing, keeping his trepidation to himself.

Lei yelled, "Whoop, whoop!" and the walls reverberated.

"Shhhhh," said Bo. "We don't know who's in here."

As they walked along the abandoned platform, things crunched and rolled at their feet. Turning his chocklight to the floor, Lei saw empty meck ampules and wine bottles sparkling amid the rubbish. He kicked and they rolled away, one of them stopping next to a heap of trash.

"Hey, look at this," said Lei, holding his light to a stack of material.

Leaning against the wall was a small shelter held together haphazardly with tape and metal wire. Inside, trinkets hung from its low cardboard ceiling: toys and spoons, and bits of holographic foil. Leon reached in and plucked a plastic harmonica from one of the strings and wiped it on his trousers. Putting his lips to it, he blew, but only air rushed out. He threw the harmonica to the ground and reached for something else.

"Gross," said Lei. "I'd never put my mouth on something like that."

"He's a little piggy," said Bo, yanking his brother's arm. "Come on, give us an oink."

Pouting, Leon looked back at the shanty. His brother yanked him again. "Let's go."

416

Walking a few paces farther, they heard a rustling noise behind them. As they swung their lights to the spot, the heap of trash next to the shanty rustled again.

"It's a rat," said Bo.

They relaxed and began to turn when suddenly the heap shifted to one side. The pile of trash slowly rose, pieces of plastic and foil shedding from it. A big chunk slid off, crashing to the floor. The mound tilted and twisted and another chunk went crashing to the ground. Then slowly a human form, covered in a ragged coat, emerged. The thing began to straighten from its crouched position. A grimy face glared at them, stained teeth and hollow cheeks, eyes in narrow slits looking at them. Raising a gnarled fist, the figure growled like an animal. The boys took off running down the tunnel, legs churning furiously, their chocklights bouncing.

"Rats!" yelled Bo as he kicked one out of the way.

The sound of metal banging on concrete reverberated from the tunnel behind them.

They ran faster and faster, crashing into to a wall of trash piled almost to the ceiling. Looking up at the rubble, Lei yelled, "There's no way out!"

"Up and over," said Bo, scrambling up the pile. At the top, there was just enough clearance for them to crawl through. Sliding down the other side they continued to run, down one tunnel and across another. They ran and ran, following Bo, hoping he knew the way. At last they came to a cavernous, empty room, water dripping from the ceiling. Fresh air was drifting in from above and they could see light filtering in. There was a grate high above and the green of trees beyond.

The sound of metal banging on concrete came again.

Their chocklights flicked across the walls. They were in a dead end.

"What are we going to do? We can't go back that way," said Lei, nervously feeling for the lucky rabbit's foot he kept in his pocket.

"How are we going to get out of here?" cried Leon, panicking.

"Get on my shoulders," said Bo, standing directly under the grating. "I can hold both of you. We'll go out the top."

Grabbing Bo's shoulders and stepping on his knee, Leon climbed up, then paused and jumped off. "You need to be near the wall so I have something to hold on to."

Bo repositioned himself next to the wall and Leon quickly remounted, climbing onto his brother's shoulders. He called down to Lei, "Come on."

Lei began to climb, feeling uneasy as the bodies of his friends flexed under his weight. With his hands against the wall, he managed to get to his feet on top of Leon's shoulders.

"Go ahead, Bo," he said. "Walk over to the opening."

Bo moved slowly, one small step at a time. His knee threatened to buckle under the weight and he grunted, slowly trudging away from the wall.

The sound of metal banging against concrete became louder. The grime creature, as they would later refer to it, was getting closer.

"Hurry," said Leon.

"Don't move," said Lei, as he studied the grating. What he saw was not good. The grate was wet and encrusted with rust. Pushing his chocklight against it with both hands, it wouldn't budge. He thought for a moment.

I can make it . . . but they'll see me. I promised mother I wouldn't, but there's no other way. I have to . . . just this once.

Bending his knees, Lei crouched down. He concentrated and particles began to swirl around him. As hard as he could, he pushed off from Leon's shoulder. He went flying, and Leon fell to the ground.

The force of Lei's jump knocked both of them to the ground. They looked up to see Lei standing on top of the grate.

Getting to his feet, Bo yelled, "Hey. Find a rope or something."

418

"Yeah," came the answer came from above. "I'm looking. Hold on."

The banging noise came again from the tunnel, this time much louder.

Bo aimed his chocklight at the ceiling and said incredulously, "The grate's still closed. How'd you get out?"

"Wait," said Lei, "I'll be back."

Lei returned a moment later with a long branch and wedged it into one of the open squares of the grate. He called to the boys below, "Watch out."

At the other end of the branch, he brought all of his weight to bear. The grate moved slightly. He began to kick up and down, swinging his legs higher each time, coming down hard on the end of the branch. With a dull crunching sound, the rusted metal suddenly broke free and Lei fell to the ground. Picking himself up, he flipped the grate over and lowered the branch down into the darkness. Leon scrambled up. Shaking with adrenaline he took up a position next to Lei. Together they held on as tight as they could while Bo climbed up, grabbing their clothes at the last to haul himself out.

Dropping the branch into the abyss, they heard a growl from the chamber below and took off running through the park. Reaching a safe distance, they stopped at a park bench, laughing nervously.

"Whoa," said Leon. "That was something!"

"Yeah. We would have been dead if he had caught us," said Bo.

Lei was uneasy. He wasn't sure what the others had seen. They were down on the floor when he passed through the grate and appearing on top of it wouldn't be easy to explain. His mother forbade him to go to that other place, the place with the particles. He would have to tell her, and she would be angry. She would stare into his eyes and talk a lot. She often did that when he did something he wasn't supposed to do.

They were happy to have a whopping good story to tell—they escaped the grime creature and, in the telling of it, the creature would become more terrifying with each iteration.

On the way back to South Point, Bo asked Lei how he was able to pass through the grating. Lei lied, saying the grate was loose and it flipped open when he jumped through. Then it must have fallen shut by itself and he had to pry it open. Lei left out the bit that would have been impossible to explain. In mid leap, in that moment when he closed his eyes and entered the world of churning particles, he passed through the grate unimpeded – assisted by something unseen—something that pulled him up to the top.

About the Author

Jack Phillip Hall began writing science fiction and general fiction in 2001. In an earlier life he was a product design engineer in Silicon Valley, working with corporations such as Sony, Apple, IBM, Motorola and Intel. He collaborated on the world's first laptop computer and the world's first handheld GPS locater. He currently lives above the white water in Southern California.